SOLOMON'S DREAMS

THE PRICE OF FREEDOM

ERIC SUDDOTH

RISING SMOKE PUBLISHING

i

Unless otherwise indicated, Scripture quotations are from:
Holy Bible, New International Version®, NIV©
1973, 1978, 1984, 2011 by Biblica, Inc. ®
Used by permission. All rights reserved worldwide.

Rising Smoke Publishing
ISBN 978-1-949869-19-4

Then Solomon awoke –
and he realized it had been a dream.
1 Kings 3:15

SUNDAY

CHAPTER 1

He closed his eyes and waited on the park bench, tracing the hundreds of initials etched in the wood. His heart was racing, but it wasn't the brisk jog through the woods on a lonely winding path that caused his blood to pump harder than usual. He lowered his head, allowing a few drops of sweat to roll down his nose, sliding down the slender curvature. He licked his lips and smiled at the saltiness.

It was the last Sunday in June. He had often wondered what this time of year would feel like in a less humid area, but sadly, he was stuck in Washington D.C. He often thought about picking up and heading to the Rockies where snowcapped mountains could be seen 365 days a year, but he knew that wasn't in the foreseeable future. This was where he was meant to be. For now.

Raising his head, he watched as a few lightning bugs chased one another, lighting up the desolate park. He knew it wasn't safe to be in a park this time of night for some people. But he wasn't one of those people. He was the one people should be warned about. He looked down at the Fitbit on his wrist, showing him his heart rate was still spiking at 134 beats per minute.

He took a few deep breaths, closed his eyes, and let his body sink into a relaxed posture. He slumped his shoulders and exhaled. He inhaled again, letting the craziness of the world into his psyche. He didn't want to let it go, didn't want to exhale. He wanted to hold in all the animosity swirling in his lungs. But he couldn't and eventually let out the air.

He heard a pair of sneakers hitting the paved path in the distance. He wondered if this was the one he was waiting for. The pounding started to get louder. The pace wasn't anything extravagant, easy to overtake if necessary. He kept his eyes sealed and listened to the crickets chirp, feeling like a kid camping in a pitched tent with his two brothers. He'd had a good childhood, no matter what the news might say. So what if his father abused him? So what if he learned to bob and weave his father's punches before he could ride a bicycle? It had taught him more than the rest of the world would ever understand.

The sound of jogging feet was getting closer. He thought about opening his eyes and seeing if this was the main attraction for the night, but he knew there were other ways to find that out. Instead, he waited patiently. His grandmother had always told him that patience was a virtue. He used to roll his eyes at her condescending tone and wonder what Bible story she was going to force down his ears before supper. Some people would have regrets over tarnished relationships, but he never let that emotion grow enough to give it a second thought or a period of remorseful mourning. She was dead, and life went on.

He heard an owl hooting as if singing along to the melody of the crickets' legs and the drumming of the runner's steps. He listened intently as the runner came within a few feet of the park bench, inhaled deeply, and started to exhibit a crooked grin. He knew he didn't need to open his eyes to start the chase. All he had to do was smell him.

The man jogged by and left a trail of musky cologne that was just one notch up from a feminine perfume. He chuckled to himself that just because a smell was bottled for a man didn't mean it deserved to be on one. He opened his eyes and watched Tuck, a twenty-seven-year-old former college baseball stud slowly jog away in his green jersey shorts and gray muscle tank shirt with a pair of expensive earbuds plunged deep into his canals. He rolled his eyes at the man's cockiness; wearing earbuds to tune out the surroundings this late at night wasn't the smartest thing. But then again, Tuck wasn't known for his smarts. He flaunted his good looks as if it was his only good quality. Many women had fallen victim to his playboy ways. Too many.

He stood up and stretched his legs and started to run in Tuck's direction. He didn't care about being loud. The man's deafening music would drown out any sound. He looked down at his Fitbit and saw his heart rate was creeping up to 147 beats a minute. He felt like his heart was about to explode, but he didn't care. By time he finished, the device would probably tell him to stop and cool down.

He watched Tuck follow the paved path into an area of trees. He looked around, but there wasn't a soul in the park. What crazy person would be running through the park at ten o'clock in the evening?

Just good ol' Tuck.

Too bad for him.

He took a deep breath and ran full force in Tuck's direction. He was within an arm's reach of him when he caught a whiff of his Abercrombie or Hilfiger cologne. The revolting smell surged through him like a lightning bolt. His legs went into overdrive. Tuck might have played baseball in college, but an unprepared baseball player could not compete with a hurling linebacker.

Tuck didn't see it coming.

He didn't hear it either.

CHAPTER 2

Tuck couldn't get a scream out as his body was falling like dead weight to the ground. He was helpless and out of breath after his three-mile steamy run. Sweat was pouring off him as if someone had just doused him with a bucket of hot water. His body collided with the asphalt, and he felt his knees slam onto the concrete as his hands tried to soften the fall. He sensed the scraping of his palms and knew the top layer of skin was tattered and torn.

Tuck tried to turn his head around to see who he was about to fight, but his ego got the better of him.

"You son of a …," the attacker hissed as he squatted on Tuck's back and punched him on his right cheek, causing his head to whip around, slamming his forehead onto the concrete. "Don't look at me!"

The attacker grabbed the back of Tuck's head, weaving his fingers into the man's blond curls. He lifted up the weakening head and snarled, "How's it feel?" before slamming Tuck's head back into the concrete.

One of Tuck's hands quickly slid between his face and the paved path, slightly softening the blow, but it only caused his crippling fingers to feel the aftermath. He reached back with his other hand, trying to grasp onto something to pull the attacker away or inflict some pain on him, but it was useless. He had never been in this position before.

He had never been the inflicted.

Sadly, unremorsefully, he had usually been the inflictor.

"Stop!" Tuck moaned as the man sinisterly gripped Tuck's strands of hair tighter, pulling his head in different directions like a wounded marionette.

4

"You never stopped for them!" he remarked, lifting Tuck's head, causing his back to arch, pinching each vertebrae's sensitive nerve endings. He watched as Tuck's lips quivered in fear as streams of blood trickled from his forehead down to his chin. He was thankful for the lighted pathway tonight, so he could see the effects of his massacre. "Did you?"

Tuck grimaced in pain as he timidly shook his head no.

But it wasn't enough.

The attacker dug his fingers deeper into his hair, his fingernails scratching Tuck's scalp as he asked once again, "Did you?"

Tuck started to cry, tears mingling with the blood. "No!" he yelped like a wounded coyote caught in a bear trap.

But the attacker wasn't satisfied. He shook Tuck's head back and forth, moving it side to side as if Tuck's neck were a piece of rubber and not made of fragile, breakable bones.

"No, you didn't!" he snapped, throwing Tuck's head back down onto the concrete as if he had just scored a touchdown and this was his victory dance. He got up from Tuck's back, and the runner tried to quickly get onto all fours to stand up. But the attacker wasn't done.

He was just beginning.

A touchdown was always followed by a field goal opportunity, but instead of a ball, he aimed for Tuck's midsection. He planted his left foot and kicked his right one below Tuck's ribs. He made contact and watched Tuck flip over onto his back.

"Please, stop!" Tuck moaned with what little breath he had left as he tried to curl his body into a ball. But it wasn't quick enough. The attacker started kicking Tuck's side as quickly and repeatedly as a kid hitting buttons on a pinball machine.

"I will," the man hissed with a smile. "But not yet. Have you ever touched a little kid?" he asked, taking a break from his ruthless attack.

"No, never!" Tuck moaned.

"Promise?" he asked. "Because if you have, and I find out, you'll wish you were dead later."

"No!" he moaned once again as the kicks started up again.

"Good answer," he snarled. Tuck rolled his body into a ball, trying to protect his vital organs, but the attacker didn't care what he kicked. He was just there to hurt him until he was on the verge of death.

He didn't want to kill him. He wanted to teach him a lesson that he would never forget. Sometimes killing someone was giving them the easy way out. He wanted Tuck to suffer.

"Not much of a fighter, are ya?" he laughed as his legs started to tire from the manic kicking. "I haven't done this much cardio since my wife made me go to a kickboxing class." He stooped down until he was inches from Tuck's face. Tuck slowly opened his bloody eyes and realized he knew his attacker.

"If you rat me out, Tuck," he started, "so help me, I will kill you next time."

"I, I…" Tuck started to say feebly, "I won't. I promise I won't."

"Good boy," he said as he patted his head before standing up. "Do you want to call the paramedics?"

Tuck looked stunned. "I think I can make it," he said fragilely.

The attacker started to chuckle to himself. "I think you better call the paramedics."

Tuck swallowed and looked around the darkened area. He breathed in deeply. "My car isn't that far away. Just let me lie here a minute, and I'll make it back," he said. "I won't rat you out."

"Oh Tuck," he said stooping down once again and lifting Tuck's woozy head. "Do you really think I'm finished with you? You call the paramedics, and then we can start round two."

"Round two?" Tuck coughed out a few bloody bubbles as his eyes widened in fear.

"Round two."

"Please," Tuck started to beg as the attacker grabbed the phone attached to Tuck's bicep. He pressed three digits through the plastic guard and then wiped his prints away.

"911," an operator answered. "What's your emergency?"

Tuck looked up at the attacker's towering stature and bowed his head. He shook his head as more tears started to flow. He mouthed, "Please, no, please stop."

The attacker didn't say a word. He just pointed at the phone.

"Hello?" the female voice asked again. "911."

The attacker squatted down until his eyes were inches from Tuck's and whispered, "You better do this now because you won't be able to call when I'm done with you."

"I've been attacked," Tuck moaned as he answered all the operator's questions.

"Someone will be there sir. Just stay with me," she said optimistically.

The attacker smiled devilishly and reached down to end the call as the operator continued to speak good, life-giving words. Once again, he wiped his fingerprints clean.

"Smart decision, Tuck," he said.

"Please, no!" Tuck groaned in agony.

"Round two," the attacker grinned as he stood up while Tuck pleaded for his life. "I told you I'm not going to kill you." He shook his foot, loosening his leg muscles before looking around to ensure no one was around. He looked down and took aim for Tuck's chin. "I'm just going to make you wish you were dead."

"Please, no. I'll do whatever you want," Tuck groaned as his cell phone rang.

He looked down at the crying man. "It's too late for that. Isn't it, Tuck?"

Tuck's head flung back when the attacker's foot connected slightly below his chin. He listened as Tuck's breathing started to soften. The groaning had stopped. He watched as Tuck's eyes rolled like marbles behind his quickly bruising eyelids. He had succumbed to unconsciousness. The only sounds were the crickets chirping and Tuck's annoying ring tone.

He continued to kick the lifeless man. Tuck's lean and ripped physique wasn't any match to his muscle-packed body.

He kicked him a few more times and thought it was best to leave the scene.

But before he walked away, he checked himself for any battle scars. He looked around his hands, arms, and legs and couldn't find any wounds. He knew that his DNA was all over the scene of the crime through his sweat, but that was all.

He trotted away, heading to where he parked his pickup truck a few miles away. He didn't want the cops to see him getting into his getaway vehicle. They would probably ask him questions and then start to suspect him as the heinous citizen causing havoc on this poster child of the rich and guilty who had somehow been found innocent by a jury of his peers.

He knew he was safe.

His DNA wasn't in the system.

He wasn't a criminal like Tuck. Even though Tuck had been acquitted on all charges of rape and violence, he was still a criminal. Who knew money could buy someone's freedom?

Tuck knew.

Tuck knew it all too well.

CHAPTER 3

"Do you ever think we are playing God?" Elizabeth asked as she pulled out of Wint and Elizabeth's neighborhood speaking into her car's handless device.

"Playing God?" I asked with a wishy-washy tone. I had often asked myself the same question, but I never got a definitive answer. It changed depending on my mood.

"Yeah, Solo, playing God," she said snarkily. I could hear her roll down her windows and pictured the nighttime air blowing through her brunette hair. "Don't tell me you haven't thought about that," she remarked. "And you know, Jesus doesn't like liars."

"Why do you do that?" I laughed. "You throw down the Jesus card as if that card trumps everything."

"Doesn't it to you?"

"Well, you don't have to use his name like a tool," I snapped.

"Like a tool?"

I closed my eyes, and I could see her facial expression twitch in annoyance. She would ruffle her nose and huff anytime I pushed her buttons, and she knew my tell-tale sign of when she pushed mine.

Some people would look at us and see a jaded pair of individuals who bickered more than they agreed, but that was our relationship. It started rocky last October when I unknowingly slighted her abilities of seeing future events in her nightly dreams. I had stated I didn't believe in people having revelations from God like they did in biblical times, and that had ruffled her feathers to no end.

I'd stated my case and she'd stormed off like a spoiled brat in her BMW.

That was when my life drastically changed.

That night I'd had a few dreams that I couldn't comprehend, but somehow, each dream occurred the next day. Then the next night, I dreamed again. And then those dreams happened.

I had to swallow my pride and tell her I believed her, but she didn't easily trust my quick attitude change.

Luckily, her opinion changed the night Wint, my best friend and Elizabeth's brother-in-law, caught the infamous Carbon Monoxide Killers who wreaked havoc last October by killing poor, defenseless tourists. I'd helped Wint apprehend the estranged siblings, Jenny Ascot and Alexei Lechov. Wint still didn't understand why I showed up at Huntington Station that night. But if I hadn't been there, Wint would have been another victim of the two killers.

Wint arrested Jenny and shot and killed Alexei. I left the scene of the crime to save a future suicide victim from drowning in the Potomac River. Unbeknownst to me, I was the drowning victim.

Elizabeth came to my rescue. It was the first time in her life she had ever done anything to help the person in her dreams. In the past she had always just crossed off the dreams as they occurred. No matter what the dream was, big or small, she never interfered. Until me.

That night after she saved my life, I knew I was indebted to her, and she knew she was somehow grafted to me. It wasn't a perfect friendship, but we were learning.

Well, *I* was learning.

She was too stubborn.

"Are you still there?" she barked through her speakerphone. "Or did you tune me out like you do most nights?"

"I'm still here," I said opening my eyes as I lay on my worn-out couch in my bachelor pad apartment that even cockroaches were too proud to live in.

"You didn't answer my other question," she snarled.

"I think the fact that I didn't answer the question actually answered the question." I smiled as I grabbed the remote control sitting on the end table and turned on the television to see if anything newsworthy was on.

"Whatever, Solo," she kidded as she proceeded to drive the quieting roads home to her gated community.

"Anyways," I said getting back to her first question, "I don't like to think we are playing God."

"We pick and choose who to help," she rebutted like her attorney father and sister.

"Why didn't you become an attorney like your family?" I grinned as I noticed the news was only showing the forecast for the steamy weather for the upcoming Fourth of July.

"I can't stand to be around criminals," she said disgustedly. "I think they all deserve to rot."

"Innocent until proven guilty," I snuck in.

"Well, the judicial system sucks sometimes!" she said raising her voice in aggravation.

We had all experienced the flaws of the judicial system when Jenny Ascot, one of the Carbon Monoxide Killers, and former best friend to Wint's wife Veronica, was found not guilty on all counts of murder. She had clearly killed all those people, and everyone knew she'd killed them,

12

yet she walked out of the courtroom a free woman two and a half months ago.

The day after she was released, she tried to kill Elizabeth. I saved her from being tortured to death, and I had the scars along my legs from where Jenny stabbed me mercilessly trying to kill me as well.

Luckily, I'd remembered Elizabeth was a Second Amendment-supporting, gun-toting woman. I'd grabbed her purse and fired several bullets into Jenny's body.

Sadly, she survived.

Something I regretted daily. So, in a way, I wished I could play God, because if I had another go-around with Jenny, I wouldn't aim at her chest. No, I would aim at her head. Right between the eyes. And I wouldn't lose any sleep over stealing her last breath. I often wondered if that was wrong of me. The grace taught by my faith encouraged me to forgive Jenny's horrid past with the phrase, "Everything isn't excusable, but everything is forgivable."

I hated that line.

I wasn't ready for forgive.

"Yes, it does suck," I said remorsefully. I wanted to stand on the virtue that everything would be made right in the end, but in the meantime, I didn't want to have to wait. I wanted everything to be made right then. Not in the end.

"So, have you heard anything about your assault victim, Tuck?" she asked, her rage dying down as she changed topics like it was a radio station.

13

"I'll call the hospitals tomorrow and track him down," I said watching a commercial for cheap car insurance with their annoyingly bad acting.

"Why do you think God didn't tell us where the attack was going to happen?" she asked solemnly. "Why did God show you a guy was going to be brutally attacked in a park somewhere, but that's all? Were we supposed to figure out where it was going to happen with the cryptic clues left in a foggy dream? I mean…" She stopped and I heard her pound her fist on the steering wheel. "Come on, throw us a bone. We could have stopped it."

"Maybe we weren't supposed to," I feebly said. Those words hurt coming out of my mouth as much as they probably hurt Elizabeth hearing them.

"So God is cruel?" she yelled with a judgmental tone. "He picks and chooses who He wants to help? Don't you say we are all His children?"

I listened to her heartfelt plea. I had often wrestled with the notion of pain and how God could use it. But when I was in pain, I didn't want it to be a tool for my future. I just wanted some relief and healing during the crisis. If given the choice between a hard lesson learned or an easy life, I would jump on a cruise ship and sail away on the small pleasure-filled town.

"I wish I knew all the answers," I said disheartened. "I wish I knew."

"Yeah," she said compassionately. "I know you do."

I heard her ignition stop and the sound of her rustling through her belongings in her car. "Well, I'm home now. See you tomorrow morning at Verny's. I'll bring breakfast."

"Bring something good," I smiled.

14

"Don't I always?" she laughed as I pictured her walking into her townhouse, dropping her purse on the kitchen counter, and grabbing an imported bottle of water from her refrigerator.

"Please don't try to enlighten me with some new cuisine. Just keep it simple. Donuts will be good."

"Donuts?" she scoffed. "You know you'll get a sugar rush and crash by lunch, and we have a busy day of moving them."

"Fine," I huffed. "If you bring something healthy *and* some donuts, I promise I'll eat a little of both."

"How old are you again?" she laughed hysterically. "'Night, Solo."

I flipped the channels a few more times, but knew I needed to get to bed as well. It was going to be a long day. We were going to be moving Wint and Veronica the next day, but I bet there were going to be some dreams we were going to have to resolve too. I just hoped Wint didn't ask too many questions.

He was a police officer, and when things didn't add up, he started investigating.

I didn't know how much longer Elizabeth and I were going to be able to hold him off. I felt like I had lied to him by not telling him the truth, but the truth seemed so farfetched. I just hadn't been ready to see that look of disbelief on my best pal's face.

But he always told me the same thing when something didn't seem right: "You know you can trust me, Solo."

Sadly, I always nodded my head and agreed.

I knew I should trust him.

I just couldn't.

MONDAY

CHAPTER 4

A twelve-year-old girl poked her blonde head into a darkened room, looking startled with widening eyes and jarring head movement. She started to talk, but she didn't step into the room. She stayed fastened in the dimly lit hallway. Her lips were moving, but no sound came out. There was only silence.

She shook her head no and continued to talk, poking her head into the room. She looked around as if it were the first time she had seen the room. Her eyes darted left and right, taking in all the knickknacks and wall hangings. Suddenly she stopped dead center.

She continued to talk, but still nothing was heard.

She was talking to someone, but the other person or people couldn't be seen. She was the star of this attraction.

Her lips stopped moving, and she nodded her head in agreement as her eyes sparkled with intrigue and curiosity. She timidly took one step forward, crossing over the threshold from the familiar hallway into the foreign terrain.

She showed a brilliant smile and even started to giggle as she took another step forward into the deadly silence. She started to talk once again.

"You," she said as her voice engulfed the room.

She continued to speak, but that singular word was the only one heard. Her mouth was moving faster. Her feet were moving forward. She was taking more small steps until she was in the center of the room. But her eyes were fixed on one thing.

The room looked like a darkened home office with a desk and an old large computer monitor. The walls were decorated with gold and blue-striped wallpaper with artistic portraits similar to Rembrandt hung sporadically around the room. She tapped her fingers rhythmically on the desk, swirling her fingers around the hardwood as she walked around the large piece of furniture.

As she came around the desk, the perspective changed from staring forward at the door to looking behind at a large glass window overlooking a darkened yard with strings of colorful plastic lanterns below hanging between poles on the ground. She peered out the window, looking down at the festive lights as the window reflected her beaming smile.

She stopped talking.

Her smile started to fade until it was gone. Her bright eyes of curiosity changed to a glaze of fearful concern.

She turned around and shook her head as she started to mouth something.

A hand reached up and placed a finger on her mouth to silence her words.

Her lips started to quiver at the touch of the adult finger as another hand reached up from the side, grabbing her shoulder and pulling her in.

Her mouth gaped open as if she were screaming, but suddenly she stopped. Flashes of colorful lights filled the sky behind her. Fireworks were being detonated in the backyard.

But still, there was only silence.

Sparkling blues, reds, and yellows glittered the nighttime sky like pieces of fiery confetti as the colors shimmered into the room.

The young girl was pulled in closer by a pair of large-knuckled hands. She tried to fight them off, but they were too strong. Her body was tossed around as tears started to trickle down her cheeks.

She started to talk but her words, though silent, were easily recognizable. She was begging and pleading to be let go as a pair of hands left her bony shoulders and moved down where no child should be touched.

The room went dark except for the flashes of light from the fireworks.

"You," the young girl's voice repeated.

I woke up dripping in sweat.

I couldn't move. I was sickened at what I had just dreamed. I wanted this to be just a sick nightmare I could forget. I wanted to roll back over, go back to sleep, and have no memory of it when I woke up again in the morning.

But that wasn't going to happen.

A young girl was going to be sexually attacked somewhere, and I had no clue where it was going to happen.

Even though it sickened me to retrace my dream's steps, I knew I had to get all the information I could about this dream so I could try and stop it.

I closed my eyes and thought back. I looked around to see if there were any geographical points of interest that could shed some light on the location, but there weren't any. It was a dark room on a dark night in a two or three-story home with a backyard displaying a colorful string of

18

lights. I tried to remember if I could see anything in the distance. Any landmarks, but I saw nothing.

I mentally went back to the room where it happened, and I tried to be as delicate as I could to uncover something. But the only thing I uncovered was the disgust of a young child being victimized. She was probably molested by someone she knew since she was talking to them from the hallway. She had been friendly and bubbly at the beginning.

But then it changed drastically.

No child deserved to be in that position. None.

I lay in bed and wanted to cry. I wanted to get all the filth of what I had just witnessed out of me, but crying wouldn't do any good.

"You," the girl's voice echoed in my mind.

Why did she say "you?" I wondered. Why was that the only word I heard?

My body convulsed in a heart-wrenching thought.

Was she talking to me?

My heart sank at the thought, and I couldn't believe what I was thinking.

Was I the perpetrator?

Was I the person she was talking to?

"Please God, what's going on?" I prayed aloud as my fingers clenched and all the muscles in my body tightened like I was experiencing a full body charley horse.

I lay perfectly still in my paralyzing state and tried to breathe, but it was hard to do with everything colliding in a chaotic mental state.

I closed my eyes and all I could hear was the young girl's only word echoing in my mind.

"You."

"You."

"You."

CHAPTER 5

I left my apartment and started running down the sidewalk with no end in sight. I didn't have any plans for where I was running to or for how long. I just needed to run. I popped in my earbuds, cranked up the music on my phone, and ran as if I could leave my dream behind.

The sun still hadn't risen, and it would probably be another couple of hours before it would start to peek its summer rays over the horizon. Yet, the darkness still had a mugginess that blanketed over me like a pair of damp pajamas.

I came to a crosswalk and quickly looked both directions. The sign was telling me to stop, but there weren't any cars on the street at 4 a.m. It was like I was running in a city of one.

The tempo of the music was causing my legs to pick up speed as my feet tried to keep up with the fast beat. After a minute my mind was begging for the song to quickly end so my feet wouldn't feel the need to sprint much longer. I eventually started to ignore the music blaring in my ears.

This was a bad decision.

When my mind drifted into the region of peaceful silence, it was quickly shattered with the haunting voice of the young girl's singular word.

I tried to switch my brain's mode to listen to the music again, but now the two noises were competing for domination. The drum beat and synthesized loops were commingling with the girl's voice.

Her voice was resounding, repeating the word as if forming a beat of its own.

"You, you, you," and break. "You, you, you," and break. "You, you, you."

I tried to listen intently for the guitar strings, the singer's raspy vocal cords, the keys in the background, but the chaos soon started to sound like an operatic symphony. They were harmonizing in a way that my mind could have never concocted.

I grabbed on the cords of my earbuds and pulled hard, ripping them from my sockets, screaming at the top of my lungs. Thankfully, I wasn't around any homes. I had ended up at a nearby park with old rust-covered playground equipment that hosted drug deals at the swing set like it was a drive-thru McDonald's. I was alone. I guess even cocaine addicts were sleeping off their snow powder highs.

I screamed in hope of drowning out the girl's voice. I pleaded for God to show me what I was supposed to do. I begged that the girl wasn't saying I was the one who was hurting her.

My stomach lurched at the thought of me hurting a child in that way. Suddenly, the contents of my stomach were lying at my feet. I closed my eyes and waited for the second wave to come up. I wanted to release everything inside me because if I continued to think of hurting a child, I couldn't live with myself.

Eventually, the girl's voice disappeared, but I could still see her.

She didn't look familiar.

I didn't want to keep watching my memory, but I needed to. I needed to figure out if I knew this young girl. If I knew her, maybe I could stop whatever was going to happen. I went through my inner circle of friends with children, but none of them had daughters her age. She was a cute, precious little girl with innocence in her sparkling eyes.

I wanted to help her keep that innocence.

I needed to help her.

As I straightened up and refocused my thoughts, I started debating with myself. The devil's advocate within me was playing both sides brilliantly.

Quit thinking of her! You pervert!

You're not a pervert. You're just trying to sort out this mess.

Yeah, perverts never think they're perverts.

Quit calling me a pervert. I have never done anything or ever thought anything like this.

There's always a first time for everything.

That voice knocked me off my feet. I almost fell into my vomit on the sidewalk as I let my body fall to the ground. The voice was right. No matter the sin, it always started with a thought. There was always a first for everything.

"Please, God! Please!" I mumbled with conviction mixed with dread. "Please don't let this be me."

I rested my hands on each side of me, feeling the wetness of what I had heaved a few minutes earlier.

I looked over and realized the bile between my fingers was nothing compared to the corrosion eating away at my heart.

Nothing.

"Oh, God," I groaned in confusion. I knew beyond a shadow of a doubt I would never be able to commit such a horrid and gruesome act. The mere thought of it caused a cold sweat to engulf my body. The thought was wrecking me to my core. I couldn't even dare to imagine what I would be feeling if this were truly a sign of my future.

"Why did you show me the dream?" I yelled out as I looked up at the cloudy sky. "Is this a warning?" My emotions were shifting from confusion to anger. "Why show me something like this if there isn't anything I can do about it?"

I stopped my animosity-fueled words and let my anger shift once again to cynicism. "If you're really God, you can tell me what I need to do. You could tell me! But…" I stopped and scraped my hand clean on the grass behind me.

"But you never do." I moped like a disgruntled, spoiled kid. "You're never here when I need you the most."

CHAPTER 6

"Don't say I've never bought you anything," Elizabeth smiled, waving a box of five-star donuts from District Donuts. She untied the blue string around the white box and let the intoxicating aroma dance around like sugar plum fairies.

I planted on a pain-filled smile as Wint grabbed the box and devoured the vanilla bean crème brûlée donut creation. Elizabeth rolled her eyes at my lack of appetite.

"I specifically went and got these freakin' carb circles for you, Solo, so you better smack that stupid grin off your cheesy face before I stuff one of these obesity-inducing heart attack-causing goodies down your skinny throat," she growled menacingly. "You got me, jogger boy?"

Nodding my head, I grabbed a funfetti donut with inviting, colorful sprinkles. I tried my best to swallow every bite, but I couldn't keep it down. Every time a little piece slid down my throat, my stomach quickly heaved it back up with venomous acid.

I had hoped Elizabeth wouldn't catch me spitting up a few bites into Wint's bushes in front of their house, but she saw me when she came marching out the front door with a pair of matching black and white Pottery Barn lamps.

I pretended that a piece choked me, but she saw through the charade.

Elizabeth, Wint, Veronica, and I were on a mission to get the last of Wint and Veronica's furniture out of their gigantic former home they'd put on the market two months earlier to move into a two-bedroom townhouse in a suburb of Alexandria, Virginia. They were leaving their well-to-do neighborhood with politicians and diplomats to slum it in an up-and-coming trendy neighborhood of young professionals.

If Wint had told me a year ago he would be moving away from the lavish lifestyle of the rich and elitist, I would have laughed in his face. Veronica was the poster child of trust-fund kids. She had been given the best education and a great position in her father's law firm, Manfield & Hyde, on the fast track of becoming partner one of these days. All that came to a halt three months earlier when she was defending her former best friend and accused killer, Jenny Ascot. Wint had told me the story of what took place just a couple of months prior.

Veronica had always had a nagging thought that her father never loved her, but she'd always tried to dismiss that notion by proving her worth to him. The illusion came to an end when Luther Hyde sided with Jenny Ascot, a woman who'd stated she wished she had killed Veronica when she'd had the chance that fateful weekend about nine months earlier when Veronica stayed with her after she and Wint had a spat.

"How does Cooper Law sound?" Veronica had asked Wint a couple of weeks after Jenny was found not guilty.

"I will support your decision, Veronica," Wint had always replied with a considerate boyish grin. "I will always be here for you."

So, Veronica went to work on a Thursday morning and resigned.

Some of the firm was in disbelief, some saw the writing on the wall, and one person was indifferent with the decision – Luther Hyde.

As Veronica was packing up her belongings, Luther had stepped into her office and closed the door.

"Don't think this place is your fallback plan," Luther had said unremorsefully as he continued to grip the door handle as if he'd had many other places he would rather be.

"I would rather work as a sewer cleaner than work for you, Father," is what she'd wanted to say, but she had just smiled and nodded. "I know. Thank you for the privilege of learning from you, Mr. Hyde." She wasn't allowed to call Luther Dad or Father while at work. He was always Mr. Hyde or sir to her.

"You didn't learn this from me," he said snidely. "I don't teach quitters."

A few months prior, those words would have crushed her, but not anymore. She was stronger after all the years of his verbal assaults. "I'm sorry you see me in that way, sir."

"I'm sorry too," he'd said as he turned the door handle and quickly walked away.

There were no goodbyes. There were no plans to see one another at dinner. There was no cordial politeness. It was business as always for Luther.

Veronica had picked up her box of belongings and left before eleven that day. She'd said she would give two or three weeks' notice to help in a smooth transition for her clients, but she didn't care anymore. She had read and reread her employee contract, and her father had made one error. He had never made her sign a non-compete contract. She was free to leave and take as many clients as she could.

She'd known the law firm might go after her, but she'd had the law in her back pocket. She had all her documents scanned from when she started working at Manfield & Hyde. If they said she signed a non-compete contract, she would cite it as a forgery.

And if her father went after her, she would have had to go after him with the secret she had been holding for years. He'd had an affair with an employee and had her killed by Miloslav Alexeev's Russian mob. She hadn't wanted to go there, but if she was backed into a corner, she wouldn't stay there long. She hadn't wanted to ruin her father's life, but she knew he wouldn't have had any concern ruining hers.

"I did it," Veronica had said unfazed as she'd called Wint sitting in her parked car that Thursday morning.

"I thought you were going to wait a few more weeks," Wint had said, concerned. "I thought you needed to get a few more things lined up."

"I couldn't take it any longer," she'd said gruffly. "We were in a meeting and they brought up Jenny's next court appearance and they were deciding who was going to defend her this time."

"You've got to be kidding me," Wint had said agitatedly.

"No, Wint, they were talking as if Jenny was innocent and started planning her defense," she'd said gripping her steering wheel and gritting her teeth. "So, I just stood up and did it."

"What did your dad say?"

She'd stopped and thought back to that moment. "He never even looked up," she'd said scornfully. "A few of my colleagues were asking questions, but he said, 'Can we get back to the point of this meeting? Mrs. Cooper, you may be excused since our clients no longer pertain to you. Please close the door behind you as you leave.'"

There had been silence on the phone.

"Wint?" Veronica had asked, wondering if he had gotten disconnected.

"I'm so sorry, Veronica," he'd said sniffling. "You don't deserve that."

Veronica had heard the emotion in Wint's words. She knew if she'd thought much longer, her voice would be cracking soon. "Well, I'm going to go look at a few office spaces if you want to come join me."

"Always," Wint had said sounding more chipper. "I'll meet you wherever."

Veronica had found a quaint little office space, nothing spectacular, that would work for her. It was a blank canvas with five rooms and white walls. It was formerly a dietician's office, but when the police figured out it was a front for trafficking drugs, they had quickly shut the place down. Unfortunate for the drug dealers, but the landlord needed someone to pay the rent, so Veronica was able to slide in with her negotiation skills and get a nice two-year lease, utilities included.

That same day they had put their home on the market.

"These are a lot of big changes," Wint had remarked as his eyes pierced into Veronica's. "Are you sure you're up for all of this?"

She'd grabbed his hand and kissed his knuckles. "If you promise to be here beside me through it, I'm up for anything."

"Then let's sell this baby."

Two months later, I was chugging some water trying to wash away the aftertaste of the upchucked breakfast as Elizabeth snuck up behind me.

"You're hardly moving. You didn't appreciate the breakfast I bought for you, and you are actually throwing it up," Elizabeth said with a disgruntled gesture. "What gives?"

I thought about what to say. Should I tell her about my dream? A dream, the meaning of which still left me confused? Did I tell her that I was on the brink of losing it again, like I was any time I was pressed too hard? Should I pretend like everything was fine and she was the one who was losing it? So many choices. Which one to choose.

"Uh…"

CHAPTER 7

"Uh?" Elizabeth snapped, smacking the back of my head like I was her little brother and not a full-grown man five years older than she. "Really, that's all you have to say?"

"I'm just not feeling it this morning," I said with a weak sigh. "Maybe it's the emotional toll of them moving," I lied.

"Emotional toll?" she asked, cocking her eyes at me with a questioning stare. "They're moving across town, not to Cambodia."

"It's just…" I started to say as she interrupted.

"It's just, it's just, it's just," she said in her mocking nasally tone. "Give it a break, Solo," she stabbed hatefully. "You are just a lazy bum. I now see why you live in your run-down place you call a home. Maybe if you tried a little harder in life, you could make something of yourself instead of living on your friends' coattails."

"Coattails?" I whispered, closing my eyes and shaking my head in disbelief.

I stepped aside, walking past her into the house to help Wint start carrying out the heavy furniture. I could hear her saying something as I walked away, but I didn't want to listen to her judgment.

Not today.

I hustled into the living room and found Wint and Veronica holding hands. They stood like a bride and groom on their wedding day, looking around as if the reality of moving was finally hitting home. I stopped and felt the heaviness in the room. I looked down at my own empty hand and knew I would never be able to stand that way with my true love, Chelsea.

Chelsea had been killed in a drive-by shooting as she was reporting on the increasing crime in the inner city. She was the love of my life.

I continued to stare at my trembling hand as another suddenly swooped into mine. "You know I didn't mean what I just said," Elizabeth said softly, whispering into my ear.

I nodded my head.

Deep down I knew Elizabeth had my back, but she had a strange way of showing it.

"I'm just pissed you wasted that donut as I'm starving myself to stay thin," she said, squeezing my hand tighter before letting go. "Veronica, if you and Wint are going to keep standing there like horny teenagers, you are going to have to start paying us for wasting a day."

Elizabeth turned her head and winked at me. It was a wink that assured me she spoke to everyone with disdain. And that was true. Even the pope wouldn't be safe from her twisted remarks and cruel backhanded compliments. "Nice pointy hat, Father, but you have more bling on than a drag queen J Lo on karaoke night."

I shook my head and walked over to one side of the couch as Wint straddled and squatted on the other side.

"Ready?" Wint asked.

"Ready."

CHAPTER 8

"How did that make you feel?" Ally McDermott asked Jed Poston, one of the members of her anger management circle, as she tried to put on a sympathetic front.

"I wanted to kill 'em!" Jed answered angrily as he recalled the moment two months earlier at the soft drink fountain machine in Chipotle. "That moron took the last cup of ice out of the machine and he snickered at me like a moron would and started to taunt me like I was a stupid kid."

Ally loved her work. She loved digging into people's psyches and uncovering the unresolved issues they had buried deep in the inner regions of their troubled minds. Except for the court-mandated anger management sessions. She knew this group of delinquents was not going to change. They had to come to at least twelve of these *life-changing* group meetings to erase their indiscretions. At first, she'd had hopes of changing these people, but as the years went on, she had come to terms with the fact that she could not change those who didn't seek to be changed.

"Can you think of anything else you could have done besides beat that kid's head against the straw dispenser?" Ally asked while drawing a meadow of flowers in her notepad. She had begun to loath these hour-long sessions each day. She looked at her watch on her medically taped left wrist and stared in agony that her hour with these criminals still had ten minutes.

"I could have stabbed him in the eyes with the plastic fork," he grinned menacingly. "But I tried to hold my temper."

"Jed, you caused the teenager to go to the ER."

"He's eighteen," Jed said smoothing out his crimson silk tie as he winked at the auburn-headed Chantelle. "He's an adult. I don't hit kids."

"You got lucky you didn't do this to him four months ago when he was still seventeen," Ally remarked, looking into his calloused eyes with her own flare of malice. "Anger management training would be a class you could be taking at the state pen."

"Maybe I'll buy a lottery ticket today then, hon."

"Not cool," Lex Wetzmann said as he popped his knuckles, watching Jed with malicious eyes. He twisted his upper body, exposing a portion of bold tattooed Hebrew letters that trailed in a vertical line down the back of his neck under his fitted camouflage t-shirt. He gripped the back of his chair and popped his back with chiropractic force. "Not cool, man."

"Whatever shylock," Jed said, ignoring Lex's condemnation.

"What did you call me?" Lex asked, jumping up with his fists ready to fight.

"What?" Jed asked, leaning back in his chair with a sly smile. "I thought that was a good thing for your people."

"Lex, sit down! We don't settle things with fighting in here," Ally said trying to control the testosterone-fueled room. "And Jed, if you keep running your mouth, you'll meet someone one day who will stop it for good."

"I'll like to see them try," Jed said with a smile.

"I'm willing," Lex said under his breath, taking his seat in the circle.

Ally felt her blood boil with their disregard for the sanctity of her work. She needed to move on to her last participant for the day.

"How are you doing today, Kristopher?" Ally asked, lifting her eyes from her drawing to give her favorite member of the circle her undivided attention.

"I'm trying," the soft-spoken man in his forties said as he looked around the room as if feeling the eyes of judgment from each of them.

"What are you trying?" Ally asked with a tone that would ease the most frightened of kittens.

"I'm doing your breathing exercises when I feel the pressure starting to rise. I'm trying to look at the person I am having a conflict with as a person and not just as an adversary. I'm taking nighttime walks to alleviate some stress; I actually took one last night."

"And how is that helping you?"

Kristopher lifted his head with a newfound charisma. He didn't sink back into the shell built from his violent past. He was tired of hiding. He started to nod with a slight smile on his face. "I'm feeling better."

Ally reciprocated the smile. "These exercises may not work for everyone, but that is why you have to try to find something that channels this pent-up energy. Some people prefer painting or doing something with their hands. Getting the creativity out is a way to get the stress out. Others find great relief in exercising. Kickboxing or running is a great way to release your anger in a safe way."

"What about sex?" Jed asked, winking once again at Chantelle. "That releases a lot of pressure for me."

"Jed, when you need to release anger, do not bring sex into it. That will only lead to more problems down the road," Ally said biting her tongue at the audacity of the male ego. "Rape, torture, bondage, and sadism are just a few things that could be byproducts of an act of love when done with wrong motives."

"But what if she likes it rough?" Jed asked, smiling like a cocky playboy in his $800 suit as another participant, Moe Holmes, snickered and agreed.

"Jed, that is outrageously inappropriate," Ally scorned, slamming her notepad closed and dropping it on the ground beside her. She grimaced in pain and clutched her tightly-bound wrist.

"You okay, Mrs. McDermott?" Kristopher asked from across the room as his eyes softened with compassion.

Ally looked down at her wrist, rubbing it with her tender right hand. "I was walking my dog over the weekend and had the leash around my wrist. When someone lit a firework, it startled him," she said shrugging her shoulders. "He didn't mean to hurt me, and I will be okay. Thanks for asking, Kristopher." Ally smiled warmly at her favorite member as he nodded in condolence.

"Looks like the time is up, Ally," Jed interrupted, standing up and striding over to Ally's chair. "Can you sign the judge's order, and I'll be on my way."

Ally leaned over and picked up her pen from her notepad. "I hope you have changed, Jed. This program isn't supposed to be a fix-all. I can recommend some good therapists or counselors for you to continue working with."

"I think I'll be fine, sweetheart," he smirked with a fetching wink he used at the bars to pick up his nightly flings.

She quickly signed the paperwork and stood up to join the remaining members at the table getting their free snacks and signing their attendance sheets.

"Anyone know where Tuck is?" Chantelle asked, quickly losing interest in the answer as she signed her name and followed Jed leaving in his well-fitted suit. "Jed, wait up."

"Wish she worried about me," Moe said under his breath.

CHAPTER 9

Ally waited until the majority of the members left before starting to clean up the room and wipe down the table with spilt Dr. Pepper and crumbled Goldfish crackers.

"You don't have to help with that, Kris," Ally said as she turned around and found him folding the chairs and leaning them against the wall. "I can get that."

"I thought I would help with your wrist being hurt," he said with a kind expression on his face. Ally had to remind herself she was happily married, but there was something about how Kris looked in his light purple polyester polo shirt. The contrast of his tan complexion to the soft pastel caused the hairs on the back of her neck to rise. She had to turn her head and shake out the tantalizing thoughts, or she could have watched him bend over and pick up the chairs all afternoon.

He's your patient and you are married, she told herself. She had a moral obligation to keep this relationship strictly professional. She had an oath to help this patient, and she was seeing a change in Kris, a change she had never seen before with court-mandated anger management classes.

"That is very kind of you," she said as she threw away her wet napkins and sealed up the crackers in the cabinet. It was just the two of them in the room as the last member left without saying goodbye.

"Kris, can I ask you a question?" Ally asked with a tone of apprehension.

"Sure," he said folding up another one of the chairs in the circle.

"You don't fit the mold of someone needing anger management," she said with a compassionate look in her eyes that glistened in contrast to

38

the overhead stale lighting. "What happened, if you don't mind me asking?"

"I wish I could say someone made a mistake, but I was in the wrong and had been for a while," he said looking down at his brown loafers for a few seconds before returning to the remaining chairs.

He took a deep breath and started to tell his story. "I wasn't always angry all the time, and I don't mean to make excuses, but when I was deployed to Iraq, I saw some things that I wish I could forget. Then as I started working here in the states, I started to drink a little more. There would be some days that I would come into work drunk. I have given up drinking, but a few weeks ago I lost it at work. It seems like this time of year is always the hardest."

"I didn't know you were in the military."

"Yes, I had two stints in Iraq, and then I came back home. I tried my best to keep my rage hidden from my family and friends, but there were some days when I would just explode on anyone who looked at me the wrong way. I tried to not scare my wife, but sometimes, it just took over."

Her eyes continued to soften as he told his story. She was allowing his words to enter deep into her soul. She felt the pain in his story. A story that was way too common.

"Have you considered going to counseling? Didn't the military recommend it for you?" she asked. "My husband has bouts of PTSD from his duty in Afghanistan." As soon as she said the words her insides clenched.

"I didn't know your husband was in the military," Kris said, stopping dead in his tracks.

"I'm sorry, Kris. I should have never said that to you. Please do not tell anyone. I am not supposed to release any personal information to anyone in our group. Please forget that I ever said anything."

"Ally, your words are safe with me," he said with a kind disposition as he folded up the last two chairs and aligned them on the wall with the others.

"Thank you, Kris, but I think it would be best if you seek a counselor or therapist who will help you with your daily struggles. Just as I told Jed, this anger management class will not fix all your issues. This is just an intro, you could say, to getting more personable and consistent treatment."

"I'm thinking about looking into that," Kris nodded.

"I can give you a few good counselors who specialize with military personnel," Ally said walking over to him.

"I'd appreciate that," he said as he looked towards the door and saw someone turning the knob to come in. "Well, you have a good rest of your day, Ally."

"You too, Kris. See you on Wednesday."

Kris waved goodbye as a gentleman just slightly taller than him entered the room in a postal uniform with a messenger bag strapped across his chest.

"Want to go to lunch?" Gordon asked as he strutted in with his grey shorts and light navy shirt.

"Love to," Ally said, walking over and greeting her husband with a welcoming kiss. "Looking good today," she said admiring his tan, strong legs.

"What can I say?" he said with a seductive smile. "I love my job."

CHAPTER 10

"I can't believe it's all in there," Veronica said in awe, staring at the moving van as Wint laid in a shadow on the driveway, drenched in masculine sweat. I, on the other hand, just looked dirty and gross.

"Can we just sit here for a few minutes before we head over to unload it all?" Wint begged.

"I guess," Veronica grinned as she leaned down, rubbing her husband's head like a dog. "You are so wet," she laughed. "Disgusting."

"What did you expect? Glitter?" Elizabeth chimed in with wide-eyed sarcasm. "They've been working like dogs all morning. I'm surprised they haven't started slobbering on themselves from exhaustion as well."

"Kind words just fall from your mouth like lemon drops, you know that?" I kidded.

"I was giving you a compliment for your hard work, Solo," Elizabeth replied with a high-pitched cackle.

"I prefer your silence more than your compliments," I returned with an over-dramatic wink that the neighbor kids up the street could have witnessed with the strange contortion of my face.

"Close your mouth, Solo," Elizabeth said busting out laughing. "You look like you're having a stroke."

"See," I said glancing over at Wint who had raised himself up onto his elbows. "Silence is better."

"He's got a point," Wint grinned looking over at Elizabeth sitting neatly on a step on their front porch. "Your silence is golden sometimes."

"Well, you're never going to get it from me then, because gold causes my skin to turn green," she laughed. "My skin requires the highest quality of metal, like platinum."

"Wasn't that a test they used back in Salem to see if you were a witch?" I joshed as Wint fell back in laughter. "Sorry to say, sister, but you would be dead now."

"How do you know I'm not a witch?" Elizabeth asked with scathing eyes.

"Oh honey, you're not a witch," Veronica said maternally. "You're a bitch. It's easy to misunderstand when people are yelling that to you all the time."

"Hardy har har," Elizabeth smiled as she stood up. "Want to help me get some drinks for the boys?"

"Can't you just wiggle your nose like Samantha or point with your finger and get us the drinks?" I asked with a playful tone.

"I can't do that," Elizabeth said brushing her pants clean. "But I can do this with my finger," she said with a hoity smile as she gave me an obscene gesture.

Elizabeth and Veronica left me and Wint to relax for a few minutes alone.

"Are you sure there is nothing between you two?" Wint asked, rolling over onto his side as if we were twelve-year-old boys at a camp out.

"I promise you, I'm not man enough to control Elizabeth," I said with an eye roll. "Lord help Jeremiah."

Wint nodded his head in agreement. "But it would be nice to have you as a brother-in-law," he said with a softer tone.

"I would need a shot to get into that family."

"I got mine," he smiled. "It was worth it."

"Some people are meant to be friends and not lovers," I said looking up into the blue sky with the white fluffy clouds hovering motionlessly. "And I think if I made one too many wrong moves, she would snip me in the middle of the night just for revenge."

"You're not right, boy."

"I swear," I laughed. "I don't trust her with a pair of scissors."

"But you have to admit, you two have some strange connection. Are you ever going to tell me what's up between you two?" Wint had been asking this question more and more over the last three months, and it hurt me to not be honest with my best friend, but I wasn't ready to tell him yet.

"You two?" Elizabeth oohed as she walked out with a few water bottles in her hands. "Solo has a--"

Multiple deafening popping sounds echoed around the street. It sounded like a war zone of firecrackers two houses away. We quickly darted our eyes to where the screams were coming from and saw a pack of pre-teen boys shooting off bottle rockets and roman candles. The street shimmered in a fountain of colorful sparks that shot up ten feet before flowing down.

"Kids," I laughed before I noticed a look of confusion on Wint's face. I turned my head toward where he was looking and saw a shaken Elizabeth with water bottles rolling around her feet.

"I hate this time of year," she groaned as she carefully bent down, trying to grip the wet bottles.

"I got it," Wint said jumping up to help her. "Catch, Solo," he said as he threw me one of the bottles.

I quickly opened the bottle and chugged the refreshment. "I love this time of the year," I said recalling childhood memories of when Wint and I were just like the kids up the street. I looked down at my ankle and caught a glimpse of a scar. "Remember when you shot me with a bottle rocket?"

"You should have jumped," Wint laughed.

"You shot me though!"

"You could have jumped!"

"You shot six of them at me at once. I couldn't dodge them all!"

"Oh yeah," Wint said thinking back to that teenage summer as a smile landed on his face. "Those were good times."

CHAPTER 11

"I'm going to head out and get some water. I'll meet you all at your new place," Elizabeth said as she looked with cruelty at the kids up the street.

"I can get you some more water," Veronica said slightly bewildered. "Or is that code for something?"

"Yes, dear, getting some water is code for hooking up with my boy toy Enrique," Elizabeth kidded with a twinkle in her eye. Her twinkle turned to a wink as she looked in my direction. I knew getting water was a signal she was going to go handle one of her dreams she'd had the night before. Sadly, I couldn't remember what she told me that morning when she'd rambled on about her dreams from the previous night. We usually split up each other's dreams and took the ones that best suited our abilities, but I lied this morning when we were going over our list and told her I had already resolved my two dreams since they were going to happen early in the morning.

"Early bird," she'd laughed as she'd succumbed to the idea of taking care of her own predictions.

I didn't have the heart or the nerve to tell her about my fear-ridden, pedophile-filled dream. I didn't have the stomach to watch her eyes look at me in disgust as the young girl's only words were "You." I didn't want to hear her relentless questioning.

Why did she say 'you'? Are you a sicko, Solo? You are a middle-aged single man and you fit the profile for child abusers since they hide in the church so well. Just turn yourself in, or better yet, go kill yourself. Stop the cycle before it ever begins.

I wasn't ready for her innuendos and badgering. I wasn't ready for her tirade because I hadn't healed from my defense mechanisms of trying to justify how I would never hurt a child.

But didn't everyone think that moments before they decided they were going to do something they knew they shouldn't do?

As I sat and debated myself, I knew these discussions were better with a neutral party. I needed the person who wouldn't judge me when I spoke politically incorrectly or in fractured run-on-sentences. I needed to speak to Elizabeth's boyfriend, not her fictitious cabana boy. I needed to meet with Jeremiah for one of our hypothetical ponderings.

"Be safe," I said to her as she walked by while I quickly texted Jeremiah and asked him to meet for a late-night snack. I didn't want to interfere with any romantic shenanigans they might be having with dinner. Although Jeremiah would welcome my presence as a third wheel, Elizabeth would rather slice my tire.

"Always," she said as she got into her BMW and skirted down the street, blaring her horn at the kids who'd startled her.

"She's something," Veronica said as she walked back in the empty house.

"That's an understatement for the ages," I said with a slight chuckle.

I stood up shaking my wobbly legs awake as I braced myself against their garage door. I walked over to Wint, who was still on his back, his legs sprawled out like a sleeping dog on his favorite cushion. "Ready to get this over with?"

I reached out my hand and pulled Wint up. That was what friends did. When someone was down, a friend would always be there to lift them back up.

46

Sadly, I couldn't do the same to myself.

All I kept seeing every time I closed my eyes was the petrified glazed look of impeding terror in that child's eyes.

I looked up the street for the pack of boys who must have scattered after Elizabeth left. I would have begged them for another firework to go off because all I could hear now was the poor girl's trembling voice echoing inside my tossing head.

You.

CHAPTER 12

"Are you two ready?" I asked, walking into Wint and Veronica's home as they were looking at the emptiness of their living room one final time. "Oh, sorry," I said as I quickly stepped back outside.

"It's okay," Veronica said as she kissed Wint, tugging on his hand to follow her outside.

"Are you two sure about this?" I asked, swaying on the front porch like a nervous kid waiting for a doctor's appointment.

"Definitely," Wint said locking the door one last time. "This is just a house," he said looking at me and then Veronica. "It's time to move past the past."

Wint headed towards the van as I took a seat in my old beat-up Honda, crossing my fingers that it would start on the first try.

"Let me check the mailbox before we leave," Veronica said. She sifted through the mail on her way back to her vehicle as a certain envelope caught her attention. She ripped it open and unfolded the letter as pieces of paper fell onto the ground. She clutched her mouth as she started to gasp.

"What is it?" Wint shouted, jumping out of the truck and running to her side.

He grabbed the letter from her trembling hands, and his face turned white as he scanned the piece of paper.

"What?" I asked, coming up beside them.

"It's from Jenny," Veronica said with a shallow breath, craning her neck to read the letter once again.

I looked down and saw a few pictures scattered on the pavement. I bent down and picked them up, seeing that they were images of Veronica dressed in a pair of red capri pants and a red gingham short-sleeve button-up. She was stunning as ever in her designer sunglasses and Birkenstocks.

"Who took these?" I asked, handing them to Wint who handed the letter back to Veronica. "Jenny's in jail."

"I don't know," Veronica said. "I don't know."

"Wasn't this what you wore yesterday?" Wint asked, handing Veronica the pictures.

She looked stunned as her knees started to shake. "I need to sit down."

"Solo, hold these," Wint said as he walked his wife to their front porch, helping her every step of the way.

I knew that I shouldn't look at the letter since it wasn't addressed to me, but I couldn't help but drop my leering eyes down onto the ransom note-style cut up letters.

Sis,

You may think you are safe since I am behind bars, but let me remind you, I have my eyes on you. You can move from your fabulous house, but I will find you at your new home. You are really slumming it in your new abode. But I guess with Wint's cop salary, you're going to need to start slumming it to make ends meet. I heard you quit your job. How did Luther take it? Never mind. I already know since he met with me when he came to my grave. Even though he killed me, he still comes and visits regularly. He seemed...what's the word...uncaring. He didn't care that his daughter left him. He

49

seemed unfazed. Funny, isn't it? He cares more about my well-being than your employment with him. You may not see the laughter in it, but from where I am, it's one of the few things getting me through the solitude. And I think about it often.

I hope you enjoy the pictures. I just wanted you to know you are not safe. I can kill you any time I want. All I have to do is ask, and you will be dead. It would be horrible to get blood on that nice shirt, so I'll ask them to not shoot you. They can kill you in other ways that won't damage your clothes. And I bet your mother would prefer to have an open coffin. I mean, with her socialite status, it would be horrible to not make your death into some public spectacle. Anything to impress the Joneses.

I know Wint is going to read this, but if you let anyone else see it, I will go public with what I know.

Even from the grave, I can bring you down. I mean, we were co-workers, and I know more than you could ever imagine.

Always yours,
Mia Rosenburg

"I thought you said this letter was from Jenny," I said with confusion radiating from my furrowing brow. "Who is Mia Rosenburg?"

CHAPTER 13

"Where are you?" Elizabeth asked as she drove to Wint's new home after her adventure-filled afternoon.

"I could have asked you the same question," I said pulling out of Wint's narrow driveway after unloading furniture all afternoon.

"I had a little snag in my plan," she huffed. "Why do kids always have to make things more difficult? I don't understand why more parents don't invest in leashes."

"Leashes are for dogs," I laughed.

"Well, rabid dogs are more well-behaved than the two little demons I was dealing with for the last two hours."

"Do you know how hard it's been coming up with excuses as to why it's taking you so long to pick up water?" I asked, looking both ways before proceeding through the four-way stop.

Elizabeth cursed, probably realizing she needed to stop and get the water like she said she would. "What did you say to them?"

"I ignored the question a few times," I said shrugging my shoulders. "Wint was getting into police mode with his interrogation tactics. So…" I took in a long deep breath. "I said I had to use the bathroom."

"How many times did you say that?" Elizabeth asked hesitantly.

"Seven." I laughed as she too busted out in her loud boisterous cackle. "I think they are worried about me. Wint mentioned diabetes and going to see a doctor."

"Veronica was worried about you?" Elizabeth scoffed before she told me she was pulling into a convenience market.

"I'm pretty sure she was more worried about me pissing on her furniture that I was carrying."

"Typical Verny," Elizabeth said. I could hear her quickly getting out of her car and running in to get the case of water. "So, are you still there helping out?"

"No, I'm done," I smiled. "You can go help Verny with decorating and go play nicely with Wint as he nags you with a million questions. *Nicely*, Elizabeth," I said, emphasizing the word.

"When am I not nice?" she asked sarcastically.

"This morning as you were commenting on Wint's shorts."

"They had holes in them," she defended.

"He's moving and was going to get sweaty. Let the man wear whatever he wants."

"Well, when I'm seen in public with him, he's got to step up his game," Elizabeth said. "Excuse me, can you get that case of water? My hands are full," she said to someone in the store.

"You're only holding a cell phone," the teen groaned. I pictured him rolling his eyes when I heard him add, "You can get that yourself, ma'am."

Elizabeth went ballistic on the poor kid. "Ma'am? Ma'am? Do I look like a ma'am to you, kid?"

"How old are you? Thirty?" he naively asked.

"Thirty!" Elizabeth croaked. "Solo, I have to get off here and teach this kid a lesson," she said in a muffled tone.

"Nicely," I said with a laugh before she mocked me with a snide laugh and ended the call.

I wondered if I needed to say a prayer for the poor kid, but I knew nothing was going to stop Elizabeth's tirade. Not even a heavenly miracle.

I proceeded to drive to my next destination. I wasn't sure if it was the right place, but I knew I would eventually find Tuck.

I parked my car and walked to the entrance of the Sibley Memorial Hospital. I worked out a story in my head, rehearsing the dialogue like I was reciting my lines for *Death of a Salesman*.

The lobby was typical for a hospital setting. Cheap art décor highlighted under dim lighting to enhance the atmosphere, as if mood lighting was what was needed in a hospital where the sick came to die or live. I had never heard anyone say, "Want to go check out the artwork at the local hospital? I hear it's to die for?"

I strolled up to the guest services desk with a smile on my face from my whimsical thought and asked what room Tucker Stevenson was in. The retirement-age woman slowly found the letters on the keypad one finger at a time.

"304," she smiled warmly and then proceeded to point the way.

I was surprised it worked. I didn't expect to find him on the first try. Now I had to quickly figure out what my next step was going to be.

Hello Tucker, I'm Solo…I had a dream about you.

That line hadn't worked out very many times. And it probably wouldn't work out again today. I needed to come up with another introduction.

Hello Tucker, I'm Solo…

Yeah, that's all I had.

CHAPTER 14

"Who are you here to see?" the police officer asked as the man walked into the correctional facility with all his belongings in his hands.

"Jennifer Ascot," he said calmly handing over his wallet, phone, keychain, and chewing gum as he went through the security procedures like the many times before.

"Is this your first time here?" the guard asked, eyeing him suspiciously as he looked over his identification.

"First time today," he answered cunningly as he quickly shook his head. "No, sir. I have been here before."

Another guard took him to the room with a line of cubicles with a flimsy plastic chair slid under each table. The partitioned glass had fingerprint smears from loved ones trying to hold hands during this trying time. "Can I have a sheet of paper and a pencil to write with?" he asked the guard who nodded and left.

He sat down and untangled the phone cord like he did every time he waited on Jennifer, or as he liked to call her, Jenika Lechov. The guard returned with his pencil and paper, and a few minutes later his guest arrived.

"How are you doing?" he asked as she held the phone's earpiece haphazardly in her hand.

"As well as I can," she said. "I met with my attorney earlier today. They are optimistic, but they want to claim an insanity defense."

"But you're not crazy, Jenika," he said defensively.

"If that's the best defense," she said as her eyes started blinking at various rates of speeds.

"Is your head hurting today?" he asked as he started to scribble without looking down at the paper, never taking his eyes off Jenika.

She rubbed it instinctively and gave a weak nod.

"It's really good to see you today," she said with a forced smile that seemed more obligatory than friendly.

"Always a pleasure," he grinned as he kept the pencil in his hand.

"What are you writing?" she asked playfully.

"Nothing much," he said as he continued to look in her direction and not down at the paper. "It's just a nervous twitch."

"Coming to a jail makes you nervous?" she asked with a gleeful smile.

"Not from this side of the glass," he returned. "I wish I could show you the pictures I took this morning. They were beautiful."

"Tell me about them," she asked, leaning on her elbows as her eyes continued to flutter like a schizophrenic without her medication.

"I don't want to bore you with cheap imitations of descriptions. One day I'll show them to you," he said. "But the emotions were pure. Just like you would have liked them."

She closed her eyes and imagined the scene. He watched as he could only imagine what she was thinking. He wondered if she was picturing it like it happened. He wondered if she was visualizing a woman she'd commanded him to follow and could see the letter she'd had him dictate and mail. He hoped she was enjoying the game she was playing from behind the plexiglass.

A sinister smile grew on her untouched face as he saw the scheming in her eyes. It was a game she played so well. He wanted to laugh at the idea of Veronica thinking safety was within reach since Jenika was placed behind bars.

But bars couldn't stop everything.

Jenny opened her eyes and he locked onto them. He hoped he had been a friendly face in the last month coming a few times a week. He remembered the time when he saw the connection between the two immediately, as Jenika's eyes started to well up with tears at the first sight of him. She hadn't expected to have any visitors besides her attorneys. Her biological parents had both been killed; her father had killed her American mother and was then killed in prison by an enemy gang. She had killed her grandparents as a young girl when her father ordered her to silence their testimony. She'd also killed her adoptive parents a couple of years earlier when her estranged brother reappeared from her forgotten past. She had become so angry with her parents that they hadn't adopted her brother, Alexei, that she'd killed them. Then last October, Alexei was killed by her best friend's husband, Officer Winston Cooper.

He had quickly become a new member of her circle, and he hoped she was already starting to see his true loyalty. He had already done everything she had asked him to do.

He wished he was going to be brave enough to do everything she needed him to do. But he still didn't know everything. All he knew was a new step in the plan arose with each visit.

They talked for another ten minutes before the guard returned and told Jenny's guest their time was up.

"Do you have anything else you want Mia to know?" he asked sincerely as he stood up with the red phone in hand.

"I think that will be enough for right now," she said hanging up the phone and walking away.

"Bye," he said into the phone even though it was pointless. She was already out the door heading back to her cell. "Thank you for the pencil," he said handing it back to the guard.

He walked behind the guard and glanced at the paper with his scribblings that no one else would be able to read. That was the benefit of being Russian.

He folded the piece of paper and stuffed it into his pocket as he came to the desk to sign out. He scribbled a name and waited for the guard to give him back his belongings.

"Alexei Lechov, right?"

"That's me," he said with a twisted smile. "Alexei."

CHAPTER 15

I roamed the hospital hallways, turning left and then right until I found the ICU. I didn't know if they would let me in, but I knew I had to try to see Tucker even if he didn't want to see me.

Room 304 had the door closed when I approached, so I politely knocked and waited for someone to welcome me in. I didn't hear anything. I knocked again, but once again I was left waiting outside.

Cracking the door ajar, I poked my head in and heard the beeping of the medical machines. "Hello?" I said before stepping into the room, but once again there was no response. I tiptoed into the room expecting to see someone sitting at his bedside, but the room was void of visitors. The only person in the darkened room was a sleeping bruised man hooked up to life-saving machines. I wasn't a medical person, but I could tell that he desperately needed ICU.

I closed the door behind me and stepped further into the medically musical room with beeping, breathing, and mechanical sounds of blood pressure machines. I scooted my chair over to his side and watched silently. I had planned an entire dialogue of introducing myself, only to become a one-man mime show. The silence inside my head was deafening as I watched a man around my age sleeping in what was probably a medically-induced coma to help alleviate the pressure from the beating he took last night.

I couldn't stand my awkward silence anymore.

"What happened, Tucker? Who did this to you?" I asked.

I knew he wasn't going to answer, but I needed to talk. I couldn't sit and watch this person on death's doorstep knowing I dreamed about him two nights earlier but couldn't do anything to stop it because I couldn't figure anything out except for his name.

I remember waking up, my ribs and side hurting just thinking of the kicks he endured. I looked over at his face and noticed his handsome features were swollen and bruised; he had stitches lacing up his face like Dr. Frankenstein's monster. The doctors and nurses did the best they could to mend his wounds, but now he was going to have to wait and let time work its wonder.

That was always the hardest thing – waiting for time to heal the wounds.

I looked down at my hand and noticed I was rubbing my finger where my wedding band used to proudly reside. I had a nervous tendency to search for the gold until my finger would redden. A few times I had even rubbed it until my fingers were bloody.

Sadly, time didn't heal all wounds. I had succumbed to the idea that some wounds would linger until time was no more. No matter how well my life was going, there were moments the pain of Chelsea not sitting behind her laptop in bed working on her latest article cut me to the core. *Talk some more Solo,* I told myself.

"So, Tucker, I know you know who did this to you. I don't want to scare you, but I want to help. Please help me help you."

As soon as the words escaped my mouth, I couldn't help but roll my eyes at the sound of the after school special that was being broadcasted in this room. *Don't stop.*

"So, do you have any family?" I asked looking around the room for flowers or balloons or any sign he'd had some loved ones visit him. But the room was bare of any encouragement except for the cheerful drawings by the nurses on the white dry erase board.

"Does your family know you are here? I wish I could track them down for you and let them know, but I'm pretty sure the hospital is working on that." I stopped and looked at the sad room and felt the solitude. "I bet they would be here if they knew. I bet there are many people who love you."

I closed my eyes and listened to his heavy breath that seemed forced, as though if the machines were suddenly unplugged, his lungs would be gasping for just a sweet taste of oxygen. I breathed in and out and felt the relief I didn't have to worry about anything. I had a good life. My phone vibrated in my pocket signaling someone I knew was contacting me. I breathed once again in peace knowing I was loved.

I didn't know what else to do but bow my head and say a gentle prayer. I prayed for healing. I prayed for support. I prayed for protection. But in the middle of the prayer my focus shifted and my prayer for Tucker switched to things I was thankful for. I gave thanks for my healing. I gave thanks for my support. I gave thanks for my protection.

"What are you doing in here?" a woman's voice shouted startling me.

"I, uh, I was just visiting," I stammered in shock as the large nurse in pink scrubs walked in my direction.

"Visitors are not allowed up here right now. Get out!"

"I didn't know," I said as I stood up and headed toward the door. I turned around and bid my sleeping companion ado. "See you later, Tucker."

The nurse quickly checked Tucker over, probably making sure I didn't do anything to damage or hinder his recovery. She came out and gave me a dirty look.

I once again apologized and asked how he was doing and what his prognosis looked like.

She softened a little, like when an ice cube slightly began to melt in a glass but was still too hard to chew. "It's going to be a long road, but he should recover," she said casually. "Now leave."

We concluded our dialogue as I told her to enjoy the rest of her evening and she snarled at me. "My shift just began an hour ago, and I have a long night ahead and don't even know where the rest of my help is. One's probably off shacking up, doing God only knows what in a closet somewhere with some guy she met three hours ago. Sadly, she does that more often that I care to share. And hopefully there aren't any other visitors hiding that I have to kick out," she said snidely standing in the middle of the hallway watching me leave the ICU like a menacing neighbor. As I turned to leave, I saw her scurry off and pace the floor like a lion searching for a wounded gazelle.

Poor gazelle.

I pulled out my phone and saw a text from Elizabeth. *Yeah, Wint thinks I'm sick now too. I lost count how many times I went to the bathroom.*

I warned you, I texted back as I smiled picturing Elizabeth hiding out in their bathroom for most of the afternoon.

Poor Elizabeth.

Hopefully you got the water.

Oh, I got the water. But they think that I drank most of it before I got back since I kept skirting off every time Wint asked something I didn't know how to answer. We really need to come up with a story.

I'm not ready to tell him the truth.

Definitely not! she quickly returned. *Can you picture him telling us to be careful every time we go out?*

He means well, I responded.

I know. Well, I'm about to leave the bathroom. Wish me luck.

Nope, I texted back with a ruthless grin on my face.

She just sent me a picture of her middle finger.

Thank God for friends.

CHAPTER 16

The telephones had not rung in the Washington D.C. metro police station in twenty-three minutes, which caused the dispatch operators to enjoy the reprieve of silence. Usually, during the week of Independence Day, the police were ramping up the security in the city to safeguard the citizens from juvenile delinquents and possible terrorists. But now two of the operators were actually able to complete the Sudoku puzzles they had started the day before.

"That's a seven," Rachel said, looking over her co-worker's shoulder. "At the top right."

"Oh, yeah," Cleo commented as she quickly jotted down the missing number and looked around the puzzle for any other blanks.

"What are you two doing?" Detective Smith Young asked as he strutted into the operators' room that had only females working this evening. He smiled his boyish grin, winking at Rachel who had become his latest plaything during work hours.

Detective Young wasn't the most respected officer on the force. In high school he might have been picked first for dodgeball, but in the real world, when loyalty and work ethic mattered, he wouldn't even be allowed to play with the big boys. He had a history of backstabbing anyone near him to make him look like the prettiest rose in the garden, even though a hidden bee lurked within the petals. When someone on the force got stung, the rest of the unit learned from their mistake.

"Just talking." Rachel blushed like a gawky teenager admiring the school quarterback.

"Hopefully it wasn't about me," he winked before turning around and bending over to tighten his shoelaces. He knew he was being watched and he loved it. He straightened up and looked over at the two, who were both checking him out in his fitted uniform. "Later, ladies."

"Bye."

He listened to Rachel's voice trail off as he almost skipped down the hall to get to his desk, getting his kicks from their lustful gazes.

"Young, any news?" Chief Johnson asked as he walked up, jostling Young's thoughts of the ladies talking about him. Chief Johnson had the stature that commanded respect and authority. His build was comparable to a linebacker, not slim and toned, but bulky and muscular. He might not be able to run a mile without huffing and puffing, but he could take anyone down with his bare hands if they were within reach.

"I was about to start on it, Johnson."

"That's sir or Chief Johnson," he corrected with a growl. Chief Johnson and Young had had many run-ins in their past, and Chief Johnson knew he would probably have many more in the future since Young was protected by the mayor.

"Sorry, sir," Young corrected as he walked faster to get away from the gnarling man who often caused Young to put his tail between his legs. He turned his head and noticed that Johnson turned into another office.

Young got to his desk, but he wasn't ready to start working on the stupid case he was given. He sat down and twirled around in his chair, looking at up the ceiling, wishing the hours would pass quickly.

"You know, it's easier to work if you stop spinning like a ballerina," Chief Johnson barked as he walked into the room, causing Young to stop immediately and sit straight up.

"I, I was fixing my chair," Young stammered, shocked that Chief Johnson caught him.

"We don't pay you to fix your chair. We have maintenance for that," Chief Johnson said with annoyance. "Now get to work."

Young flipped open his case and read the few details that the paramedics and first responders had notated.

"Tucker Stevenson," Young started to mumble to himself. "Attacked at Rock Creek Park on one of the trails. Severely beaten. Taken to Sibley Memorial Hospital." He looked around the room and wished he had something more important than a random beating to handle. A murder, a kidnapping, a drug trafficking case. Anything would be more interesting than a guy getting beat up while hitting a trail.

He flipped over the sheet and saw the photographs of the poor soul. His face was disfigured from the swelling. His nose and cheekbones were fractured in multiple places. He had multiple broken ribs and was fortunate that none of the fragments pierced any of his vital organs, or he could have easily died.

He glanced over the final page of contact information from the hospital records. He knew since Tucker wasn't able to talk, he had to start somewhere else to try to find out if this attack was on purpose or a mugging gone horribly wrong. He found Tucker's address and his next of kin. He casually looked them both up on his computer to get an idea of where he would be heading. He had to start somewhere.

But first, he wanted to grab a granola bar and a whey protein shake to help keep his muscular form intact. It wasn't like Tucker was going anywhere tonight.

Or tomorrow.

CHAPTER 17

"So, did you find him?" Elizabeth asked as I was walking along the Korean War Veterans Memorial as the sun was setting in the distance. The sculpted soldiers' shadows slinked towards me as at least one seemed to be looking at me.

"I found him, but he was unconscious still, so no luck finding out anything," I said as I approached the statue whose eyes appeared to follow me wherever I was standing.

"So, do you believe this attack is a one-time deal?" she asked rationally and systematically. "Or could this be something bigger?"

"I don't know," I said, hoping this vigilante wouldn't kick another person within an inch of death. I continued to walk around the memorial, nodding my head at strangers paying their respects.

"You okay, Solo?" she asked sincerely.

The tone caused my hand to twitch. I wasn't used to the kinder side of Elizabeth, and I silently debated if she was reeling me in for a low blow. "I'm doing," I said casually. I wasn't chipper in my tone, but I wasn't depressive either.

"Something was just off about you today," she said. Her tone didn't cut me like many times before, but it was layered with compassion.

"I know," I said, stepping away from the nineteen stainless steel statues and strolling along the cement path beside the mural wall.

"So," she said in an exaggerated breath, "what is it?"

I felt the smoothness of the mural wall, looking at the brave faces of soldiers past. Each face had a story to tell, although I would never know them. I didn't know how to respond to her question. I felt shallow with my feelings of fear and guilt, especially because it was about an act I hadn't committed and had only dreamt about, like a type of warning.

"Elizabeth, I have to go," I said ending the call. I couldn't stand to listen to her calming voice. I looked up and caught a pair of eyes etched into the mural. They were eyes that had seen much worse heartache than I could ever imagine. I wanted to lift my hand and cover them so they couldn't look into my sad existence. But I couldn't. I couldn't disrespect the soldier for his valor.

I looked closer and noticed that the soldier looked to be about eighteen years old, probably weighing about 130 pounds with all his gear strapped on his back. He wasn't wearing a smile like some the soldiers; rather, his expression was drained and tired. Even though his eyes were young, they had a hardness encasing their edges. There weren't any wrinkles, but his eyes had aged quickly on the warfront.

A few older tourists with cameras draped around their necks placed small American flags in the grass beside the mural. I felt a connection with people humbly showing their gratitude for the sacrifices made by the fearless and fearful. I watched as a husband helped his aging wife back up to her feet, straightening her back after she plunged the flag into the welcoming soil. I grinned politely as they both smiled and walked away hand-in-hand, heading to the Vietnam War Memorial nearby.

I turned back to the mural wall and caught a pair of eyes that looked saddened yet had a flavor of contentment and wonder. I stared into the eyes and sunk deeper into his story. I dove headfirst into the lucidity of the eyes. I wanted to swim in the tossing waves until I could find the peacefulness of the aftermath that crashed along the iris. I wanted to float and drift away to a simpler time when life was without a tidal wave or a hurricane brewing or even a mere ripple from a raindrop that could travel for miles. I felt the wall of the mural and awoke as I stared into the pair of eyes.

The eyes blinked. I had been staring into my reflection and felt an uprising deep within my core. It wasn't of fear or confusion. I didn't even feel sickened or defeated. I felt like my story wasn't over. I felt like my story was here and now. It wasn't written yet. I just hoped I could convince myself of that.

I am not my dream.

CHAPTER 18

He nursed his gin and tonic like he was nursing his bruised knuckles, tender and slow. He rolled his eyes at Jed's cockiness that oozed out of him like the puss on a pimply-faced teenager's chin. Looking around the bar, he felt Aristo's was not the type of watering hole he would normally frequent, but he had to admit his drink was one of best he had ever tasted. However, he still didn't agree with the outrageous robbery of the price tag.

Jed stood near the bartender, laughing and carrying on, making a gaudy spectacle like a reformed street performer. In a matter of minutes, he was enclosed by a crowd he wowed and mesmerized with rich-boy theatrics, pandering to their taste of elitism.

The stalker watched from the shadowy corner, gently swirling his drink in his hand, not wanting to gulp it like he would have at the sports bar two blocks away. The drink swirled into a whirlpool in his glass as the lime wedges danced smoothly with the few lingering ice cubes.

"What kind of drink do you want, love?" Jed asked like it was a line from a romantic comedy he was starring in.

"Appletini," the woman said flatly as if she were above everyone in this place. And based upon her appearance, she looked the part she was playing.

Jed snaked his arm around her waist, pulling her into his side. He tilted his head until his lips could have licked the lobe of her ear and whispered something. He backed away with a thunderous laugh, as she joined in politely, but he wasn't fooling anyone. Especially Jed.

"If you don't want to be here, Melanie, then leave," he barked, causing everyone in the room to fixate their attention on the fighting couple.

"Have it your way," she said snidely, stomping away in her stilettos.

The gentleman in the corner licked his lips, tasting the acidity of the lime, although she looked like she would have been better than any drink with her tall, lean legs that would cause any man's eyes to follow up her perfectly-fitted skirt to the curvature and voluptuous backside.

"Moron," he said to himself as he watched Melanie close the door behind her and gulped the rest of his gin and tonic to quench the fires burning inside. He glanced up at Jed, smiling with his lackeys around him, pulling out his newest cell phone and causing his crew of imbeciles to ooh and awe as he quickly texted.

"This may be a long evening," the man sighed to himself, pulling out his wallet to see how much cash he had.

He snapped his fingers and raised his empty glass to the barmaid nearby. "Another, please," he said in a course husky voice that sounded like many years of screaming had stripped his vocal cords raw.

She nodded cordially with a coy smile before returning with another glass that looked like water but tasted like heaven. He went ahead and paid the bill, giving a tip that was polite for his standards but meager compared to what she was used to. He didn't want to have to fumble around if Jed decided to leave at a moment's notice. He didn't want his next victim to have to wait.

That wouldn't be polite, he thought as he smiled to himself.

He watched Jed, studying his every move like a basketball player replaying videos of Michael Jordan in his prime.

70

His eyes darted to the door when he saw Jed wave at someone from the distance. The woman walked in and he thought she looked familiar, but she was too far away to make out all the details.

"Nice to see you, Chantelle," Jed winked with a half smile. "Glad you could make it so quickly."

CHAPTER 19

I arrived earlier than intended that evening at Jeremiah's favorite coffee shop and ordered something sweet. I wasn't usually a coffee drinker, but a cold iced coffee in the middle of summer sounded ideal.

"Good evening, Solomon," he said as he sat across from me after ordering his espresso.

"Isn't that too much caffeine this late at night?" I asked.

"My body has become immune to the jitteriness of espresso beans. Your body can too with any gradual increase. It's when people drink an espresso on vacation that they shock their body. That is when they feel the wear and tear of the caffeine," he said as he sipped the hot concoction. His eyes widened at the large plastic cup of dark liquid. "And what do you have?"

"I know," I smiled shaking my head in disbelief. "I thought I would mix it up today."

"And mix it up you did," he laughed heartily. "Have you ever had a coffee with me?"

I quickly thought back and shook my head. "I don't recall. But I probably have at least once."

"I need to tell Eugene about this later," he snickered to himself as he pulled out his phone to make a note.

"How is Eugene? Have you talked to him today?" Dr. Eugene Wright was a professor of theology and lifelong friend of Jeremiah's who welcomed me into their philosophical circle to discuss and debate anything from capital punishment to whether orange was really the new black. A few months earlier, he discovered he had an inoperable brain tumor, yet his faith hadn't weakened one bit.

"There's practically not a meal that goes by that we don't communicate in one way or another," Jeremiah said placidly. "But he is doing well for the sake of saying he is doing well."

"I need to call him but keep forgetting."

"Isn't that interesting? People always remember things at moments when it's not polite to follow through and then forget to continue on the winding path when time is available. The human mind is a fickle companion," Jeremiah said taking another hot sip, savoring the white foam on the top. "That's why it's best to take notes, Solomon. Always take notes. You never know when you will forget, and then by that time, you don't remember you have forgotten because you have forgotten it."

"Very true," I agreed as I sipped my Reese's-mocha iced coffee. "I think I could get used to drinking this," I said licking my lips, enjoying the peanut butter sweetness that overpowered the bitterness of the coffee beans.

"Are you forgetting something?" Jeremiah asked, tapping his fingers on his phone on the table.

I quickly picked up my phone and saved a note to call Eugene later.

"Better?" I asked facetiously.

"Just trying to teach you ways to better yourself," he said smugly.

That was the thing with Jeremiah. His tone may come off as smug, or gruff, or even arrogant, but his tone never conveyed his true meaning or character behind the words. One would think that Jeremiah was egotistical and snobbish with his daily attire and mannerisms, but that was Jeremiah. Not cocky, just oblivious to his own undertone. Even after all his studies of anthropology, he still didn't cave or bend to the social standards of the day.

Months ago, I had asked him why he didn't just act like everyone else.

"Then it would be acting," he'd said with a grin that shot me down faster than a slingshot. "I am not an actor. I am Jeremiah. I could say the same to you. And then I could ask, who is everyone else? Which majority are you speaking of? Because on this vast diverse planet we are on, the majority that I could conform to would be Asians with their expanding population. Do you want me to start speaking Mandarin and eating noodles and rice with every meal?" he'd asked as he then started speaking Mandarin Chinese fluently.

"I get your point," I'd said with a laugh.

"Nǐ ne?"

I took another sip of my intoxicatingly good drink and dove into the reason I'd asked for this meeting. I needed his viewpoint on my hypothetical situation.

"I have a question for you," I started as he nodded for me to go on. "Do you think it is possible to stop yourself from doing something you don't want to do even though it seems probable you will do it anyway?"

"It is possible if your want to not do it outweighs your want to do it," he said in a theorizing tone. "For example, a person who wants to lose weight goes on a diet. They decide giving up chocolate will help them lose weight. If they really want to lose weight, they will give up the chocolate. But sadly, the desire to lose weight will eventually be outweighed by the instant gratification of eating a Hershey bar. They have a decision to either abstain or indulge. It's been human tendency to indulge since the beginning of time."

"But that seems so trivial," I said, considering my issue was more disgusting and vile.

"But every situation is like this. It may be trivial to you because you don't feel the need to withdraw yourself from chocolate, but it's very serious for the dieter who may have lowered him or herself so much as to do despicable crimes, even kill for a piece of chocolate."

"Kill?" I scoffed. "I think you are going to extremes in your examples, Jeremiah."

"Really? People do cruel things for irrational reasons all the time. Look at why Cain killed Abel. What is your Sunday school answer for that reasoning?"

"Jealousy," I said. "Abel was commended for his offering to God, and Cain hated him for it."

"Is jealousy a good reason to kill someone?" he asked as he took another sip of his espresso.

"No," I quickly answered.

"But people kill for jealousy all the time. In their mind it is justified at the time they take the other person's life. They are starving for a piece of chocolate, and that gas station attendant has a counter full of it." He stopped and looked me in the eyes. "It doesn't make it right, Solomon. But people do not think coherently when they want something they cannot have."

"So, do you think people can stop their incoherent thought processes?" I asked, looking at the blueberry muffin behind the glass case.

"People can do whatever they want to do. Sadly, people's intentions change, thus causing them to do things they don't want to do."

"So, let me throw this moral dilemma out there," I said pretending like it was a thought that just popped into my head. "What about a pedophile? Are you saying they don't want to do those sick things but succumb to the pressure and do them anyways?"

Jeremiah bowed his head and nodded in respect. "Sadly, I do. That is a grave topic. Hypothetically, we can discuss all people's decisions, whether they're about a piece of chocolate or jealousy or abuse, but the underlying factor is people lose the will to fight off the urges they have. As the expression goes, they fall off the wagon. Sadly, some falls take other people down with them, which is a disheartening thought."

"Very disheartening," I agreed.

"But I truly believe people can change. Psychologists have been studying this for centuries, and they continue to explore the human psyche to try to understand why we do what we do. And as someone told me long ago, everything we do is connected to our wants. So, if someone wants to lose weight, they will do whatever it takes to lose a few pounds. If someone wants to be a great soccer player, they will practice for hours in the rain if need be. If someone wants to not kill someone, they will find a way to battle their inner torment. But sadly, people journey down the road of least resistance. So they nibble on the piece of chocolate and say they will start over the next day. Or they sleep in because they feel their dream of being a soccer professional is too lofty of an aspiration. Or, sadly, they allow their unstable emotions to come to the forefront of their decision-making process and shoot someone over an unbecoming glance."

I looked at him with saddened eyes.

"Someone once told me, Solomon, and this is a graver thought..." He stopped and looked at me with compassion. "Never think you are above a certain circumstance, because once you say something is impossible, the world has a way of showing that it is indeed possible."

I shivered. "I don't like that thought."

"But you need to know it. If we have these discussions on morally taboo topics and ask people their opinions on them, that will engage a discussion. They need to mentally state their preferences of where they stand on these issues then come up with a path of how to deter from falling into the pitfalls of these corruptible decisions. If someone decides they will never be a drug addict, that is great. But too often you read obituaries of habitual addicts who wanted to be clean and tried rehab multiple times, but once again failed. But if you have that mistake-laden path already planned out, you know what segments to detour when you come face to face with those situations. Am I making sense?"

"I think so," I said. "So, basically make up a storyline of cause-and-effect events that could lead someone to choose a situation when their decision-making process is flipped and their answers that used to be 'no' are then changed to 'yes.'"

"In a way, yes."

"So, do you believe you will ever do something you will regret?" I asked solemnly, forgetting about the blueberry muffin and digesting his words like my last meal.

"That is the question. Right now, I do not believe I will do anything I will regret because my focus is on making the right decisions that will better myself and the people around me. But am I immune from ever making a decision I regret?" He stopped and strummed his fingers on the table a few times. "Sadly, I am not immune; no one is."

"So, regretful decisions are a part of life?"

"I wouldn't say it that way. I prefer to say regretful decisions should be a part of your life in order to keep you from making the decisions that will end up causing you regret."

"You have given me a lot to consider," I said glancing once again over at the blueberry muffin. "I may regret this decision, but I'm going to buy that muffin," I said with a slight laugh.

"Then it is my responsibility as a fellow human to try to sway you from making that regrettable decision," Jeremiah said with a smile. "But if you are ordering, would you mind getting me a slice of chocolate cheesecake? We can commiserate together tomorrow."

"Did all the chocolate talk get to you?"

"Moreso the philosophical banter. I need to taste something good after wrestling with the toxicity of the world."

"Taste and see that the Lord is good," I said before I ordered our two dishes.

"There are many good verses of wisdom in the Psalms," he commented as the waitress brought out our two pieces of cheesecake. He looked up at me shocked. "I thought you were getting a blueberry muffin?"

"I told you, I'm going regret this decision later."

"You said you *may* regret it," Jeremiah said digging his fork into the creaminess of the dessert.

"Well, I saw the path of least resistance while I was standing in line and decided to just go all in."

"I think you missed my point," Jeremiah said with a wink. "Once you see it, you're supposed to turn from it."

"But look at this, Jeremiah," I said lifting my fork as the caramel trickled down. "Look at all that ooey, gooey caramel. I couldn't say no."

"That's what they always say when handcuffed," Jeremiah said closing his eyes to savor the sweetness.

CHAPTER 20

"What if she comes after me?" Veronica asked, sitting up in bed beside the drowsy-eyed Wint.

"Come after you?" Wint asked, blinking his eyes awake. "She's in jail. She's going to be in jail for a long time. She is just trying to scare you." He tried to calm her nerves because his own felt like they were on the San Andres fault line. He leaned over and kissed his wife, looking into her dark beautiful brown eyes. "You have nothing to be afraid of."

She laid her head on his chest as she looked around her new bedroom setup. All their bedroom furniture wouldn't fit, so they had to put some of it in storage. Wint looked down and noticed her roaming eyes.

"Do you regret moving here?" he asked tenderly, rubbing her back gently.

She lay in silence for a minute as Wint's mind started to wander down a lonesome path of self-deprecation. He knew she was the moneymaker in the family. He loved his job and had fulfillment in trying to make a difference in a rotten world, but his payroll wasn't what Veronica was used to with her lavish lifestyle.

He started to wonder if she got bored with this quaint home, when was she going to get bored with his mediocre self? That thought crushed him.

"I'll get a second job," Wint burst out. "People always need security in the evenings. I'll do it, Veronica. I'll do whatever to keep you happy."

A tear trickled down her cheek as a big smile swelled on her face. She looked into his eyes. "Would you?" she asked.

"Oh, Veronica, if it meant you would be happy, I would do whatever," he said kissing her forehead.

Her tears continued to flow as she laid her head back down on his chest. "I don't know how I fell in love with you."

That sentence crushed Wint's fragile heart. His eyes started to feel the pain as they began to water. He gulped hard, trying to control the hurt he was feeling through and through. His nose started to run as he lifted his hand to rub it. He inhaled as his sniffles echoed through the room.

Veronica lifted her head and saw the man of her life stifling his emotions. "Honey, no," she said kissing him on the lips. "I love you," she said holding his face in her soft, delicate hands. "I don't know how I fell in love with you because you are so much better than me," she said as she traced her fingers around his face until her thumb caught one of the falling tears. "I love you, Winston, because I know you would take a second job for me and work like a dog to make me happy. But…" She stopped and looked around the small, cramped room with a bed and dresser. "I'm happy just being next to you, wherever we live."

"Promise?" Wint asked with a stoic look to stop any lies she was holding back.

"Promise you'll never leave, and I'll promise to be happy, whatever comes our way," she gushed. "And promise me you'll be right here beside me every evening. I don't want any more time away from you."

Wint's desire went into overdrive as their lips connected with an explosion of emotion. Their bodies were fueled with a passion that neither had felt before. Veronica lifted his shirt, exposing his muscular chest. She placed her hand there, feeling his strong torso that rippled like waves in the ocean. She moved her hand higher until she found what she was searching for.

His heart was beating for only her.

"I love you," they said in unison as their passionate fire burned into the early morning.

TUESDAY

CHAPTER 21

The scene looked like a 1950s private eye detective movie as a stranger lurked under a light pole across the street from the apartment he was watching. He had his ball cap pulled low, shadowing his face so he could go undetected.

There were three windows lit on the side of the four-story apartment building. The first floor was Daisy's, a small flower shop welcomed by all for funerals, weddings, and apologies. He ignored the window displays of baby's breath and sunflowers and focused on one of the three windows two floors up.

A figured passed by the window, appearing to be putting on his pants and shirt as the man below on the street continued to watch with bated breath. He knew the time was coming to an end and quickly pulled out his cigarette and lighter for one last puff. The flame lit up the stranger's wristwatch, 1:07 a.m. He inhaled the tobacco and blew out the nicotine, flicking his ashes below with the four other cigarette butts around his feet.

Once again the figure walked past the window and then left. A few seconds later, the light went off.

He dropped his cigarette, stepping and twisting the burning fuse to put out the remnants. As he walked across the street, the front door opened, and out walked a man dressed in black slacks, a white Stafford untucked shirt with the top two buttons left undone, and a crimson tie trailing like a tail out of his back pocket.

The man walked down the steps of the apartment and turned left. He started to whistle as he walked the deserted street.

The stranger walked behind him, smoothly and quietly, watching the other man's movements like a hunter watching a deer. He picked up his pace a little as he tightened his fists, getting ready for when the right moment struck.

The whistling man came to a four-way intersection at Eighth and S Street and turned left once again, still whistling softly, oblivious to the intruder a few steps behind.

The stranger turned to follow. He looked up and saw a small alley to the left, about fifteen strides ahead. No one was nearby. The road was desolate. All the apartments were dark, their inhabitants most likely sleeping. He knew there may be security cameras nearby, but his black attire and baseball cap would be good enough to hide his identity.

He dug into his back pocket and pulled out a roll of white tape. He quickly wrapped his knuckles until his skin was covered with white. He placed the roll of tape back, never losing focus on his deer ahead.

Figuratively, the gun went off, and he exploded from his starting line when the man was two strides away from the dark alley. The man in front never saw or heard him coming as he continued to whistle up until the final moment when the white-knuckled man collided with him and punched him in the back of his neck. The prey went down.

The attacker quickly grabbed the man's struggling arms as he feebly tried to put up some kind of a fight. He dragged him into the hollow of the black alley where even rats and mice were too afraid to reside.

That's when the man started his ruthless attack.

Kick.

Kick.

Kick.

He knelt down and rolled the man onto his back spreading his arms and holding the left one down with his combat boot. He didn't hear any bones break, so he lifted his foot and quickly slammed it down, twisting to make sure that a few were crushed.

The lying man whimpered as the attacker bent down, getting within an inch of his face. The two looked into each other's eyes as recognition sank in.

"If you say anything, I will kill you. So man up, Jed," he said in a whisper.

Jed nodded his head in agreement.

"Have you ever hit a kid?" he asked softly, still an inch away from Jed's face.

"No," Jed muffled with a stifled cry.

Tsk-tsk, the stranger sounded. "I said to not say a word." He pulled out a small roll of duct tape from his other back pocket and tore off a piece. "If you can't follow my orders, how are you going to not scream out when I keep you from dying?"

He placed the silver tape over the man's mouth.

"Much better," he said standing up to kick the man in the side. All the man let out was a soft moan. "See, isn't that much quieter?" he asked as he looked down over the crying man. "Didn't your dad teach you not to cry? Real mean don't cry, Jed. I guess I'll teach you then."

He stooped down, kneeling on Jed's legs and started pummeling his stomach like a boxer's punching bag with a quick jab to his face every so often to keep him from passing out from the pain.

"I said no crying, Jed," he said calmly, like a father telling his four-year-old. "Big boys don't cry."

I woke with my side splitting in pain. I rolled over and heaved a breath that caused my lungs to sting from the fresh air. Turning my head, I noticed the time on my alarm clock. 12:56 a.m.

My mind went into warp speed.

It was about to happen.

CHAPTER 22

"Elizabeth, where are you?" I called, waking her up.

"Where am I?" she answered drowsily. "I'm in bed talking to a dead man if he doesn't let me go back to sleep."

"This is serious," I said, not caring about her attitude. "The guy is going to attack again, in about ten minutes."

"Solo, why are you just worrying about this now?" she said, sounding much more awake and bright-eyed. I pictured her slinging her duvet off and grabbing some nearby clothes. "Why didn't you say something earlier if you needed help? I thought you said you already took care of your dreams yesterday morning?"

"I just had the dream a minute ago!"

"Are you sure it's going to happen now and not tomorrow night?" she asked, slowing her pace.

"I don't know!" I shouted, grabbing my wallet and keys and running to my front door in my blue navy pajama pants and grey fitted t-shirt. "I'm heading there now."

"Where is 'there'? Solo, where are you going?"

"I saw Eighth and S Street in my dream," I said running down the outside steps of my two-story apartment building.

"Eighth and S Street?" she huffed. "Solo, you can't get there in ten minutes."

"What would you suggest?" I barked, running toward my car sitting under the parking lot lights.

"Call the police," she said with authority. "Call the police and tell them you saw someone following someone and you think they are about to be attacked."

"What if I'm wrong and it's tomorrow?" I asked unlocking my car door and starting the engine.

"The police get prank calls all the time. Just call them and wait and see. That's all you can do."

"Well, I'm heading there now," I said pressing on the gas and fleeing the parking lot like I was leaving the scene of a crime.

"Solo," Elizabeth groaned, "I'm on my way too. But you're going to owe me."

"Owe you?" I smiled as I looked both ways as I slowed to a stop sign without fully stopping. There weren't any other cars on the road. "What else would you be doing right now?" I laughed, knowing she always had a comeback.

"Wrapping my dream arms around the neck of Brad Pitt's *Ocean's 11* body."

"That's a pretty specific dream," I smiled.

"He's still fine, but he's aged," she said as I heard her garage door open followed by the slam of her BMW's door. "I prefer the early 2000s Brad Pitt."

"You are so vain," I chuckled as I pulled onto the freeway.

"Vain? I just know what I like. If given a choice, you would pick a twenty-year-old Cindy Crawford over a forty-year-old one. And if you say you wouldn't, you're such a liar."

I knew she was right. I didn't want to say so, but my silence was the reward she was wanting as she laughed with hysterics.

"Oh, Solo," she said between breaths. "Your reluctance to answer is the pay for this stupid night."

We continued to talk once she stopped laughing at my expense. We discussed our strategy and logistics, specifically whether we would hide or go to the scene.

"Wait, Solo, have you called the cops?"

"I'm on it," I said ending the call and dialing emergency. "Yes, someone is being attacked around S and Eighth Street."

"Can you describe the attacker?" the operator asked as she reported to patrollers on the street.

"Dark clothes, baseball cap, um…" I stopped and thought for a second. "That's all I saw."

"They are on their way," she said, trying to ask me a few more questions, but I ended the call.

I proceeded to drive toward S Street when my phone started to ring.

My stomach dropped.

I knew who it was before I looked. The dispatch operator was calling me back.

CHAPTER 23

He looked back a few times as he walked away from Jed, making sure the body wasn't moving even though he was still alive. He jogged down the alley trying to get away from the scene as quickly as possible.

Just like the night before, he allowed Jed to call for a paramedic, but interestingly, the dispatcher had said that help was already on the way. He ended the call and quickly went into overdrive with kicks and punches. He didn't want to rush through the beating, but he didn't want to get caught either, so fast punches and kicks would have to do.

He exited the alley and continued to jog down the sidewalk when he realized someone must have seen him and called for help. *What if they are watching me now?*

He picked up his pace with a mad dash, crossing the street and ignoring the crosswalk signs. His ears perked up when he heard sirens in the distance, and his heart started pounding. A glance up the street brought relief as no cars were coming his way. He continued to run, his combat boots pounding against the concrete. They were not ideal for running, but he didn't care. He could run for miles in them if necessary to escape handcuffs. He could overlook the discomfort.

He was four blocks away from the alley before he pulled off his ball cap and threw it in a nearby trash can. Stopping behind a tree, he took off his shirt, leaving a white ribbed tank top undershirt. He unzipped his pants and let gravity pull them to the ground. Bending down, he took off his boots and pants and turned to face a storefront window. He looked at his reflection and didn't see someone who had just attacked someone in an alley nearby, but rather a runner with black compression shorts going for a late night jog. No one could tell he was wearing his Jockey underwear. He picked up his pants and boots and hid them behind a trashcan near a stoop on the sidewalk.

He started to smile as he felt the humid, nighttime air rush past his bare skin. At first he felt exposed running in his underwear, and his black socks didn't absorb the concrete as well as his boots, but he only had a few more blocks before he would find his pickup truck parked on the street.

Suddenly, he saw a police car turn two blocks ahead. Its sirens were blaring and the blue lights spun, painting the street with the lively color.

Just keep running, he told himself. *You are just a runner.*

He didn't try to hide. He watched as the police car came speeding toward him. He held his breath as the police car came to a screeching stop. The cop rolled down his window and shouted, "Have you seen someone in a baseball cap and dark clothes around here?"

"No sir," he answered coming to a stop, wiping his head, noticing that he hadn't taken the white tape off his fingers. "I haven't seen anyone."

"If you do, call the cops and let us know," the blond police officer said before proceeding up the street to the real crime scene.

The attacker looked at the police car leaving and smiled. *Well, that was easier than I thought.*

He considered turning back and getting his pants and boots but reconsidered. He enjoyed running freely in his underwear. *I might do this more often,* he thought with his smile growing wider as he pictured how his neighbors would react.

He ran a couple more blocks and saw his pickup truck parked in front of the closed convenience store. He got into the driver's seat and breathed a sigh of relief. As he gripped his steering wheel, he felt his pent-up tension and stress vanish. Who knew beating someone senseless was so therapeutic?

He closed his eyes and felt the beads of sweat dripping down his neck, ending their trail at his damp tank top. He took off the white tape that still had blotches of Jed's blood and let his fingers free from their confines. Not wanting any of Jed's DNA in his truck, he got out, rolled up the tape, and threw it away in a nearby trashcan. He stretched his arms and legs, trying to relax, but he knew sleep wasn't going to be an option that night. Not anytime soon, anyway. He looked up and down the street and felt the calmness in the air. The sirens had vanished. It was too quiet. He started to whistle the tune he had heard earlier before returning to pick up his clothes and boots.

CHAPTER 24

The ambulance passed me with its sirens wailing as I started down Eighth Street to arrive at the crime scene. I didn't know what that meant. Did I call the cops in time to stop the beating? But since the ambulance had its lights flashing, I knew someone needed some immediate assistance.

My mind started spinning wildly with all the possible scenarios that could have arisen from my phone call. What if the police arrived and there was a shoot out and some one was seriously wounded? Or what if the attacker turned on himself when he saw the cops arrive and tried to commit suicide on the spot? Or what if the attacker jumped the police officer and critically wounded many people because he knew his time was up?

My phone rang; it was Elizabeth.

"Are you nearby?" she asked softly.

"Almost. Are you there?" I asked knowing I had a few more blocks before I would get to S Street.

"I'm here."

"Why are you whispering?" I asked.

"I don't know," she snapped. "I felt like I was eavesdropping on the investigation, and when you eavesdrop, you whisper."

"Are you in your car?" I questioned. "Because if you're in your car with your windows up, they're not going to hear you."

"I know that now," she said rolling her eyes as she continued to watch the police officers cordon off the crime scene with yellow caution tape. She had lowered her seat as soon as she'd parked five minutes earlier so her eyes were just above the dashboard.

"So, what happened?"

"All I know is that the paramedics left a few minutes ago," she started as I interrupted.

"Yeah, I passed them on the way."

"I don't know who they were taking back to the hospital, but I saw them only put one person on a stretcher."

"Did you notice which hospital?" I asked, realizing I hadn't thought to look at the screaming ambulance.

"Howard University," she said. "It's pretty useless to come down the street. The cops are just walking around and scratching themselves."

"Elizabeth!"

"Well, it's that blond guy that Winston can't stand. You know, the one with the last name for the first name. I hate it when parents do that. They think they are being unique and cute, but I think it's just idiotic. I mean, come on, you deserve to have a first name. I'm like, do you remember his name? Turner or Smothers or Phelps. I don't know, he's walking around grabbing himself so much I feel like I'm at a baseball game."

"Oh wow," I said wide-eyed as I stopped at the corner of 8th and S Street. "And I think it's Smith."

"Smith! Yes! Thank you!" she exclaimed louder than a whisper. "He looks like a Smith. Cute surfer boy type."

"You're just ready to get back to dreamland and make out with Mr. Pitt," I said parking my car but staying behind the steering wheel.

"A girl can dream, can't she?"

"Dream all you want," I said with a slight grin. I leaned my head and saw Elizabeth's BMW parked down the street with no sign of her in the driver's seat. "You're hiding yourself pretty well. I can't see you from where I am."

"Where are you?" she asked, raising her head up and swiveling it around. "Oh, there you are," she said with a wave. "This is pointless waiting around here. There is nothing we can do now."

"But I thought you would like to spend the night here and watch Smith strut around town," I teased as I turned on my ignition.

"I've watched him long enough. It's like a pool boy. Once you see his goods, you don't have to stay and watch him clean the gunk out of the pool."

I shook my head at her analogy. "You have a way with words."

"What can I say? I majored in literature. I'm a wordsmith."

"I bet you'd love to make Smith into your wordsmith," I said, trying to make a pun but failing miserably. Once I said it, I knew I shouldn't have. I knew she wasn't going to let this one down.

"Really, Solo? Smith into my wordsmith? Was that supposed to be a dirty innuendo or something, because I don't get it," she billowed with ruthless intent.

"I know, I know."

"I mean, do you think before you speak sometimes?" she continued as she started her BMW.

"You can drop it, you know."

"Drop what, your word prowess? You're such a sesquipedalian, Solo. I need a dictionary with your aristocratic vernacular just so I can decipher your big words," she said continuing to bust my chops.

"I'm glad I made your night," I said turning to head back home.

"Oh, Solo, that truly did," she said with a cruel laugh. "That might have helped me get through this week. Drive safe, Solo," she said as I watched her pull away.

"What do you mean?" I asked, but she had already hung up. I guess after the dream last night and the day of uncertainty and sickening thoughts, she thought I needed a good laugh as well. I looked at my clock and noticed the day ended almost two hours ago. It was officially Tuesday morning.

Even though I felt relief to not be part of a tragic story that day, it broke my heart to know a young girl was victimized by someone she trusted. I let out a sigh because I knew I wasn't the monster in the dream. I knew I could never do anything so barbaric. But then my thoughts circled back to a young girl who was hurting while I was incapable of helping her.

That thought crumbled me. I was startled to realize there were millions of people hurting every day, and I turned a blind eye to the unidentified. It sickened me that I didn't do more to find the chains that bind people and smash them to bits all because I didn't know who had a chain that needed breaking.

But to see the face of a victim. To look into a pair of innocent eyes and do nothing. That was more than I could take. I could only think of one thing to do.

"Please God, protect that little girl tonight. Please. Please. Please."

CHAPTER 25

A twelve-year-old girl poked her head into a darkened room, slightly startled as indicated by her widening eyes and jarring head movement. She started to talk, staying safely in the dimly lit hallway as only her shadow seeped into the room. Her lips were moving, but no sound came out. There was only silence.

She shook her head no and continued to talk. She poked her head into the room and looked around as if it were the first time she had seen it. Her eyes darted left and right, taking in all the knickknacks and wall hangings. She slightly turned her head as something caught her attention. Then she suddenly looked dead center in the room.

She continued to talk, but still nothing was heard.

She was talking to someone, but the other person or people couldn't be seen. She was the star of this attraction.

Her lips stopped moving, and she nodded her head in agreement as her eyes sparkled with intrigue and curiosity. She timidly took one step forward, crossing over the invisible boundary line.

She smiled brightly, even started to giggle somewhat as she took another brave step forward. Her shy demeanor vanished as she glided into the room. She started to talk, and one word was heard in the middle of the sentence.

"You."

She didn't stop talking, although that singular word was the only one heard. Her mouth was moving faster and she barely took time to catch a breath as her feet skated on the hardwood, taking more steps until she was in the center of the room.

The room looked like a darkened home office with an old large monitor nestled in the middle of an ornate desk. The walls were decorated with gold and blue-striped wallpaper with artistic portraits similar to Rembrandt hung sporadically around the room. She tapped her fingers rhythmically on the desk, swirling her fingers around the hardwood as she walked around the large piece of furniture.

As she came around the desk, the perspective changed from staring forward at the door, to looking behind at a large glass window overlooking a dark yard with strings of colorful plastic lanterns. She peered out the window, looking down at the festive lights as the window reflected her beaming smile.

Her lips started to move once again as a single word was vocalized.

"Can't."

Then she stopped talking.

Her smile started to fade until it was gone. Her eyes, brave a minute ago, now had a look of fear and fragility.

She turned around and shook her head as she started to mouth something.

A hand reached up and placed a finger on her mouth to silence her words.

Her thin lips started to quiver at the touch of the finger as another hand reached up from the side and grabbed her shoulder, pulling her in.

Her mouth gaped open as if she were screaming, but suddenly she stopped. Flashes of colorful lights filled the sky behind her. Fireworks were being detonated in the backyard.

But still, there was only silence.

Blues, reds, and yellows lit the sky like pieces of fiery confetti as the colors shimmied into the darkened room.

The young girl was pulled in closer by the pair of hands. She tried to fight them, but they were too strong for her. Her body was tossed around as tears started to rain down her cheeks.

She started to talk, but her words, though silent, were easily recognizable. She was begging and pleading to be let go as a pair of hands left her bony shoulders and started trespassing down where no child should be touched.

The room went dark except for the flashes of light from the fireworks.

"You can't," the young girl said once again.

My eyes shot open as tears started to run down my face. The dream continued to replay in my mind like a skipping record player.

I wanted to scream for her to run, but I knew it wouldn't do any good. There wasn't anything I could do. I felt like a patron in a movie theater watching a horror flick screaming at the screen for the actress to stop going up the stairs and run out the front door instead. *No, turn around! Turn around and run out the front door. The villain is waiting for you upstairs. Always run outside and try to get help from a neighbor. Go find a parent! Go tell an adult! Go turn in the guy who is about to hurt you!*

That's what I wanted to tell the little girl as I stared up at my chipped ceiling. I commiserated with it, feeling as though I was falling to pieces and there wasn't enough plaster in the world to keep me intact.

You can't. You can't. You can't.

The words softly echoed in my mind, getting louder as they repeated. I continued to see the young girl walking closer to her known abuser as the words kept repeating and increasing in volume until they were screaming at the top of the young girl's lungs.

The fear in her voice turned to anger.

You can't! You can't! You can't!

"What can't I do?" I moaned in the middle of my bed. "Please God, tell me, what can't I do?"

I rolled over and cried into my pillow with gut-wrenching agony until the room went black.

CHAPTER 26

Elizabeth opened her eyes and let out a deep yawn. She wasn't ready to seize the day but knew she couldn't continue to lounge in bed. She had promised Veronica she would work for her and answer the phones at her new law office a few days a week until she was able to hire a permanent receptionist.

Today was one of those days.

She rolled out of bed, leaving her best friend – her goose feather pillow. She looked at her phone, wanting to make sure her alarm hadn't gone off early by accident. It hadn't.

"Solo," she muttered under her breath, thinking of the late-night drive to a crime scene just to drive back home. She missed her sleep, but she knew if it were the other way around, he would have driven to meet her as well. But she wouldn't let him know that. She could use last night's poor excuse of helping someone for her leverage in the future.

She liked leverage.

Wake up! she texted to Solo with a smiling emoji. She sent him two dreams that she had and asked him to take the one that needed to be accomplished in the late morning since she would be at work. She rolled her eyes at the idea of saying she had work.

Gotcha, he replied quickly, making her wonder why he was up at this God-forsaken hour in the morning.

Why are you up? she texted as she threw open her closet pulling out some business-friendly attire.

It's 8:00.

She looked down at the message and rolled her eyes. *What does that have to do with anything? Aren't you tired from last night?* She went into the bathroom and started putting on her makeup and fixing her hair.

I got plenty of sleep. Don't work too hard today. I think this gig will do you some good! See how the working women do it.

She read his text and grimaced at his upbeat attitude this early in the morning before she'd even had a cup of coffee.

I work! She was starting to get annoyed at his implication she didn't do anything.

Sure you do.

The flames inside her rose higher. *If you only knew.* She dropped the phone on her bathroom vanity counter and looked into the mirror, puckering her lips to apply the right amount of lipstick.

She heard her phone vibrate, alerting her that Solo had probably sent another text, but she didn't care to look. She had 45 minutes to get to Veronica's office, and she didn't have time this morning.

Running to her kitchen, she turned on her Keurig and dropped in a K-cup with a single serving of a cinnamon hazelnut coffee. She put her tumbler under the spout and waited like a child on Christmas morning for that heavenly aroma to circle her kitchen. As the machine started purring, a smile enveloped her face.

She closed her eyes and let her other senses bask in the goodness as she inhaled the luscious fragrance. It was almost down to its last drop when a loud explosion outside startled her.

"Stupid kids!" she screamed looking out her kitchen window and seeing remnants of bottle rockets lying in her grass. A cold chill ran through her veins as she heard the popping of fireworks. She felt a coldness that shouldn't be felt in summer. She grabbed her steaming tumbler and gulped.

She knew it would burn, but she didn't care. She needed the heat.

She stomped to her car in the garage and quickly pulled out. She saw the group of preteen boys swarming on the sidewalk like locusts around one kid with a lighter. She pulled up to the kids and lowered her window and tried to be polite.

But politeness wasn't her strong suit.

She watched as the boys ran off in different directions, scattering like cockroaches to their mothers. Some had never heard the words she let roll off her tongue so effortlessly. She rolled up her window and hummed on her way to work.

She expected to be notified by the HOA, but she didn't care. She paid her dues. In fact, she may even put a little more into the special reserves fund for safe measure. She knew how to play the system. She knew all too well the power of money and how it could buy silence and cooperation.

CHAPTER 27

My morning jog wasn't as long as I would have liked, but the dream of the little girl still rattled my nerves. I kept thinking of the two words she said: You can't.

As I ran around the neighboring streets of my apartment, I watched my neighbors poke their childish heads out the window staring at me as I jogged by. I usually ignored the watchful eyes as I sprinted by, but this morning, I waved at every eye that looked my way. I knew the dream wasn't about me. I knew there was another meaning behind the words, You can't.

But what can't I?

The only thing I knew I could do right then was visit Tucker and Jed and hopefully figure something out before a third person was attacked. Sadly, it looked like this was going to be a trend.

I went home and quickly showered, planning out my day as the jets of water sprayed my sweaty chest. I let my mind drift into a daydream of possible outcomes for the day. I saw myself walking toward the ICU of Sibley Memorial Hospital.

An hour later, I passed through the swinging doors and found Tucker's room once again. This time, a nurse saw me as I approached and smiled. I guess I had arrived during visiting hours this time.

"Can I go in?" I asked the young nurse sitting behind her desk as I pointed at Tucker's room.

"Yes, you can go on in," she said softly as she picked up the ringing telephone. "ICU."

I walked into Tucker's room, but I didn't see anything different from the night before. He was still lying in the same bed with his eyes closed and several tubes protruding from his arms and chest. The room was still bare of any personal belongings. It made me sad to not see any balloons or get-well cards spread over the table. It looked more like a prison cell than a hospital room.

"Tucker," I said pulling a seat beside his bed, "my name is Solomon, but you can call me Solo. I stopped by last night to see how you were doing."

I spoke about random topics such as the Nationals' baseball season, the latest Marvel comic blockbuster, and my plans for the Independence Day celebration in two days.

"July 4th is on Thursday," I said casually, as if speaking to an old friend. "I love this time of year. There is something about seeing all the patriotism. I guess that's one blessing we have living here is that we see so much." I thought for a moment before I corrected my sentence. "Well, I'm not saying other cities don't have celebrations, but I think it's just different in D.C. than anywhere else." I stopped once again. "Well, you know what I mean. It's just different."

I rolled my eyes, shaking my head at my phrasing. "Geez, who knew speaking to someone unconscious could be so difficult?"

"At least you are trying," someone said as they walked into the room.

I turned around to see a police officer walk into the room. "Wint?"

"Solo?"

Crap.

CHAPTER 28

"What are you doing here?" Wint asked with a confused look on his face. "Do you know him?"

I looked at Wint and then back at the silent Tucker and then back at Wint. I had a decision to make, tell him the truth or a lie. I looked into Wint's eyes and I didn't want to lie to him. We had too much history for me to do that. I closed my eyes and quickly said a prayer of forgiveness if things got tricky.

"No, I don't know him," I said, which wasn't a lie.

"Then why are you here?" he asked, taking a step into the room as his partner Dakota followed him.

I looked at Dakota and then at Wint. I knew that I looked suspicious like a methhead caught licking battery acid.

"It's for school," I answered, nodding my head enthusiastically.

"I thought you didn't have any classes right now," Wint said with doubt in his voice.

"Yeah, I don't have any classes, but I'm doing this for my hours of service that I need to graduate."

"You've never mentioned that before," Wint grilled as he looked over at Dakota who shrugged her shoulders.

"Wint, I have to have about 200 hours. I've been doing it on my days off or on weekends," I said, lying through my teeth. Some degrees did require hours outside of class, but since I wasn't close to graduating, I wasn't even concerned with that aspect yet. But he didn't need to know that.

"So, what are you doing here?" Wint asked, standing at the foot of Tucker's bed, looking with compassion at the sleeping man.

"Just talking with him," I said shrugging my shoulders. "I make my rounds at various hospitals and visit the sick," I lied once again. "You know, praying for them, talking with them, trying whatever I can to make them feel a little better."

"That is very kind," Dakota said as she patted me on the shoulder when I started to stand up.

"Yeah," Wint said unconvincingly. "That's good ol' Solo. Always around at a moment of crisis to pray for someone."

I smiled and gave an uncomfortable laugh. I hated the feeling of all eyes on me in the room, like I was being judged by my peers. Luckily, Tucker was asleep.

"Well, I will leave you two to whatever you need with Tucker," I said sliding my body towards the door in a sideways shuffle.

"How'd you know his name?" Wint asked, looking at me with an inquisitive stare.

"It's written right there," I said pointing to the dry-erase board on the wall with the nurse's name scribbled on it.

"Hmm," Wint said with a dubious nod.

"Hmm what?"

"Nothing," Wint said as he looked at the board and then back at me. "Just strange."

"Tell me about it." I smiled as I turned, breathing a sigh of relief as I walked out of the room. I froze when Wint called out my name.

I took a deep breath and turned around. "Yeah?"

"Thanks for helping us move yesterday. We really appreciate it. We'll have you over for supper soon."

"Sure," I said stuffing my hands in my back pocket. "Sounds great."

I walked away as Wint and Dakota started talking and then started fast-walking to the exit of the ICU. As soon as I got through the swinging doors, I pulled out my phone and started texting.

You'll never guess who I just saw in Tucker's room!

CHAPTER 29

No! Elizabeth replied as she sat behind her temporary desk answering the phone and getting the door for Cooper Law, LLC. *You better watch yourself 'cuz you are walking on thin ice.* She had spent most of the morning critiquing Veronica's new office. "Have you thought about putting a picture over that chair, V? Or what about painting the walls a bolder color? I mean, this space isn't bad, but it isn't good either," she'd started out as Veronica huffed and went to work in her office. "Just trying to help you, sis."

I know! Solo texted. *I was sweating through my shirt. I wonder if he noticed.*

Well, he's nicer than me. I would have said something rude to you if I saw sweat marks, she texted as the desk phone rang.

"Cooper Law, how may I help you?" Elizabeth warmly answered with a fake receptionist voice that sounded welcoming and friendly. "One minute," she said as she put the phone on hold. "Yo, V, phone!" she shouted to Veronica in the adjacent room.

"Can you say it a little less brashly?" Veronica asked from behind her desk. "This is Veronica," she started as Elizabeth went back to her text.

You can keep your remarks to yourself, Solo responded. *Luckily, I have another shirt in my car. I'll head to Jed's later, but first I'll take care of your tripping hazard down at Union Station.*

Thanks, love, Elizabeth quickly sent back as a young man with an envelope walked into the room. "May I help you?" Elizabeth asked with a priceless smile. She showed all her pearly whites for the dimple-faced stud in his ultra slim chinos and white polo shirt. She examined the bulging bicep vein that slithered under the tightly fitted sleeve. She always enjoyed seeing a piece of eye candy. She may not indulge in the delicacies, but she was an observer of fine art.

"Is Veronica Hyde-Cooper available?" he asked.

"One minute," she said looking down at the phone system to see that Veronica was no longer on the other line. She stood up and strutted to her office, swinging her hips to the music of Beyonce in her head. "You have someone here to see Veronica Hyde-Cooper."

"Who is it?" Veronica mouthed as Elizabeth stepped into the office.

"I don't know, but you have to see him," she said with a purr.

"Elizabeth, I can't be sued for sexual harassment already. And you're just a temp."

"Oh, I'd let him sue me any day," she winked as she walked out quickly followed by Veronica.

"Good morning. I'm Veronica Cooper," she said, enunciating Cooper and dropping the Hyde as she held out her hand in greeting.

He lifted his hand with an envelope, dropping it in her open palm. "Veronica Hyde-Cooper," he said enunciating the word Hyde. "Will you please sign this?" he asked, pulling out a pen from his pocket.

Veronica quickly signed her name and took the envelope.

"You have been served," he said with a grin. "Have a good day."

"Served?" Veronica exclaimed as the office runner left, giving Elizabeth a wink before leaving.

Elizabeth gave a flirty wave with only her fingers. Fingers that would also say come hither if she didn't have standards against slumming it with the lower class. "He was cute."

"Elizabeth!" Veronica stammered in haste. "I'm being sued."

"By whom?" Elizabeth asked, waking up from the daydream of pouring hot honey all over his tan arms.

Veronica ripped open the envelope, quickly read the legal jargon, and almost dropped the paperwork as she felt her world crashing down.

"Dad."

CHAPTER 30

"He's doing what?" Wint asked, pacing the hospital ICU hallway. "How? Why? Why would he do that?"

"It's Dad," Veronica said feebly. "He always sues people when they leave, just out of spite."

"But you didn't sign the clause, right?" Wint questioned, remembering Veronica had said something about a clause when she first mentioned starting her own legal firm.

"That's correct. I never had to sign a non-compete clause, so that's the one thing we have going for us. But..." she stopped and looked out her office window and watched a yellow bird sitting on a perch.

"But what?" Wint asked, pushing through the ICU swinging doors to find a place with a little more privacy. "But what?"

"That's what big firms always do," she sighed. "They drown little people with paperwork and dispositions and court hearings, hoping they will cave because the little guys don't have the manpower to focus so much time on nonbillable work."

"But you have the law on your side," he said with a convincing tone. "You are right on this."

Veronica continued to stare out the window at the people passing on the sidewalk. They were smiling and eating their ice cream cones. She was envious of the vacationers enjoying their summer break, ready to sit on the Washington Mall for the firework extravaganza.

"It's not fair!" she screamed at the top of her lungs as the tourists continued to lick their melting chocolate and vanilla swirl cones. "He's my dad! He should be the one telling me to better myself!" She stopped and closed her eyes as she shook her head in belief. "Not suing me because I left his firm to work at my own."

"Are you sure it's him?" Wint asked with a ray of hope. "Maybe it's not him, and it's another one of the partners going after you. Did you take anyone else's clients?"

"No, Wint," she said with rage flaring as her defense mechanism. "This has Dad written all over it."

"Don't jump to conclusions just yet," Wint said finding a stairwell and taking a seat on the top step of the gray room. "Just maybe," he started as Veronica stopped him.

"Don't defend him," she snapped. "Don't you ever defend him to me again. My family isn't like yours," she said with a verbal slap.

"What does that mean?

"That didn't come out right," she said, brushing off his emotions to focus on the main problem. "You know what I mean."

"No, tell me," he said, switching hands holding his phone.

"Your family is just the typical American family," she said casually. "And I really love that about them. They aren't flashy or civilized," she started.

"Civilized?" he scoffed. "Is that an insult?"

"Wint, no," she started to sniffle as she once again looked out the window. There were so many other places to be than this misconstrued conversation. She swallowed her pride, something that she used to never do, but she knew the problem was her and not Wint. "I'm sorry, Wint. I'm just losing it here," she said as tears started to run down her face. "I thought enough time had passed and this was over, but it's not. It's like he's playing with me. As soon as I thought I was safe, he dropped the gauntlet."

He didn't say anything but just listened to the love of his life.

"Wint," she said.

"Yeah, I'm here," he said with a delicacy in his voice that melted her pain like the ice cream she just saw. "I'm always here."

There was silence on both ends of the line. Neither knew what to say, but they knew they had each other's back. They couldn't have said that nine months earlier.

"Wint," she said softly.

"Yes."

"I love you," she said with the purest of motives as she wiped away her remaining tears. "I hope you know that."

"Always," he said with total assurance.

She felt the unity in his words. She needed his shoulder now more than ever. She ended her call and walked out to Elizabeth.

"You have a client coming in fifteen minutes," Elizabeth said professionally before switching to sister mode. "Are you going to be able to handle it, or should I reschedule?"

"I'll get through it, but I may leave early this afternoon," Veronica said with a tiredness in her voice that a candle and a long bath would help alleviate. "You are so lucky you didn't ever let Dad take advantage of you," she said as she smiled and walked away.

"If only you knew," Elizabeth said under her breath as the phone rang. "Cooper Law, this is Elizabeth."

CHAPTER 31

The ICU of Howard University Medical Hospital was much smaller than the one at Sibley's Memorial Hospital, but its smaller size didn't mean the quality of service was any less. I walked up to the nurse's station and asked for Jed's room number.

"Jed Poston?" the nurse asked as I nodded my head. "He's right there," she said, pointing at a room behind me with the door open.

"Thank you." I stopped before turning to leave. "How is he doing? Have they found out who did it yet?"

"The doctors are hopeful he will fully recover, but it might be a while. He was messed up real bad," she said grimacing with a grandmotherly expression. "I've never seen anyone look as bad as him and live." She stopped and popped a piece of popcorn in her mouth.

"Have the cops been by lately?" I asked.

"I haven't seen 'em," she said grabbing another handful of her snack. "But I heard they were here early this morning checking on him."

"Thank you," I said turning to go into the room able to breathe a little lighter knowing Wint wouldn't catch me.

I walked into the room and found a visitor sitting beside his bed. It was a young woman holding his hand as she watched a soap opera on the television.

"Hello, my name is Solomon," I said quietly, trying not to startle her. "How's he doing?"

"He's resting," she said with a slight smile. "At least that's what I call it."

I nodded my head and agreed.

"Let me turn this off," she said lowering the volume on the television. "How did you know him?"

I looked at the soap opera that had layers of lies in every episode. I hoped one I pulled out of my hat would appease her.

"I, well, we worked together," I said.

"Oh, you worked with him at WestMinor Financial."

"Well," I said recalling that name somewhere. "I work with him, but not there. We work together on some other things."

"It's very kind of you to stop by and see him," she said, shaking her head as if she just realized something. "I'm sorry, I'm Melanie," she said standing up and releasing Jed's hand to shake mine.

"Nice to meet you, Melanie," I said trying to read the social clues. "So, you're the Melanie he's always talking about."

She blushed as she sat down, grabbing his hand and patting it tenderly. "He talks about me?"

"Well, we don't talk about personal things much, but he did bring you up a time or two," I said as I wondered what I was doing.

"He's a good guy," she said as she started to cry.

"Don't cry," I said, rushing over to her side and patting her shoulder awkwardly like a guy putting sunscreen on his brother's back. "The doctors said he'll recover."

"It's not that," she said, grabbing a tissue from a nearby box. "We had a fight last night and I stormed out of the bar we were in. Then I got a phone call in the middle of the night saying he was attacked not far from here." She stopped and looked up into my eyes. "I didn't realize I hurt him that badly. I mean, why else would he be walking around late at night? I was told they found him in an alley a few blocks away."

"I wouldn't blame yourself," I consoled.

"But why else would he be that far from his home? Or the bar that we were at?" she asked. "What was he doing there?"

"I, uh," I stammered for some solid answers as I looked up at the television. "Maybe he went to a friend's place last night to talk."

"Maybe," she nodded as she looked down at Jed and stroked his cheeks with hands as soft as rose petals. "But I wonder who he was seeing. I don't know anyone around there."

"I don't," I started to say as I suddenly remembered where his work name sounded familiar. Last October I had dreams of a kidnapped girl and I went to her parents to help find her – the Fiddelsteins. Jed worked with Isaac Fiddelstein. My mind started to race as I wondered if there was a connection. Maybe Isaac would be able to give me some understanding of what had happened.

"Uh, who are you?" an annoyed female voice asked from behind.

"I'm Solomon," I started as she walked past me to get to Melanie.

"Not you," she said rudely. "Her!" she said pointing at the woman holding Jed's hand.

"I'm Melanie," she said with a wicked smile. "His girlfriend. And who are you?"

"I'm the one he was with last night, ho!" she said, grabbing Melanie's perfectly styled hair and yanking her up from her chair.

"Let go!" Melanie screamed as she started smacking at the new woman's face.

"Is that all you got?" she laughed. "No wonder he called me up last night for a little fun."

"Let her go," I said, trying to break up the fight without knowing exactly what to do. "Nurse! Nurse!" I screamed as I tried to untangle the woman's hands from Melanie's hair.

I wasn't trained for this predicament.

With the help of two nurses, we finally got Melanie free from the scorned lover and separated the two.

"I've never seen that before," I whispered to one of the nurses.

"It actually happens more often than you would think," she said with a judgmental grin. "Poor guy, he had two women last night and when he finally wakes up, he'll have none. Karma, I guess."

"Karma?" the second woman screamed as one of the nurses started pushing her out of the room. "There was a third woman? You can have that dog!" she yelled in rage. "I'm okay being the other woman," she said flicking her hair. "But, I won't be his third."

"Oh honey, you're never gonna be a man's first choice," Melanie stood up, stomping out of the room. "But he's all yours now!"

"What did you just say to me, ho?"

"You heard me," Melanie said with about as much fierceness as an over-inflated kitten to a mountain lion.

"No, you didn't!" the first woman screamed as Melanie turned the other way and started running in her high heels down the ICU hallway. "I'll catch you!" she screamed as she bent down and grabbed her stilettos holding one in each hand as she ran past Jed's door to catch up with Melanie.

"See," the nurse said, "karma. It's better than most soap operas in here some days."

I sat there stunned. "Aren't you going to go do something?"

118

The nurse looked at me and laughed. "Once they're out of my hallway they are someone else's problem."

CHAPTER 32

"I'm heading to WestMinor to talk to Isaac Fiddelstein," I said into my phone as I drove through midday traffic that was bumper to bumper, creeping at a pace that made me wish I had kept my car parked at Howard University Hospital and used the nearby subway. "Jed worked for him."

"Who's that?" Elizabeth asked as she trolled the internet for Independence Day Sales. "Do you think I would look good as a redhead?" she asked, finding a wig that seemed attractive.

"He's the father of the girl I saved last year, remember?" I said annoyed as I contorted my face, weaving in and out of stalled traffic as best as I could. "The kidnapped girl last October?"

"Oh, her, yeah, I remember," she said with a passive tone, almost dismissive. "So, back to my wig idea, would red work?"

"I don't know," I huffed. "You've got money. Buy it, and if it doesn't work out, use it for Halloween," I said annoyed at both Elizabeth and the soccer mom in the minivan in front of me that kept letting anyone with a valid license plate get in front of her.

"So, you think he may know something?" she asked, returning her attention to the attacker dreams.

"It's a stretch, but I thought maybe he could give us some insight," I said. "Want to meet me?"

"Can't," she said. "Veronica would dock my pay if I left." She chuckled at the idea of getting a paycheck from her sister.

"How much is she paying you?" I asked, staring up at the blue sky through my windshield. Oh, to be a bird and fly over all this chaos.

"Zilch," she said flatly. "I'm doing it out of the goodness of my wee heart," she said with her impersonation of a welcoming soul with a thick southern drawl.

"I don't believe that," I grinned. "You always have something up your sleeve. You don't just do anything for the kindness of strangers, missy," I said, bantering back with my own southern charm.

"Oh, I see how it sounds now," she said with distaste. "You can't do that; only I can."

"Why only you?" I scoffed.

"Because I can't hear my own voice when I'm doing it," she laughed while her work phone rang. "Cooper Law," she said in a shockingly professional voice. "I'm sorry, but she's in a meeting right now. Can I take a message?" There was a brief moment of silence. "Oh, okay. Sure, you can call back, but I'm not sure when she's going to be available. She has another appointment this afternoon." She stopped, allowing the caller to reply. "You have a good day. Bye now."

"Bye now?" I smirked. "What are you on *The Beverly Hillbillies?*"

"Remember Solo, they had money. They can talk any way they like. That's what money lets you do." She stopped and quickly searched the top one hundred billionaires in the United States on her computer.

"Next time I see a billionaire with a hick accent, I will remember that."

"Oh, they're out there," she said with wide eyes as she read the computer screen.

"So, how's Verny?" I asked, recalling her tears and raw emotion yesterday from the letter.

"Not good, but who would blame her," she said softly, making sure she couldn't be heard through the closed door of Veronica's office.

"So, did she find out it was from Jenny?" I asked, pulling up to the next traffic light.

"Jenny?" she asked confused. "It was from Dad."

"Your dad sent that cryptic letter yesterday? How did she find that out?"

"Yesterday?" She asked in shock. "What letter?"

"What letter are you talking about?" I quickly replied, slamming my fist onto my horn to alert the car who was about to take off my front bumper in order to gain a few inches in the traffic.

"Is that your horn?" she laughed. "Sounds like a dying goose."

"Back to the letters. The threat was from your dad?" I asked, trying to inch my way down the street.

"Well, I guess being sued is a threat."

"Sued? She's being sued? By your dad?"

"Hold up, did you say a letter from yesterday?" Elizabeth closed her internet browser to focus on the conversation. "She didn't tell me anything about that."

We each told the sides of the stories we knew. I went straight to the facts, whereas Elizabeth had to give every tiniest detail as if she were writing a legal novel.

"Poor V," Elizabeth said. "No wonder she wants to go home this afternoon. Who wouldn't after the last 24 hours?" She stopped and looked up as she heard the office door jiggle. "Hold on," she said.

I stayed on the phone for five minutes. I finally realized she had forgotten about me as I heard Veronica start to cry and Elizabeth casually mention something about getting her gun from her purse, so I ended the call. I knew Elizabeth would mention getting her gun for little annoyances like the mailman being late so I didn't think it was anything major from her tone of voice.

CHAPTER 33

"That didn't help much," Dakota said as she and Wint stepped into the elevator.

"We had to give it a shot," Wint said with a frigidness in his words.

"You okay?" she asked, pulling out her phone to check her messages.

"Just a lot of stuff on my mind," he said as he grinned, changing the topic. "Any missed calls from your new beau?"

She shook her head as she put up her phone. "No, Stew's working and doesn't usually call through the day."

"Hmm," Wint said.

"Hmm what?"

"Oh nothing," he said. "I just thought of something about the two cases."

"What?"

"Do you think they could be connected?" he asked, looking up at the tiled ceiling with two security cameras at opposite corners.

"Haven't thought of that," she said.

"Both men were mandated by their employers to comply with anger management classes in order to keep their jobs. You don't think they somehow knew each other and the attacker through that?"

"It is suspicious come to think of it," she agreed. "So, are you going to call to get ideas of when they attended their classes?"

"When we get back to the car, I'll give someone a call." He continued to feel that they may actually have a lead on these two crimes.

"It does make sense though," she said. "They were both beaten in the same way."

The doors opened and they proceeded to find their way out of WestMinor as Wint looked up and saw someone he knew jogging up the sidewalk to the entrance.

"That's really strange," Dakota said turning to Officer Cooper who was eyeing the incoming guest.

He nodded in agreement as though trying to uncover a hidden secret. He watched as the man was about to open the door but quickly opened it for him.

"Thank you," the man said, at first oblivious the two knew one another. He lifted his eyes and stopped. Shock smacked him on the face like a spoon of whip cream at a Mexican restaurant on someone's birthday.

"Solo?"

CHAPTER 34

Crap! Not again.

"Hey, Wint," I said cordially. "Hey, Dakota. What are you two doing here?"

"I was about to ask you the same thing," Wint said with a twisted smile that brought a chill to my core.

More lies!

I quickly thought up a story that he could possibly believe. Possibly.

"I'm here to see my financial advisor, Isaac," I said with confidence in my tone and my posture upright.

"I didn't know you had a financial advisor," Wint said unconvinced.

"Do you want to know my blood type too, because I have a doctor's appointment next week if you want to see that," I quipped with a hint of jadedness, a hint I didn't drop subtly. I glanced down at my watch, pretending I was almost late. "Sorry, but I have to go. See you later," I said and hit the button on the elevator, which magically opened immediately.

Stepping inside, I pressed the floor button and watched as Dakota and Wint stared at me unsurely as the metal doors closed. I breathed a sigh as I leaned against the side of the tiny box, trying to calm my sloshing thoughts.

I exited the elevator and entered the floor of WestMinor Financial. People were walking casually to their desks with idle chit-chat, oblivious that last October I thought someone was going to be logging into Isaac's computer to steal all of his clients' money leaving some of these people without a job. But instead, his nephew had gone to Isaac's house to try to embezzle funds, but was caught instead. Today, I didn't blend in well with my blue jeans and t-shirt. Today I was visiting an old friend.

I approached his personal assistant who had replaced his nephew after he kidnapped his daughter with a ploy to deplete his funds. The new assistant was a forty-ish looking woman with neon green 1960s style glasses. The contrast was odd, yet it actually was becoming on her.

"Is Isaac available?" I asked kindly, giving a polite smile as I rapped my knuckles on her counter. "I know him."

"One minute. Can I ask who you are?"

I gave her my information, and she picked up her phone. "Mr. Fiddelstein, Mr. Solomon Davis is here to see you, sir," she said as she smiled politely at me and turned around to try to not be heard. "I don't know sir, but he said he knows you," she said softly.

"Tell him I haven't seen him since last October," I said trying not to interrupt. "That may jog his memory."

She relayed the message and asked me to sit and wait.

Isaac walked around the corner in his three-piece suit with a blank expression on his face. "Hello, Mr. Dav--" he started as finally our eyes connected and he remembered. "How have you been?" he asked in a much friendlier tone as he shook my hand and patted my shoulder leaning in for an embrace. "Come, please come in. Amanda is going to be thrilled when I tell her tonight that I saw you."

"You didn't remember me," I smiled as I winked to his receptionist as we walked by.

"You got me," he smiled as he offered me a seat on the couch in the more personable side of the office that housed his family relics and treasures. His family portrait with Amanda and his cute daughter glowed

127

in the museum-style lighting that one would have showcasing a Picasso. But he was more proud of his family than any artwork.

He closed the door and took a seat in his armchair.

"You know, we only spent a few hours together, but you became a part of the Fiddelstein family after that day," he gushed, and I could tell that this systematic and statistical man wasn't pulling my leg. "I feel horrible not remembering you when my secretary said Solomon Davis, but you're not Solomon. You're Solo when Amanda and I talk about you."

"Your family holds a dear place in my heart as well, Isaac."

"So, why are you here?" he asked, looking down at his watch. "I would love to reconnect. Maybe we can do supper soon. Amanda would love that."

"That would be great," I beamed. "But I have a favor."

"Name it, Solo, anything you need," he said as he placed his elbows on his knees to give me his undivided attention. "You risked your life to save my little girl. Want my Tesla? It's yours."

"Tesla?" I asked shocked as I quickly toyed with the idea of being behind the wheel of that vehicle. I shook my head to focus. "No, it's nothing financial," I quickly corrected as I remembered he had tried to give me a lot of cash when I helped him get his daughter back. Suddenly, I looked over and saw his daughter's smiling face in the picture. That face gave me so much joy to know that she was safe from the evils of this world. Peace flowed over me as my other haunting dream shrunk. I knew I could never hurt anyone like my dream was showing.

I helped people, not hurt them.

I looked over at Isaac who watched with anticipation. "It's nothing about you or your family, but I had a dream about one of your employees, and I'm trying to figure something out."

"Who?" he asked.

I loved the idea of not having to lie to someone. I had already showed all my cards to Isaac last year, who at first didn't believe my dreaming tales when I knocked on his front door at midnight. Now, instead of questioning my authenticity, he jumped to action. That leap of faith caused me to wonder if I could open myself to others.

"Jed Poston," I said plainly. "He's not at work today, is he?"

"I'm not sure, let me check," he said as he started to walk out the door.

"Well, I know he's not because he's lying in a hospital bed right now," I said as he turned and gave me a grave look after he verified the information with his assistant.

"You're right. He didn't come in today and Shirley said--" he stopped as I started to snicker. "What?"

"Her name is Shirley with those glasses. Where is Laverne?" I smiled as he too had a quick laugh. "I'm sorry, it just caught me wrong."

"Well, Shirley said the cops were in here just a while ago asking some questions," Isaac said taking a seat back down. "What do you want to know? I will try and find the information for you."

"Is there anyone you know that would want to beat him?" I asked.

"Oh, Solo, I don't know all my employees that well," he said solemnly. "But I know someone who might," he said with a wink. "But you have to be polite. She's the best assistant I have ever had."

Shirley walked in with a nervous expression with a pair of black slacks and white button-down top with neon green heels and belt that matched her eyewear. Isaac explained a little of what I was doing as he asked her to sit down beside me on the couch. She was a free-flowing fountain of office gossip.

She told us the story of Jed's temper tantrums that had caused human resources to write him up for how he was treating his assistant. That incident only culminated to the criminal problem he had with a brutal attack on someone that forced him into anger management classes.

"I hear that he's good at what he does, but he thinks he's a god," she said slyly as she crossed her legs and got a little more comfortable. "I'm not sure about this, but I overheard someone say he was beat up pretty badly after leaving another woman's place last night."

"Do you have any idea who could have beat him up? Was the other woman in a relationship with someone? Could this be a jilted lovers' spat?" I asked as more questions and theories started to sprout like sunflowers, leaning my thoughts toward a proverbial sun.

"I wish I knew for his sake," she said. "I watched as the cops left, and they didn't seem like they had learned anything new after talking to a few of the people here."

"Well, I know the cops who were here, and they are two of the best," I said looking over at Isaac. "Officer Cooper is my best friend, and he's not going to stop until he figures this out."

Isaac leaned down and whispered in my ear, "And knowing you, you aren't going to stop either."

I wasn't so sure. I had no frickin' clue how these two crimes connected, but I felt it in my bones that they did. There was a common thread somewhere.

I just hoped it wouldn't strangle me as I went searching for it.

CHAPTER 35

Veronica left work shortly after her last client for the day. She loaded up her laptop since she could work just as well at home this evening as she could in the office.

She almost started to drive towards her old house out of habit since she had only been in the new place less than twenty-four hours. She quickly fixed her route and headed toward Alexandria. She flipped on the radio to alleviate the silence and didn't even get bothered by the mind-numbing jingle of Sips, a local coffee shop that was proudly singing about the opening of its newest location in Baltimore.

Usually, she would have flipped the station or called a client as she drove, but that didn't matter right then. She just wanted to get home, pour a nice glass of merlot, light a few aromatherapy candles, and recline in her new bathtub, even though it wasn't anything fancy like her previous one that had the hot-tub style jets around the sides. No, this tub was a plain Jane, clawfoot tub that exuded character. At least, that was what she was telling herself.

Her telephone rang, but she didn't take the call when she realized it was an unknown number. She let her voicemail get the pesky telemarketer or needy potential client.

She pulled into her driveway, grabbed her laptop and purse, and checked her mailbox.

She flipped through the junk mail, but one envelope wasn't junk. She ripped it open and saw photographs of her standing in her driveway with a moving truck in the background. She stood trembling as her laptop slipped away from her arm and collided with the concrete. Looking closer at the pictures, she noticed she was holding a letter in her hand.

The pictures were of her yesterday opening the first letter she had received.

She spun around in a circle, looking up and down the street. One side of her was petrified, because if they took a picture yesterday when she opened the letter, maybe they were doing it now.

On the other side of her mental state, she was boiling with rage at the audacity of someone trying to scare her to her last hanging thread. Were they watching her now? Were they within striking distance? Could this be her last thought?

Her legs were shaking. She didn't know if it was from fear wanting to run into the house and deadbolt the door or run and attack anyone taking a picture of her right now if she could find them.

She wasn't the type of girl to sit by and let someone else do her dirty work.

Not anymore.

Her purse strap was over her shoulder. She continued to survey the houses nearby, looking for anything out of the ordinary. The problem was *everything* looked out of the ordinary. She hadn't been here long enough to know what cars were not her neighbors'. She dropped the mail into her purse and pulled out a gun. The gun Elizabeth had given her earlier that day.

I didn't think I would need this, sis, but thanks, she said to herself.

She held the gun tightly with both hands. Wint had taken her to a shooting range a few times to teach her how to be safe, and she kept her concealed weapon license in good standing, but she never carried a gun.

Lurching up the street, she held her gun straight out, ready to shoot if anyone jumped her. But the only thing she saw moving was her own shadow leading the way up the street.

Suddenly, she saw shaking in the bushes, two houses down from her and across the street. She looked back at her house and then at the bushes. It was a perfect place to hide to get pictures.

"I've got a gun!" she screamed at the top of her lungs. "Come out from behind the bushes or I will shoot you!" The bushes started to shake more as she walked quickly past the sidewalk into the grass.

"Do you hear me?" she billowed. "I've got a gun. Why are you stalking me?"

The bushes stopped moving.

"Come out! I know you are there!" she said, getting close enough that her gun barrel could almost touch the leaves. She breathed deeply, keeping her finger on the trigger as she took a step back. She didn't want the attacker to jump out and get her. She had taken off the safety when she first saw the bushes move. She was ready to defend herself. But mostly, she wanted answers.

She walked around the bushes aligning the house and aimed.

"Please don't shoot! Please!" a young boy around eight years old cried with his shorts and Captain America briefs around his knees.

Veronica lowered the gun and quickly apologized. "Is your mommy home?" she asked as he continued to cry with his lower half fully exposed. "You can put your pants back on," she said softly.

"But I got to pee," he cried as his little bladder suddenly released, spraying the bricks of the house.

"I'm going to go find your mom," Veronica said, quickly turning to walk up to the front door as the little boy wailed.

"Don't shoot my mommy!"

She rang the doorbell as she tried to calm the little boy who continued to scream from behind the bushes. That's when she saw it from the corner of her eyes. An older red four-door car squealing its tires as it fled away.

"Can I help you?" a woman opened the door.

Veronica ran to the street trying to get some of the license plate, but it had already turned. She didn't have anything but a red four-door car.

"Why do you have a gun?" the woman yelled from her front porch. "Richie! Get inside!"

The little eight-year-old came running with tears streaming down his face and his underwear up, but his shorts unfastened.

Veronica lowered her gun, fastening the safety as she walked up the grass to the front door. The mother quickly ran inside and locked her door.

"I'm sorry," Veronica said stupefied through the front door shaking her head. "I know how this looks, but let me explain. I'm your new neighbor from two houses down. My name is Veronica Cooper. My husband is a cop if that makes any difference." She thought about saying something else, but she knew it wouldn't do any good.

She walked away from Richie's house and knew to never expect to get any invites for any of the neighborhood block parties. She knew that she was blackballed already.

CHAPTER 36

Veronica tiptoed the walk of shame back to her new home as she felt the eyes of judgment peering through the window blinds of every house of the street. She didn't think the day could get any worse, but then she remembered she never read the letter sent by Jenny.

She sat down at the kitchen table and slowly unfolded the paper, ignoring the pictures she already had memorized. She laid the letter flat on the table and closed her eyes. She wanted to prep herself for the demoralizing words that were most likely written.

Dear Veronica,

I hope you enjoyed my letter and pictures from yesterday. I was rather taken with how well it came out. Are you scared? You should be after what you did to me. You should be very afraid. It's not every day you have someone come back from the beyond to ruin your life. And by the time I am finished with you, it will be ruined. Just like you did to me.

Your father didn't come see me yesterday, but I know he will be back. He always comes back.

I hope you enjoy your new home. It looks lovely from the outside. I can't wait to see what the inside looks like. I wish I had the luxury of moving to a new place, but since you killed me, it's a little hard to move plots. But you'll be right beside me soon enough.

Trust me, you will be. I have plenty of people who would do anything to get justice for me.

Anything.

If you think these little letters and photos are frightening, you've seen nothing yet.

Once again, love, if you say anything, you'll be next to me sooner than I originally intended.

Sincerely,

Mia Rosenburg

Veronica stared at the letter with its ransom-note style of cut up letters and felt the uneasiness wrap around her like a magician's straitjacket. She didn't understand Jenny's use of smoke and mirrors, but she couldn't deny her illusionist abilities.

Just like all great magicians, she was a liar.

She took a picture of the letter and sent it to Wint and quickly called him.

"Did you see it?" she asked as he answered his phone.

"It's just now coming through," he said as he waited for the image to download onto his phone.

"We need to find out who's visiting her, Wint," she pleaded. "Because I'm pretty sure now this is going to be a daily occurrence. I think I saw someone watching me."

"Watching you?" His body tightened up, and he slammed his fist into the wall. "Where are you now?"

"I'm home," she said. "I'm safe and at home."

"Have you called the security system people yet?" he asked, hoping they had one deterrent.

"I'm calling them as soon as I get off here," she said.

"Get one of my guns from the safe," he said. "I know you don't like them--."

"Elizabeth gave me hers, so I've had one today," she interrupted.

"Should have figured she always carried one," he grinned. "It may be safe to have her come in each day for a while. Just to have someone else in the office with you."

"You mean, someone who wouldn't have a second thought about shooting anyone?"

"Let's just call her your bodyguard," he smiled. "I bet she would appreciate that job more than being your receptionist."

"Scary, but you're right," she said as she pulled out Elizabeth's gun from her purse. "On a lighter note," she started to laugh at the ludicrous chain of events of the afternoon. "I caused a neighbor kid to piss on himself today."

"That's my girl," Wint said with pride.

CHAPTER 37

"Since you are new to this setting, Manuel, why don't you tell us a little something about you?" Ally asked as she looked at the faces of her Tuesday afternoon anger management group. She had a few members who came to the majority of the sessions, even after their court-mandated appearances were tallied and verified, but Kris was the only one who came that day.

"Can anything I say be reported back to the authorities?" Manuel asked with a thick Mexican accent as he looked around the room, trying to read each person as if playing a game of high-stakes poker. And it was high stakes when a life was on the line.

"Even though this group is for counseling," Ally answered as a disclaimer, "if anything is said that could impede an investigation, I am bound to the state to disclose my findings. Since technically, this is something the court is requiring, we do not have doctor-patient privileges."

"Okay," Manuel said with a bright white smile that accented his mocha skin. "I'm good then."

"I think you misunderstood me, Manuel," Ally said laying her pencil down on her paper of doodles from the last thirty minutes. "You can talk freely about anything you want to talk about. You need to talk to get out some of your emotions and aggression."

"Nah," he said passively as he leaned back in his chair and crossed his arms. "I plead the fifth."

Ally huffed at the uncooperative manner of some of her group members. Manuel wasn't the first person to not want to share, but she couldn't in good conscience sign off on his attendance if he didn't participate in the program.

"Listen, Manuel," she said gruffly, "since this is your first time joining us, I am not going to push you, but you will have to talk a little more next time if you want me to tell the judge that you participated in this program. If not, I can let the judicial system take the next appropriate steps in your rehabilitation."

"Rehabilitation," he chuckled. "I don't want any rehabilitation."

"Well, then why did you sign up for this program?" She felt her blood pressure rising as she tried to control her temper with a few of the techniques she taught her members. She closed her eyes and unclenched her fists. She was ignoring the pain in her wrist that was still taped from her accident over the weekend.

"My attorney forced me to," he said nonchalantly. "He said that if I did this, I wouldn't have to serve any time."

"I think your attorney intended for you to participate," she said with controlled contempt. "If you don't participate, you get no credit for this."

"That blows," he groaned like a teenager sitting in the back row of math class.

"Yes, yes it does blow," she mimicked.

"Are you mocking me?" he asked, turning his head as if trying to figure out the easiest way to snap her scrawny neck. "Because I don't do well with people who mock me."

She looked him in the eyes without backing down. "I don't do well with threats."

The silent standoff lasted a few seconds until Manuel rolled his eyes and looked away, but Ally had learned to never step away from a challenge. Once she did, she allowed them to have the upper hand.

She wasn't used to having anything but the upper hand in most situations.

And this wasn't going to be any different.

"Come on, man," Lex said, leaning over to whisper into his ear. "Just do your part so she can sign off on her paperwork and we all can get out of here."

"Okay, let's break off into pairs for some role-play scenarios," she started and quickly looked at Moe to squash his perverted mind. "Not that type of role-playing."

"Don't you want to be my partner, Dr. McDermott?" Moe asked, wearing a creeper's smile that showed years of tobacco use.

"It would be unfair to partner with you," she said as she shook off the filth from his improper glances. There wasn't anything wrong with role-playing with her group members, but she didn't have to endure the punishment. She'd never been convicted for beating a man's skull into a hotdog cart when he put mustard instead of ketchup on the bun.

"Isad, you and Moe work together on this round, and Kris, would you mind being Manuel's partner today?" Kris shrugged his wide shoulders and walked over to the uncooperative Manuel. Ally smiled to Kris and started explaining the rules for this lesson. She glanced down at her watch and almost fell over when she realized she still had twenty minutes with this group.

Twenty agonizing minutes.

CHAPTER 38

"What are your plans the rest of the day?" I asked Elizabeth, who had promised Veronica she would answer the office phone and door until closing time.

"Nothing much," she said typing on her laptop she'd brought from home. "Just killing some time. You?"

"I don't know what else I can do," I said walking the sidewalks like a tourist. "I think I may go to a museum and just relax the rest of the day. Tucker and Jed are both still unconscious, and even if they wake up soon, the cops will be questioning them."

"You mean Wint?"

"Yes," I nodded as I stopped to get a popsicle like a kid at one of the convenience markets before heading to one of the Smithsonians. "He knows something is up."

"He's known since last October," she said fingering her keyboard. "But he's not going to do anything about it."

"Are you sure about that?" I asked, biting a piece of icy cherry from the top. "Because Wint's job is to investigate."

"Investigate crimes, not us."

I let her words repeat in my ears as we ended our call and I started to walk through the Air and Space Museum. It was decked out with red, white, and blue decorations, celebrating the lineage of great American explorers bravely searching for new answers.

I passed through the planes on display and came to a room where kids were running around, trying out the scientific experiments without comprehending they were actually learning and not just playing. I immediately joined in on the fun.

I played with one of the exhibits explaining the common law of inertia when it hit me. I was placing the poker chips on the paper and quickly pulling the cardstock away allowing the chips to fall into the cup below. Kids were stacking as many chips as possible to see who could drop the most. Technically, it shouldn't matter how high the stack of chips towered, they should all fall uniformly down if a steady hand pulled the sheet. I watched as uncoordinated kids tried to master the skill of dropping the chips, but they either flinched or jumped in excitement. That little twitch caused the chips to topple away and miss the cup.

I wished my life were like the tower of poker chips I was building, neatly stacked with grooves pressing them firmly between one another. Sadly, life wasn't always as easy as a routine science demonstration.

But why wasn't it? I looked around the room with time-tested examples. Wasn't everything in life just like this experiment?

Wasn't everything aligned to some extent?

It may not be associated in a way that I preferred or imagined, but someone had already ordained all of life's inner workings.

And if God had already designed the future as he had the past, that would mean that these dreams could be figured out just as inertia.

I smiled as I watched the kids believing that the impossible wasn't really impossible. It just hadn't been achieved yet. But it might one day. I stepped away from the chips, laughing with the kids as they tried and flopped when I bumped into a couple holding hands watching their three-year-old girl swing a weighted string as a pendulum. I apologized and proceeded out the door when a pain shot through me faster than the speed of sound.

If everything was aligned by God, that would mean both the good and the bad. It was one thing to hold that reverence when life was going well, but it was another to maintain that respect when life was just like the toppled tower of poker chips, falling all over the place with no hope of finding its way into the elusive cup. To know and believe that everything was planned out from the equation to entropy, the number of legs on a caterpillar, when and where Chelsea was murdered.

That thought hurt.

CHAPTER 39

He took a seat and waited for Jenika to be brought into the visitors' room. He watched in anticipation, ready to tell the story of the sight he'd captured today. The sheer terror in Veronica's eyes as she walked the street, gun held high, aiming the barrel at mailboxes and lawn decorations. The memory of the last two hours caused him to snicker to himself.

Looking down, he noticed the pencil the officer gave him wasn't to his liking. He slid the sharpened side against the paper until the point was sharp enough to inflict pain if need be. But mostly, he was ready to take down the morse-coded message that Jenika would blink to him.

He'd been trained from an early age by his father who was originally in the KGB and was infiltrated in the 80s in the United States as a Russian spy. Years passed, and he'd fallen in love with an American woman. He'd tried to hide the truth from her, but her beauty unraveled him. He'd had a decision to make, to remain true to his homeland or to flip sides.

He had chosen the beauty of a blonde American over the cold winter nights in Siberia. He'd had to guard himself from other Russian spies as they thought he had betrayed them, but it wasn't an act of disloyalty. He was just ready to move on to something else. When the Cold War ended, he was left as somewhat of a free man, even though he knew Russia wasn't going to take its watchful eyes off the Western world.

So he'd befriended fellow Russians with similar histories. They met at darkened bars, spoke mostly in Russian, regaled on times of old, and sung the Russian anthem with pride-filled masculinity. One of the men he'd befriended was Jenika's father.

He was used to being in a secret organization unable to tell anyone he was KGB because he never knew who he could trust. Moving to another organization wasn't a far leap. Even though this organization from the outside wasn't ethical with his Eastern Orthodox Christianity, neither was the KGB. But he'd learned to ask for forgiveness then and he learned to ask for forgiveness again, just in English to a priest during his weekly confession.

He left one brotherhood and joined another. Each one had his back and each one held a gun to his head if he made a wrong move. He had seen the KGB kill his brothers for acts of believed treason that were later absolved as mistakes. Later, he watched as ruthless cutthroats of his new family ignited fires to kill a backstabber's family.

It was a treacherous life, but it was the only life he had known.

He had two girls with his American bride, but he'd wanted a son. A strong, burly son to keep up the family tradition in his new family circle.

He eventually had a son after two miscarriages, who became his pride and joy. He loved his daughters, but a Russian son was better than a dozen daughters. He taught him to fight and how to hold a gun and hold his vodka. He taught him the secrets of the KGB. All the formal training he'd had at sixteen years old, he taught his son at six. That was the one thing about his current family; he couldn't guarantee he would be around for another day if the right person said something about him.

Jenika walked up without sitting down and picked up the phone. Her eyes started to blink quickly as he watched for the message. "Leave and don't come back unless I call you! If you show up again, I will not come out to see you. Understand?"

146

He didn't respond for ten seconds as he scribbled her message. "I understand," he said stringing out each syllable as she continued to blink. "Can I ask you a few questions?"

"No," she said.

He watched with a look of sadness as his pencil continued to unveil her next step.

"But give Mia my love," she said, hanging up the phone. She stopped her rapid blinking and waited for his pencil to stop.

Looking up from his paper, he nodded and said, "Okay," with the telephone still in his hand.

She turned and walked away.

He heard the words and looked past the hurtful intent. He had his next step.

CHAPTER 40

Wint hadn't come home yet, and Veronica was halfway done with her bottle of wine. At first, she sat on the couch in her living room for an hour clutching the gun, holding it in her lap in case anyone tried to barge through the door. She finally relinquished that guarding stance and took a bath with the door open, her trusty gun within arm's reach.

She was feeling like a victim once again. And she didn't want to feel like that anymore.

She got out of the tub and put on her purple terry cloth robe. The only way to quit feeling like a victim was to quit playing defense and take the offensive position.

She looked at the complaint Manfield & Hyde claimed, a breach of employee non-compete agreement. She read over the ten-page legal document citing 39 allegations of petty findings, which were easily defendable. But allegation 26 was a blatant lie, stating that on the date of her employment she'd signed a non-compete agreement. She started to fume at the fraudulent intent of her father and wondered if he'd gone so far as to forge her name on a document.

Her mind was running over the various countermeasures she could take. At the top of the list was turning in her father to the police for the death and cover-up of Mia Rosenburg. She didn't want to go there, but she had it in her arsenal if it ever got that messy. He wouldn't have any regrets throwing her under the bus, so why should she?

She opened her laptop and started typing her counterclaim. The words were flowing like an Alps stream in springtime. She was taught in law school that there were always three ways to handle a bad judgment: cry, do nothing, or get even.

She wasn't going to let her father make her cry anymore. It was time to show him her bones were not brittle but were strong and able to withstand any storm he sent her way. She wasn't going to stand like a child with an umbrella and galoshes. She was going to put on her battle gear with many rounds of ammunition and crawl through the mud if she had to. She wasn't his little girl anymore.

Sadly, she never was.

Wint walked through the door and found his wife behind her laptop with no dinner in sight. "Hungry?" he asked as he walked up behind her, kissing her on the cheek.

"Let me finish this and then let's go out," she said with a determined look in her eye.

"Go out?" he asked shocked. "I would've thought you would want to stay in tonight."

She shook her head and continued to type. "Not tonight," she smiled, looking up at him with a strong will and determination. "This is my first meal as a free woman," she said with a twinkle in her eye.

"Free woman?" he asked, confused about how the last twenty hours had gone with the various letters from Jenny and the lawsuit. "Are you feeling okay?"

She raised her hand to give her one more minute. Her fingers were running over the keyboard, jumping over the letters like hurdles for a track and field athlete. She was on a mission to complete this document, and she could see the finish line. She buckled down and stared at the screen as the letters were popping up faster than she had ever typed before.

"Done!" she huffed, breathing out a sigh of relief. "I am more than okay," she said saving her documents and closing her laptop. She looked over at Wint in his police uniform and untied her purple robe. "But before supper, let's work up an appetite," she smiled wickedly as she stood up letting her robe fall to the ground.

She was going to start living the life she'd always wanted to live.

Unashamed. Unafraid. Undefeated.

She walked towards her bedroom and turned around seeing Wint standing shocked. "Well, are you coming, officer?"

CHAPTER 41

"You're not going to call me while I'm sleeping tonight, are you?" Elizabeth asked in a warning tone that didn't exude any comic relief. She was serious. "Because I'm beat."

"You're beat from one day of work?" I laughed as I lay on the couch watching a movie.

"Don't judge," she said as I heard her pour pasta into boiling water. "And I do more than you realize."

"Like what?" I asked, knowing that today she didn't respond to any of her dreams since I caught the tripping man before falling down the steps and breaking his neck.

"Wouldn't you like to know."

I stopped and thought for a second. I felt like she was playing a game of hide and seek. "I kinda would," I said shocked I was about to take a bite of the dangling carrot.

I think I caught her off guard because she coughed, as though trying to change the subject. I had never pressed upon what she did throughout the day. It was never my business. Just because I didn't grow up with a trust fund didn't mean I could discriminate against someone more fortunate than myself. If she considered her day busy doing whatever she did, that was not my concern.

"Oh, you don't want to hear about that," she said, sidestepping the request with a new conversation starter. "So, did you go back to the hospitals to check on the two guys?"

"I didn't," I sighed. "I didn't know what else to do because both their nurses told me they may be out for another day or so. They are both in a medically-induced coma to help with the swelling. I think I'll go back tomorrow afternoon and check on them."

"Can't you just call and see if they're awake?"

"I guess. But that just seems so impersonal."

"You don't know them," Elizabeth said flatly. "You don't owe them anything. We had a dream. They got beat up, and now there is nothing you can do. It's up to the doctors now."

"But what if I'm supposed to do something?" I asked as if I was standing on a path that forked in twelve different directions.

"Solo," Elizabeth groaned. "You go be your Solo self, but I'm not going to worry about those two guys anymore."

"But what if these crimes are connected?" I said, getting up from the couch to find something to snack on in the kitchen.

"Well then, the cops will find the perp and arrest him," she said casually as if we were discussing what paint Veronica should use in their living room. She felt distant. She sounded aloof. There was something different about this conversation.

"Fine," I said not wanting to argue with her on our different stances of action. "So, back to what you did today that kept you so busy."

"You know," she said in a restrained voice.

"No," I countered. "I don't know."

Elizabeth made a failed attempt at an excuse and then ended the call. I scratched my head and thought she had no idea what a busy day really was.

CHAPTER 42

The house was silent as he lay in bed beside his wife. She was lightly snoring, which he always thought was cute, even though she refused to believe she did it.

He couldn't sleep and looked at the clock on his nightstand. It was just 10:11 p.m., but this was the first night in the past two he was able to catch up on his sleep. He was going to try and take advantage of it, but something in his body wouldn't let him. It was like his body was telling him it needed to release some pent-up rage.

When he turned to get out of bed, it squeaked a little. He looked beside him, hoping he didn't wake his wife. She rolled a little more to the middle, causing his body to lean away to get out of the bed. He stood in the doorway, looking at his sleeping wife as she rolled back onto her side of the bed, stealing a little more of the covers. Another thing she refused to believe, even though he would often wake up with nothing but his boxer briefs covering his body.

He strutted down the hall, turning on the bathroom light and shutting the door. The mirror showcased his muscles as he massaged his tightening bicep. He wasn't hurting, but his muscles were sore. He loved that feeling. The feeling of a good workout.

His knuckles were showcasing a swollen purple hue from the punches from the last two nights. He had perfected hiding the bruises with his wife's makeup. He couldn't hide the puffiness, although he always had a reasonable excuse if anyone ever dared to ask.

But no one ever did. People knew not to ask too many questions.

He closed his eyes and recalled the sounds of the grown men crying, begging for sympathy, pleading for surrender, hoping the torture would end. He smiled to himself as he thought that torture always came to an end one way or the other. No one was tortured forever.

He glanced down at his thighs that bulged from all the squats he did at work. He was never into soccer as a kid and could not see why kids enjoyed the thrill of kicking a ball into a goal. He wondered if the adrenaline was just as intense as when he was kicking the men in their sides. He considered the sound a goalie made as they leaped for a ball and collided with the ground, only to see the ball slip past their reach. The groans of failure. He'd liked hearing the groans the last two nights as well.

He turned off the light and left the bathroom. He was feeling an invincibility he hoped wouldn't fade. He strolled into the blackened living room and unlocked and opened the front door. He stood behind the glass door and stared out at the deserted street, remembering the feeling of jogging through the city streets in his underwear the previous night. It was empowering to let everything out and know no one was the wiser.

He stepped outside and stood in his driveway. He stared up at the sky, knowing there were a billion stars overhead, but he couldn't see any of them due to the city's light pollution. He walked around to the chain-link fence surrounding his backyard, but he wasn't getting the same feeling of boldness as last night.

It wasn't the same. He needed something more.

Just as druggies needed to always get another hit more intense than the last, he needed something as well. He looked down and slipped his thumbs into his shorts and pulled them down. He felt the openness of being exposed. He walked into the middle of the yard and looked at his

154

neighbors' homes. If anyone looked outside, they would see him. But if they did, he knew they wouldn't dare say a word. They were all afraid of him.

He felt the high he was needing. It wasn't an erotic or sexual feeling. It was more of brutal control and fierceness -- the knowledge that he could do whatever he wanted, and no one would say a word. He walked back towards the front yard with his underwear in hand. As he stood on the front porch, legs spread and hands resting on his hips, he felt like Neil Armstrong landing on the moon. He felt untouched. He felt unashamed. He felt unabashed.

He saw a pair of headlights turn down the street and immediately wanted them to drive by and see him. He wanted them to see he didn't care. He stepped further into the yard, making sure to be seen if the car drove by. He watched as the lights started to brighten and the muffler on the pickup truck chugged closer. He knew that sound. It was Porter's old beat-up Dodge. Porter, who lived four houses down.

The old truck puttered closer as the beams from the headlights started to spread across the front yard, slowly coming closer to his bare feet on the grass. He began to smile as the light hit his exposed skin, inching up until the light shone over his nude body, standing in the grass like a Roman god.

Porter looked over as he passed, eyeing the naked man suspiciously.

But he felt in control. He felt domineering. He felt strong.

He smiled as Porter drove by, saluting his America flag decal on the back of his truck. He felt like a young soldier again ready to take on the world. He still had more battles to contend with this Independence week.

God bless America.

WEDNESDAY

CHAPTER 43

The scene was black with the commotion of several people talking. The dialogues evaporated as a deafening sound from a machine billowed and echoed around. It stopped. The hydraulics boomed and sputtered as the sound of sliding metal was singled out. More loud laughter and shouting swarmed the scene as it seemed like thousands of voices suddenly appeared.

"Watch that!" a woman yelled.

"Don't push!" shouted another.

The voices trailed off until it was barely a murmur of noise. The sound of the sliding metal broke through the void as it clasped shut, silencing the voices. The hydraulics snapped, and the sound of movement engulfed the place.

A lone pair of feet came running followed by a fist pounding on the glass. "Hey!" the man shouted, infuriated. "Stop! Let me on!"

By the disgusted groan and colorful Spanish words, the man didn't get on.

"There'll be another one in six minutes," a husky voice said from behind. "We have time."

The other man huffed, clearly annoyed by the optimism of the calmer man.

"Just sit down," he said. "Take a load off."

The silence was broken by a strange question. "Have you ever hurt Ally?" the gruff man asked.

Silence.

"I know you…you're the…" the accented man said as a scuffle ensued. Groans and yelps escaped their mouths. A fight continued and heavy breathing encapsulated the sounds like a vacuum.

"Get your hands off me," the man said with a hint of a Mexican accent as his voice was stifled. The sound of skidding shoes on the concrete lingered in the air like a trail of smoke. Suddenly, the fighting ceased with the sound of a broken bone.

"Oh man," the second man said with a twinge of fear. "Get up, man, get up!"

A bubbly gurgling sound soothed the room like a meditation record of a peaceful brook.

The gurgling stopped, and a pair of feet was heard running away.

The stomping feet switched to a ticking sound of a clock until the ticks overpowered the sound of the feet.

"Cut the blue wire," a man heard through his radio as he looked down at a box with a timer counting down.

"Are you sure?" the man asked holding a pair of scissors. "There is a white wire that is coming from the same section."

"No, believe me, cut the blue wire," the man commanded.

The man clutched the scissors and looked down at the time. "We have six minutes left. Can we get the robot up here to do this? I'm feeling unsure of this wire. It's a 50-50 gamble."

"I wouldn't gamble on your life, Garrison," the radio emphasized.

Garrison took a deep breath, wondering if this was going to be his last taste of oxygen. He touched the blue wire with the sharp blades and thought of his wife. He said a quick prayer and cut.

The radio connection went dead as a newspaper clipping for July 4th had "Bravery Will Not Be Forgotten" as the headline on the front page with a picture of Lieutenant Jamal Garrison under it. The story opened with, "Lieutenant Jamal Garrison, a 15-year veteran of the DCMPD, was killed by a bomb blast at First American Bank at 2:24 during an attempted robbery gone horribly wrong. The robber, Xavier Needlestone, was shot and killed by Garrison who arrived first at the scene. But as his body fell, it activated the bomb."

Elizabeth woke up with her eyes crusty. She wasn't ready to retrace all the information in her dream. She wanted to roll over and forget and catch some more z's. But she knew she couldn't do that.

Two people were going to die that day.

At least.

CHAPTER 44

A twelve-year-old girl poked her head into a darkened room, looking slightly startled with her widening eyes and jarring head movements. Her lips started to move, but no words were heard. She didn't step into the room but held onto the doorposts with her arms spread, swaying back and forth as if gathering the nerve to step in.

Her hair tossed back and forth as he shook her head no, but she still peeked her head into the room. She looked around as if it were the first time she had seen the room. Her eyes danced around, exploring the sights as if uncovering a new land. Then suddenly her head stopped dead center.

She continued to talk, but still nothing was heard.

She was talking to someone, but the other person or people couldn't be seen. She had center stage.

Her lips stopped moving, and she nodded her head in agreement as her eyes sparkled with intrigue and curiosity. She timidly took one step forward, crossing over the threshold from the familiar hallway to the foreign terrain.

She smiled brightly. Silent laughter radiated from her toothy grin. She started to talk, and only one word was heard in the middle of the sentence.

"You."

As that singular word broke through the void, she continued to talk. Her mouth was moving faster as her feet moved a little more, taking more steps until she was in the center of the room.

The room looked like a darkened home office with a desk and an old computer monitor that took two hands to carry. The walls were clothed with gold and blue-striped wallpaper that looked of satin with artistic portraits hanging sporadically around the room. She tapped her fingers rhythmically on the desk, swirling her fingers around the hardwood as she walked around the large piece of furniture, scraping her short nails along the groves.

She came around the desk and the perspective changed from staring forward to the hallway, to looking behind at a large three-pane window overlooking a dark yard with strings of colorful Chinese lanterns below. She peered out the window, looking down at the glowing lights as the window reflected her blonde hair.

Her lips started to move once again as a single word was vocalized.

"Can't."

Then she stopped talking.

Her smile dissolved until it totally disappeared. Her eyes, bright a minute earlier, now had a glaze of concern and fear.

She spun around, shaking her head no as her mouth quivered. "Stop."

A lone finger came into view as it landed on her mouth to hush the frightened child.

Her trembling lips shook more as another hand reached up from the side, grabbing her shoulder and pulling her in.

Her lips parted, and she looked like she wanted to scream, but suddenly she stopped. The sky sparkled behind her as fireworks exploded in the distance.

But still, there was only silence.

Different shades of the rainbow colored the sky like a Jackson Pollock painting with splashes of reds and yellows bursting into the scene.

The pair of hands tightened their grip on the young girl. She maneuvered her body as best she could, but the hands were too masculine for her small frame. Her body was tossed around as tears started to rain down her cheeks.

Suddenly her eyes went lifeless as the stranger's hands went elsewhere on the innocent child.

A blanket of darkness covered the room except for the glittering colors of the fireworks cascading the nighttime sky.

"You can't stop," the young girl said once again.

My eyes shot open, and I rolled over, punching my pillow with all the force of the world behind me. It was the power of unfairness that ran rampant in the world. It was the energy of darkness that tried to blow out any light that someone tried to shine. It was the vigor of evil that coursed through every human's veins.

Even myself.

I wasn't innocent of doing any wrong. I knew the gift of grace that I held, but this act -- this dehumanizing act of violence was one that God should never turn a blind eye to.

"Where are you?" I pleaded out loud, not with tears, but with pent-up hostility. "Where are you when these bad things happen?"

I looked at my alarm clock as it went off.

Time for another day.

Many people with ethical dilemmas would turn to a priest or rabbi or other religious figure in their life. Interestingly, my first thought was to talk to my atheist friend.

Want to meet for breakfast this morning? I texted, crossing my fingers that it wasn't too early or too late for him.

Sure, he quickly replied. *Same place as usual, say 45 minutes?*

I rose out of bed and knew a shower was needed. *Better make it an hour.*

An hour it is.

CHAPTER 45

"I had two dreams last night," Elizabeth huffed. "Each one had someone dying."

"So, we got a two-fer today," I said driving to my breakfast spot with Jeremiah.

"It's not funny," she said with a sick feeling rising within her. "One was a bombing at a bank, which I have information on, but then the other was a beating in a subway." She stopped and let out a disgusted sound. "I don't know anything about the second death."

I wiped the smile off my face because death was a serious matter. We dealt with it so often, I sometimes felt like a funeral director. But instead of planning funerals, we tried to divert them.

"With both of us, we can try to figure it out," I said with an assurance that calmed her nerves but rattled mine.

"I have to go to Veronica's again today, but maybe you can come by and we can formulate some type of a plan," she said getting her head back into a logical framework. "We've done it before, right?"

"Absolutely," I said, slowing my car to park. "I'll try to be at Veronica's by ten."

"Ten? It's only 7:00. You can't get there any sooner?"

"I'm meeting your boyfriend for breakfast."

"If I was the jealous type, I would start to think there was something going on with you two," she said with a questionable tone.

"Get off it, Elizabeth," I said brushing off her ignorant remark. "I'm straight."

"Keep telling yourself that," she laughed. "People change."

"Not me."

"Before I let you go, send me your dreams so I can look them over," she said in a friendlier voice. "So I can make sure we don't miss anything."

I didn't have any dreams to share. I thought I could send this dream, but it just seemed wrong talking about it with a female. Also, I didn't have any idea of when the dream was going to happen. It now seemed like it would happen tomorrow night, at someone's house with fireworks shooting off. Hopefully, I would get another dream tonight with more intel.

Hopefully.

"I already took care of my dream this morning," I lied. The sad thing was, I didn't feel guilty like I used to feel after I told a white lie. It was like my heart was getting calloused. I didn't like that feeling. Even though I felt like I couldn't get hurt, I still didn't feel like I was all there either. Like a piece of me had broken off.

"Well, that's good," she remarked. "More time to focus on mine."

"Yes, that is what I always want, more time for you, Ms. Hyde," I said in a cynical monotone. "My loftiest dreams have come true."

She let out a curse and told me not to be late.

"I won't. I'll probably be there before ten," I sighed.

"I wasn't talking about me, I was talking about your breakfast date," she laughed as she quickly hung up.

Why did I put up with her?

CHAPTER 46

Jeremiah was diving into his eggs Benedict and wheat toast as I played with my French toast scooting around the pieces in the maple syrup. I thought I was hungry, but my eyes were bigger than my stomach.

"Why do you think bad things happen?" I asked as he buttered his toast.

"What do you consider bad?" he asked with a coy grin.

"I think you know what I consider bad, but what do *you* consider bad?" I asked, turning the question around to him. "Do you think there is right or wrong in this world?"

"Solomon, you are talking of two different things. Wrong isn't always bad. Those are two different adjectives on a different scale. It's like comparing a cougar to an apple. You can compare the cougar's size to an apple, but if you compare the animal instinct of a cougar to an apple, those comparisons are not going to be relatable."

"Okay, then let's go back. Do you believe in right and wrong?" I asked, laying my fork down to give him my undivided attention.

"I'm not a fundamental atheist," he corrected before he started to give his speech. "As a human, I believe there are things that are right and there are things that are wrong, not because of what a religious text says, but because I would feel wronged if they happened to me. I am less stringent on the philosophy because sometimes notions are only good in the confines of theoretical scenarios and textbooks." He stopped and took a sip of his water.

"Murder, for example, is wrong, and I don't believe any atheist could deny that because it's wrong on many levels. One, it is universally unlawful to end someone's life by means of your own hands. Two, it is emotionally hurtful to others. Three, depending on particular convictions, most religions prohibit murder. Four, and the most relatable to me, is I don't want to be murdered."

"Well, we can nix out number three for you, because if religion is worthless, then it shouldn't hold any merit in your reasoning," I said as he nodded his head.

"I just put it in there because the majority of the world has some type of religious affiliation."

"I understand that," I said, "but I don't see how number four can be put into this category either. You said murder is wrong because you don't want to be murdered, but there are many things in life that I don't want, but that doesn't mean they are wrong." I stopped and looked around the restaurant, lowering my voice. "Like constipation. I don't want it, but it doesn't mean that it's wrong. It's just a matter of life."

Jeremiah started laughing and clapping his hands. "Good point," he said with a hearty and impressed tone. "Very good point," he said as he started to think.

"What?" I quickly said. "What are you thinking."

"Well, isn't constipation wrong?" he asked, rubbing his chin. "Your body has a specific anatomical chemistry, and when something is wrong, your body tries to fix it."

"Well, then is it murder when an animal kills another animal to fix the ecosystem that is its habitat?"

"Hmm," Jeremiah said as he looked down at his plate, taking a bite of his toast. "You have given me a lot to think about."

"Well, can I go back to my first question?" I asked, wanting to get back to the purpose of this breakfast. When he nodded, I continued. "Why do bad things happen?"

"Solomon, I wish there were a simple answer to that complex question, but there isn't. If you ask each person in the world that question, you will likely get many different answers. Each person has a reason for why bad things happen, and in a way, each one could partially be correct."

"But why do *you* think bad things happen?" I asked. "I know if I ask the cashier, she will tell me something, but her opinion doesn't matter to me. I don't know her, and there isn't a bond between us more than her taking my money," I said with a laugh as he smirked. "But you," I started with sincerity, "I value your opinion."

"That is very kind of you," he said. "Many Christians wouldn't care to know my opinion on matters important to them because they see me as cynical or argumentative or stubborn, but for you to say that to me, that means very much."

"I don't see you that way at all," I said giving him a warm smile. "All I see is a man who is a friend who eats a disgusting breakfast."

"Disgusting?" he scoffed. "It is delicious."

"How are runny eggs delicious?" I asked with my eyes sealed shut while contorting my open mouth into a grotesque expression. "It looks more like a bad sinus infection."

"Don't knock it 'til you try it," he said with a comical smile.

I started to laugh after hearing Jeremiah say such a common expression. "Are you still studying Elizabeth's phrase-a-day calendar?"

"Why do you judge me like that?" Jeremiah laughed as he dipped his toast in the remainder of his egg yoke. "Scrumptious."

"Because you do things like that."

He finished his breakfast and started to answer my question. "Why do I think bad things happen, Solomon?" He stopped once again, licking his teeth to make sure he didn't have anything showing. "You got me."

I looked amazed at how easily he said that without an ounce of remorse in his eyes.

"Doesn't it get to you?" I asked. "I mean, doesn't it make you upset or sad when bad things happen?"

He nodded his head. "Just because I don't understand why things happen doesn't mean I am sheltered from the ramifications of them."

"So you agree that bad things happen?" I asked, making sure I was speaking to a human and not a robot.

"Oh, yes," he said with a passionate expression. "No one is that blind. But I cannot intelligently say that the cause of the bad things that happen in this world started at a precise moment of time that had a ripple effect through the ages."

"So, no big bang for bad things?"

He shook his head. "Exactly. There is no big bang for bad things." He smiled at the phrasing. "That is a tongue twister."

"It's a twister all right," I said.

"So, why do you believe bad things happen?" he asked me as he folded his arms across his chest.

"Well, it may sound simplistic to you," I started as he stopped me.

"Don't ever think your ideas are simplistic," he said as if lifting me up on his shoulders with encouragement. "Some of the wisest men are those

168

that delve in simplicity. There is a beauty and a wonder in that realm, like Giotto's perfect circle."

"Who?"

"You've never heard of Giotto?" he asked amazed.

"Never."

"Well, sit back," he said, and I reclined in my chair. "In the 14ᵗʰ century Pope Benedict XI commissioned the painting of St. Peter's Basilica in the Vatican. The story goes that the Pope sent a courier to get some artists' works around Italy. He went to Florence and asked for a drawing to take back with him. Giotto took out some red paint and painted a perfect circle. 'Here's your drawing,' he said. The courier thought he was kidding and requested a better painting. 'This is enough, and more than enough.' The courier returned to the Vatican with all the artists' drawings and showed them to the Pope. He was questioned about Giotto's circle, and when he explained that he painted it without any assistance, the Pope was amazed. He got the job with just painting a red O.

"So, don't ever believe your simple acts are simple acts." He stopped and took a breath. "Your simple acts could be monumental to the world."

I let his words drip over me. That was what I needed to hear at that precise moment. It especially meant the world with two people possibly dying later that day.

Our simple acts could be monumental to them if we succeeded.

I bowed my head and said a quaint silent prayer.

May I be as round as Giotto's O. Amen.

CHAPTER 47

Veronica sat behind her laptop in her office, rereading her counter-complaint for Manfield & Hyde. Every time she went through the pages with a fine-tooth comb, she found something new to add or take away.

She was used to writing complaints and could quickly write one in her sleep for a client, but when it was her complaint, it deserved a little more attention.

"What are you doing?" Elizabeth asked when she walked into the office with two iced coffees in her hand.

"Thank you," Veronica said, taking a sip of the sweet mixture, hoping that the burst of caffeine would invigorate her. "Reading this again."

"Reading what?" Elizabeth asked, walking around the desk as Veronica groaned like a teenager whose little sister was invading her privacy. "Just trying to help," Elizabeth said walking away.

"It's a counter-complaint to Dad," Veronica said, looking up over her laptop to see what Elizabeth's expression would be. It was a look that Veronica wished she hadn't seen.

Elizabeth's eyes went wide as if asking if Veronica was sure about this.

"Don't look at me like that," Veronica said, pushing her laptop away so there weren't any barriers between them.

"Like what?" Elizabeth asked naively, even though she knew how she looked. She didn't want her sister to get hurt.

"Like you are on his side."

"Oh, is that how you thought I was looking, because I was looking like I thought you were crazy," Elizabeth jabbed with hurtful honesty.

"Crazy?" Veronica screamed. "Crazy? You think *I'm* the crazy one?"

"Well, your actions don't seem so un-psychotic right now."

"He's suing me, Elizabeth!" Veronica erupted. "He is suing me, his flesh and blood, for taking a handful of clients that I worked to get. Clients that no one else at the firm has ever spoken to. And he is suing me for damages. Now, that's a load of crap and you know it."

"It's not right what he's doing, V, but…" she started as Veronica shut her up.

"There are no buts, Elizabeth! None!"

"Then talk to Mom," Elizabeth said, trying to sound reasonable. "I bet she would talk to him if she knew."

"You think Mom matters to him?" Veronica asked, shaking her head knowing their father had had multiple affairs and their marriage was one of convenience and strategy. "If she died tomorrow, he would be annoyed that she messed up his golf plans for tomorrow evening."

"I'm just trying," Elizabeth started, but Veronica didn't want to hear it.

"You always side with him. Always. Why do you do that?"

"I don't always side with him!" Elizabeth roared.

Veronica rolled her eyes like she did in high school when they would argue over everything; nothing was off limits.

"It's sad. You are so far up him, and you don't even see it." Veronica shook her head and grabbed her laptop to try to refocus herself on her work and not this family spat. "Why don't you just leave? It's not like you need to work here since you are still living off Daddy's allowance."

171

Elizabeth looked at her sister and stood silent. She was beyond hurt.

"What? No response?" Veronica mocked. "I see you're using your literary degree exceptionally well with your outstanding communication skills. Father would be so proud knowing you've been out of school all these years and finally got a job. Sadly, it's just because I was desperate."

"If only you knew the truth, Veronica," Elizabeth said stomping out and slamming her office door. "If only you knew," she said as a lone tear fell down her cheek. The telephone started to ring, and she turned to get it. "Cooper Law, this is Elizabeth."

CHAPTER 48

"So, do you think calling the police will work with the bomb threat?" Elizabeth asked as I sat beside her at her desk. "Won't they think that you're part of the robbery?"

"Why would they think that?" I asked perplexed with my hands in the air.

"So, you want to call the police, tell them that there is going to be a robbery at 2:00 today at First American Bank, and when the bomb is about to explode not to cut the blue wire but cut the white wire, all because of your gut instinct?"

"Yeah. What's wrong with that idea?"

"Because that sounds crazy to be so specific with the details," she pointed out. "Whatever dispatcher picks up is going to ask a ton of questions."

"Well, then, I'll just hang up," I said, crossing my arms as if that solved all the problems.

She tapped my forehead with her finger. "How well did that go the other night when you called them about the beating? How many times did they call you?"

"I eventually blocked their call," I said, shrugging my shoulder.

"They still know you called that in, Sherlock," she said with a stupefied smile. "Even though you stick your head in the sand, the rest of the world sees your butt up in the air like a moron."

"I thought people liked my butt," I smiled. "I've been working on my glutes."

"We need another plan," she groaned, leaning back in her chair and stretching her arms. "We need a plan that will not get us killed or locked up."

"I'm too pretty to be locked up," I grinned.

"Why is that always your comeback?" she asked with exasperation.

"Because it's always true," I smiled, grabbing a few of the chocolate candies in her candy dish and popping them in my mouth.

"Not with that haircut of yours. And I wouldn't eat those candies. I didn't bring them. I think they were here when Veronica moved in."

My eyes widened as I quickly spit out the non-melting so-called chocolates. "You could have said something earlier," I said getting up to clean myself.

"I could've," she said shrugging her shoulders. "But I knew this would make me happier."

"I need a drink," I said, grabbing her iced coffee.

"Hey now," she said with a bewildered look. "I don't know where your mouth has been."

"Isn't that ironic coming from you?" I joshed as I quickly took a sip and wiped the plastic straw clean before putting it down. "Better?"

We continued to come up with various plans when a loud, blood-curdling scream came from Veronica's office.

"Veronica?" I yelled as we both ran to her office.

She was standing up watching her laptop as she continued to scream, pointing at the screen and mumbling.

"She…got….how…she…"

"Veronica. What?" Elizabeth asked, walking around as she too gasped at the image on her laptop.

"What is it?" I asked, running around to see what was causing the commotion.

The three of us stood watching what looked like a home movie of Veronica running up the street, aiming a gun and screaming.

"Veronica, what's going on?" I asked watching the video and then looking at Veronica who was crumbling beside me.

"It's Jenny," she said, her voice trembling with fear. "She's having someone follow me."

CHAPTER 49

"Follow you?" Elizabeth shouted, closing the video on the laptop to see that it was an attachment in an email. "What did the email say?"

"Read it. You're going to anyway," Veronica said walking around the desk to sit in a different chair. She didn't want to see the email or video anymore.

Dear Veronica,

I hope you are enjoying these little messages from the grave. Apparently, there is life after death after all. Please don't try to reach out to me. If you try, I will find out. And if I found out, there will be grave consequences.

I know you told Wint about me, but if you tell anyone else, I will be forced to shut you up so my name isn't tarnished. And I don't mean with duct tape.

I hope you love the video. Do you have a license for that?
With love,
Mia Rosenburg

"I thought you said this was from Jenny," Elizabeth said, looking up at me and then across the desk at Veronica. "Is Mia Rosenburg one of her aliases?"

Veronica swayed in the chair, biting her nails -- a nervous twitch she had outgrown when she was nine. "It's her alias now."

"What do you mean *now*?" I asked, looking over Elizabeth's shoulder to reread the email.

"I shouldn't say anything," Veronica said, chipping away at her nails like a beaver cutting down a tree. "Just forget about the name."

Elizabeth looked up at me and I stared into her eyes. We both knew there was something she was hiding, and that name was one we would never be able to forget.

I saw the email came from a Gmail account. "Can't we find who sent this email by the IP address?"

"Do *you* know how to do that?" Elizabeth asked unconvinced.

"No," I answered undaunted with a nasally tone. "But anyone with some IT experience can."

"Well, I don't think V is going to want to forward this email to anyone."

"No," Veronica said defensively. "No one can know about this."

Elizabeth minimized the email and quickly did a search on the internet.

My eyes went wide at the top finds. She clicked a newspaper link, and an article from years ago covered the screen.

We quickly read the article and gave each other a look of suspicion.

"You don't think?" Elizabeth mouthed as Veronica stared at a blank spot on the wall.

I shrugged my shoulders. "Suicide?" I mouthed back.

"Huh?" Veronica said, waking up from her trance. "What did you say?"

"Nothing," I lied.

CHAPTER 50

"I need to stretch my legs," I said, stepping out of Veronica's office to walk outside. I quickly called Wint.

"Solo, what is it?" he asked, sounding annoyed.

"It's Veronica," I quickly said, dismissing his tone.

"What about Veronica?" he jumped in response.

"She got another email from Jenny with a video of her toting a gun yesterday," I said. "And she's freaking out with good reason."

"Stay with her, Solo," he said as he quickly told Dakota he needed to leave.

"I'm not leaving."

"Thanks," Wint said breathing heavily as I pictured him running down the police station hallways. "Solo?" he asked with a sense of confusion. "Why were you with my wife?"

"I was visiting Elizabeth," I answered casually as I leaned against the building, feeling the mid-morning heat radiate from the concrete. "Do you think someone could actually cook an egg on the sidewalk?"

"Don't change the topic," Wint replied. "I wish you would be honest with me," he said as I heard him slamming his car door and turning on his siren to head to Veronica's rescue.

"Wint," I started, but didn't know what else to say. "I promise you, I'm not in any trouble."

"But you are hiding something from me, aren't you?"

I didn't respond. I let his question linger in the air like a painful punch to the gut as his doubt in me caused all the air inside my lungs to escape. But I didn't hold that against him. I'd felt hurt when he had kept things from me in our past.

"You just have to trust me," I said, pushing myself away from the building to go back inside to check on the women. "I'll see you when you get here."

"Solo," he said, but I ended the call and put my phone on silent.

I walked back into the office and found Elizabeth and Veronica where I left them. Elizabeth lifted her eyes from the laptop, looking concerned and frazzled.

I glanced over at Veronica who continued to sway in her chair. "I called Wint; he's on his way."

Veronica didn't respond but continued to bite her nails as the confetti of clippings covered her blouse.

Elizabeth got up from Veronica's desk and walked me back into the waiting area. "I think there is a problem with this whole Mia thing," she said in a whisper. "Something doesn't seem right. Mia Rosenburg worked for Dad and committed suicide." She stopped and took a breath. "You don't think Jenny knows something that could bring Veronica down, do you?"

"Veronica is a lot of things, but I don't think she would do anything to cause someone to kill herself," I said, scratching my head and messing up my hair.

"Hmm," Elizabeth said, skidding around that statement.

"What?"

"Veronica isn't the nicest one in the family," Elizabeth remarked.

I thought back to all the verbal daggers Veronica had thrown in my direction. She didn't have very many tactful bones in her body, whereas

Elizabeth slithered like a rubber snake. "Neither are you," I said, not trying to be argumentative, but pointing out a fact.

"True," she agreed. "But what if Mia didn't know Veronica well enough to know how to read her?" She stopped and spun around looking at her fragile sister. "What if Veronica rode Mia so hard she snapped? Jenny and V were best friends before Jenny went psychotic. What if she was getting her guilt off her chest and now Jenny is using that against her?"

The more Elizabeth spoke, the more it made sense.

"We have to get to the bottom of Mia," I said, "but I don't think it will be best to ask her. I think we better talk to Wint when he gets here."

Elizabeth nodded and looked down at her watch as her mouth gaped open. "What about the bomber?"

I started picturing a scenario that might work. "Why do we have to wait for the guy to die and detonate the bomb by accident?" I closed my eyes to picture a totally different outcome. "What if," I started to say as Wint came barging into the office.

"Where is she?" he asked galloping in with chivalry.

He was Veronica's knight in police armor.

CHAPTER 51

The man went to the microwave to fetch his bag of popcorn. He was watching a video that had died down in excitement, but he thought the action was going to be picking up fairly soon.

He returned to his laptop and watched a screen that displayed a desk ledge, an empty leather chair and half a diploma hanging on the wall.

"Come on, come on," he said, watching the live feed and hoping he wouldn't be watching a motionless screen for long.

"Veronica," he heard a manly voice say near the hacked laptop. "It's going to be okay," he said soothingly. "It's going to be okay."

Here we go, he thought as he stuffed a handful of popcorn into his mouth and waited for the drama to intensify.

When Jenny had asked him a few weeks ago if he knew someone who could send an encrypted email to access the recipient's web camera, he'd beamed. He didn't just know of someone who could do it. He, himself, could do it. His father had taught him all his tricks for spying on friends and foes.

"You can never be too safe," his father would tell him. "It's not wrong if you are eavesdropping on nothing important. And it's wrong of them to lie to you if you catch them doing something they shouldn't be doing. Son, it's not wrong to look out for yourself. It's only wrong if you get caught." Then his father had emphasized his most important lesson. Don't ever get caught.

He sat behind the laptop and listened in on Veronica and this stranger's conversation. As he consoled, she cried, he vowed to protect, and she cried some more.

He was actually surprised by how quickly everything had happened. He had set up a dummy email account through a burner phone because he didn't want anyone to track his IP address, just as the other guy had mentioned. He knew cop shows made it look simple to track someone down, but it wasn't that easy. He could be tracked if he didn't watch his tracks, but just as his father had said, he didn't want to get caught, so he was doubly safe.

He had attached the video of Veronica that he recorded yesterday and encrypted it with a hacking tool to access the computer undetected. As soon as Veronica started the video, he was able to download a program to get into her computer. She was so engrossed with the video that she didn't see the mouse moving in the background. All she saw was her terror-ridden face screaming for the person to get away from the bushes.

As she watched the video, he had easily bypassed firewalls and had full access to her computer. He watched as another woman, Elizabeth, was searching on the laptop. He watched her eyes widen as she read something on the screen. He hit a few buttons on his keypad, and instead of seeing the webcam footage, he was able to see what she was looking at on her laptop.

Technology, he thought. *It's not always your friend.*

He leaned back in his computer chair and stretched his neck. He didn't expect anyone to be behind the computer any time soon. He closed his eyes and heard another pair of voices enter through the computer speakers, a man and a woman.

"Veronica, come with me," the other woman said. "Let's get you some sunshine. That may do you some good."

182

"Yes," the other man in the room agreed. "Vitamin D is a good thing."

"Go on, honey," her husband added. "I'll be right here."

There were a few seconds of silence, and then the storyline picked up. "Who is Mia?" the unknown man's voice asked.

"Solo, I can't tell you."

Solo? What kind of name is that?

"Wint, come on, Elizabeth already looked her up, and the story she found doesn't sound good."

"It's not good," Wint said as he sat behind the laptop wearing a police uniform.

Nice to see you again, officer.

"Wint, you can't keep this bottled up," Solo said. "You can trust us."

"Like you trust me?" Wint asked with a raised eyebrow.

CHAPTER 52

The room was silent as everyone in the circle watched and waited for Manuel to say something. Anything.

"It doesn't have to be like this," Ally said, giving up any hope of breaking through the wall that stood between her and Manuel.

"It doesn't have to be like what?" he asked, jaded by years of watching his back from perpetrators and former friends.

"Man, just answer the question," Lex said, exhaling in disgust at the show Manuel was putting on. "Just say anything. We won't know if you're telling the truth or not, so just do us a favor and say something so she can check your name off that you participated today, and she can move on to someone else."

Ally didn't want to side with Lex and his demeaning tone regarding her line of work, but he had a point.

"Just give it a try, Manuel," Ally said with a tender voice as if watching a butterfly emerge from its cocoon. "What harm will it do?"

"You want me to talk?" Manuel said with a voice that shook down the wall. "This," he said with his arms waving around the room. "This isn't going to do any one of us any good. I've lived on the streets since I was fourteen, and you, Dr. Know-It-All, want to tell me how to control my feelings. Well, try controlling your feelings when you watch your sister get capped in the street just because she didn't say hola to el jefe of the hood. Or when you watch your dog get beaten by a group of druggies because they are too high to realize that it's a live dog."

"That's horrible, Manuel," Ally said, feeling the barrier drop as she figuratively rushed over to his side with her kind words. "You may have lived a life that I haven't, but you don't have to live it anymore."

Manuel looked around the room and smiled. "It's good. If those things had never happened, I wouldn't be where I'm at now."

"And where are you now?" Ally asked, sitting on the edge of her seat.

"I'm el jefe of the hood now, so it's all good," he said closing his eyes and leaning his head back as he wore a twisted smile. "I talked. You can check me off now."

Ally didn't know how to respond to the sadistic demeanor he showcased. "You can rise above this lifestyle, Manuel. You can change."

"I don't want to change," he said with a smile that transfigured to wickedness. "Kids look up to me. They do whatever I say because they want to be just like me," he said. He stopped and looked into Ally's eyes. "They don't want to be like you." He stopped and waited for the fear to rise into her pupils. To watch the dilation take effect like an animal backing away from its prey. "You're just a sad, pathetic, white woman who doesn't know anything about the streets."

"Manuel," Lex said, patting his knee to calm down. "Cool it, man."

"You're right," Ally said, jotting a few notes down on her paper. "I don't know anything about your life. But I know I don't want to live like you do."

"Yeah, you wouldn't make it a day on my block," he grinned. "Want to come for a visit? I'll make sure to have something extra special for you," he said in a deep tone as if yearning for her to take him up on his offer. "Or I can bring it to your place. It's your choice, doctora."

In her past, Ally had had a few patients who'd crossed the lines causing her comfort level to skid, but seldom had anything ever happened.

She watched as Manuel leaned back in his chair, but this time he kept his eyes open and glued on her. She felt the uneasiness in his words because for the first time in a long time, she believed him.

"Kris," she said trying to move past tension that was suffocating her. "How are you doing today?"

Kris started talking, but she wasn't listening to him. She wasn't watching his lips, wondering what they tasted like. She wasn't undressing him with her eyes, imagining the tight stomach that was hidden underneath the layer of cotton. She wasn't being hypnotized by his dazzling smile that she desperately wanted to touch.

No, she was still watching Manuel watching her.

CHAPTER 53

I didn't want to arrive at the bank too late, because all Elizabeth knew was the time the bomb was going to go off, not the time the entire fiasco would go spiraling down. I had a plan and I hoped it worked, but the main thing was being at the bank before it went down. Elizabeth gave me the name of the supposed robber, Xavier Neddlestone. I searched through social media until I found an image of him as I sat in the lobby waiting for my appointment.

I didn't want to look conspicuous, so I exchanged a twenty for two rolls of quarters and asked to open a savings account. I didn't think it would do any harm to get another savings account drawing less than a penny on the dollar, but it was a good excuse to be at the bank for a long period of time. Especially at a desk where I could see the entire lobby.

"Your name?" Lydia, the customer service representative asked as I looked around the spacious lobby with cream tiled floors, the stereotypical teller windows with four individuals behind depositing people's paychecks, and the quiet that loomed over the space like a lingering fog.

"Solomon Davis," I smiled, turning my head back to give her my attention, even though my mind was far away from this measly transaction.

I tried to focus as she started to type, beginning the round of questions as if I were at a doctor's office. I was polite and cordial in my answers. I smiled and gave playful small talk, but I was worlds away from where we were sitting.

Every time I heard the entrance door swing open, my head jerked.

"Are you waiting for someone?" she asked with a professionalism that was scripted through years of sitting on her side of the desk.

"Oh, me, no," I stammered, clutching onto the roll of coins in my hands, fidgeting nervously. "I just…" I stopped and took a breath. "Just a nervous twitch of mine," I said lowering my head. "My apologies."

"No apologies needed," she said as she started her second line of questioning. "Can I have your driver's license?"

"Sure," I said, putting down one of the rolls of quarters and pulling out my tattered wallet that had aged through the years, although not as fine as a nice bottle of wine. I played this up, frowning with a little humiliation. "I really need to break down and get a new one."

"As long as it does its job," she commented, taking my license and scanning it into her computer. "Here you go," she said, handing me back my plastic card as the door swung open again. I had my body tilted sideways on my left hip as I saw a familiar looking man walk in.

I looked at Lydia. "Hit your silent alarm," I said grabbing my roll of coins and standing up.

"What?" she asked in shock.

"I know you have one. Hit it now!" I said sternly, looking her in the eyes as a threat. "Oh, I forgot my license in my car. Let me go get it," I said loudly as I started to quickly walk away.

"But sir," she said as her voice started to trail. I lost focus on Lydia and saw my new target in sight. He was fidgeting at the center counter, writing something with the pen that was chained down. The closer I got to Xavier, the surer I was that it was him.

"Xavier!" I said loudly, his name echoing through the lobby. I was surprised at the acoustics in this aged building; another time, I would have marveled more at the architecture.

He looked up at me with squinting eyes but didn't answer.

The moment our eyes locked, I knew.

I knew that I had just said his name.

"Xavier Needlestone! You dirty scumbag!" I said, gripping my fist tightly around my newly exchanged roll of quarters and throwing a punch. "Why are you sleeping with my wife?"

CHAPTER 54

My dad had taught me to defend myself when I was eight, but I knew I was never going to be able to knock someone out with my skinny arms. "When you hit someone, hold something firm in your fist," he'd said with a wink. "Like a roll of coins."

"Isn't that like cheating?" my eight-year-old self asked as I was sporting a shiner under my left eye.

"Did the guy who did that to you play fair, Solomon?" he'd asked with firmness. "When it comes to defending yourself, you have to watch out for yourself. No one else will."

"So, kick him you-know-where?" I'd asked in shock.

"If you're down and it's not looking good," he'd frowned. "Kick as hard as you can." He'd patted my shoulder with a wink. "If you don't, he will," he had said and lifted his palms for me to start aiming and punching.

"What are you--" Xavier started to say as I felt my clenched fist connect with his lean cheekbone. He groaned and covered his head, trying to shake off the shock. When he lifted his head again, he looked disgruntled and perturbed that I'd disrupted his agenda.

I was ready and swung with my other hand, landing a sweet shot on the other side of his face. His head quickly turned as a large glob of spit, mixed with a little blood splattered onto the bank counter.

Screams erupted in the lobby, but I couldn't let him go. I had to stop him before he took an innocent life. I looked at his frame. His forearms looked like those of an MLB homerun derby winner, and I knew that his biceps probably showcased the same muscular features. I knew my

190

weighted quarters could not compare to the dents he was going to put into my skull if I let up.

"I'm sorry," I mumbled to myself as I saw three men in suits running in my direction from their offices. I grabbed Xavier's shoulders and his eyes locked onto mine. He grinned a bloody smile as I closed my eyes and swung my right leg into his groin.

I felt his pain as he moaned and sputtered, his knees going instantly weak at the sudden impact on his masculinity. He fell forward onto his knees, and I caught him under his armpits.

A man grabbed me from behind. "He's got a bomb!" I shouted. "He's got a bomb!"

I wasn't going to let Xavier fall to the ground. I didn't want the bomb to accidentally detonate. I continued to cling onto him as I felt the man try to pull me off him.

"Will you stop!" I yelled. "He's got a bomb!"

Two other men stood nearby, confused. This was never in their routine trainings.

"Get something to tie his hands with!" I barked the order like I commanded the scene. Neither one of the men moved an inch, probably wondering if they should listen and obey. "Do it!" I yelled, continuing to hold Xavier to his knees. His moaning was growing quiet, and I knew that I wouldn't be able to hold him off forever, especially with a man on my back.

"Will you please get off me?" I asked, trying to keep my voice calm, although I knew it didn't come out as reasonably as I had hoped. "He's got a bomb, and I'm trying to stop him."

"Do you have a bomb, sir?" the man on my back asked Xavier, who shook his head no.

"Do you really think he's going to say yes?" I asked in disbelief. "He was going to rob you."

I could feel Xavier's strength building as I was having to use more of my energy to keep him in place.

"Sir, let him go!" one of the gentlemen shouted while standing like a fool to my left, watching the fight like we were in high school and he wasn't sure who to cheer for.

"I can't!" I yelled as I tried to throw the guy off my back. "He's got a bomb, you moron! Do you want to die?" I continued to rock my body, gyrating it around, trying to toss the guard onto the ground. He wasn't moving. His grip clung around my neck, causing my airflow to lessen. "Stop," I gasped as I felt another pair of hands grab my arm that was holding up Xavier.

It was Xavier's.

The words of my father echoed in my head.

I looked down and spotted the target. I kicked again. Harder than before and more precisely. Xavier's eyes rolled back into his head. I couldn't keep him up as the other two men pulled me to the ground.

I looked over at Xavier, rolling around like an injured dog as his shirt came untucked, exposing a small black strap underneath.

"He's got a bomb!" I shouted as I heard Xavier chuckle in pain.

"You're right," Xavier moaned, looking in my direction. We were both on the ground, our heads pressed against the tile floor -- his from the pain of getting kicked in the groin and mine from having three grown men pushing me down. "I do."

Xavier painfully lifted his shirt, exposing his midsection with a powerful package of explosives a few feet from my face.

"You should have listened to him," he groaned as he pressed a button triggering a countdown display.

Sixty seconds.

CHAPTER 55

"Grab him!" I screamed as the other people in the lobby, employees and patrons, screamed and sprinted toward the door.

Suddenly, the three men on my back jumped up. Two of them sprinted toward the exit with the rest of the crowd, but one stayed by my side looking confused and bewildered.

"Help me!" I screamed to the idle man as I started to crawl on all fours toward Xavier, who continued to lie on his back, laughing like a mad man with no reason to live.

"Hold him down!" I barked as the room suddenly went silent in my head. The building was in chaos, but all I could hear was the ticking of the time bomb as I watched the red numbers quickly decrease.

"I have a family," the man said with downcast eyes as he started to run away.

"You don't have to do this, Xavier!" I yelled as I crawled closer to him.

"I have nothing to live for," he said casually, as if we were having coffee and not 40 seconds from death.

"Yes, man, yes you do," I said looking around the room wondering how I got myself into that position.

I reached my hand toward the bomb, focusing my attention on the red numbers. That's where I went wrong.

I focused on the bomb.

Not his foot.

He swung his leg and caught my hip. As I fell forward, I tried to catch myself, but the shock was too much. My hand slipped on a puddle of his spit as my head crashed onto the hard tile floor.

"You shouldn't have hit me, man," he said as he rolled over and pulled himself to his feet. "You messed with the wrong man."

I raised my head and saw a pair of combat boots swinging toward my face.

My energy surged.

My fight or flight instinct kicked in.

I swerved my neck, missing his boot by inches as I rolled over and leaned up. He didn't see the next punch coming, but it wasn't just a punch. It was something my dad never taught me, but at this moment, he would have been proud.

I punched, grabbed his delicates, and twisted. His breath was stolen as he fell to his knees. His eyes crossed in pain, but I didn't let up. I continued to twist.

I gripped my fist tighter until he fell onto his back. He was kicking and twisting his body, but this time I was watching his legs.

My grip turned deadly as I started to dig my nails deeper through the denim. I knew I was getting through when his legs quit moving. I eyed the bomb.

27 seconds.

I let go and jumped up. I became my eight-year-old wrestling hero Hulk Hogan as I kicked Xavier in his face and body flopped onto his chest. I felt his lungs exhale all his oxygen as I saw the bomb.

21 seconds.

Two wires protruded from the bomb, one white and one blue. Just like Elizabeth's dream had said.

I reached for the white wire and pulled, but nothing happened.

It didn't come out.

17 seconds.

It had to be cut.

My heart fell what felt like a thousand feet. I didn't have anything to cut the wire.

Fight or flight screamed in my ears. It was time to flee.

Jumping up, I started to leave as my stomach launched another thousand feet into my throat. Xavier grabbed my foot.

I looked back at his smile as the red numbers glowed 14 seconds.

"Where are you going?" he smiled wickedly, holding as firmly to my foot as I'd held onto his scrotum. "You're not leaving."

11 seconds.

My life flashed by.

I jumped with every ounce of energy I had left in me. But as I landed, I aimed once again. I heard a snap followed by a shriek of pain.

7 seconds.

CHAPTER 56

"Wint! Wint!"

"Dakota, what is it?" Wint asked startled by her frantic tone. He heard the urgency and fear before the two words.

"It's your friend," she said. "Solomon Davis."

"Solo? What about him?"

"I'm down at First American Bank, and there's been an explosion. They say he was in there."

"Explosion?" he asked once again. "He was there?"

"Wint, what is it?" Elizabeth asked, leaving her desk as her heart dropped. "Is Solo all right?"

"Yes, he was here," Dakota said as her phone started to cut out. "He hasn't come out yet. A bank teller said he was opening an account and jumped a guy. He said the guy was sleeping with his wife," Dakota said shocked. "I didn't know he was married."

"He's not," Wint said, breathing a sigh of relief. "It must be another Solomon Davis."

Elizabeth started to shake her head and reached up to take the phone from Wint. "Elizabeth, stop, it wasn't him."

"Wint," she said in a trembling voice. "It was him."

"Dakota, I'll be there soon," Wint said as he ended the call.

"No, it was just another guy with the same name. They said a guy with that name attacked a guy who was sleeping with his wife," he said casually since he saw things like that often. "A bomb went off and that guy never came out."

Elizabeth crumbled to the ground as she started to wail in painful sobs. "Wint!" she billowed between her sobbing groans. "He told me he was going to that bank when he left here."

"But I didn't say what bank this happened at," Wint said in a suspicious tone.

"Wint, now is not the time," she exploded. "It's Solo!"

"Elizabeth, I think you are confused," Wint said. But as he was speaking, all the things that seemed to not fit started to swirl into a hodgepodge of possibilities.

She grabbed her purse and stormed toward the door. "No Wint, it's him," she said running out and down the sidewalk to get to the parking garage two blocks down as tears were streaming down her face.

"Elizabeth, get in!" he shouted as he jumped into his patrol car, turning on the lights and siren. Elizabeth sprinted back to his car and got in as fast as possible.

"Go!" she barked. "Go! Go! Go!" she cried as her tears streamed trails of mascara down her cheeks.

"Why did he go to that bank?" Wint asked quietly, running the red lights in his way, letting his police privilege bypass traffic violations.

Elizabeth closed her eyes and bowed her head. "Please God, please," she moaned a fragile prayer. "Save him."

Wint looked over at his sister-in-law, reached over, and grabbed her hand. He, too, started to pray for a miracle.

"Dakota, what is it?" Wint quickly asked, picking up his cell phone when it rang. "Did you find out something new?"

"It was him," she said timidly.

"Did you find him?" Wint asked as Elizabeth lifted her head, straining to listen to the phone call.

"Wint, I'm sorry," Dakota started when his hand went numb, and he dropped the phone between the console and driver's seat.

Elizabeth crumbled.

"I should have stopped him."

"Elizabeth," Wint said, choking on her name. "Why should you have stopped him? What's going on?"

She started to sob as she caught her head in her hands. Dry heaves started to sneak through the gut-wrenching bawling. He had never seen her in such a state. He tried to calm her down, but his words weren't getting through. Probably because he couldn't get any words out himself.

He was feeling the weight of the acknowledgement that his best friend may be gone as tears started to flow freely down his stubble.

"What did I do?" she groaned in agony. "What did I do?"

CHAPTER 57

"Let me in!" Wint shouted when he was blocked at the entrance of the bank as the place was surrounded with emergency personnel.

"Stay back," one of the members of SWAT said as he guarded the shattered glass door.

Elizabeth stood behind the yellow caution tape, looking at the shards of glass coating the sidewalks of the windows and doors from the blast. Clouds of smoke were fleeing the building through any opening they could find.

"My friend is in there!" Wint screamed to the SWAT guard. "He's in there."

"I'm sorry," the guard said, "but they are looking around for any survivors."

"He's got to be alive!" Elizabeth screamed from the barricades. "He knew better."

Wint watched Elizabeth from the entrance. His thoughts were swirling around him like a tornado, and the glass he was stepping on was proof of the deadly force. With each step he took, he heard the scraping underneath his shoe that cranked up the grave realization.

He knew better?

Those words stung Wint's ears. He looked over at Elizabeth who was hiding something. He knew there was something going on, and he needed to find out what lurked beneath all the wreckage and debris.

"Sir, how much longer?" he asked the guard who shrugged his shoulders and kept his back to the door.

"I don't know," he said. "I'm just doing my job, so let them do theirs."

"Fine," Wint said taking a step back and turning away. But as he looked at Elizabeth, he couldn't move any closer to her. He had to find something out. No matter what.

He walked down the sidewalk and saw a broken window with pieces of hanging glass barely clinging to the sides. He looked around and tapped the glass until it fell and left a clean opening. Elizabeth saw what he was doing and immediately wailed and collapsed on the ground, creating a diversion.

Wint jumped through the window and walked through the office to the open lobby. His heart dropped as he saw blood splatter and bodily remains in the middle of the floor. There wasn't a body, but rather pieces of one.

"Solo!" he moaned to himself as he saw a shoe on the floor. He knew whose shoe that was.

He stepped out of the office and caught the looks of four other SWAT members.

"What are you doing, officer?" one of them asked, walking over to Wint.

"Have you found any survivors?" Wint asked, trying to control his lunch from coming up as he smelled the mixture of blood and explosive fumes.

"You need to leave. How did you get in here?" the SWAT member asked.

"I have some inside information," Wint answered as the SWAT member looked at him dubiously. "I know the other guy who was in here, Solomon Davis."

"You need to leave," he said walking him to the door.

"Before I do, have you looked all around?" Wint asked like a kid pleading with his parent.

"We are doing that, officer," he said defensively. "Let us do our job."

"Have you tried shouting?" Wint begged as he started to shout. "Solo! Solo!"

"Officer, please!" the SWAT member barked. "You need to leave so we can secure the scene."

"Secure the scene?" Wint huffed. "Solo! It looks secure to me. Solo!" he shouted at the top of his lungs.

"Garrison," the SWAT member said into his radio. "Please escort this officer out."

Garrison walked into the lobby, staring at Wint with disapproval. "I told you, you weren't allowed in here."

"Solo! Come on, buddy! Solo!" Wint continued to yell as Lieutenant Garrison pulled him to the door.

"Solo!"

A light moan pierced the smoky air.

"Did you hear that?" Wint jumped.

"Hear what, officer?" Garrison asked, ignoring Wint's excitement. "You need to leave."

"He's alive!" Wint shouted. "Solo! Come on, Solo! Say something! Solo!"

He waited but heard only silence.

"I don't hear anything," Garrison said with remorse. "I'm sorry, but it doesn't look good from what they are saying."

Wint was about to respond when something else caught his attention. He heard a faint moan from somewhere in the rubble of disheveled ceiling tiles, splintered wooden beams, and broken crumbling bricks.

"Help."

CHAPTER 58

"Please God, please." Elizabeth stood behind the yellow tape and wooden barriers placed around the bank. She had heard someone say the blast was powerful, even shaking the foundations of nearby buildings. She turned her head and noticed some of the adjoining buildings had broken windows and a few more loosened bricks on the exterior, but nothing compared to the desolation inside the bank.

She leaned as far as she could over the blockade, trying to get a peek of the inside, but it was useless with the dustbowl and smoke still swirling around any openings in the building. The entrance looked like a fog machine was plugged in by the door, leaving any details sketchy at best.

"Please God," she murmured as she heard Wint's screams for Solo inside the building.

"Solo! Come on, buddy! Solo!"

She heard the tone. It wasn't a sound of miraculous findings. It was the utterance of fleeting hope in the depths of despair.

She crumbled, falling to her knees that already had a coating of dirt from the last time. She didn't care. She wouldn't care if her body were covered in tar and feathers if it meant her dream didn't kill one of her closest friends.

Tears flowed.

Her eyes couldn't stop the incessant gushing. She tried to take a couple of deep breaths and compose herself, but the more she watched the door, the more she cried.

"Wint," she softly whispered, "find him."

She closed her eyes and felt herself falling apart.

She hated this week. This holiday had always been the week of remembering tragedies and mourning the past. The thought wrecked her that next year there would be another nail in the coffin of why she hated Independence Day. Picnics and barbeques were outings she ignored. Fireworks and sparklers only ignited disdain and remorse. Her agitation at people's patriotism only caused a sickening feeling in her stomach because she longed to have that enthusiasm.

She yearned for the feeling of freedom during this pain-filled week.

She needed a miracle.

"God, please," she said as a group of paramedics barged through the entrance. Her interest piqued at the idea of paramedics instead of coroners entering the war zone.

Her praying continued with rapid-firing prayers. "Please, God."

She waited for what seemed like a day, but it was less than a minute before one of the paramedics left followed by the remaining two a short period later with their bags in hand.

But no wounded victim.

There was no medical emergency.

"Please, God," she yearned for any sign of hope. Just a sign.

The door swung open, and a group of police officers exited the building as a few others went in.

Through the commotion she saw something hobbling through the windowless door pane, coming closer to the hanging metal handrails. It was two men, leaning onto one another.

They were both covered in dust and coughing.

"Solo!"

CHAPTER 59

"Stay back," Wint said as Elizabeth jumped over the barricades circling the exterior of the bank.

"Happy to see me?" I grinned, leaning on my friend for support as Elizabeth embraced the life out of me. "I'm okay," I said with a hint of laughter of the awkwardness of the situation. But a few minutes earlier I wasn't laughing.

"I thought…" she started to say as her lips started to quiver. "I thought you were…" She stopped as she pulled my other arm around her neck to help alleviate some of the pressure from Wint.

"Yeah," I said with a casual flare. "You're not going to get rid of me that easily."

They walked me back to the paramedics who were grabbing their gurney. "No need for that," Wint said as he tightly hugged my side.

"We told you to stay," one of the paramedics barked as he quickly sat me down on the back ledge to get an oxygen mask on my face.

"He wanted out," Wint smiled at me prompting me to grin in return.

"You look filthy," Elizabeth said, brushing herself clean. "I need a lint brush."

The paramedic's eyes went wide, and he stared at me and Wint. "You know…" he started to say as I interrupted him.

"I know, I'm sorry to get your new blouse messy," I said with a playful jab.

"Oh, it's not new" she quipped. "I've been thinking of taking this to a thrift store for awhile. Guess it's about time. I'm not sure I'll be able to get your blood out of my sleeve."

"My apologies."

The paramedics took my vitals. I was fine.

"Where's your shoe?" Elizabeth asked, looking down at my left foot.

"Somewhere in there," I said pointing inside the bank.

I didn't care where my shoe was. I was just relieved it wasn't still attached to my body. Xavier had clung onto my foot as I felt my life trickling away. I couldn't think of any way to make him let go, so I jumped. Somehow, as I was jumping, my foot started to slide free of the shoe he was holding. I landed my free foot on his wrist, breaking it instantly.

I didn't have long, and as I ran, my shoe slid the rest of the way off. I didn't think I could make it through the two sets of doors and outside before the bomb went off, so I took a few long strides away from the crying Xavier and hurled myself over a desk. I slid under as fast and nimbly as I could and curled myself into a ball.

The explosion shook the entire place, and I somehow blacked out.

"Where were you?" Elizabeth asked, dropping her calloused persona.

I looked up at Wint who was able to answer.

"I found him under a broken desk and pile of debris," he said as he looked at me with suspicion. "He was lucky."

"I won't be opening an account at that bank again," I said as I winked at Elizabeth.

I guess I wasn't too coy because Wint looked immediately at Elizabeth and then back at me with a disbelieving look.

"Why did you…" Wint slowly started to ask as Elizabeth interrupted.

"Not run outside?"

"I didn't have time," I said. "The only thing I thought was to dive somewhere safe like they do on the movies and duck and cover."

"Are you hurting anywhere?" the paramedic asked as I mentally scanned my body, checking for any discomfort.

"Nope, just a little sore in places, but not hurting."

"Let's take you in for some tests just to make sure," he said, jotting down some information on his clipboard. "Just to be safe."

"Yes," Elizabeth grinned. "Just to be safe, and so they can bill you."

The paramedic shot her a dirty look, but she didn't care.

"What? Is this a free visit?" she smiled enthusiastically. "Are you going to stop and get him some ice cream too while you are at it for being such a good boy?"

I started to laugh and then painfully coughed before laughing some more as the paramedic stepped away.

"I could use some ice cream," I said looking at Elizabeth with puppy dog eyes.

"Don't look at me," she said condescendingly. "What do I look like, Baskin Robbins?"

Wint stood silent, watching our interaction with a jaggedness in his body language.

"You okay?" I asked, feeling the unfamiliarity in the air between the three of us. I had felt a change in our dynamics a few times, but this felt uncomfortable and disjointed.

Wint nodded his head and slowly built a grin. "Just thinking of how lucky you were today."

"Fine," Elizabeth groaned. "I'll buy you some ice cream. No wait," she stopped and looked at me motherly. "Some frozen yogurt. Fewer calories. You could stand to lose a bit."

The paramedic returned and looked at us. He didn't know how to respond. "Is she your wife?" he asked softly as he leaned down and shone his flashlight in my eyes.

"Oh, God no," I smiled as I caught Elizabeth looking over the paramedic's shoulder, watching his every move like a concerned friend would.

"Don't blind him. You already know he can see. If he couldn't, he would have said something by now," she ridiculed as she clapped her hands. "Can you just take him to the hospital and make sure he won't die in a day or two? I have some errands I need to run before it gets too late. And this is really cutting into my *me* time."

CHAPTER 60

A twelve-year-old girl poked her head into a darkened room, looking slightly startled with her widening eyes and jarring head movement. She started to talk, but she didn't step into the room, instead staying safely in the dimly lit hallway. Her lips were moving, but no sound came out. There was only silence.

She shook her head no and continued to talk, peeking her head into the room. She looked around as if it were the first time she had seen the room. Her eyes darted left and right, taking in all the knickknacks and wall hangings. Then her eyes suddenly stopped dead center.

She continued to talk, but still nothing was heard.

She was talking to someone, but the other person or people couldn't be seen. She was the star of this attraction.

Her lips stopped moving, and she nodded her head in agreement as her eyes sparkled with intrigue and curiosity. She timidly took one step forward, crossing over the threshold from the familiar hallway to the foreign terrain.

She smiled brightly, even started to giggle somewhat as she took another step forward. She started to talk and one word was heard in the middle of the sentence.

"You."

She didn't stop talking after that singular word was heard. Her mouth was moving faster and her feet were moving as well, taking more steps until she was in the center of the room.

The room looked like a darkened home office with a desk and an old large computer monitor. The walls were decorated with gold and blue-striped wallpaper with artistic portraits similar to Rembrandt hanging sporadically around the room. She tapped her fingers rhythmically on the desk, swirling her fingers around the hardwood as she walked around the large piece of furniture.

As she came around the desk, the perspective changed from staring forward at the door, to looking behind at a large glass window overlooking a dark yard with strings of colorful plastic lanterns hanging below. She peered out the window and looked down at the festive lights as the window reflected her beaming smile.

Her lips started to move once again as a single word was vocalized.

"Can't."

Then she stopped talking.

Her smile started to fade until it was gone. Her eyes, bright a minute earlier, now had a glaze of concern and fear.

She turned around and shook her head no as she started to mouth something.

"Stop," her mouth quivered.

A hand reached up and placed a finger on her mouth to silence her words.

Her lips started to quiver at the touch of the finger as another hand reached up from the side and grabbed her shoulder, pulling her in.

Her mouth gaped open, and it looked like she was screaming, but suddenly she stopped. Flashes of colorful lights filled the sky behind her. Fireworks were being detonated in the backyard.

But still, there was only silence.

Blues, reds, and yellows lit the sky like pieces of fiery confetti as the colors shone into the room.

The young girl was pulled in closer by the pair of hands. She tried to fight them off, but they were too strong for her. Her body was tossed around as tears started to rain down her cheeks.

She started to talk, but her words, although easily recognizable, were not heard. She was begging and pleading to be let go as a pair of hands left her bony shoulders, the fingers working their way down where no child should be touched.

The room went dark except for the flashes of light from the fireworks.

A soft-spoken man's voice narrated through the fireworks with a single, simple word.

"This."

The fireworks continued to flash through the dark, bursting into a million flickering sparks of light.

"You can't stop," the young girl said once again.

"This," the man softly said.

You can't stop this.

I rose in the hospital bed dripping in sweat. I was shocked to see Elizabeth sitting by my bed with her phone in her hand.

"Quick cat nap?" she asked as she continued playing on her phone.

"How long have I been asleep?" I asked, looking around the room to see the sun was still shining.

"Just about ten minutes," she said putting up her phone. "They said you can leave when you're ready, but I didn't want to wake you."

"It must have been the yogurt," I smiled as I slid my feet off the bed. "I'm ready." I stopped and felt a chill in the air.

"Why are you so wet?" she asked, feeling the back of my head. "You're drenched."

I looked at her and she knew.

"What did you dream?"

CHAPTER 61

"It's nothing," I lied, wiping the sweat off my forehead. "Just a dream."

"Then spill it," she said with her hands on her hips, standing in front of me so I couldn't stand up without invading her personal space.

I'd been lying to Wint so much lately, I didn't want to keep on covering my tracks with different stories. I skimmed through the options.

Tell the truth.

Tell a lie.

Tell nothing.

Each scenario brought a little comfort, but it also had the backhand force of regret. I started playing the possible conversations in my head at lightning-fast speed. The devil's advocate in me started debunking and countering faster than I could persuade.

I felt the thin pillow I had restlessly slept upon and it was soaked. Not with tears knowing I couldn't stop the painful event from happening, but with pure adrenaline-forced sweat as if I had just jogged ten miles. The room was bare with a small patient table, a few medical posters plastered on the wall detailing the effects of diabetes and smoking, and a small counter with the bare minimum of a faucet and sink. It resembled a five-star prison cell.

I could relate to the feeling after the week of sickening dreams that repeated like a prisoner's regret during a lifetime sentence.

My thoughts were scattered, which happened often when I was pushed into an uncomfortable corner. A corner I had named Elizabeth's shrine.

She eyed me with hesitation before she began coaxing. "Come on," she said, wanting me to open up and share the message in a bottle that I was hiding.

I didn't feel at ease with any decision, which signaled it might be time to confess. Confession was good for the heart, they said, or so I was praying.

"It's bad," I said, looking at her for support but not expecting it.

That was one of the strange things about life. It rewarded people in unexpected moments sometimes.

"We can handle it," she said with a tender smile and a pat on my arm. The word *we* resonated loudly in my heart. It felt warmer than the friendliest of pats. It spoke a vocabulary of words I didn't know, but I knew that we could handle it.

I relinquished my dream. When I finished, I waited for her to look at me in disgust for dreaming such filth. I anticipated her smacking me on my cheek, like she had done many times before without any good reason. I dreaded the look of shame she would scan over me with judgmental eyes.

"You are not that guy," she said through her rough exterior.

"I've been hoping I wasn't all week, but when the girl said 'You' in the first dream and then 'You can't stop' last night…" I stopped and raked my fingers through my hair. "I was hoping I wasn't that kind of guy, but I've always been told to never count myself out."

"Oh, honey," she said with the warmest smile I had ever seen her wear. "It may be my guilt of what I put you through today, but you would never harm a child, Solo. I can guarantee that was not you in that dream."

"How can you be so sure?" I asked, wanting to see some proof with my own two eyes.

She looked around the room as a tear started to trickle down her face. "Believe me," she said. "You're not like that."

She turned her face and wiped her eyes so I couldn't see. "Come on, let's get out of here," she said as she motioned for me to stand up so we could get out of the room.

Something didn't seem right. Something really didn't seem right.

As she started to walk to the door, her blonde hair caught my sight. The strands sparkled under the fluorescent lighting like a radiant gold sparkler. As she walked, I realized I had seen the same stride but had never noticed it before.

"Elizabeth?" I asked, heightening my tone as the puzzle pieces started to flip over, aligning themselves with things that she had said over the last year. Most recently, her anger at kids shooting off fireworks and her distaste for this week.

She stopped and turned to me with a slight smile.

"I told you that it wasn't you in the dream," she said as a tear started to slide down her cheek.

I jumped out of the bed and rushed to her side, consoling her as she gave way to the years of secrecy.

"See, Solo," she said sinking more into my arms as her tears started to flow freer than ever before. "You would never hurt anyone." She stopped and hid her face into the cleft of my chest. "Not like he did."

We stood in silence as I continued to let her cry. I didn't try to stop what was a decade overdue.

CHAPTER 62

"Cooper, this is Officer Blackwell," he said as he looked over the reports he was asked to compile. "I have the listing of people who have been visiting Jennifer Ascot while she has been in our custody."

"Perfect," Wint said ruffling through their kitchen drawer looking for a pen and paper.

"Ready?"

"Uh huh."

"Milo Alexev came to visit her once at the very beginning of her confinement. Then we have Luther Hyde who has come eight times; Jacob Westing came with Luther Hyde five of those times," he said.

"Yeah, those are probably her attorneys."

"Brooke Payton came twice with Mr. Hyde."

"Okay," Wint said as he started taking down the names of all the various attorneys that Veronica used to work with, wondering if any of them could be responsible for the vicious taunts.

"And lastly, Alexei Lechov has come twelve times," Blackwell said, flipping through his papers.

Wint started to write the name down when it hit him. "You said Alexei Lechov, right?"

"Yes," Blackwell answered, looking through all the names and signatures. "Why? Does that name sound familiar?"

"That's her dead brother," Wint said confused as he circled the name multiple times on his yellow notepad. "I killed him last October."

"Well, there seems to be another one of him."

Wint started thinking of a plan. "Thanks, Blackwell," he said and then added, "Hey, can you get me video image of when Alexei Lechov came to visit?"

"Sure thing," he said. "Give me a little time, and I will send you the video footage as soon as I get a free minute."

"Thanks. I'll owe you one."

"Yeah, you will," Blackwell snickered as Wint ended the call.

"Who was that?" Veronica asked as she walked into the kitchen and straight for the coffee pot.

"Why don't I fix you some tea or something to help you relax?" he said, dodging the question. "You go relax, start a bath, and then I'll bring you a cup."

She leaned up and kissed his whiskery cheek. "You are too good for me."

He covered the notepad with his hand and smiled. "You deserve the best," he said, kissing her on the lips. "Only the best."

She left and turned on the faucet for her bath as he started to boil water for her tea. He flipped open her laptop on the kitchen counter and logged into his police email.

"Come on, Blackwell," he said when he saw he didn't have any new emails. He knew it was unlikely he was going to get something that night, but he could hope.

How's your friend? a text from Dakota chimed on his phone.

He's alive, he typed and stopped. The text made him realize he didn't know anything else. He felt like their brotherhood bond was fading and there was nothing he could do. No matter how much he tried to uncover some answers, more questions rose to the top.

He sent the message and laid his phone down.

He finished the tea and brought it to his lovely wife hidden underneath of blanket of bubbles. "Need anything else?"

"Just you," she said as she took a warm sip.

"Always," he smiled as he left the bathroom and quickly changed out of his uniform and into something more comfortable. He walked into the kitchen to start rummaging through the refrigerator for supper when he heard a notification from the laptop. He jumped over in his grey lounge pants and saw he had a new email from Blackwell.

There were five videos with a message saying more would be coming as soon as he could get to it.

He clicked on the first security camera feed inside the police station and watched as Alexei Lechov approached the sign-in counter.

"What the…?" he said as his appetite vanished.

CHAPTER 63

His computer flashed signaling that one of his hacked computers was being used. He was tired of lounging on his couch watching Netflix but thought it better to be safe and inspect what was going on. He could always re-watch the footage later, but who knew what would be happening later?

He typed in a few security codes and found the file with the footage of a man on Veronica Hyde's computer.

"Let's see what you are looking at," he said as he hit a few buttons making the screen immediately split in half between the man and the laptop screen. He watched as the man viewed a grainy black and white security camera feed with six different angles. He straightened up and took notice that he'd needed a haircut a month ago from the timestamp on the video. He raised his hand and ruffled his hair, which was neatly trimmed and not shaggy looking like on the video.

"What the...?" Winston Cooper said as he watched the video.

"What are you thinking, Officer Cooper?" he asked the computer. He knew he was safe watching from the confines of his apartment on the outskirts of metropolitan D.C. This wasn't like a Facetime video. No, this was like what the police did all the time with their one-sided windows when they interviewed suspects. He was just doing what the cops had always been doing.

"Who are you?" Winston asked the computer as the watcher started to laugh.

"Wouldn't you like to know," he smiled and turned off his Netflix because he thought this was going to be more entertaining for the night.

"Pleased to meet you, Officer Cooper. My name is Mikhail Lebedinsky. But you can all me Alexei. That's what one of my driver's licenses says."

Winston leaned closer to the computer, getting within two inches of the screen, squinting his confused eyes.

"A hair cut and change of color does wonders when you are trying to copy someone," Mikhail snickered as his doorbell rang. "Isn't that what all your CIA movies show?"

He got up, paid the delivery guy, and opened the lid. He inhaled the aroma and smiled at his family favorite, pizza mockba. It was a delicacy in Russia with tuna, sardines, salmon, and mackerel. He'd always thought it was funny how closely his family still held onto the Russian traditions, even though he had never been to Russia.

He took a big bite, allowing the different flavors to merge into one heavenly taste.

Winston opened another browser window and did a search for Alexei Lechov to compare the images. He froze the video on one of the frames when Mikhail seemed to be looking directly into the security camera.

He found a newspaper clipping of Alexei's death with his picture in it. He enlarged that image and tried to compare the two, noticing that even though they were similar, they were definitely not the same.

"I knew I killed you," Winston said with a smart-aleck tone as he picked up his phone and dialed. "Hey, can you do a search through the database for images of who this may be? It's not Alexei." He stopped and listened to the other person on the line.

"And can you put a note in the system that if this guy comes back to visit, they will call me ASAP? Thanks." He grinned and ended the call with pleasantries.

"When you go back to see her, we will get you," Winston smiled as he stood up from the laptop.

"That's why I'm not going back," Mikhail said with his mouth full. "Not any time soon. Better luck next time."

CHAPTER 64

"Why didn't you ever tell me?" I asked from Elizabeth's passenger seat.

"When would that ever come up in conversation?" she asked in sarcasm. "Um, hey, Solo, let's go have lunch, and by the way, I was molested when I was twelve."

I understood what she meant and nodded in agreement.

"I just want you to know that you can share anything with me," I said tender-heartedly as I looked out the window, watching the pedestrians on the sidewalk packing their bags of groceries home.

"You don't share everything with me," she snapped. "Some things are just best left unsaid."

"So, what happened to the guy?" I asked, hoping I wasn't prying too much into her family history.

"Not much." She shrugged her shoulder. "I try not to think about it much."

"Not much?" I answered in shock. "You told your parents, didn't you?"

"I told Dad," she said focusing on the road and less on the conversation. "But that was all."

"That was all?" I asked in sadness. "So, not your mom, Veronica, a counselor? No one else knows?"

"No one," she said as she flipped on the radio. "Can we drop this? That was a long time ago, and I've moved on."

"Have you?" I asked with compassion, although her expression told me otherwise. I quickly apologized, saying I didn't mean it that way and she nodded.

"I know," she said softly watching the red streetlight. "You can't tell anyone," she said, turning her attention away from the light and staring into my safe eyes.

"I promise," I said as the car horn behind us started honking.

"Oh, whatever," she said, flipping off the driver in her rearview mirror. "Get some patience."

I thought back over the last week and the same dream that I had been having. It saddened me to know the sickening thought I had been having for four days was something Elizabeth had been living with for years.

I knew I would respect her boundaries, but I hoped she knew she had a place where she could crash-land when she needed it. No questions asked. Only a place where she could feel safe, guarded, and protected if that time ever came.

"What are we going to do about tonight?" she asked. "About my other dream?"

"I don't know," I groaned. "I didn't do well saving the last one."

She looked over at me with warm eyes. "But you saved the cop's life."

"But I didn't save Xavier's," I said, folding my arms onto my chest. "He still died."

CHAPTER 65

Jenny lay on her bed in her solitary cell staring up at the ceiling, pretending to count the stars like she did with her father when he was alive. Those were happier times. Lying in an open field with her father as her brother was usually running wild catching lightning bugs or pretending to be an airplane with her mother.

"Papa," she would say, "who do you love more?"

"Oh, Jenika, I love you and Alexei the same," he would say with his arm nestled under her head like a pillow.

"But you've known me longer. Doesn't that mean you love me more?"

"I love you differently than I love Alexei, but I love you both equally," he'd said, hushing her frantic thoughts.

"But…" she would start.

"There are no buts when it comes to me." He would smile and kiss her on her forehead.

After her mother was killed and her father was sentenced to prison for the murder, she was adopted by the Ascots while her brother was tossed around in the foster care system. She'd lived a privileged life of never having to worry about anything, while he'd lived the treacherous existence of worrying about what, or who, was behind his back.

"I miss you, Alexei," she said as she rolled onto her side reminiscing on the havoc they'd caused last October. They reunited by their name. They connected by their history. They bonded through their hatred.

She missed the subway chats as they were surveying possible victims. She longed to have another car ride to a deserted park sharing stories of

225

their innocent childhood before it all fell apart. She wished to have another moment of ecstasy when they would embrace and congratulate each other on their accomplishment.

But then, she was all by herself again.

Until she met Mikhail.

She enjoyed his company, even if he didn't know it. She had a role to play, and she wasn't going to let emotional attachments ruin her future. Her prospects were as broad as the summer skies she used to gaze upon with her father as they counted the stars.

"What are you going to wish for, Papa?"

"For moments like this to never end," he would say.

But they did end.

Just like every good thing.

"I will always love you, Alexei, but I have to let you go," she softly said as if singing herself a lullaby. "I have to let you go."

She rolled onto her other side to stare at the brick wall that had become her closest companion. She reached out her hand to feel the hard, cold surface and began tracing her fingers along the crevices, as if routing a path through the rectangular maze of intersections.

A smile appeared on her face as she visualized the stars aligning for her big revenge. She just hoped Mikhail was able to keep the process moving forward.

And she was able to lure the sacrificial lamb to its demise.

CHAPTER 66

"So, do you think it has happened yet?" I asked Elizabeth as I lay on her couch.

"I don't know," she said breathing out in dread. "I just feel so useless. Do you think we should have called the police?"

"I thought about that, but what would you have said? Excuse me, I don't know where or why or when, but someone is going to be beaten tonight at one of the many subway stations. Good luck," I mocked in frustration. "It's horrible. This whole day has been one that I want to move past and forget."

"Amen," she said as she took another sip from her wine glass.

"What's Jeremiah up to?" I asked, wondering why she wasn't with her boyfriend.

"He's doing something," she said, waving her hand as if she didn't care. "Researching for a book, or a class, or I don't know, researching for the fun of it, because you know, it's him."

I agreed.

"I'm not sure how much longer I can hold out on keeping us a secret from Wint," I said, breaking the silence.

"Us?" she remarked with perplexity. "There is no *us*."

"You know what I mean," I smiled as she laughed.

"Yeah," she nodded. "I'm actually surprised you have lasted as long as you have."

"Why?" I asked, rising from the couch. "What is that supposed to mean?"

"You know," she said taking another sip. "You're needy."

"Needy?" I balked. "If anyone is needy, it's you."

We eyed each other as if deciding who was going to fire the first bullet. We both surrendered and laughed off the remnants of our words.

"Are you feeling okay?" she asked, pouring another glass of wine into her goblet. "Do you need anything?"

"Nope," I said trying to relax. "Thanks for letting me stay the night. When does the pillow fight start?"

"As soon as you try to sneak in and steal one of mine." She raised her fists. "Fight, fight to the death, I will."

"You really take your pillows seriously," I smiled as I readjusted her decorative couch pillow.

"After living with Veronica, I learned to take my pillows seriously. She's a pillow hog."

"Poor Wint," I said. "Poor, poor Wint."

"Yeah, but he picked her," she kidded. "I just got lucky by birth."

She turned on the television to find something to watch and flipped through the channels like a teenager. I pulled out my phone and started a conversation I knew was long overdue.

Thanks for being the best friend a guy could ever ask for.

I watched my phone for a few minutes. I thought maybe he would respond quickly, but I knew he had things on his mind other than me. And that thought gave me a little peace. I wasn't at the top of his priorities meter, and that consolation eased my guilt over the lies I'd been telling him.

"How's Veronica?" I asked Elizabeth, but she didn't know anything new.

"No news is good news, I guess, when it comes to that psycho."

"Do you think Jenny will try to do anything to her?" I asked. "I mean, she's in jail. What could she really do?" I wanted to believe those words we let hang in the air as if it gave off a warm apple pie smell that soothed our hearts and minds. But Elizabeth had to cut into it and extinguish the ignorant bliss.

"Oh, Jenny has something up her sleeve," she said nonchalantly. "I just hope it backfires again like last time."

"Last time?" I said in shock. "I was almost killed last time, and I have the battle scars on my legs as proof."

"Oh, get off it," she remarked. "You now have a cool scar to show to the ladies as you jog in your short shorts."

"Those are jogging shorts."

"You're not a track star, Solo." She rolled her eyes. "You wear those shorts to show off your legs," she said taking another sip as I started to say something. "I see how you look at yourself as you walk past a mirror. You check yourself out more often than a porn star on a webcam. If you even try to deny it, God help me, I will throw this at your head and give you another concussion."

"I don't think your little glass will give me a concussion," I said with a snarky expression.

"I was talking about the bottle," she said as she poured the rest of it into her cup. "All gone and ready for throwing."

"Did you drink that whole bottle tonight?" I asked in amazement.

"Don't judge," she said, her words starting to slur. "I can sleep late tomorrow. I don't have to work."

"That's right," I said forgetting that the next day was Independence Day. "How many fingers am I holding up?" I asked, raising three of them.

229

"I don't know," she remarked. "How many am I?" she said raising a singular middle finger in my direction.

"And those shorts keep me from chaffing and getting overheated," I quickly spit out as I jogged to the bathroom.

"Solo!"

I was washing my hands when my phone went off in my back pocket.

Love you too, man, Wint replied.

I was staring at the phone, so proud to call him my friend as he sent another text.

But we have to talk soon. Seriously.

I didn't feel like dealing with it that night when I could deal with it in the morning.

That was the thing about problems. There was always a tomorrow.

Until there wasn't.

CHAPTER 67

He had spent the last three hours following Manuel, trying to get a feel for his antics and work out a plan for where to attack. He had heard Manuel say he was heading to Wheaton to make a drop, which was a stop on the Red Line subway. He looked on his phone to see if there was any place in that area that would be a safe location to jump him. There wasn't. On one side of the Metro stop were residential homes, and on the other was a shopping district. He didn't see any nearby woods or alleyways to drag him to.

This may not be the night, he thought as he watched Manuel eat a Big Mac and french fries at the McDonald's on 13th Street, a block away from Metro Center Station. He grabbed a drink to not look conspicuous, but he didn't want to eat anything heavy. He still didn't know what the night may entail.

He was hopeful.

Manuel took his last bite and finished the remains of his soda as he started heading down F Street before turning to head north up 12th Street where Metro Center Station was located.

He quickly sped past Manuel; he had an idea. It may be a long shot, but it was something. He got into Metro Center Station and looked at the time on the overhead mechanical clock beside the times of the oncoming subway trains. The train heading toward Glenmont, the last stop on the Red Line, was still four minutes away. He knew that would give Manuel plenty of time to get down and onto the subway.

He wondered about hitting the emergency button on the escalators, but that wouldn't slow anyone down. They would just walk down instead of riding down lazily. He got to the automated ticket dispenser and stared at the simplistic machine, hoping that Manuel was going to need to buy a ticket. Maybe he could slow him down there. He stood in line and watched as Manuel came into view riding down the escalators, but instead of stopping to buy a ticket, he pulled out a MetroCard from his wallet.

Crap!

He ran out of the line, grabbed a map hanging on the wall, and slid his MetroCard into the ticket counter as the sliding doors opened for him to proceed through. He watched as Manuel turned to head towards the Red Line and glanced around the Metro Center with its confusing hub of Blue, Orange, and Red Metro Lines. He wondered if that was his way to get Manuel off the subway.

He dashed ahead of a few people trying to catch up with Manuel. He slid on his sunglasses and new baseball cap and tapped Manuel with a polite smile and a southern drawl.

"Excuse me, sir, you look like you can help me," he said in his Georgian accent he used to mock his military friends.

"I'm sorry," Manuel said, "I need to get somewhere."

"Please, sir," he pleaded. "I'm needing to get to…" He stopped and unfolded his map looking for a place that may take a little time for directions. "Prince George's Plaza. I think that is what my daughter said." He stopped and wiped his forehead. "If I don't get there soon, she's going to send out a pack of huntin' dogs to come find me."

Manuel didn't try to control his laughter at this stereotypical southern character, but he did start to give directions.

"Man, you just take the Red Line up to the next stop and get off there and get on the Green Line toward Greenbelt," he said as he started to walk away.

"What's the next stop called?" he asked as Manuel motioned to follow him.

"Follow me," he said.

The man felt a little remorse for his need to attack Manuel, but he needed to get his frustration out. And after how Manuel treated Ally earlier that day, he wasn't going to let his sudden politeness erase that rage.

"You are too kind, sir," he started. "Really you are." He stopped in his tracks. "Oh, gosh darn it, I told you wrong. I'm needing to go to Court House. I met my daughter for lunch at Prince George's Plaza. I'm so sorry," he gushed with apologizes. "Can you tell me how to get to Court House?"

Manuel huffed in aggravation.

Yeah, that's the attitude I need.

"Man, you just go find the Orange Line and ask someone there," he barked in rudeness.

"Where's that?"

"If you make me miss my ride…" Manuel started as he stopped and looked around the tunnels. "You walk that way, and you should see Orange Line signs. You want to go toward Vienna."

"Vienna?" he chuckled. "I didn't know I was heading to Europe," he said with a hickish laugh. "Wait till I tell all my friends."

"Yeah, you do that," Manuel said as he turned to head towards his subway train.

233

"Thank you, sir!" he said with a warm expression. "I hope to see you again, real soon."

Manuel ignored the closing and started to pick up his pace.

The attacker watched from a safe distance and then started to slowly follow. A smile formed on his face as he saw a caution sign and a detour route due to painting. He could hear Manuel shouting in Spanish, which caused his smile to widen.

Well, golly, that's a real pity.

CHAPTER 68

"Stop! Let me on!" Manuel shouted as he ran toward the subway after the sliding doors had already closed.

The attacker watched, walking up behind as he heard Spanish cussing ensue while Manuel stomped his feet and pounded his fist in the empty corridor.

Manuel looked up at the subway schedule hanging over the waiting area to see when the next train would be arriving.

"There'll be another one in six minutes," the attacker said in his normal voice. "We have time."

Manuel didn't turn around to see who was speaking.

"Just sit down," he said. "Take a load off."

Manuel didn't sit. He stood with his hands on his hips, visually perturbed for missing the train by a few seconds as he huffed and took a couple of deep breaths.

"Have you ever hurt Ally?" the attacker asked, eyeing Manuel seven feet away.

Manuel slowly turned as silence engulfed the place. The last straggling passengers had all left the terminal, and it was just the two of them.

He slowly walked toward Manuel.

"I know you. You're the--" Manuel started with squinting eyes and a curling upper lip as the attacker lashed out with his first punch.

The two started fighting like professional cage fighters. Their bodies were contorting and bending like boxers as they bobbed and weaved, trying to outwit each other with their expertise. Manuel's nose started to trickle blood as his fist collided with the attacker's lower cheek. The two groaned and heaved as if their lives depended on it.

The attacker got in two quick jabs under Manuel's nose, causing his eyes to close and water.

"Get your hands off me," Manuel hissed as the attacker threaded his muscular arms quickly around his thinner body, catching Manuel in a body lock. The attacker tightened his grip of the nelson hold, maneuvering Manuel away from the tracks.

Manuel was strong, but his slight frame was no match for his opponent. The attacker looked around the terminal; it was still empty. He moved to a darkened alleyway behind him along the corridor. Manuel was trying to break free from the wrestling hold, but his arms were not inflicting enough pain.

The attacker took a few steps back and noticed that Manuel's weight wasn't an issue. He could practically pick him up if he needed to. Manuel tried to plant his feet on the ground, but they skidded back with the attacker's larger steps. Suddenly, the two men found themselves in some privacy.

Terror seized Manuel. Excitement radiated from the attacker.

He kept the nelson hold on Manuel as he tried to scream despite his air flow starting to be cut off. The attacker saw a wall a few feet ahead and ran with all his might toward it, smashing Manuel's body between the two hard surfaces.

Manuel's lungs emptied as his head smashed into the concrete barrier. The man dragged Manuel's legs back a few steps and then launched forward once again.

Manuel saw the wall coming and raised his legs, stopping the collision and pushing back like it was the world's most important leg press workout.

Manuel screamed, but it didn't scare the man; it just egged him on more.

"Wanna play with the big boys, huh?" the attacker whispered into Manuel's ears as he eased his nelson hold and scooped him up in his arms. Manuel was sideways with the attacker's bicep between his legs. He started to pound his arms in his back and chest, digging his teeth into the fabric on his shoulder and kicking his free legs. But none of it did any good.

The attacker held little Manuel's body like he was rocking a seven-year-old and ran at full force into the wall.

Manuel groaned at the impact.

Then he did it again and again.

Manuel's body was drained; his arms were not hitting as hard; his body was zapped of all its strength.

But the attacker was just beginning. He took a deep breath and tightened his grip around Manuel and powerslammed him onto the concrete.

Manuel crumbled as the attacker heard a hard break.

He got up, about to start his round of kicks, when he noticed something that he didn't want to see. Blood was spilling out of Manuel's mouth as his eyes stared lifelessly.

"Oh man! Get up, man. Get up!"

He leaned down and heard a light gurgling as blood bubbled through Manuel's crimson lips. Then it stopped. Silence. Manuel's soft groans vanished. His gurgling for air ceased. His head fell with the gravity of death.

The man stood in the darkened alleyway. He knew the next train would be there any minute. He started to run into the light but was met with pedestrians waiting for the train. The sound of the waiting area vibrated in his ears, echoing his regret that he'd been seen. He stopped running and started to walk away from the crowd, but as soon as he made it to the stairs he started running up, taking two at a time. He heard the braking sound of the oncoming train and the loud commotion of people exiting.

Then he heard what he didn't want to hear.

A loud soprano scream at the top of her lungs, soon followed by others.

He took off once again in a sprint.

He knew he was fast. That was one of his strengths. He knew no one would catch him.

CHAPTER 69

A twelve-year-old girl poked her head into a darkened room, appearing slightly startled with her widening eyes and jarring head movement.

"What are you doing up here in Dad's office?" she asked.

"Please, come in, Elizabeth. Your dad won't mind," a soft-spoken man said from somewhere in the room.

She shook her head. "No, I can't. I'm not allowed in his office."

"It will be okay," he said. "Your father has a beautiful office. Come on, take a look."

"It is really nice," she said peeking her head into the room. She looked around as if it were the first time she had seen it. Her eyes darted left and right, taking in all the knickknacks and wall hangings. Then she suddenly stopped dead center.

"I always loved that painting with the ducks," she smiled looking at it intently from the door.

"Oh, it is a beautiful painting," he agreed. "Come on, come get a better look," he said trying to lure her in. "You can't see all the details from all the way over there."

Her lips stopped moving, and she nodded her head in agreement as her eyes sparkled with intrigue and curiosity. She timidly took one step forward, crossing over the threshold from the familiar hallway to the foreign terrain.

She smiled brightly.

"See," he said in the void. "Nothing happened because you came in here. No alarms went off. No sirens. You are fine. Come on," he said politely.

She started to giggle as she walked further into the foreign room. "I guess you are right."

"Come look at this beautiful painting."

She walked into the room and stared at the beautiful painting. "He's my favorite one," she said pointing at one of the ducks.

"If you were in the painting, you would be my favorite."

"Oh, Mr. Manfield," she said blushing.

"Call me Charlie," he said softly. "Okay, Elizabeth? You can call me Charlie."

"Okay, Charlie," she giggled once again. "What are you doing up here?"

"I'm up here to see the fireworks, of course," he said with enthusiasm.

"The fireworks?" she asked with a surprised expression.

"Come here," he said.

She tapped her fingers rhythmically on the desk, swirling them around the hardwood as she walked around the large piece of furniture.

As she came around the desk, the perspective changed from staring forward at the door, to looking behind at a large glass window overlooking a dark yard with strings of colorful plastic lanterns hanging below. She peered out the window, looking down at the festive lights as the window reflected her beaming smile.

"See, you can see everything from up here, but they can't see you."

"They can't see us?" she asked in shock. "Really?"

"Really. I bet it's beautiful to watch the fireworks from up here. Away from everyone. Don't you think?"

"Maybe, but I think I better go back," she said.

"Please Elizabeth, please watch the fireworks with me," he pleaded with a breathless ache in his voice. "I want you to watch it with me."

Her smile started to fade from lighthearted until it was gone. Her bright eyes now had a glaze of concern and fear.

"I better go," she said.

"No, you're not going anywhere, or I'll tell your dad you went into his office when you weren't supposed to," he said sinisterly.

"You tricked me," she said angrily.

"Well, if you give me a treat, I won't trick you, just like at Halloween. Do you like Halloween, Elizabeth?"

"Please stop, please," her voice quivered in fear.

He reached up and placed a finger on her mouth to silence her words.

Her lips started to quiver at the touch of the finger as another hand reached up from the side and grabbed her shoulder, pulling her in.

Her mouth gaped open, and she let out a scream.

"Don't scream," he said sadistically. "They can't hear you over the fireworks," he said as he lowered his zipper. "You are very beautiful, you know that? You are one pretty, pretty girl. Do you think I'm handsome?"

Flashes of colorful lights filled the sky behind her. Fireworks were being set off in the backyard as loud booms and bangs started to collide with her screams and sobs.

Blues, reds, and yellows sparkled in the sky like pieces of fiery confetti as the colors shone into the room.

241

The young girl was pulled in closer by the pair of hands. She tried to fight them off, but they were too strong for her. Her body was tossed around as tears started to rain down her cheeks.

"Please no, Mr. Manfield," she said begging and pleading to be let go as his hands left her bony shoulders, and he started walking his fingers down where no child should be touched. "Stop!"

"If you just relax, you will like this," he said softly, his disturbing words sickeningly sweet like cotton candy.

The fireworks continued to flash through the dark, bursting into a million flickering sparks of light as the girl continued to cry and scream for him to stop in vast darkness.

"Charlie!" another voice said, breaking into the unseen room.

"Daddy!" the young girl screamed.

"Luther, I can explain," Charlie said with urgency as he straightened and zipped his pants.

"Get your clothes on, Elizabeth, and go back to the fireworks," Luther said distantly. "And don't tell anyone!"

"But Daddy!" she cried with pain and fear as she tried to fix her dress.

"Elizabeth! Now!" he shouted as her tiny feet ran out of the room.

"And Charlie, I want to be partner now," Luther demanded as the fireworks kept exploding and flashes of light filled the room. "You understand? Effective tomorrow. Or else."

"Absolutely," Charlie said. "Welcome, partner," he said unsurely.

"And I want a bigger office," Luther remarked again with a loud boom and a sprinkle of colors. "Your office."

"That's ridiculous," Charlie huffed in the blindness. "Why should I give you my office?"

"I think you will be giving me whatever I want. If you don't, I will call the police. Understand?"

"Yes," he said feebly. "I understand."

"Daddy," Elizabeth moaned from the doorway.

"Elizabeth, I told you to go outside!" Luther barked accompanied by a loud shriek of a firework. "Now scat! And stop your crying!"

Her little feet slipped away like the sound of her tears until all that was seen were beautiful fireworks filling up the emptiness.

I woke up on Elizabeth's couch and felt a sadness that froze me to the core.

Poor Elizabeth.

CHAPTER 70

Detective Young lifted the yellow caution tape blocking off the crime scene in the Metro Center Station of the Red Line. He loved the feeling of power of raising that thin piece of plastic. He just wished more people were around to see him strut under it. He hated crimes at 1 a.m.

"So, tell me what you have," Young said to the first officer at the scene of the crime.

"Officer Jeffrey, sir," the young officer said, greeting the detective. Young didn't care what his name was. "Manuel Perez, 31, appears to have been beaten to death around 11:25 when the train heading to Glenmont stopped and some passengers found him bleeding and not breathing." The officer tapped his pen on his brand new notepad.

"So, did anyone see anything?" Young asked.

"No, no one."

"Have you met with security to get the footage?"

"They are working on it," he answered. "They said they should be able to have it to us by morning." He shrugged his shoulders. "The person who handles video footage wasn't answering his phone."

"Well, maybe they should go to his place and wake him," Young commanded.

"Yes, yes sir," the young officer replied, walking over to the security guard to tell him what his next step should be.

Dr. Raul Santiago, the chief medical examiner for Washington D.C., knelt over the dead body. Officer Young wasn't fond of Dr. Santiago -- not because he wasn't good at his job, but he never remembered his name, even though they met a few times a month.

244

"Dr. Santiago, what do you have?" Young asked with an egotistical tone as he hovered over the medical professional with enough degrees and credentials to make his initials longer than Young's entire name.

"Ah, Officer Hong," he said with a smile.

"It's Detective Young," he corrected.

"Sorry," he lied as he grabbed his bag and stood up. "It appears Mr. Perez was beaten to death. I don't know what was the final blow that ended his life, but his body is lying in an uncomfortable twisted manner, so I'm waiting to hear back if CSI believes that he was murdered here or if his body was disposed of here. I would suspect he was murdered here, by the blood splatter on the wall," he said pointing in front of him.

"So, you can't tell us anything else?" Young asked surprised.

"What would you like to know, Young?" Dr. Santiago replied. "I can give you my theories, but theories are not reliable unless I am able to conduct all my tests and analysis."

"I was just thinking," Young stammered in the tunnel, now brightly lit with the police lighting system.

"Let's wait until we have the results before we start making assumptions," Dr. Santiago lectured. "There are fewer lawsuits for the city that way," he said patting Young's back as he walked away.

Young stood wounded.

That was how he always felt when Dr. Santiago walked away. He never understood why everyone loved the guy so much while he hated him with each fiber of his body.

"If you get the body to me soon," Dr. Santiago said to a few officers standing at the end of the tunnel, "I'll send over a box of donuts to your precinct."

Young rolled his eyes.

Yep, everyone loved Dr. Santiago.

CHAPTER 71

"Top story tonight, 14 dead at the Independence Day celebration this afternoon at the Memorial Mall in downtown D.C.," Trisha Kensington, the Channel 5 newscaster read from her teleprompter. "I am deeply saddened to announce that we lost two of our own this afternoon during this horrendous attack."

Two pictures appeared showing a man and a woman. The man had a gray buzzed haircut, light hazel eyes, plump rosy cheeks with a double chin, and wrinkles under his eyes. The woman had long blonde straight hair, stormy blue eyes, a tan complexion, and a heart-shaped face.

"Harrison Peters had been a cameraman for the station for 22 faithful years. Juliet Knowles had recently graduated from Howard University and had only been a part of the Channel 5 family for two months. We are deeply saddened, and our thoughts and prayers go out to their families and loved ones," Trisha said as she dabbed her eyes dry.

"They were killed while reporting from the National Mall when Ira Quill, 42, attacked, tied, and locked them in the news van. He then went on top of the vehicle and shot 22 people, killing 12 of them while they participated in the Independence Day celebrations at 3:24 this afternoon.

"Here is footage of Ira Quill on top of the news van from one of the other news outlets."

The video showed a man, a little shorter than six feet and weighing around 175 pounds wearing khaki pants, a red button-up shirt, and a white Nike hat standing beside the news van antenna with a semi-automatic rifle resting on Harrison Peters' camera.

"Ira Quill was shot and wounded by the Secret Service on guard. Video footage shows that while he was wounded and lying on the roof of the news van, he detonated a bomb that was inside, killing himself, Harrison Peters, and Juliet Knowles.

"Our thoughts and prayers go out to everyone affected by this tragedy today," the news reporter said as they went to a commercial break.

I shot up from the couch and quickly found my phone and started dictating all the details of the incident. It was a short dream, but all the important clues were there.

I leaned back and breathed a little easier knowing all the crucial information was readily available. No one should be dying today.

The harder part would be figuring out how to stop it.

But it would be stopped.

CHAPTER 72

I wasn't normally one to fix breakfast, but I also wasn't one to have a refrigerator full of groceries. Elizabeth, on the other hand, had everything anyone could ever want.

"Good morning," I said in a chipper tone as the sleepy-eyed Elizabeth reached out her hand.

"I smell coffee," she said with her eyes barely open.

I handed her a cup as she inhaled the caffeinated coffee beans mixed with a splash of Irish cream.

"Better?" I asked as she walked over to her kitchen bar and took a seat.

"Getting there," she said drowsily as her eyes hadn't fully awakened to the sunrise. "What time is it?" she yawned with a groan of distaste.

"It's a little after seven," I said with a grin.

"Seven?" she groaned with her eyes still closed. "Solo, if you sleep over here again, you're going to have to follow some house rules."

"I made you waffles," I said with a toothy smile.

"Unless those waffles are fat free and coated in angel dust, I'm not touching them," she snipped. "I'm not going to waste a day's worth of calories on breakfast."

"How many calories are in your Irish cream?" I asked.

"Just hush," she said covering her coffee cup's imaginary ears. "He doesn't need to hear that."

I sat down and devoured a couple of buttery waffles with Vermont maple syrup and a surprisingly good cup of soy chocolate milk. I watched as she started to open her eyes to their full width.

"So, what did you dream last night?" I asked as she pulled out her phone and read me her dream in all its murderous horror.

"That's strange," I said. "I had the same dream."

This had happened a few times over the last nine months, but it was very rare.

"So, what do you think we should do?" she asked, leaning her elbows on the bar counter.

"I think we should call the cops and give them all the details and let them handle it."

She listened to the idea. "That just seems too simple," she said. "We both got this dream, and you think calling the cops will do it?"

"After yesterday," I said rinsing my plate, "I'm fine with the cops having the guilty conscience instead of me if it doesn't turn out right."

She nodded and swiped one of the waffles as I took the plate away.

"I thought you said you weren't going to eat it," I laughed heading to the refrigerator.

"Well, it's a holiday," she said. "I thought I deserved a treat."

I nodded and agreed, especially after learning the truth of the memory this day held for her. I would let her eat a tub full of ice cream if it helped with dulling the pain or healing some of the wounds she had buried deep.

"How are you doing?" I asked softly, pouring her another cup of coffee.

"I should be asking you that," she said playfully with a smile. But she knew what I meant. "I'm doing fine, Solo," she said pouring the golden syrup onto her waffle. "Just fine."

CHAPTER 73

Ira Quill watered his small garden in his backyard, pulling the weeds that had taken over where his carrots and cabbage were supposed to be growing. He loved this time of day to stand and look at his bounty as the rising sun kissed him on his forehead. It was peaceful listening to the rushing water from the hose, drenching the dirt, forming puddles of mud before the water sank deep down to the roots.

He wished the whole world could be like his backyard.

But that was a delusion.

The world was in chaos. It was a brewing storm that constantly spun into a bigger mess, pulling in anything that its whirlpool could grab. Anything good would turn bad. Anything pleasant would tarnish. Anything valuable would get stolen.

He tossed the water hose down, letting the water pool into his pot of gardenias as he leaned down to smell the fragrant blooms. The aroma tickled his nostrils causing him to chuckle to himself.

The laughter ended as his eyes caught sight of his old, shabby tool shed.

He twisted the faucet knob, and the water flow ceased as the last bit of water sloshed onto the grass. He watched as the cool water trickled out but hoped he would be seeing a warmer liquid coming out later today, a thicker, redder liquid.

As he stomped toward the shed, his shoes trekked through the wet grass, squishing with each step.

He got to the door and looked around the yard. He was guarded by his eight-foot fence that kept out unwanted eyes. He opened the shed door and immediately smelled the red plastic containers filled with gasoline for his worn-out lawnmower. A ray of sunlight snuck through the opening, spotlighting his treasured possessions.

On the wall hung pruning shears and trowels of various shapes and sizes, but those weren't his favorite tools. The sunlight grew wider, shining on his grassy rakes and mud-crusted shovels. But still, those did not cause his heart to beat faster.

He walked over to his metal toolbox, spun the lock, and put in his three magical numbers. He heard the last click and pulled down. His eyes widened as he saw the first of his many toys. He reached in and petted the hard, cold metal as if it were a German shepherd, giving the semiautomatic the praise he thought it deserved.

"You'll be good today, won't you?" he asked as he pulled out his most trusted friend. He often spoke to it like it was his companion. He aimed the gun and looked through the scope. It was precise and on target, as it always was.

He laid down his gun and grabbed the JanSport navy backpack hanging on the wall. He unzipped it to reveal packages of explosives he had been yearning to detonate since he'd first learned how to create the powerful bombs from an easy YouTube video. He dreamed of the fire and smoke he was going to cause that day.

He was ready to go out with a blaze of glory.

"This is for you, Carl," he said as he looked over at a picture hanging over the toolbox. It was a small newspaper clipping, about the size of three postage stamps, of a United States soldier that was killed in Afghanistan by a terrorist mob.

He pulled out his cell phone and reread the Facebook message he had scheduled to post at 4 p.m. It was a memoriam for his beloved best friend and brother. It was his manifesto. It was going to be his legacy.

"Maybe they will remember you a little more today," he said. "But it will be a little too late."

CHAPTER 74

"Peterson," Dakota said as she picked up her phone in the precinct, listening with complete attention for about a minute before saying anything else. "They said *what?*" she asked as Wint's ears perked up at the dialogue she was having with the operator. "Okay," she said with a disbelieving tone as she eyed Wint and shrugged her shoulders. "Did they give you their contact info?" she asked, grabbing a pen from her drawer but flicking her notepad instead of writing. "Okay, we will look into it."

"What was that about?" Wint asked.

"Someone called in and said the guy who was killed last night at the subway is connected to the two guys that were beaten earlier this week," she said standing and pushing in her chair.

"Connected? What does that mean?"

"The caller said the person who killed the guy last night is the one who also beat the other two guys."

"*Our* two guys?" he asked baffled. "They're connected?"

Dakota shook her head. "I don't know, but that's what he said."

"I guess we need to go check it out," he said as they started down the hallway to leave the precinct. "Was it a reliable source?"

"I'm not sure. He didn't give his name or number, but he said something else that confused me," she said walking by his side. "He said the killer mentioned the name Ally."

"Ally?" Wint responded. "Who's Ally?"

"I don't know," Dakota sighed. "He didn't give me anything else."

"Hmm," Wint said, thinking out loud. "That could be anyone."

"Yep," Dakota said unfazed as her cell phone started to ring. "Oh, it's Stew," she said. "Give me a second."

"Tell loverboy cheerio for me," he said in a British accent, winking at her. Dakota rolled her eyes as if annoyed at being taunted by her older brother, but deep down she liked it. She liked the feeling of having someone who would call her out but also have her back at the same time. That was how she defined family.

She got off the phone. "Happy?" she laughed as Wint boyishly grinned.

"Always," he said as they got into their patrol car. "So, how's the greatest guy on this side of the pond?"

"Making sure I'm going to be off for his family get-together tonight," she said, brushing lint off her uniform.

"Family get-together?" Wint groaned. "Already? Are you sure you are ready for that?"

"Why wouldn't I be ready?" she snapped. "I'm perfect."

"If Stew thinks so, that is all that matters," he laughed as he drove toward Sibley Memorial Hospital to see if there had been any changes for Tucker.

"I'm charming when I want to be," she snickered. "His friends love me."

Wint stopped at the light and turned his head. "Why aren't you ever charming with me?"

"Aren't you funny?" she hissed comically. "Just ha-larious."

He turned and proceeded down the road. "I think I am," he grinned.

"You're the only one," she joshed as she started to read over the documents on the death of Manuel Perez.

CHAPTER 75

"Jeremiah's coming over," I told Elizabeth as she returned from taking a shower and putting on some comfortable lounge clothes. I was just finishing the dishes after having called the police to inform them of the maniac's plan to ambush the celebrations today.

"You know I have a dishwasher," she stated as she poured herself another cup of coffee.

"Are my hands not good enough for you?" I quipped, showing my soapy digits.

"Nothing you have is good enough for me, Solo," she smiled as she sipped her caffeinated beverage.

"Anyways," I said, allowing that smack to slide off my back. "Too much caffeine isn't good either."

"Don't you know by now," she posed with a dramatic flare of feminism, "I'm immune to what's toxic in the world. I actually thrive in it."

"Uh huh," I said, rinsing my plate to be free of any soap suds. "I believe that."

"So, why's Jeremiah coming over?" she asked, sitting down at the bar to watch me slave behind the sink. "This is a pretty nice view," she winked. "I'm not used to seeing a man in the kitchen."

"Jeremiah never cooks for you?" I asked surprised. I had imagined he would have some culinary skills since he was so sophisticated and cultured.

"He used to always try and make new dishes that he learned through his research of strange cultures and cuisines. One night he made a stew

256

with crickets, grasshoppers, and other bugs," she groaned. "Literally, they were jumping around on the counter, trying to flee for their lives, as if the ones that he grabbed and threw in the pot were screaming for the others to run. 'Save yourselves!' From then on, I banished him from making me dinner. We go out now."

"Understandable," I nodded as I dried my hands and leaned over the counter. "He's a good guy," I smiled. "A little quirky." I stopped and gave her a wide-eyed expression when she nodded in agreement.

"True dat."

"So, what's your favorite movie or binge-worthy TV show you would like to watch today?" I asked, switching subjects with a bumpy transition, not smooth like a playboy would at a bar with a cocky smile and a tantalizing wink.

"You don't have to do that," she grinned. "But thanks for the offer."

"Nope," I smiled, walking towards her living room. "This is your day. If you don't tell me what you want to watch, I'll enlighten Jeremiah with a *Police Academy* marathon."

"That's insidious," she gasped as she held her cup and followed me into the nearby room. "I would need an aspirin after just a few minutes of it."

"Well, you better tell me what you want to watch, or I'll play my feel-good movie," I smiled as I picked up the remote.

"Have you ever seen *Orange is the New Black*?" she asked with a wicked grin.

"No," I said shaking my head. "Why?"

"Oh, nothing," she said stealing the remote from my hand. "I think you'll like it."

"What is it?" I asked, unaware of what type of show it was. "I'll watch it if that's what you want to watch."

"Oh, Solo," she said clicking her remote to open her Netflix app on her smart television. "I think you'll like it," she said with a demonic laugh. "Really."

I looked over at her with a mixed feeling of confusion and fear as Jeremiah stepped through the front door.

"Hey, you," Elizabeth said, finding season one, episode one. "We're going to give Solo here a lesson on colors."

"It's a painting show?" I asked in surprise.

"Oh, Solo, you'll be painting yourself so many shades of red, I may watch you watching the show more than the show itself," she teased like a giddy teenager.

"What have we done?" I asked, looking at Jeremiah.

He shrugged his shoulders.

"Don't look at him," Elizabeth said with a large toothy smile. "He hasn't a clue either." She pressed play and the show began. "Thanks boys. And Solo," she said looking at me, "you can't close your eyes or cover your ears. That will ruin the experience for me."

"Say what?"

CHAPTER 76

Officers Cooper and Peterson went to Sibley Memorial Hospital and found Tucker Stevenson still unresponsive. The nurse in his room was optimistic he would be waking that day or the next as his body had shown improvements and stabilized a great deal over the last twenty-four hours.

"Has he had any family come to see him?" Cooper asked.

The nurse showed an empathic frown and shook her head. "His next of kin has been called, but he's only had a few visitors since I've been around the last few days," she said with a soft whisper, hoping the sleeping man couldn't hear. "Sad, really," she said looking over at the young man in the bed. "To be so handsome and yet alone."

Peterson's eyes looked over at Cooper's at the oddness of the statement, and he silently agreed with the eeriness of her words. The nurse brushed Tucker's forehead, parting his hair. "But I'm here," she said with a tender coo before leaving the room.

"Poor girl," Peterson said as soon as the nurse was out of earshot. "I wonder how many daydream relationships she has with her patients."

"Everyone wants a little love and attention," Cooper said with a softness in his voice. "I bet this happens more than we would like to believe."

Peterson looked down at the once attractive man with bruises and stitches piecing together his face as she pulled up his case information on her phone. Looking at his before and after photographs, she couldn't help but admire his boyish good looks from a few days earlier. "If she goes *Misery* on this guy, I couldn't forgive myself."

"I think she would prefer the pottery scene from *Ghost*," Cooper said weakly, "over a sadistic hostage."

"I bet she checks her makeup before sponge bath time approaches," Peterson said with raised eyebrows.

"Dakota!" Cooper scolded as he tried to cover up his laugh with a cough.

"You know it's true," she said as she looked through his records. "Huh."

"Huh, what?" Cooper asked looking over her shoulder to see what was causing her intrigue.

"He was in court-appointed anger management classes," she said. "I totally missed that the first time."

"Wasn't Jed also?" Cooper started as Peterson nodded in agreement.

"Yeah," she said opening his file. "I think he was." She scanned through the uploaded documents and found a possible common thread. "He was." She stopped and looked at Cooper. "Do you think they went to the same class?"

"It's a shot," Cooper said. "What about the guy from last night. Was he in a group as well?"

"I'm already looking," Peterson said as her mouth gaped open in surprise.

"I think we are on to something," Cooper said as they left Tucker's room.

"Do you think we should tell the nurse to not get involved with a possible future wife-beater?" Peterson asked. As they passed the nurses' station they noticed she had a pocket mirror in her hand, checking her mascara.

"Sadly," Cooper said shaking his head, "it wouldn't do any good. They always think they can change them. But they never do." They continued to walk down the bustling hallways. "Sadly, these women are the ones that eventually change."

"People can hope," Peterson said unconvinced. "Can't they?"

"They can," Cooper agreed as they stepped into the elevator. "But when they crash…" He stopped and thought for a second. "It's not pretty."

CHAPTER 77

Veronica sat upright on her chaise lounge with her laptop on her thighs. She was reading the countersuit for the sixth time. Each time she had found something minor that needed to be changed, a word here, a phrase there. Legal jargon bored the commoner, but it energized her mind like a spinning class.

She knew it was Independence Day and most people wouldn't be working, but she also knew her father wasn't most people. He would be at the office piling on his billable hours for the week while clenching his jaws at the lack of loyalty by the rest of the staff.

She grabbed her car keys and laptop and headed out the door. She wanted to print off the paperwork and have someone serve him the papers that day. She wanted this to be another form of Independence Day for her.

She dialed the number for a court clerk. "Hello, Giselle, this is Veronica Cooper. I am sorry to bother you, but I have a huge favor to ask."

Veronica gave her spiel about the need to have the paperwork filed that day. As she was talking, she noticed the above-average traffic in the Washington D.C. streets due to the holiday.

"And you can't wait until tomorrow?" Giselle asked with a slight huff. "This is my day off."

"I know, but if you do this for me, I will owe you big time," Veronica said looking into her rearview mirror and seeing a familiar red car that had been trailing her since she'd left her house. She brushed it off as a coincidence and continued her conversation. "I promise I will make it up to you."

"Fine," Giselle said. "I'll be back, honey," she yelled to her husband. "When you say big time, how big?"

They both laughed and ended the call.

Veronica made another call to have a carrier pick up the filings and deliver it to the law office of Manfield & Hyde that afternoon. "Yes, I know," she said. "Charge me double, I don't care. This just has to be delivered to Luther Hyde today. Meet me at my office in one hour."

She ended the call and felt in control of her life for the first time in a few days.

That was until she saw the same red car three vehicles behind. She turned left and the car slowly turned to follow. She turned right and watched as the car turned right. She tried to recall if it was the same vehicle she'd seen leaving her neighborhood after her public outburst the day before.

She felt like her grip was going to break the steering wheel in two. Her breathing escalated as she found herself leaning away from her state of control. She was hurdling into a drain of chaos. She turned left once again, praying and hoping the car would go straight. She watched behind her more closely than what was in front of her. Her vehicle's emergency collision deterrent system launched into a beeping alarm and braked her car to a sudden stop.

She breathed a sigh of relief at the close call with the vehicle ahead of her. Closing her eyes, she quickly muttered an urgent prayer. She looked into the rearview mirror for the red car, but it was nowhere to be found. It wasn't following her anymore.

It must have gone straight.

She figured it had just been her imagination.

CHAPTER 78

Mikhail watched as Veronica's vehicle turned left and felt her zigzagging through the busy city streets was a warning sign he had been noticed.

On the last few turns he would have run a red light to keep up with her, but he knew where she was going. He watched her car turn left as the streetlight changed from green to yellow to red. He stopped and looked over at his laptop playing the audio being recorded from Veronica's laptop.

He smiled as he drove straight when the light switched to green and decided he had time to stop for a quick bite before heading to Veronica's office.

He didn't have any specific intentions for the day's adventure. He didn't have a script he was playing out since he didn't get to see Jenny. But he knew something was going to be coming down the line and wanted to be ready to act when Jenny called.

He heard a faint strumming of guitars coming from his laptop. Veronica had turned on her radio as she headed to the court to file her paperwork.

He listened to the music; it wasn't his preferred genre, but it broke the chasm of silence. He let the melody take him on a journey, one that didn't have a finish line.

He recalled his first few meetings with Jenny when he'd had to win her over.

"My father and your father were best friends," he'd said as he started to blink. He wasn't sure if she would think he had something in his eye, but she never commented.

She never asked if he was okay.

After he finished with his morse code, he waited as she said nothing. She just continued to look at him with a protective stare as if deciding her next move of chess.

"Oh, they were?" she replied with a rapid-fire of blinks.

A smile engulfed his face as hers remained stone cold.

"Yes, very much so," he responded as they carried on two simultaneous conversations with voices and a blinking code.

They were in the same group, Mikhail had blinked.

Prove it.

Russia forever in our heart and in our thoughts. But now we are more than compatriots, no we are brothers in this new land.

So you know a motto, she blinked. *What else do you know?*

Milo is sick, he blinked with a sad expression that didn't mix with their lighthearted verbal conversation.

He's never said that to me.

When he dies, Oleg will take his place.

That name doesn't sound familiar.

His face had twitched thinking that she'd misunderstood his blinks. *Oleg.*

I don't know that name.

He'd shook his head in surprise. *Oleg, your uncle.*

I don't know that name.

My father never cared for Oleg. He never trusted him.

Why are you telling me this?

He needs to be stopped.

Why do I care?

We can become something.

I don't need to become something out there, she blinked.

You need us, Jenika. We can protect you on the inside, and then you can return to us. My father has a spot for you.

Your father?

Yes, Jenika. We need to stop Oleg.

He stopped his car and ran into a small diner to pick up a deli sandwich, bag of chips, and water. He didn't know how long the afternoon was going to last, so he threw in a couple more dollars for a red, white, and blue cupcake.

He often wondered if Jenny knew he was playing her. Or did Jenny think she was playing him? He didn't care who was pulling the strings between the two of them.

Either way, whoever was playing whom, didn't matter in the long run. He knew his father was playing them both, but his father's goals benefited his future as well.

Oleg must be stopped.

CHAPTER 79

Ira Quill entered Channel 5's parking lot and hoped his plan was going to work out. Sneaking behind parked cars, he waited until he saw an older employee carrying a large video camera. Ira scurried through the parking lot, following the gray-haired man as he approached the back of the news van.

The cameraman opened the back door, climbed in, and fastened the camera securely so it wouldn't slide around during the drive.

"Where are you heading?" Ira said, sneaking into the back of the van while the cameraman had his back turned.

"Down to cover the festivities," he answered stooping down to bundle the wires scattered around the back of the van.

The cameraman froze in his place when he heard the back door squeak as it closed. Ira swiveled the rifle strapped onto his back, gripping it firmly, ready to attack.

"Who are you?" the cameraman asked as he turned around. His eyes widened at the sight of a stranger with a rifle in his hands.

But it was too late. Ira lurched forward and swung the butt of the rifle under the cameraman's chin, causing all the air in his lungs to freeze. He gasped as his head flung back, hitting the van's walls. He tried to grab onto one of the shelves on the side but missed as he slid down the wall. He watched in fear as Ira stepped forwarded and rammed the butt of his rifle on the side of his face, knocking him out cold.

Ira pulled out a handful of black, thick security ties from his backpack and quickly fastened the cameraman's hands and feet. He threw his bag on the ground and rifled through it until he found the duct tape. He pulled a strip and placed it on the cameraman's mouth.

Ira heard the front door of the van open. "Harrison, are you in the back?" a female voice asked.

"Uh-huh," Ira said. "Can you come here and help me?"

"Give me a sec." Ira could hear her shoes stomping beside the van heading to the back. He found a blanket in the corner and threw it over Harrison's limp body.

Ira leaned the rifle against the wall with easy access as he heard the snap of the back door opening. He stooped down, pretending to reach for something.

"Can you get this for me?" Ira asked as he heard the woman step into the back of the van.

"Are you feeling okay? Sounds like you have a cold," she said standing over Ira.

Ira grabbed his rifle to his side and spun around so the barrel was aimed inches under the woman's chin. "If you scream, you're dead."

Fear seized the woman as she looked around the back of the van and saw a pair of shoes escaping from under the old woolen blanket they used during late nights or mid-afternoon naps.

"Please, no," she gasped.

"I'm not going to shoot you," Ira smiled as he quickly flipped the gun so the stock whacked the side of her face, causing her to fall unconscious.

"That was easier than I thought," Ira said to himself as he got up and closed the back door.

He tied up the newscaster like he did Harrison. Then he fastened the two individuals together at their hands and feet so they looked like mismatched conjoined twins.

Ira searched through their belongings and found Harrison's Channel 5 employee identification to show to security as well as keys to the news van to start his unforgettable journey.

And it was guaranteed to be unforgettable.

CHAPTER 80

"So, all three victims were in an anger management class?" Officer Peterson confirmed on her cell phone as Cooper was driving to Manuel Perez's home to question his family.

"Did they go to the same one?" Cooper asked as he crept through the snail-like traffic.

"Can you tell me if they went to the same class?" Peterson asked. "Oh," she said with discouragement before being quickly reassured. "Really?"

"What?" Cooper asked as Peterson shook her head. "Can you put that on speaker?"

Peterson spoke as she clicked her phone so Cooper could hear. "Francis, can you repeat that?"

"I'm not sure if they were in the same classes," Officer Francis Brady said in a deep tone, "but it shows that they were assigned to the same facilitator, an Ally McDermott."

"Did you say Ally McDermott?" Cooper asked, staring in amazement at Peterson.

"Yes," Brady responded.

"Can you give me her address?" Peterson asked, grabbing a pen.

"Can you give us her home address as well?" Cooper added. "She won't be working today."

"Sure thing," Brady said, typing into his database.

"Can you believe that?" Cooper asked astounded. "Ally McDermott. I think we found the common thread."

Peterson nodded her head as Brady gave them Ally's work and home addresses. "If you find anything else that connects these three, let us know, Brady."

"Will do," Brady said as Peterson ended the call.

"So, I guess we're not going to Perez's home anymore," Peterson said typing Ally's home address into their GPS.

"Detour it is," Cooper said as he started following the new electronic directions.

"Hopefully, she will be able to help us," Peterson said. "You know, doctor-client privilege."

"Technically, I don't think she is their doctor, and they are not her clients," Cooper said. "It's court-mandated, so she shouldn't be able to use that as an excuse to not answer our questions."

"Should we call in a warrant just in case?" Peterson asked. "Just to be safe?"

"Wouldn't hurt," Cooper said. "It never hurts to have a plan B."

CHAPTER 81

"Are you okay?" Elizabeth asked as I sat silent after three episodes of *Orange is the New Black*.

"I'm just..." I hesitated as I couldn't find the right words to say.

"I think you might have broken him," Jeremiah said with a smile. "Anyone want something to eat?" he asked walking toward the kitchen. "I was thinking I could make--" he started before I interrupted, remembering what Elizabeth had told me earlier of his culinary tastes.

"We had a big breakfast this morning," I said as Elizabeth nodded.

I pulled out my phone and went to Channel 5's website for breaking news and headlines. I wanted to see if anything had been said so far about the potential terrorist attack.

Elizabeth must have figured out what I was doing. "I don't think anything will be on the newsfeed for a diverted attack."

"You never know," I said, swiping through the news stories. I didn't find anything listed, but I hoped the police were going to take my warning seriously.

"Ready for another episode?" Elizabeth asked with a wicked smile. "Can you handle it?"

"I think I need a shower and a stiff drink," I said, grabbing the pillow in my lap I had used as a stress reliever.

"Stiff drink?" she laughed as Jeremiah returned with a bowl of cheese crackers. "What's a stiff drink for you?"

"After today, I may need something to erase the memories of what I have seen."

"You're a brave little boy," Elizabeth joshed as she grabbed a handful of crackers from Jeremiah's bowl.

"I asked if you wanted any," Jeremiah kidded her before turning to me. "What do you think of the show?"

"That's what we were just talking about," I said with wide eyes. "I don't think I can ever forget what I have seen."

"I can help you with hypnosis," Jeremiah answered sincerely.

"I think I'll be okay. But if I'm not sleeping in a week, I will give you a call."

"Promise?" he asked. "I would love to evaluate you in this line of studying."

"Like a lab rat?"

Elizabeth laughed out loud, coughing out a few crumbs. "Sorry," she said brushing her lap clean. "But if you start some shock treatment, can I push the button?"

"I bet you would enjoy that," I laughed.

"I really would," she gushed with a scheming smile. "Can we try it now? Every time you start to cover your eyes, I get to smack you."

I huffed. "You're doing that now anyway."

"I know," she laughed. "But now I can say I'm doing it for the love of science and not because I'm cruel. I love science," she winked to Jeremiah. "A lot."

"I don't believe you are doing it for the love of science," Jeremiah snorted. "Or you would have watched the documentary on black holes and the growing universe last week."

"Anyways," she said grabbing another handful of crackers and pushing play on her remote control. "Next episode, boys."

I shook and yelped out in pain.

"What's wrong?" Elizabeth jerked as the episode started to buffer.

"Just wanted you to know what it would sound like if you shocked me when you hit the other button."

She looked into my eyes and thought for a second a blank expression on her face. "Scream, little boy, scream," she hissed with fiery eyes as she held down the play button on her remote. "I don't hear you," she laughed.

I grabbed my pillow, smothering myself and screaming into the goose feathers. "Better?" I asked.

"Much," she said as she leaned over and whispered in my ear. "Thanks for today, bud."

CHAPTER 82

"Can I help you, officers?" a tall man wearing sweatpants and a camouflage t-shirt asked as he opened the front door of his home to Officer Cooper and Officer Peterson.

"Is Ally McDermott here?" Cooper asked standing on the front porch.

"Yes. I'm Gordon, her husband," he said with a confused smile. "What can we help you with?"

"We have some questions about an ongoing investigation she may be able to help shine some light onto."

"Sure," Gordon said as he went into a nearby room to get his wife.

"Hello, what can I help you with?" she asked rubbing the tape on her injured wrist.

"We are investigating the beatings of Tucker Stevenson and Jed Poston, and the murder of Manuel Perez. Do these names sound familiar to you?"

She gasped, covering her mouth in shock. "I didn't know," she said as she corrected. "I mean, yes, I do know these men, but I didn't know they were harmed."

"Can you tell us if these men were in your anger management class recently?"

"I can't tell you what we discuss in these sessions," she said.

"We understand the conflict of doctor-client privilege, but technically these people were not clients; they appeared in your presence due to court mandates. You have an obligation to provide the court with discoveries during your sessions," Peterson pointed out, having just researched this issue in the passenger seat of the patrol car.

Cooper nodded his head, admiring her quick findings.

"Yes, okay," Ally said, offering the officers a seat in their living room as her husband sat down beside her, holding her hand for support.

"We are just trying to get to the bottom of this," Cooper said. "Anything you can tell us would be greatly appreciated."

She looked at her husband, who nodded his head.

"All three of those men were recent participants in the anger management program I lead. Jed Poston actually finished his required hours earlier this week while Manuel Perez just started attending a couple of days ago."

"What about Tucker Stevenson?"

"Yes, he was also in the classes and is still required to attend a few more hours before I can release him," Ally remarked.

"Is there anyone you have had in these classes in the last week that seems capable or willing to attack these three men?" Cooper asked, getting to the meat of the questioning.

"It's anger management, officers," Ally replied. "Everyone who takes these classes has, at one time, shown attributes capable of harming themselves and others."

"Have there been any disagreements this week that seemed out of the ordinary?" Cooper asked, leaning forward.

"Most of the people who take the class are not taking it seriously. They do not take it to change, but to fulfill an obligation they signed," she said with a disheartened expression of losing hope in making an impact.

"So, are there any candidates in your class that could do this?" Peterson asked once again. "Can you give us a list of names and addresses so we can ask them ourselves?"

"I really cannot think of anyone standing out," she said shrugging her shoulders. "Sadly, anyone in the class could have done this. Anyone."

"I've often worried about something like this happening," Gordon said, speaking up. "I'm sorry, honey. You always want to try and change the world, but some just don't want to change."

Ally nodded her head and got up from the couch. "Let me go get the list of names. I should be able to access it. Just give me a few minutes."

"Has your wife seemed scared or different lately?" Cooper asked while she was out of the room.

"I haven't seen anything different," he said shaking his head. "But I'm not the best at noticing things like that. I should do better, but she doesn't like to talk about work because I get protective."

"Why is her wrist taped?" Peterson asked.

"Oh," he said scratching his head. "She did something last weekend that hurt it. Fell I think."

Ally came back into the room and handed the list of names and addresses to Cooper. "Here is the list of students I have had in the last two months during the times of these participants."

"Thank you," Cooper said looking down at the long list of names that filled an entire page.

"Did you say Manuel just started this week?" Peterson asked as Ally nodded her head. "Sorry, but can give you give us a list of names of people in your classes this week that were in class with the three men?"

"Oh, yes," Ally said as she started to walk back to her office. "Give me another minute."

"Take your time," Cooper said as Gordon gave a polite smile.

"If you think of anything, or remember anything," Peterson said, handing him her card, "give us a call."

"I will," he said, sliding the contact information into his pocket. "I hope you catch this guy."

"We will," Cooper said with a positive smile.

Ally returned with the list that was now only a dozen names. "If you need anything else, let me know," she said handing them her business card.

"We will probably be in touch," Cooper said as they stood up and thanked each of them for their help.

Gordon hugged his wife on the front porch while Ally waved to the patrol car as they drove away.

"Good thinking," Cooper said to Peterson. "You really got that list shortened."

"Not to be sexist," Peterson said, "but I think we can remove the women on this list."

"I would usually agree, but what if one of the women told a man about something that happened during group?"

"Wint," Peterson scolded as she looked down at the short list of names. "You just doubled or tripled the list," she huffed.

"Anything is possible," Wint frowned.

"I know," Peterson said tapping her foot on the floorboard. "But let's go to the men first, and then we can follow your thought process. Okay?"

"That's fine with me," Cooper said. "So, who's first?"

"Isad Jahandar."

CHAPTER 83

Ira Quill maneuvered the news van like it was his pickup truck, just a little longer and much more expensive with all the technology and satellite signals attached. He slowly drove to the Washington Mall, making sure to follow all traffic rules and speed limits, but he didn't have to worry too much. Traffic was bumper to bumper, with very little chance of speeding or running a red light.

He approached the magnificent Washington Mall and saw the Washington Monument in the distance. The brilliant white obelisk towered over the trees as if the peak could touch the fluffy clouds overhead.

"Where to park, where to park?" he murmured to himself as he drove past the National Gallery of Art. He knew if he drove around, he would find the news vehicles parked together like they were food trucks for informed viewers.

He wanted to turn and head back up, but various side roads were blocked as waves of tourists and families lined the streets walking with festive hats and t-shirts celebrating their freedom. He turned his head and saw what he desired across the grassy square: four news vehicles had already parked and had their cameras out.

He smiled as he made his way, estimating it would take twenty minutes to drive two blocks. But he had time to spare. Showtime wasn't going to be until later that afternoon. He wanted to have an early show for the people who wore their nauseating red, white, and blue one time a year. He cringed at their ignorance even though people were dying for their freedom around the world daily.

He tapped his steering wheel, humming "God Bless America" with reverent disdain.

He loved his country. He would die for his country.

He just hated its citizens.

It was the ungrateful citizens in their $20 t-shirts that caused his blood to boil with rage and contempt.

CHAPTER 84

"I did it," Veronica beamed as she pulled into her garage and pressed the button causing the door to slide down.

"Has he called you yet?" Wint asked as he sat in the patrol car with Dakota waiting for the surveillance footage of Manuel Perez's murder in the subway to download.

"No, but I don't expect him to," Veronica said grabbing her laptop and iced coffee. "I feel like he's not going to be talking to me very much for a while."

Those words hurt Wint. He hated knowing his wife had to have thicker skin than him in order to combat the emotional abuse she had endured through her lifetime. He hadn't known of the secret wounds she had been mending silently for years before their counseling sessions began. He thought their sessions were for their marriage, but he realized their marriage couldn't be fixed if there was unresolved baggage in other areas of their lives. Her family needed an entire storage unit for past skeletons and ghosts.

"I'm sorry, hon," he said as Dakota sat in the passenger seat texting her boyfriend for the evening's plans.

"It's okay," she sighed. "Well, it will be one day."

"Why don't you go to Elizabeth's," he suggested, watching the download percentage increase a dime a minute.

"I'm not sure," Veronica said, disgusted by how her sister had treated her the day before. "Maybe I just need to give them all up."

"Veronica," Wint said shaking his head. "You need Elizabeth as much as she needs you." He stopped to rub his forehead. "She probably feels the exact same way."

"Probably not," she said. "She was always his favorite."

"She says *you* were his favorite."

"Winston," she snapped. "I went to law school and work hard for what I have. She lives off his fringes." She stopped and laid her laptop down and slurped her iced coffee. "My trust fund couldn't keep us up in the lifestyle she has been living the last few years."

"Maybe she invested it," Wint started to say before Veronica interrupted.

"Are you going to say Elizabeth knows how to handle her money better than I do, when I'm the one who took business law and finance classes?"

"I'm just saying maybe there's something you don't know," Wint said. "I feel like you both are keeping things from each other."

"What do you know?" she asked with skepticism as she muttered something under her breath.

"I know you are just now telling me some of your secrets," he said with a saddened heart. "If you have secrets, she must have them too."

"I'm not sure about that," she said as she ended the call.

Wint looked down at his phone and punched the ceiling in the patrol car.

"Trouble in paradise?" Dakota asked as she continued to text Stew.

"I wouldn't say paradise," Wint sighed as the download finally finished and the video started playing.

They watched the black and white grainy footage of a large white male attacking and manhandling a smaller man.

"Look how big that guy is compared to Manuel," Dakota said. "He's like a giant."

"I guess that's a start," Wint said as he looked down at Manuel's driver's license showing he was five and a half feet tall. "Yeah, our attacker is easily over six feet."

They watched the video and then replayed it, hoping they missed something. All they got was the killer was a strong, tall man with some anger issues.

"Ready to start the questioning?" Dakota asked.

Wint looked down at the list. "Hopefully only one guy will fit those descriptions."

Dakota nodded. "Hopefully."

CHAPTER 85

"I'm hungry," Elizabeth said, stretching as she stood from her couch where she'd been sitting between me and Jeremiah. "Anyone else want lunch?"

"Eh," I said, getting up from the couch and following her to the kitchen.

"I thought you said you weren't hungry," she said raising her eyebrows.

"You know me," I said with a cheesy grin. "I can always eat, even if I'm not hungry." I looked down at the watch I'd had since middle school and noticed it was after one. "Do you think they stopped it yet?" I asked as Jeremiah walked around the living room, taking notice of a few new books in Elizabeth's bookcase.

"We won't know until it happens or doesn't," she said, shrugging her shoulders. "Not a good feeling, is it?"

"Nope. I need to find out." I left the kitchen as she stood in front of her open refrigerator.

I flipped the channel to find a newscast, hoping there would be some coverage of the Washington Mall somewhere. I scanned through the channels but found nothing. So, I did it again.

After my third time through the channels, something caught my eye. A newscaster was standing near the Washington Mall detailing the upcoming events with a firework spectacular for the grand finale. The video scanned the entire Washington Mall, and I saw the Channel 5 News van nestled beside a few other news trucks. I watched as they were interviewing people, asking their favorite Fourth of July memories or best side dish recipes for family picnics when someone walked by the scene in a green shirt.

My heart dropped.

"Elizabeth," I stammered, watching the television, trying to rewind the last fifteen seconds so she could see what I just saw. "Elizabeth."

Elizabeth didn't come into the living room where Jeremiah and I were standing.

"Elizabeth!" I yelled, pausing the news as she walked into the room with a cheese stick in her hand.

"What?" she quipped, but her attitude vanished when she saw my face. She ran over to the television as I clicked play.

"This was just on," I said as she watched the same news footage on the Washington Mall as a lone guy in a green shirt walked by, heading to the other news vehicles.

"How?" she gasped. "How can he be there?"

"Who?" Jeremiah asked, leaving the bookcase to see what we were watching.

"That guy doesn't belong there," Elizabeth said as she started to pace around the room talking in incomplete sentences. "What are we going to do?"

"I don't get it," Jeremiah said. "Why doesn't he belong there?"

We looked at one another, and I wished I had telepathic abilities to read her mind. Instead, I stayed silent to let her answer her boyfriend's question.

"Well, he…" she started and looked at me. "He beat up Solo last year and was supposed to be sentenced to prison for three years."

"I'm so sorry, Solomon," Jeremiah said giving me a hug. I looked over his shoulder and gave Elizabeth a dirty look.

Shrugging her shoulders, she mouthed something I couldn't understand.

"What?" I whispered, but she didn't repeat it.

"You are stronger now than you were a year ago," Jeremiah consoled as I grimaced.

"Yes," Elizabeth joined in. "Yes, you are. And who cares that you wet yourself from the scare?"

"I didn't pee on myself." I glared at her as I corrected the fake story she was telling.

"It's okay," Jeremiah said with a compassionate pat on my back. "It is your body's natural reaction to fear."

"I didn't pee on myself," I said again, trying to laugh off the tall tale.

"My bad," Elizabeth said as she motioned for Jeremiah to not say a word.

"She's lying!" I ranted. "That whole story is a lie."

Elizabeth shot me a look that could kill as Jeremiah stood to the side, lost and confused.

"I don't get it," Jeremiah said, looking at both of us with suspicion. "Who was that man then?"

I looked at Elizabeth who looked at me while raising her hands.

I groaned in annoyance and shot Elizabeth a look that warned her that the gloves would be coming off one day.

"He's the guy that beat me up a year ago," I said with a depressing tone. "But I didn't pee," I emphasized. "I did not pee on myself!"

Jeremiah patted me on the back as he walked away.

"You could have come up with anything, but you came up with that?"

"I was speechless," she said, fumbling her words once again. "When I saw him, my thoughts just jumbled."

"Mine too," I said.

"I'm sorry," she winced, "but that's the only believable thing I could think of."

"Wait a minute," I stopped in disbelief. "The only made-up story you thought was believable was a grown man beating me up until I peed in my pants?"

"What?" she said with an uneven smile. "I could see it happening."

"If I was a girl, I would come after you until you peed on yourself," I laughed. "Who knows, I still might."

"No, you won't," she said as she hugged me. "You're too good to stoop down to my level."

"True," I stopped and nodded my head. "But it sure is tempting."

I turned my attention to the television and saw the man in the green shirt positioning a camera tripod on top of the news van.

"That's where it's going to happen," I said shaking my head in fear and dread. "Just like in my dream."

"Mine   too."

CHAPTER 86

"Should we call the cops again?" Elizabeth asked, flipping the channel to see if there was other news coverage of the Washington Memorial.

"I already called them this morning, and they didn't do anything. What do you think is going to change now?"

"I don't know!" she said, throwing her hands up in the air, tapping her foot and muttering a few choice words under her breath.

"I don't know either," I said, shaking my head. "But I can call them again. Or..." I stopped and looked at her. "You call them. Maybe if someone else calls them they will take it more seriously."

She pulled her phone out of her purse and noticed the time. "It's almost two," she said forming a fist. "He's going to kill these people in less than two hours!"

"I know. So call!"

Elizabeth called the police and told them there was a possible killer on the grounds of the Washington Memorial. She told them he had taken two Channel 5 employees hostage and would kill and blow them up if he felt cornered.

"You better do something! And do it fast!" she screamed into the phone. "He's going to do this a little after three." She stopped and listened to the dispatch operator who started asking her questions. "Just believe me! His name is Ira Quill, and he's going to kill a lot of people if you don't stop it."

She listened to the operator as she put her free hand on her hip. "Listen, I'm telling you the truth. He is there now! I just saw him on the news walking by and later standing on the news truck. He's going to shoot and kill a lot of people if you don't do something fast!" She stopped and listened to the dispatch operator and gave me a sinister look.

"She put me on hold!" she screamed. "She freakin' put me on hold!" She stood with the phone to her ear as she continued to spur venom and hate. "We can't just stand by and do nothing, Solo," she said as her voice quivered. "We can't."

"What are we going to do?" I asked. "Drive down there and stop it ourselves?" I shook my head. "It didn't go well yesterday," I said realizing that yesterday seemed like a lifetime ago. "I couldn't stop the bomb." I paused and looked at the television screen and then at her on hold. "I'm not sure we can stop a guy with a machine gun and a bomb by ourselves. That sounds like a death wish."

"Well," she snapped as she hung up the phone. "We can't just stay here and wait for it to happen."

"What do you suggest?" I asked as my head was mixing a thousand thoughts until it looked like a flubbed-up painter's palette.

"I think you need to make a call," she sighed. "It's the only way."

"I've already called the cops," I huffed. "Didn't you hear me?"

"No," she said with calmness and serenity. "You need to call *a* cop. It's the only way," she said with a softness and fragility in her demeanor. "You have to, Solo. You have to tell him. He'll know what to do."

"Wint?"

CHAPTER 87

"Yes," Elizabeth said with a tilted smile. "Wint."

"You know if we tell him about the terrorist, he's going to ask questions," I said taken aback.

"I know," she said with a warm smile. "I think it's time."

I looked her in the eyes and recalled the moment she first told me of her ability. I wasn't kind with my knee-jerk judgmental reaction. I was cynical and disbelieving. I was sarcastic and doubtful. I was unknowingly hateful and rude.

I didn't want to go through that with my best friend of twenty years. I didn't want to feel like an oddity in my small circle of comfort.

All the emotions came surging back with a tidal wave of force, crashing my mind and heart against an internal wall.

"Did you believe my apology?" I asked.

"What?" she asked bewildered, staring at me in confusion.

"When I hurt you," I said. "You know, that night last October."

"I can't remember," she said. "But I believe you now. Why?"

I pulled out my phone and found Wint's contact in my favorites. I didn't have the guts to call him yet. I saw his name and number and the goofy picture I saved of him when he wasn't looking.

"Because this call could change everything," I said in contemplation. "I'm not ready to be thought of as a freak."

"What? You don't care about *my* opinion of you?" she asked with a snicker.

"It's okay if you think I'm a freak because you understand me," I said still looking down at the phone in my palm. "He won't."

"Don't judge someone before giving them the chance to show their true colors," she said.

"Where did you hear that from? Confucius?"

She shrugged her shoulders with a laugh. "Nah, nothing that meaningful. It was probably from *Sex and the City*."

"I didn't know Carrie was that introspective," I said unconvinced.

Elizabeth's eyes went wide in astonishment as her mouth gaped open.

"That was Chelsea's guilty pleasure," I grinned. "But Charlotte was my favorite."

Elizabeth looked at me with admiration. "I think our friendship just went to the next level, Solo."

"Can I take it back?" I asked with a grimace. "I was kidding. I don't know anything about that show. I take it all back!"

"I know the truth," she smiled. "Your secret is safe with me."

I looked at her in disbelief.

"What?"

"You told your boyfriend a humiliating lie about me, and now you are telling me my secret is safe?" I snarled with sarcasm. "We shall see how true your word is."

"You'll see," Elizabeth said. "But if you ever turn on me, I'll blab it to all your manly friends," she laughed. "Well, whenever you get one."

"I don't have to take this ridicule anymore," I scolded as I called Wint.

"Good luck," she said as I headed to the front door.

I needed some privacy for this delicate phone call. But mostly, I needed to be alone to deal with how my best friend responded.

293

"Hey, Wint."

CHAPTER 88

"Hey, man," Wint said as he and Dakota were leaving Isad's home. He definitely didn't meet the physical traits of the killer as he was about the same size or smaller than Manuel.

"Wint, I know this is going to sound crazy, and I promise to explain everything to you soon. Very soon," Solo started as Wint started to say something. "Please, Wint, let me just say what I need to say and then you can talk."

"Okay," Wint said getting into the passenger side of the car as he asked Dakota to drive to the next name on the list.

Solo inhaled a deep breath and spit out his words. "There is going to be a terrorist attack on the Washington Memorial this afternoon."

"What?" Wint asked, raising his voice.

"A little after three this afternoon to be exact."

Wint looked at the clock radio and noticed that three wasn't too far away.

"Solo, how do you know this?"

"I will tell you the whole truth when we have time, but for right now, you have to get the police to go to the Washington Memorial. The terrorist is a man dressed in a green shirt pretending to be with Channel 5 News. The back of the news van has the cameraman and newscaster locked up," he said as if his life depended on it. "And Wint, the van is rigged with a bomb that he can detonate."

Wint listened to every word Solo said. He listened to the fear in his voice and how his breathing heaved and vibrated with each utterance.

"Wint, are you there?" Solo asked with more fear and trepidation in his voice as he coughed and choked on the words as if taking a gulp of sour lemonade.

"I'm here," Wint said. "I'm always here for you, Solo."

"So?" Solo said in agonizing wait.

"We are heading there now, Solo," Wint said as he told Dakota they had a change of plans and needed to head to the Washington Memorial. He turned on the siren shocking Dakota. "As fast as possible!" he commanded.

"You believe me?" Solo asked in heartfelt surprise.

"Why wouldn't I?" Wint said.

CHAPTER 89

"How'd it go?" Elizabeth asked as I walked into the home like a tame zombie.

I couldn't speak. My body was numb at the emotional toll of the conversation, the excitement of warning, the uneasiness in waiting, the shock of belief, and now the sweet warmth of relief.

"He's heading there now," I said, unsure of what to do next.

"Well, then," she said grabbing her purse. "So are we!"

"What?" I asked, following her around like a dog on an invisible leash.

"Jeremiah, we are heading out for an emergency," she said with sharpness. "We will be back a little later. Why don't you stay and fix something for us to eat? Whatever you want."

"Anything?" he grinned.

"Just no crickets," she said. "Or anything else that isn't normal."

"What's normal?" he asked with an honest look.

"Jeremiah!" she barked. "You know what I mean."

We got into her car, and she put it in reverse, squealing her tires as she started to drive forward, unfazed by the speed limit signs posted along the journey.

"So, how'd he take it?" she asked as I held onto the door handle for security, closing my eyes after she drove through the third red light.

"He said he trusted me," I said with a feeling of peace enveloping me.

"What did he say about the dreams?" she asked, speeding by the traffic, weaving in and out like an experienced racer.

"I didn't get to that," I said closing my eyes and triple-checking my seatbelt.

"I have airbags too," she scathed. "Sissy."

"People still die with airbags and seatbelts," I said, bracing myself for a possible wreck.

"They also say that relaxed people survive and recover from a wreck better than tightly-wound pansies."

"Sissy and pansy." I laughed at her choice of words.

"Fine, want something more adult-like?" She finished with an unflattering term for a man, or a woman for that matter.

"You didn't have to go there," I smirked.

"What?" she said shrugging her shoulders. "You can handle it." She stopped and looked over at me. "Now that you've watched a few hours of *Orange*."

"I'm not sure I'm man enough to watch that show," I said.

"Or maybe not *woman* enough," she corrected with a hint of a smile. "So, he's going to stop the gunman?"

"I heard him tell Dakota to start driving that way, so they should get there before we do." I stopped and reiterated the most important word, "Should."

"What are you trying to say?" she asked, slowing because of the traffic ahead.

"I think you know," I said, keeping my eyes closed. I felt the car come to a stop. "Did you hit someone?"

"Hardy-har-har," she laughed sarcastically as she smacked my forehead. "Yeah, you."

"Why do you do that?" I asked, opening my eyes and rubbing my wound. "You do remember I was in a bomb blast yesterday?"

She gritted her teeth apologetically, but her words didn't say it. "How long are you going to play the bomb card?"

"As long as it takes for you to give me sympathy."

"You better laminate that card," she said shaking her head, "because it's going to fall apart as often as you play it."

"Really?" I asked unperturbed. "Anyways," I started as she smiled and giggled. "I have a good feeling about this."

CHAPTER 90

Ira Quill stooped down in the back of the news van, looking into Juliet's frightened eyes as she lay in the middle with Harrison attached behind her.

"I'm not a bad person," he said as he inched his face closer to hers. "Really."

She squirmed behind her duct taped mouth, turning her head left and right, trying to get his seething teeth away from her flesh.

"Juliet," he said with a menacing tone, holding her identification in his hands. "Such a beautiful name, but what's really in a name?" He started to smile. "By the way Harrison looks, he's not your Romeo," he said in a cat-and-mouse style. "And based upon your hand, you're Romeo hasn't come."

She lowered her head, squirming louder to tune out his psychological words.

"Shh," he soothed as he brushed her hair out of her eyes. "I want you to see this."

Standing up, he opened his backpack and pulled out four bricks wrapped in plastic. He laid one in each corner and then attached each of them with a wire, forming a circle. He connected the red wires to another box, twisting the copper-stripped wire around the main component.

Her eyes started to fill with tears as her hopes of watching the fireworks tonight were dashed.

"If you move or hit the wires or try to dismantle any of them," he stopped and smiled. "Boom."

He walked around the cramped van grabbing the blanket to cover them.

"One more thing," he said as he grabbed his rifle. "Do you want to see your death or not?"

She squirmed once again as tears flooded down her cheeks, dripping over the gray tape.

"Juliet, if you can't be quiet," he said holding his rifle in his hand "I'm going to have to make you."

He slammed the butt of the gun into her face, knocking her out. He walked around to check on Harrison, but he was still unconscious from the two earlier hits.

"Sleep tight," he said as he covered the two with the wool blanket. He strapped his rifle onto his back, then put on his backpack over the gun. He grabbed the tripod and camera, carrying both with one hand as he left the van, closing the back door behind him.

He climbed up the ladder mounted on the back door of the van. He reached the top and walked with confidence on the sturdy roof. Kneeling, he took off his backpack and gun, laying them at his feet. He looked around in all directions and felt the humid breeze only intensifying the summer sun scorching overhead. But he wasn't going to let the heat stop him. It only caused his rage to simmer more.

He looked to his right and saw the majestic Capitol building with the classic dome showcasing its architectural beauty. Squinting, he tried to see the Statue of Freedom, but he couldn't see her beauty. Although he knew what she looked like in her military garb. He stood and saluted a warrior like himself.

"Today," he said to himself. "Today, they will know what freedom looks like."

CHAPTER 91

"Why are we going there?" Peterson asked as she followed Cooper's orders on a few shortcuts.

"There's going to be a terrorist attack around the press area in about an hour," Wint said as he radioed for backup, describing the shooter the best that he could.

"I'm trying to get more details on the possible shooter," he said as he texted Solo, who responded almost immediately.

"His name is Ira Quill. He is wearing a green shirt and he is in the Channel 5 News van," Cooper said into the radio. "He has two hostages in the back, a man and woman who work for Channel 5. Proceed with caution because I've been told he has rigged a bomb."

"Where did you get this information?" someone asked through the staticky radio.

"I was alerted from a reliable source," he said. "So, whoever gets there first, don't make any sudden movements. I have been told the shooter is planning to attack at three."

"I'm on the grounds," one officer said. "I'm heading that way."

"We are close," Cooper replied. "A few blocks away."

"I can confirm," someone else said through the radio. "There is a man with a green shirt standing on top of the Channel 5 News van."

"Does he have a weapon?" Wint asked.

"It looks like he is setting up a tripod," the officer said.

"Do you see a weapon?"

"No, I don't see a weapon," the officer answered. "But I'm watching the target."

"Yes, I see him as well," the first voice on the radio said. "I don't see a weapon either."

"What are your positions?" Cooper asked.

"I'm in front of the National Gallery of Art. The press has parked their vehicles there."

"I'm on the other side of the mall, near the Air Museum. I'm heading that way."

"Once again," Wint pleaded, "do not startle the shooter. He may activate the bomb. Start blocking off the area."

"On it," one of the officers said.

"Are you sure about this?" Dakota asked as she braked, looking ahead at the traffic.

"He wouldn't lie to me," Wint said, twitching his anxious foot. He opened the door thinking he could run there faster than creeping through the traffic. "Meet me near the press!" he yelled as he started sprinting down the sidewalk.

Solo wouldn't lie about this.

CHAPTER 92

"Come on! Go, people! Go!" Elizabeth shouted as she held her palm against the horn on the steering wheel.

"That's not going to get us there any faster," I said, rolling down the window and sticking my head out.

"What are you doing?" she balked in annoyance.

"Just trying to see up ahead," I said, slinking my body back into the car and raising the window. "I couldn't see anything."

"Duh," she said pursing her lips. "What did you expect? All the cars would disappear once you stuck your head out like a freakin' golden retriever?"

"I'm just getting nervous," I winced, fidgeting in the front seat like a three-year old needing to pee.

"That's not going to get us there any faster," she smiled, echoing my earlier words.

I looked over at her as she gave me a large, toothy grin. I rolled my eyes at her candor.

I called Wint as I wiggled around in my seat. "He's not picking up. Why isn't he picking up?"

"Hell if I know," she said as she turned on her radio to hear some news. "Maybe it's already done."

"Yeah, maybe," I agreed as I looked out my window again. "But what if he didn't believe me?" I asked as a wave of realization pounded my desolate sandy shore. "What if he just pretended like he believed me? What if he thinks I'm crazy?"

"To be fair," she started in a matter-of-fact tone, "I believe you, but I still think you're crazy."

I didn't say anything. I felt the cold shoulder of the world, as if I were experiencing a personal eclipse.

"I'm kidding," she said, retracting her last statement. "You're not crazy."

Her words brought a little warmth.

Just a little.

My silence was forcing Elizabeth to bring out her security blanket dialogue to console my troublesome thoughts.

"He believes you," she said like a good friend would as she eased off the brake pedal and started to coast ahead. "I know he does."

"But how do you know for sure?" I asked, turning my head and watching her stare at a bumper sticker ahead of her claiming that the driver's kid was smartest.

"You should know better than anyone," she said, winking at me. "You just gotta have faith."

She said her words with confidence that should have eased my uncertainty, but they didn't. He just added another crack to my already thawing ice pond.

"My faith isn't as strong as you think," I said, leaning my head back and closing my eyes. "Not even close."

I thought my words were going to cause our conversation to close in remorse, but she wasn't having it.

She snapped her fingers an inch from my face. "How can you say that? I mean, I would think your faith would be ten times stronger with everything that you have seen in the last year."

I listened to her sermon, surprising as it was. "You see things no one else can and they always come true. Have any of your dreams not happened?"

I didn't answer, but my silence was my yes and amen response she was hunting for.

"You step out every day, taking broken pieces of information you have received and tether them together into making a lasting impact. Sometimes we succeed. Sometimes we fail. But at the end of the day, you follow because of faith."

I listened to her words, seeing her momentum of encouragement which was as rare as digging up a dinosaur bone in a gallon of ice cream. "Why do you follow then?"

She looked straight ahead, coasting further down the road, braking occasionally when the cars in front of her did. They were nearing the Washington Mall, but it still wasn't visible.

"Elizabeth, why do you?"

She didn't answer. She just continued to drive forward, watching people on the sidewalk passing her with their casual strolls.

"Elizabeth," I said, causing her to finally turn her head.

"You," she said looking into my eyes. "You make me want to follow," she said in a soft voice that felt like velvet to my soul.

A smile started to break through my depressed façade before she had to interrupt.

"And just to get one thing straight," she said with a twinkle in her eyes. "What we have isn't romantic or sexual, so I don't want you to start thinking that I'm in love with you or anything," she laughed. "I do have my standards."

I laughed. "Am I not good enough for you?"

She cocked her head over at me and pursed her lips in thought. "Oh, honey, with those clearance rack sneakers and knock-off shorts, I think you already know the answer to that question."

"Knock-off?" I scoffed. "I got these at Target!"

"Oh, forgive me," she riled as she fixed her attention on the road when she saw an opening from a tourist driver messing with his GPS. She skidded in front of his creeping mini-van and made a break for it. "That's right," she mocked. "I did read Target is the up-and-coming Gucci of mid-America."

"Mmhmm," I nodded. "I'll take you tomorrow."

"Oh be still my beating heart," she laughed. "I think I may have plans tomorrow."

I glanced up and noticed we were just a few blocks from the action. My heart started to pound with adrenaline.

"I don't know if it's the fact we are getting closer or going to Target tomorrow, but my heart is banging against my chest."

She sighed. "Sadly, I think it's the Target trip causing you to go all sweaty-palmed and weak-kneed."

"You may be right," I winked.

"I usually am." She looked at me. "Aren't I?"

She stopped her car, and I saw that the traffic was at a screeching halt, but I knew that Washington Mall was just a few blocks away.

"It looks like you are going to be stuck here for a while," I said opening the door. "I'll meet you down there."

"You didn't answer my question, sweetheart," she said with a southern accent.

308

"Oh, yes, Miss Daisy, you are always right, my dear," I said, slamming the door and starting to run up the sidewalk. "Always!" I shouted, but I didn't know if she heard. I was already a few car lengths ahead of her.

CHAPTER 93

Wint ran up to the Washington Mall, finding the area with the news vans huddled together like a cluster of chess nerds at lunchtime across the vast area of green. He stopped running when his feet hit the grass. He didn't want to look obvious to Ira. He looked around and found a few other police officers standing around the scene, watching the man in the green shirt as if they were watching through a hunter's scope.

"I see him," he said into his radio. "Has the street around the perp been blocked?"

"Yes, it's secure," someone answered.

"Good," Wint answered as he continued to walk along the sidewalk, keeping his head turned away from the gunman.

"Has anyone approached him?" Wint asked.

"I haven't," someone said as a few other voices confirmed the same.

"I haven't even seen him with a gun," one of the officers said.

"Me neither," another voice commented. "I've only seen him messing with the camera. Are you sure about this guy?"

Wint had a split-second decision to make. Go with the evidence or trust Solo. "I'm sure," Wint said through the radio. "Have you seen anyone around him?"

No one said a word.

"Don't you think there would be a reporter around him like all the other news channels if he was a cameraman?"

"Maybe they're late," someone chimed in.

"Or maybe they are in the back of the van like the intel I was given," Wint said in a low but certain voice. "He's got them in the back, and he's got a bomb."

"SWAT is on their way," dispatch said.

"If he sees that, he will just detonate the bomb," Wint said with confidence. "If he's standing on top of the van ready to shoot up this place, he's not worried about protecting himself," he said as he turned his head in Ira's direction. "This is a suicide mission."

"How do you know that?" someone asked through the radio.

"Trust me," Wint said. "It is."

"So, what's our next step?" someone asked. "Just stand here and wait 'til he does something?"

Wint didn't know what to say. He didn't want to overstep orders and chain of command, but based upon Solo's tip, he didn't have the time to wait.

He stopped and looked around, trying to blend in with all the celebrators. But something unexpected caught his attention.

A man was running in his direction, sprinting as if his life depended on it.

"Solo?"

CHAPTER 94

"Wint," I heaved, taking the deepest breaths my stinging lungs could hold. "Wint."

"Why are you here?" he asked in shock.

"We couldn't stay at home knowing this was going down," I said, bending over with my hands on my knees.

"We?" Wint asked.

I rose, ignoring his question as I saw Ira standing on the news van. I wasn't ready to break Elizabeth's confidence. "There," I said, pointing my head in his direction. "That guy in the green shirt. He's the one."

"We're watching him," Wint said. "We are waiting for our next step."

"Next step?" I asked in shock as I looked down at my watch. "The next step is to stop him."

"We have to follow protocol," Wint dismissed. "We can't jump the gunman, or someone could get hurt."

"Lots of people are going to get hurt if you don't do something now!"

Wint shook his head. "You need to stay back and let us do our jobs. We know what we are doing."

I didn't want to say anything rude, so I knew I was going to have to phrase the next sentence wisely. "I was the one who told you about this guy, so I think I know a little more than you!"

Well, I might not have spoken it as wisely as I had hoped.

"Solo, we can't just go and shoot the guy," Wint said with a little more force. "We haven't seen him do anything to cause an alarm. We are watching him. They have drones with cameras flying around here, and they are looking at the footage to see if there is anything abnormal with him."

I looked down at my watch and noticed it was almost three. "You don't have time," I pleaded. "What do you want to see before you make a move? The people in the back gagged and tied up?"

"Solo," he said my name with a frigidness I had never heard before. "Are you okay? Do you need to go talk to someone?"

I stood in silence at the power of those words.

"Because I can take you somewhere to go and get some help," he said, lowering his head, not able to look me in the eyes.

This was what I was fearing, his inability to look at me in my freakiness. I shook my head.

"Wint, do you promise not to arrest me?" I asked as a thought flashed through my head.

"I can't promise that," he said with a stern expression. "Don't do anything stupid."

"Wint, if I do something stupid, do you promise not to arrest me if I can get you closer to the news van?"

"I don't know what you mean," he said, looking at me with a mixture of confusion and sadness. "I have to follow the law," he said with remorse. "Solo, don't do anything you will regret."

I looked at him as I bent down. "If I do something that distracts the guy, you run over there and get him!" I said as I started to untie my shoes. "And rescue Harrison and Juliet in the back."

"Solo, who said these names to you?" he asked in surprise.

"I'll tell you later," I said as I slipped off my first shoe. "But you start walking over to the van. And then in a minute, I'll get him to look at me

313

and someone better be on the roof of the van stopping him from shooting and blowing everyone up."

"Solo, this is crazy," Wint said as he looked over at Ira who was looking around the grounds through his camera.

"I'm crazy?" I asked, looking the same direction and seeing something the others had overlooked. "Do you see Ira over there looking through his camera lens?"

"Yeah," Wint said. "Why?"

"Isn't it kinda hard to see through a camera lens when the cover is over it?" I asked. "He's not a real cameraman," I said as I started to untie my other shoe. "He's pretending so he could get a good spot to kill a lot of people. No one would expect a news cameraman to start shooting people from the top of the news van. Would they?"

Wint looked over at Ira and his eyes widened. "How?" he faintly asked as he shook his head. "I don't understand this," he said as he started to walk toward the news van.

I slipped off my other shoe, placing them where I would hopefully come back later to get them. I watched as he spoke into his radio and knew it was time for my show to start.

I just hoped my mother didn't find out.

I took a few deep breaths because I was going well beyond my comfort level. I wanted to figure out another way around this situation, but I couldn't. I knew if I didn't do something right then, many innocent lives would be stolen in a matter of minutes.

I watched as a few police officers on the other side of the Mall started to enclose the news trucks. I knew it was my time to shine.

I closed my eyes and uttered a prayer of strength and forgiveness.

"Please God, don't let me down now."

I lowered my hands, unbuttoning my shorts and pulling the zipper down.

"Oh, God," I said as I felt fully exposed. "What am I doing?"

I looked up and saw Wint was within striking distance. I lifted my t-shirt so it would cover my face but still be thin enough to see through. "Lord, help me," I muttered over and over under my breath.

I grabbed the last piece of fabric covering myself and let it slide down my legs like a firemen's pole. I kicked them off, reached down, and clutched them firmly in my hand. I took a final breath and jumped out into the middle of the Washington Memorial, naked as the day I was born.

This had better work.

CHAPTER 95

Wint walked away from Solo, unsure if he was making the right decision. But ultimately, he knew whatever Solo did, he could overstep and make the right final call.

He quickly walked toward the news van that Ira Quill was standing on. He was a little less than twenty feet away when he turned his head. His eyes widened in disbelief at the sight of his friend standing in only his boxer briefs. Suddenly, he realized what he was doing. He watched as Solo gripped his elastic waist band and turned back to look at Ira Quill.

"Do not attack the guy you're about to see," Wint commanded into his radio. "Chase him, but don't tackle him. Let him run. Three of you go ahead and chase him, but I need the others at the news van now!"

"What?" someone asked in confusion as Wint made his way behind the news van like a ninja as a loud roar of the crowd screamed and a few cheered at the spectacle.

Wint looked up and watched Ira's head jolt toward the middle of the grassy field. The diversion was working. Ira was watching the naked man running in the open and didn't notice four cops surrounding his hunting stand.

Wint signaled one of the cops behind the van, telling him to wait until he was on the top of the truck before he opened the back door.

He gripped the ladder on the back of the truck and stepped up as if trying to sneak up behind Santa as a five-year-old on Christmas morning. His head rose above the hood, and he saw Ira standing beside his tripod with the camera mounted on it. Wint took another step up and tried his best to be as quiet as possible.

That's when Wint saw it.

The barrel of the rifle lying on the rooftop and pointed at his head.

He snuck up the remaining rungs and slid his body on top of the flat surface. He scooted his body forward, staying flat and reached out his hand to grab the rifle.

Wint felt the hard metal as he gripped the barrel in his palm as his radio went off.

"How long do we need to run?"

Ira turned frantically, looking as if he were the one caught naked in the middle of the biggest Independence Day celebration.

He sneered in rage, looking into Wint's eyes.

"What are you doing up here, officer?" Ira asked with a grotesque expression of hate as he snatched up his rifle.

Only Wint was still holding the barrel.

CHAPTER 96

"Drop the gun!" Wint shouted as he jumped up, pulling the rifle away from his body, trying to twist it out of Ira's hands.

Ira didn't drop it.

Wint watched Ira move along the top of the van, like a high school wrestling match revolving in a circle, each pulling and gritting his teeth as if his life depended on it. "Drop the gun!" Wint spewed out the words like fire. He tugged at the barrel, watching Ira's hands wiggle down the butt of the gun until his finger was a few inches from the trigger.

He watched as Ira's finger continued to trek down the stock until it passed the grip, just an inch or two away from a deadly place.

Ira pulled with all his might, sliding his finger into the trigger guard.

Wint's eyes caught sight of it, and he yanked the barrel as far away from his body as he could. He didn't want to die just yet. Ira's finger was twitching, trying to wrap around the trigger.

Wint saw his opportunity.

He quickly yanked the barrel back toward him and twisted. Ira's finger got caught in the trigger guard, and he yelped out in pain.

Wint hoped Ira's finger was broken, but he wasn't going to let up. He pulled the barrel once again away from his body and twisted it the other direction. Ira's finger snapped the other direction as he yelled in anger and pain.

Ira slid his mangled finger out of the trigger guard and pushed the gun into Wint's chest. He pushed with all his body weight causing Wint to slide back a few feet with his slick-soled shoes.

"Stop!" Wint screamed, but Ira wouldn't relent.

Wint fell to his knees, gripping the barrel and pushing back with all his weight. He heard something behind him, but he didn't look.

"Freeze!" another officer shouted from the ladder, pointing his gun toward Ira, but Ira didn't freeze.

He was falling backwards from the force of Wint's will to live.

Ira reached back, wrapping his good hand around the satellite antenna attached to the roof. His body weight caused the white tower to bend and buckle, but it didn't fall.

And neither did Ira.

CHAPTER 97

Three fully-clothed policemen chased me around the open area as I heard one of the imbeciles yell into their radio, "How long do we need to run?"

"Really?" I screamed at the top of my lungs through my sweaty t-shirt. "Why did you just do that? He can't sneak up on the guy if you shout through your radio!"

The cop's face dropped as he acknowledged the mistake with those seven little words.

"I'm doing this for you!" I shouted. "I'm doing this to save you!"

I dodged and weaved, running in only my white socks, as I looked over at the Channel 5 News van. I hated what I saw. I stopped in my tracks and pointed at the deadly scene.

"Stop him!" I screamed as the three cops looked at me baffled. "Go save Officer Cooper!"

I didn't care that I was naked anymore. All I cared about was making sure my friend was saved.

One of the police officers tried to grab my hands behind my back to cuff me, but I didn't let him. "Go save my friend!" He looked over and saw the two other officers running toward the news van and started to follow them. I ran faster than I had during the streak, even though I was still technically streaking, passing the three cops who started running to the news van before me.

I loosened my fist and my underwear opened like a parachute. No one cared that I was standing buck naked with the scorching sun reddening my two butt cheeks. Terrorist attacks trumped indecent exposure any day.

I stepped into my shorts and lowered my shirt. I didn't know what to do. I felt like a parent watching his son's wrestling match. I wanted to cheer and scream for Wint to smash his face to the ground or break his neck. I didn't care. I just wanted Wint to live.

I heard the man groan in pain and then watched as Wint fell to his knees.

"Get up!" I screamed to Wint. "Do something!" I shouted to the other cops who were on the ground. One officer was helping Harrison out of the van, making sure not to trip the bomb wire as two other officers had their pistols pointed in the air at the assailant.

"There's a bomb in there!" one of the cops yelled as he helped Juliet away from the van as a new cop jumped into the back.

I felt helpless. I shook my head as fear overcame me. I couldn't let my friend die because of me. I just couldn't. I heard the cop inside the back of the van call for the bomb squad.

If the cops weren't going to do anything, I had to. I watched as Wint continued to fight. When Ira fell back, a thought hit me.

I ran around the front of the news van and looked up, seeing Ira's back. I took my socks off and scurried up the hood to the windshield.

Help me, God!

CHAPTER 98

I leaned against the glass watching Wint swing the rifle at Ira's head, but he ducked with each pass. Ira stepped back and grabbed the video camera attached to the tripod, throwing it at Wint.

Wint dropped the rifle, trying to block the flying camera coming at his head. It ricocheted off his forearm, but the hard plastic of the hurdling camera did some damage to Wint's arm.

Groaning, Wint clutched his arm as Ira looked around the scene and saw three guns pointed at him. He reached into his shirt and pulled out something that looked like a cell phone.

I don't know if it was seeing me or the detonator, but either way, Wint's eyes widened.

"Stay back or I'll blow us all up!" Ira screamed, gripping the plastic box with his sweaty hands.

A few of the cops on the ground started commanding Ira to put down the detonator.

Wint played good cop. "Ira, you haven't hurt anyone," he started. "Just surrender!"

"I can't!" he yelled. "These people deserve it!"

"These people?" Wint said a little calmer. "The only people here are us. They have already cleared the area," Wint continued as Ira looked around and saw the crowd fleeing.

I watched as Wint continued to speak sense into the man, but he wasn't biting. He wanted the world to pay for his pain and tragedy.

"They need to know!" he shouted as he looked at the detonator in his hand. "They need to know what sacrifice looks like!"

"No!" Wint shouted as Ira fidgeted with the button. "Just stop, Ira! Just stop!"

Ira looked at Wint and then at the button. "I have nothing to live for!" he shrieked, looking up at the blue, tranquil sky. "Nothing!"

"Yes, you do!" Wint said in a calmer voice, taking a step forward.

"Now, he, he had something to live for!" Ira shouted. "But I bet you don't even know."

Wint looked at me and then up at him. "No," he said shaking his head. "No, I don't. Who are you talking about?"

Ira stomped his feet in impatience. "Now, you want to know. They always want to know when they are looking death in the face. But when life is going great, they never care to ask."

The sounds in my ears were resonating with cars honking, cops shouting, men crying. It was a collage of chaotic decibels.

"Red!" I heard in the far-off distance. The voice sounded familiar, but it wasn't loud enough. "Red one!" Again, the voice sounded like a whisper. "Red!"

I looked up and waited for Wint to give me a sign, but he continued to talk. I ran over the idea in my head. If I jumped up and attacked him, he could hit the button.

And we would die.

I could reach my hand up at his foot and trip him, but he could still hit the button.

And we would die.

I could let the police shoot him, but there was a chance that when he fell, his finger could hit the button.

And we would die.

I looked up at Wint who had his eyes trained on Ira as the voice came back with a shrill.

"Solo! It's the red one!"

I looked over and saw a woman jumping and screaming from behind the barricades a block away.

Elizabeth!

CHAPTER 99

I slid down the hood and passed the cops who ignored my presence. They had their guns aimed, listening to their radios for a command to shoot.

"It's the red wire," I said poking my head into the news van as an officer examined the wires entering the little black box.

"Who are you?"

"Believe me!" I shouted. "It's the red wire!"

"Are you on the bomb squad?" he asked.

I answered the best I could. "Yes," I said jumping into the van. He gave me an awkward look at my lack of clothes. "Diversion tactic."

"Do your thing," he said as he stepped away, jumping out of the van and moving away to a more protected area.

I examined the box. I saw the red wire and hoped I would be able to dismantle it better than I had the day before.

"Please God!" I said a quick prayer as the rainbow of wires slithered in my hands like snakes.

I saw the red wire and took a deep breath.

"Who are you?" a man dressed in all black barked as he stepped into the van.

"I'm dismantling the bomb," I said as I looked at the initials on his vest.

His eyes bulged when he saw my hands on the wires.

"Back away!" he commanded as he whipped out his gun from his holster. "Just back away!"

"But it's the red wire!" I shouted. "It's the red one!"

"Sir!" he shouted, pointing the gun at my chest. "Step away."

I looked down at the box and then at the gun pointed in my direction. I closed my eyes and prayed for a sign. Any sign.

I raised my hands and stepped away from the box.

"Red wire!" Elizabeth shouted as she had run around the street to stand behind the news van. A police officer grabbed her waist, pulling her away. She was kicking and screaming. "Red wire! Solo! Pull the red wire!"

I looked at the gun and then at Elizabeth. She threw something in my direction.

"Red wi--" she started to scream as a loud popping cut through the commotion.

I jumped at the box when the SWAT officer turned his back and looked at the firecrackers exploding outside the door.

I grabbed the red wire and pulled, feeling a painful pop in my head.

CHAPTER 100

My senses smeared into one another as I felt my body being thrown, slamming against the hard metal floor. The colorful sparks continued to shoot and spray as an angry man pressed his elbow into my neck, pinning me beside bundles of cords and microphones.

The officer yelled in my ear, but I couldn't understand what he was saying. I was relieved I was alive, but I was more concerned with what was happening eight feet above me.

"I was helping," I screamed, since my eardrums felt like they'd popped at the sound of the firecrackers exploding in a confined space.

The officer grabbed my hands, forcing them behind my back, and I felt the tightness of the cuffs cutting off my circulation at my wrist. I tried to explain, but he wasn't listening.

He pulled me by my bicep, lifting me like I was a bag of leaves and not a fully grown man. He gave me a condescending expression, looking me up and down. "Where are your pants?" he mouthed as I still couldn't hear his words.

"Out there!" I shouted back. "I was creating a diversion," I said more quietly, shrugging my shoulders.

He said something rude, judging by his facial expression, but his lips didn't make sense. I was pretty sure he wasn't telling me I did a good job.

Another officer stepped into the back of the van and said something to the SWAT officer, who then looked at me and then back to the officer.

"Him?" he asked with a disgruntled eye roll. "Fine." He twisted me around and snapped the handcuffs off my wrists. I couldn't hear what he was saying since I had my back turned, but I felt him stomping out of the van as I turned around to leave.

"Where's Wint?" I yelled at the officer, who clutched his ears. "Sorry," I tried to say more quietly as the officer started untangling the bomb wire.

I jumped out of the back of the van and looked up, hoping to see Wint safe and sound, but I couldn't see him. I started shouting, "Wint! The bomb's safe!"

I ran around the news van, staring up at the sky, but I couldn't see either of them. I ran to the front and jumped on the hood once again, climbing up the windshield and poking my head over, but it was empty.

I looked around in all directions. My heart sank as I saw paramedics running toward the news van with a gurney. I slid off the hood, running to the other side of the van and found a police officer leaning over Wint's body on a bed of grass.

"Wint!"

CHAPTER 101

"Wint!" I ran over until one of the officers grabbed my arm to keep me from reaching my friend and brother. "He's my best friend!" I shouted, but I still couldn't hear very well.

The officer said something, but I wasn't looking at his lips. I was staring at the unmoving legs of my friend. I saw the paramedics running, but they didn't stop to help Wint.

They parted the officers that encircled Ira Quill. His green shirt looked like a Christmas ornament with blotches of red blood.

"What about Wint?" I yelled, but the officer just shook his head with a confused look. "They need to help Wint!" I shouted, protesting like a rambling deaf man. "Help him!"

The paramedics lifted Ira onto the gurney, cutting his shirt and applying pressure to his wounds.

I stared at Wint's legs, praying for them to move. "Please God! Please!" I moaned as my eyes started to water. "Don't take him too."

The officer leaning over Wint looked back at me with a bewildered look of concern. He shouted something, but I couldn't hear, and my eyes were blurring with tears.

The officer holding me released his grip. I ran over to Wint's side and saw blood spatter on his uniform. I couldn't look up. I couldn't look at another loved one who had been shot dead. I couldn't.

I squeezed his hand and my tears started to flow.

I looked down, and my breath was stolen when he squeezed my fingers.

My eyes shot up to his face, his kind, good-natured face that had a beaming smile on it.

"I'm okay," he mouthed. "I've been telling you, I'm fine. They are forcing me to stay here until they make sure I didn't get hurt in the fall."

"The fall?" I shouted as Wint flinched from the volume of my words. "Sorry," I tried to talk in a reasonable tone. "I can't hear," I said. "The fireworks must have temporarily messed up my hearing."

He started to say something, but I didn't let him talk. I reached down and hugged his neck and whispered in his ear.

"I thought you died, Wint. I thought I got you killed."

He just shook his head and patted my shoulder.

I wiped my eyes and sat up.

"Wait a second." I stopped and looked up at the van and then at the ground. "You fell?"

CHAPTER 102

"What happened?" I asked as another group of paramedics ran up to check on Wint.

"Excuse us," they said, and I stood up while Wint smiled.

"He's with me," he said, and they nodded their heads indicating I could stay.

"Are you going to take him a hospital?" I asked. When they nodded their heads again, I found out which hospital and promised Wint that Elizabeth and I would be there.

"Let me go get my clothes," I laughed as I realized I was still in my underwear.

"Not sure why you are worrying now," he laughed. "The whole world saw all of you today."

"The whole world better not know it was me," I winked. "I would hate for all the ladies to be hounding me."

My ears must have started to open because I heard an officer behind me say, "I don't think you'll have to worry about that." He laughed as he slapped me on the back.

"I heard that," I sneered. "Guess God didn't want me to be too arrogant."

"Guess not, man," Wint laughed as the paramedics continued to ask him to remain still.

"Okay, I'm going to leave you so you can get your tests done and then we will meet you there," I said as I started to walk away.

"Pants are required, Solo!" Wint shouted as I walked away.

I waved him off as I strutted across the Washington Memorial to pick up my clothes I'd stashed before my bold, risqué move.

I turned back and saw the police cars and ambulances and felt a breeze of peace over what had just happened. I didn't want this moment to end. The feeling of accomplishment of a crisis diverted. A monumental success.

"Get your tight white butt in my car!" Elizabeth shouted as she honked.

I grabbed my clothes and ran toward her.

"You surprise me sometimes," she said with a proud smile.

"They already told you?"

"Told me?" she balked. "I witnessed your showcase," she said with a giddy laugh.

"You couldn't have," I said in disbelief. "The traffic was too thick."

"The strangest thing happened," she said. "You got out and started running, and it was like the traffic started to flow," she commented as she started to get out of the congested area and headed to the hospital. "Maybe they knew you were about to show your goodies."

"Or maybe they were trying to flee so I wouldn't give them nightmares tonight."

"Oh, Solo," she sighed. "You'll be in women's dreams tonight."

"Can we talk about something else?" I blushed.

"Are your cheeks actually red?" she laughed. "You know, I bet your other cheeks are red too. Something that white takes just a little sun to burn."

"Can we change the subject, please?" I begged with hysterical laughter.

"Oh, Solo," she said letting out a breath, "you've given me years' worth of comebacks."

"Years' worth?" I scoffed.

"Your pale skin has its benefits; no tan lines," she laughed. "Bet you never thought about putting sunscreen on Mr. Wi--" she started as I interrupted.

"I get it," I chuckled. "I didn't know what else to do. Desperate times call for desperate measures."

"Well, I didn't measure…"

"Elizabeth," I scolded.

"You walked yourself into that one."

I nodded my head as I pulled on my shorts and tied my shoes. "I guess I did," I said as she started to say something else. "Just drive."

"Just wait for it, Solo," she said with a wicked smile. "Just wait for it."

CHAPTER 103

"Hello Milo," Jenny said pleasantly as she made her daily phone call.

"Jenika," he said with a hint of apprehension in his voice. "Why are you calling me?"

"Aren't you even going to ask how I am doing?" she hissed with disdain.

"My apologies," he said in a soothing tone.

She'd missed that thick Russian accent that she'd heard every day during her trial when he was head counsel for her defense. A defense he cunningly won with his expert legal knowledge and the simple fact that he didn't mind twisting the facts to get his client free.

"How are you doing?" he asked in a forced tone.

"I don't trust my current attorneys to handle the case as well as you could," she sighed, unfazed that she was facing spending the bulk of her life in prison if found guilty.

"Luther is a good attorney," he said with a righteous air.

"I don't want good," she barked. "I need the best." She attempted to pull at his pride strings. "I need you."

"I helped you once," he said unabashedly, not falling for her trickery. "Your father would side with me."

"Why mention my father?" she asked with scorn. "Why?"

"He taught you better than to make this kind of mistake," he lectured as if speaking to a child and not a criminal behind bars. "He taught you much better. You were not thinking."

"She deserved it," she said defensively. "If you could have seen her, you would agree with me."

"Sadly, Jenika," he said as he clicked his tongue, "it doesn't matter if I agree with you or not."

"Why do you say that?" she snapped.

"Jenika, I have a meeting I have to go to," he said, ignoring her question.

"Milo, please come and see me this week. I need to see a friendly face," she begged.

There was silence on the phone. "Please Milo," she said, speaking to her godfather with sweetness and feminine charm. "I won't ask for anything else. I promise."

He took a deep breath and succumbed to her plea.

"I can be there Saturday at two," he said flatly.

"Thank you, Milo," she said like a child on her birthday. "Thank you, Milo, thank you."

She kept the phone to her ear as she heard the dial tone. He had hung up.

"Can I make one more call?" she asked the guard.

"Tomorrow you can," the guard said with a blank expression on his face. "Next."

Jenny walked away from the phone with her hands in cuffs. She felt the prison sentence in her wrist, but she wasn't afraid. Even if she had to wait fifteen years to get out of prison, she would still be in the prime of her life. She smiled as she passed by a cell, winking at one of the inmates. She didn't know the woman, but the woman knew her. Everyone in D.C. knew Jenny Ascot's name.

She didn't know what made her smile more -- the knowledge of the infamy in her name or the fact that fifteen years would go by in a flash.

She didn't have a problem waiting fifteen years. It may even work out in her favor.

Milo would be dead by then.

If not sooner.

CHAPTER 104

Elizabeth and I walked into the hospital room and found Wint lying in a bed in a t-shirt and some shorts the hospital lent him while they examined his x-rays.

"You feel okay?" Elizabeth asked as she pulled a seat beside his bed, patting his leg.

"I feel fine," Wint said looking at both of us. "Just ready to go home."

"How did you fall off the van?" I asked.

He shook his head and started his story.

"I was talking to the guy, trying to get him to calm down and put the detonator down, but it wasn't working. He kept looking at the button and then at me. Then at the button and then at the cops on the ground," he said building anticipation in his story.

"Go on," Elizabeth said.

"Well, that's when we heard the firecrackers go off," he said.

"You're welcome," Elizabeth said.

"That was you?" Wint asked in shock. "How did you get…? Why?"

"I'll tell you later," Elizabeth said, dodging the questions. "What happened next?"

"Well, that startled everyone. He ducked and started looking around. Then when he heard the bomb was safe, he pressed the detonator with all his might. I have never seen a look of pure hate like the one he had on his face. He looked right into my eyes and basically said I was going to die.

"Well, when the bomb didn't go off, he was frantic. I stepped on the rifle so he couldn't get it. He looked down at the cops with their guns pointed at him, and it was like he just gave up and wanted to die. He reached into his pocket and pulled out a small pocketknife and started to put it up to his neck."

"No," Elizabeth said, looking around the room for a bag of popcorn.

"Yes," Wint said shaking his head. "No one deserves to kill themselves."

"Some people just don't think they have anywhere to turn," I said as I recalled those dark moments after Chelsea was killed.

"Well, I didn't want him to die, so I started to run toward him to stop him. I think the cops at the bottom thought the same thing because a few of the cops shot him to wound him, not kill him. One person hit him on the shoulder, one hit his leg, but he kept raising the knife closer to his neck. I watched as the blade cut open his flesh. That's when I tackled him. I tried to stop him, but we rolled around until we rolled off."

"You rolled off the van?" I said in shock. "Didn't that hurt?"

"Well," Wint said, grimacing with a smile. "I landed on the guy, so he took the brunt of the fall." He gritted his teeth. "But he didn't die. I stopped him from killing himself."

"You just might have paralyzed him," Elizabeth remarked before quickly backpedaling. "That came out wrong," she said. "I mean..." She stopped and looked at me.

"That is all you," I said, leaving her stranded.

"So, yeah," Wint said with a smile, rearranging himself to get comfortable. "That's the story."

"That's unbelievable," Elizabeth said with astonishment. "You're a hero," she gushed.

"I think Solo had a big part of it," Wint said, looking in my direction.

"I'm not sure you can say a *big* part," Elizabeth coughed out as her laughter became contagious.

"See what I've been having to deal with," I said, scratching my head.

"You could have done anything else, but you thought, 'You know what? I'll take off all my clothes and save the world,'" Elizabeth said with a booming laugh. "You had an hour to come up with a plan, and that's what you came up with?" she asked. "Did you know you were going to do that? Is that why you jumped out of my car, so I wouldn't see your naked self?"

"I didn't know until I got there," I said, raising my hand as if taking an oath.

"Mmhmm," she said in disbelief. "You've never played the naked card before."

Wint looked at Elizabeth, and then he turned to me before looking back at Elizabeth. I saw the look on his face as his mental wheels started to turn, cranking like a steam engine locomotive.

"Before?" Wint said. "How many *befores* have there been?"

I looked at Elizabeth's deer-in-headlights expression.

"I think it's time," I said to Elizabeth as she looked at Wint and then me, nodding her head in agreement.

"Yeah," she said standing up and walking over to close the door.

"What's going on?" Wint asked as a startled expression flashed over his face.

"You have to promise that what we say stays in this room," Elizabeth said as she walked back to her chair. She leaned her elbows onto his bed and inched her face closer to his until the only thing between them was their eager breath.

"Okay," Wint said timidly as he glanced over my way. "You're not a spy, are you?"

"Spy?" I laughed when I pictured Elizabeth working in the CIA. "Can you picture her as a spy?"

"What are you trying to say?" she asked with an attitude as her neck weaved in defense.

"Actually," Wint said furrowing his brow looking in my direction "I'd have a harder time believing you are one."

"Ouch," I said, clutching my chest at the hurtful remark.

"Yeah," Elizabeth agreed. "You're a p--."

But once again, she didn't say pansy.

CHAPTER 105

"He took that better than I thought he would," Elizabeth said as she started driving us to Veronica and Wint's home.

"He'll ask more questions later," I said. "It didn't hit me until a day or so later."

"With the fall he had, he'll probably think he was dreaming all of it today and won't remember much of it tomorrow," she said starting towards Alexandria, Virginia.

I looked out the window at the setting sun and thought about her last comment. I wasn't ready to uncover that side of us, but now that we had, it felt nice. Like a weight had been lifted off my back.

"It feels kinda nice, though," I said turning my head to look at Elizabeth. "Not hiding something."

"Yeah," she said. "I kept mine a secret for years, and you couldn't even last a season of *Grey's Anatomy*."

I shrugged my shoulders and turned to look out the window. "But it does feel nice," I said closing my eyes. "Even if he doesn't remember, I feel whole for once."

Elizabeth didn't say anything.

"Elizabeth?" I asked, not opening my eyes.

"Yeah."

"Do you feel better knowing Wint knows?"

She thought for a second. "I always thought I could trust Wint with my secret," she smiled. "I'm glad my gut was right."

I let that thought hang in the air as I tried to figure out my next move.

"Hey, Elizabeth," I said still with my eyes clenched, trying to meditate to a peaceful state.

"What, Solo?" she asked, getting an annoyed tone in her voice.

"Sharing a secret is freeing," I started tepidly. "It refreshes your soul."

"Okay," she said in a distancing demeanor.

"Just hear me out," I started as she cut me off.

"I know what you're going to say, Solo," she said with a sigh.

"So, what do you think?" I asked, opening my eyes to give her my undivided attention.

"My soul doesn't need refreshing," she shrugged. "It may get me off kilter if some of my skeletons roamed free."

"But don't you think--" I started when she stopped me.

"I know what you're doing, but I'm not ready to tell her," she said with a short breath.

I didn't say a word. I just laid my head back on the headrest and enjoyed my life with a little less baggage.

"Jeremiah!" she shouted as I, too, suddenly remembered he was at Elizabeth's home.

"I hope he isn't still waiting for us to come back for lunch," I said, squirming in my seat.

"Nah," she said as she called him. "He'll be fine. He's used to it."

"What a lucky man."

CHAPTER 106

Veronica ordered a feast from a local Chinese take-out for the five of us. I felt like we were at a buffet with the broad selection of cuisine, but Veronica had multiple reasons to celebrate today.

"I'm glad you're safe," Veronica said, stretching out her hand as Wint willingly took hold of it as if the years of troubled waters were a tranquil lake with no ebb or flow, just a relaxing paradise that fishermen dream about.

"Me too," Wint said. "Me too."

I looked around the table that looked like a glamorous photograph that could be framed and treasured. But I always saw the wear and tear on this group. We all had our issues. We all had our flaws. We were a hodgepodge, each showcasing our tattered edges with battle scars and the invisible elephant in the room from years of hurting and healing. I could see the inner demons we all had wrestled with when we were alone and in secret. It was the stereotypical arrangement of rocky relationships near the cliffs of divorce, the fearful abused still gagged to silence, the faithless searching for his burning bush, and my yard sale belongings of unneeded baggage.

"To Wint," I said, raising my glass as Elizabeth, Jeremiah, and Veronica joined in my toast without hesitation. "To the man every man dares to be and to the man that never sees himself in that way."

"Here, here," Elizabeth chimed in without an ounce of sarcasm. "I couldn't have said it better myself."

"Really?" I laughed at the rare compliment.

"I was being polite," she said, looking over at Wint and then winking at me.

Wint saw our exchange, and he, too, turned his head and winked at me.

I hated to think of the cliché at a moment like that, but we were the Three Musketeers that day.

I only wondered if the next day would be a clean slate or a continuation.

CHAPTER 107

"Who wants dessert?" Veronica asked from the dinner table as she scooted back in her chair.

"Let me," I said jumping up and taking the empty plates back into the kitchen.

"You don't have to do that," Veronica said with a hospitable tone and a warm smile.

"Let him," Elizabeth said throwing her plate on mine. "How many times do you have a man willing to do the dishes?"

"Dishes?" I balked with a laugh. "I just want a bigger slice of cake than what she was probably going to bring me."

I walked through the swinging door that separated the dining room from the kitchen and scraped the plates clean, dumping the half-eaten pot stickers, crab rangoon, and rice into the trash.

I looked behind me and saw Wint standing there holding his half-empty glass. He set his cup down, walked over to me, and hugged me.

"What was that for?' I asked, holding onto the fork and plate.

"I haven't been thinking the nicest things about you lately," he said as I heard an apology between the lines.

"It sounds crazy," I started as I rinsed the plates in the sink, "doesn't it?"

He didn't say anything but took in my words like scotch, letting the words seep into his mind.

"Well," I said opening the store-bought cake box. "I thought it was crazy when Elizabeth first told me." I found the knife and started cutting through the white cake with whole blueberries and cut up strawberries sprinkled on top of the icing.

Wint looked down at the first piece. "Is that yours?" he smiled.

"I thought Veronica would want a small piece."

"That's not a small piece," he laughed as he suggested I cut it in half. "I can understand why you didn't tell me, but then I also can't."

"I know," I said, not looking up but focusing on the sweet treat. "Elizabeth said she thought she could always trust you with her secret, but it's just that thing where you never know for sure until you say it, and sometimes it works out and sometimes it doesn't."

I stopped and showed him the piece, making sure I got Wint's stamp of approval.

"I was just afraid of it not working out," I said shoveling our slightly larger pieces onto the plates.

"Have I ever let you down before?" he asked, picking up a couple of the plates.

I shook my head. I knew that he never had, but there was always a first time for everything.

"Well, I'm glad you told me the truth, because if I'm honest, there were a few times when I thought you were in the middle of something bad," he said, lifting the plate to his face to take a bite.

My eyes shot open. "Really?"

"You've been nearby during drug raids, attempted murders, bombings..." He stopped and looked at me while shrugging his shoulders. "It just didn't add up with all the coincidences. What else could I think?"

"What did you think of Elizabeth?" I smiled.

"Oh, I definitely thought she was part of the mob," he grinned before heading into the dining room.

We distributed the slices as Elizabeth quickly traded her sliver of a slice with Wint's.

"Hey," he scoffed. "I already took a bite of mine."

She pursed her lips, indifferent to his remark. "I don't care," she smiled. "We're family."

"If you try to steal my piece, I will stab you," I smiled as I took a large bite.

"I dare you," she hissed as she reached over and dug her fork into my slice.

"You know we have more in the kitchen," I laughed as I guarded the remainder of my piece like a prisoner at lunchtime.

"Yeah," she said nonchalantly as she took a bite from Jeremiah's plate. "This is more fun though."

We continued to eat our cake as fireworks started to explode in the neighborhood. I glanced over at Elizabeth, who sealed her eyes shut trying to ignore the booming displays of thundering color.

"Anyone want to go outside and watch them?" Wint asked, and Jeremiah stood up.

"I always find the Chinese invention awe-worthy," Jeremiah said leaving his half-eaten piece of cake behind.

"I'm going to stay in here," Veronica said, holding her sister's hand. "She's never been fond of fireworks."

"I'll be out later," I said as I watched the men leave out the back door.

"It's okay," Elizabeth said as she looked at me and then Veronica. "You can go. I'll just stay in here."

I pulled out my phone and opened an app. I raised the volume and hit play.

"What episode were we on?" I asked as *Orange is the New Black* filled my screen.

FRIDAY

CHAPTER 108

Elizabeth's voice cut through the darkness, rising in volume with every sentence she barked out.

"Why do you always say that?" Elizabeth shrieked. "You always do."

"Well, it's true!" Veronica's voice shouted back. "You always side with Dad! I don't even know why I tell you some things! I thought you would support me on this!"

"I don't always side with Dad!" Elizabeth roared.

"Yes, you do!" Veronica erupted. "You will side with him as long as he gives you what you want."

"Veronica!" Elizabeth stammered. "You don't know what you are talking about!"

"I don't know what I'm talking about?" Veronica mocked. "I've seen all my life how Dad treats you better than me. All my life I have had to watch him give into everything you ever wanted. You wanted to go to Europe with your friends after high school. Done! You wanted to go to school and get a plush degree that you don't use. Done! You wanted to live in a nice home without it costing you a penny. Done! You want and you receive! Just like always!"

"I paid for all those!" Elizabeth screamed. "Not Dad! Me!"

"You paid for it using your trust fund, which Dad gave you! How much did he give you if you don't mind me asking? Because I bet it's a lot more than what I got!"

"Why are you doing this?" Elizabeth shouted. "Why are you mad at me?"

"Because you are just like him! You are greedy and selfish and think you do no wrong! You are the spitting image of what you never wanted to be!"

"Well, if you hate him so much, and I'm so much like him, why do you even want me around?"

"I don't!" Veronica said as she stomped her feet. "I hope I never see you again until you change some of your ways!"

"That's fine!" Elizabeth retorted. "That's freakin' fine! But one day you will learn that you don't know it all!"

"Oh," Veronica hissed with rage. "I know it all! I know how you play Dad for whatever you want. I'm not blind!"

"You don't know anything, Veronica! You know nothing!"

"Have a nice life!" Veronica said slamming her door.

"I wish Jenny had killed you when she had the chance!" Elizabeth huffed as she slammed the door.

A telephone started ringing before the answering machine picked up. "Cooper Law. Sorry we're not here to…" the message continued as it faded out.

White sheets of paper hung on a line in a dark room. Slowly, the blank sheets started to reveal black and white images as if telling a story.

The first sheet had an image of a man standing beside a height chart; he was five foot eleven inches. He was clean cut but wearing a sinister smile in his mug shot. It was an image that would cause some women to write him letters while in prison. He showed up again, standing in a courtroom, holding onto the lectern as if giving a toast at a wedding. The next image developed as he sat in a circle with other adults of different ages and races, looking agitated.

350

Quickly the pictures started coming faster. A different image showed up of a different man, lying in a hospital bed. Then another image of another man, lying in a hospital bed. Then another image of a man lying in a coffin.

The images slowed. The man from the first image sat in a playground swing, puffing on a cigarette, flicking his ashes into the woodchips under his feet. The picture panned out to show the entire deserted playground. There were two rusty slides of differing heights, splinter-covered picnic tables under a grouping of shade trees, monkey bars with red and blue peeling paint, and a clock that read 9:47 lighting up in the dark. The clock's face shone as large as the moon above the desolate parking lot that only had one silver beat up Volkswagen Jetta parked under the streetlight.

The man on the swing ended up lying in the grass with his eyes closed and a stream of blood running down from the corner of his mouth.

An ambulance arrived, and two paramedics rushed to the man's side.

In the distance, a lone figure stood and watched, poking his head out from behind the shade tree.

I woke up from my dreams and grabbed my phone, trying to remember all the details of both.

I didn't know what dream made me hurt worse.

They both had victims.

As I closed my eyes and retraced the second dream, the images materialized once again. The pictures started to connect into a story I had seen previously this week.

He was going to attack again tonight at 9:47.

He was going to attack my downstairs neighbor Lincoln.

He was going to attack him in the park near my apartment.

We were going to catch him.

CHAPTER 109

"How was your night?' Wint asked Dakota as they headed to question the remaining names on the list from the day before.

"It was great," she gushed. "Stew's family was amazing. They had food and games, they shot off fireworks and then we ate smores," she said, leaning back into her passenger seat. "It was a really good night. What about you?"

He nodded his head and smiled. "I had a good on too," he said. "It was a really good night too." Wint continued to drive as a thought flashed in his mind. "It just hit me, was it weird celebrating 4th of July with the people we actually fought to claim our independence?"

"That was over two hundred years ago," she smiled. "I think they are over it."

"Just making sure," Wint smiled. "You know some people hold onto grudges."

"I think Stew and his mom are fine. His dad is from here," she said opening her laptop to look over any new evidence they had received on the three beatings. "As American as apple pie."

"Picturesque."

"Have you heard about the guy from yesterday?" she asked.

"I haven't even thought about him," Wint said frowning. "I hope he made it."

She nodded and understood.

"So, how did you convince your friend to streak to cause that diversion?"

"Oh, it wasn't hard," he lied with a smile. "He said it was something else he could cross off his bucket list."

"That's some bucket," Dakota said. "So, who are we going to see first?"

"I think his name is Moe Holmes," he said as he looked over at her. "I put that address in the GPS. We can see if he's home."

Wint's phone started to ring, and he hit the button to answer through speaker phone.

"Hey Wint," Solo said. "How are you feeling this morning? Sore?"

"I'm doing okay," he chuckled. "A little sore, but nothing major."

"You beast."

"Don't flatter him that much," Dakota chimed in. "I have to work with the beast all day."

"My condolences," Solo said. "Hey, can I meet you for lunch today? I have something I need to talk to you about."

"Sure," Wint said as he suggested his favorite little Mexican place, Miguel's.

"I can eat chips and salsa any day," Solo said as he ended the call.

"Me too," Dakota said with a smile, "but I have a lunch date with my beau."

"He's going to get tired of you before you two give each other a chance," Wint said with a snicker as he followed the commands to turn at the next street.

"He won't get tired of me," she said playfully. "I'm a keeper."

Wint looked over with a quizzical look. "A keeper?"

"Yeah, what's it to you?" she snapped.

"Oh, nothing," he said shrugging his shoulders. "People keep herpes, but it doesn't mean they want to."

"Are you comparing me to herpes?" she busted out laughing. "Herpes?"

"Hey, you're the one who said you're a keeper," Wint smiled. "I'm just reiterating the differences."

"Please feel free to keep your comments to yourself."

"Now, where's the fun with that?"

"Just drive."

CHAPTER 110

Mikhail had his laptop on his bed, watching and waiting for anything interesting to happen to Veronica. Nothing was arousing his interest. It was just a boring fifth of July.

He picked up his ringing phone and noticed it was an unfamiliar number. He considered not answering, but something about the number begged him to accept the call.

He swiped to listen as a female voice came through and started talking without any type of greeting.

"0 – 6 – 0 – 7 – 1 – 4 – 0 – 0," she said in a slow, computerized tone as if forwarding an authorization code.

"Confirmed," Mikhail said as he scribbled the numbers down.

Jenika ended the call without any farewells. This was strictly business, and this was the code he'd been waiting for. He was surprised by how quickly it had happened, but he wasn't going to let this pass by.

He sent out a text with the details to a select few individuals before he closed his laptop since he wasn't concerned with Veronica for now. He could always watch his surveillance later that night. He still had to edit the video he wanted to send to her but thought he could wait one more day to send it. He picked up a small brown package and placed it by his door, making sure he didn't leave it behind. He had picked it up the previous night and thought it would be a nice treat.

He knew once he sent it, she would realize her laptop had been hacked, and then he wouldn't be able to spy on her anymore.

But if her life was anything like today, he was tired of spying on her.

It seemed like Jenika was tired of playing with her as well. Jenika had another game she was playing that took precedence for now.

But who knew? Next week when things were trying to continue, Jenika may want to reconvene her scare tactics.

But for now she had another target.

Milo.

He smiled as he received a few return texts from the chosen few. They were in.

His father's plan was working.

Tomorrow would be a day of great awakening.

CHAPTER 111

"Where are you?" I asked Elizabeth over the phone.

"Guess," she moaned with distaste.

"Aren't you a nice little sister," I smiled before I remembered my dream of Elizabeth and Veronica's vicious fight.

"Always," she said full of sarcasm. "So, I read your dreams."

"And?" I asked as I straightened up my apartment. I didn't know if I should include both of my dreams since one included her, but I didn't want to keep it hidden. I wanted her to know so she could try to diffuse the situation.

"What can I do?" she asked, but her tone was rhetorical. She didn't want an answer or an opinion. "Sounds like I see how she really feels about me."

"That's not why I sent it," I replied, folding the afghan I sometimes used for a nap and placing it on the couch.

"How can I even be sure you dreamed that?" she asked with distrust. "You've been wanting me to share my life history with Veronica from the moment you figured out I was the girl in your dream."

"Elizabeth," I huffed at the daggers behind her words. "You know better than to go down that hurtful path."

She didn't say a word. I could hear her breathing as she inhaled and exhaled her jilted feelings. I waited. And waited, hoping that after a few more seconds she would ease up and say something rational.

"So, I'll take care of the dream I had," she said as she cut me off and ended the call.

I looked down at my phone and felt a wall building between us. And it frightened me to think of the barrier between two sisters. It wasn't Berlin yet, but it could be. No one ever saw the construction of their ivory castle until they had moved in and were alone.

I didn't want to see that happen to Elizabeth.

I tried calling Elizabeth back, but it went straight to voicemail. Three times.

I plopped down on my couch and called another telephone number.

"Cooper Law, this is Elizabeth. How may I help you?" she said with a warm welcome.

"Don't hang up on me, please," I said with concern.

"What do you want?" she asked with annoyance.

"Just hear me out," I started as she agreed to my request. "Veronica has wrong opinions about you because she doesn't know the real you."

"The real me?" She sounded hurt.

"Yes, Elizabeth," I said without remorse. "The real you. You care about people even if you pretend that you don't. Veronica doesn't see what I see."

"Is that really what you see?" she asked as her hardness started to break.

"Elizabeth, what do you get out of running around the city with me each day? Nothing," I said looking back over the last nine months of how much we each had grown. "But I'm glad you're beside me."

She didn't say anything.

"I just want you and Veronica to be beside one another too."

"But," she started to say as I interrupted.

"But nothing. You are not your past, Elizabeth. And the only way you can move past it and tear down that barrier built from a decade of thinking the other sister is the favorite is communication."

"I'm not the favorite," Elizabeth said.

"But she thinks you are," I said shaking my head in remorse at what I was about to say. "Your dad is a pile of..." I stopped as Elizabeth finished the saying with one of her colorful words.

"Yes, he is, and I'm so sorry for the years you have had to deal with it," I said. I hoped she could hear my compassion. I hoped she could sense the merciful intentions behind each word. "But as you were hurting, she was hurting as well. I'm not trying to belittle what you went through, because no one, absolutely no one should ever have to go through what you did. But the secrets inside your family won't make you stronger. It will only cause your relationship to rot and crumble more easily."

I waited for her to say something, but she didn't. I couldn't even hear her breathing anymore.

"Hello?"

"I'm here," she said with a fragility as delicate as a snowflake.

"You know I'm only saying this because I'm scared of what will happen if I don't," I said, curling under the afghan I'd just folded, shaking my head at the hamster wheel of my life. "You know our dreams always come true unless we do something to stop them."

"Uh huh," she moaned. "I know."

"If you don't march in there and talk to your sister soon..." I stopped and thought of the unimaginable. "It may be years before you get another chance."

I stopped my lecture and prayed. *Please God, use my words. Use them.*

"One more thing," I said when she didn't stop me. "I love you, sis. You three are my family. I can't deal with another loss. I don't want to lose any of you."

"You're not going to lose us," Elizabeth said. "I'll let you know how it goes."

CHAPTER 112

"Do you have a minute?" Elizabeth asked as she walked into her sister's office. It was the longest walk from her temporary desk to her sister's. It was only fifteen feet, but it was fifteen years in the making.

Veronica looked over her laptop and continued to type. "Almost done."

Elizabeth took a seat and fidgeted. She started to think of what she wanted to say. All the words in Solo's dream were swirling with the words she was too afraid to say. She closed her eyes and felt the distance between her and Veronica. Even though she was just across the desk, she felt the barrier. They were not the typical sister unit. They were not the sitcom family she'd wanted to have as a teenager.

The more she thought, the sadder she became. She went through the years, recalling moments of heated arguments with no point. Screaming matches with no resolutions. Unflattering words with no apologies. They'd been sisters of opposition from the very beginning. Even before that horrid day when her innocence was stolen, and her father made his lifelong dream of partner in a prestigious law firm.

Her best intentions were never his intentions.

She looked up at her strong, independent sister and saw the characteristics she admired and wished she had. But she'd never told Veronica that. That showed her weakness and crippling self-esteem.

She lowered her head and felt a tear running down her cheek as her nose started to sniffle.

"Elizabeth?" Veronica said as her fingers stopped tapping the lettered keys. "What's wrong?"

Elizabeth looked up. She saw the concern in her sister's eyes. It was a look that she rarely saw. That look was the crack in the avalanche of their lives.

"I have to tell you something," Elizabeth said, grabbing a tissue from Veronica's desk. "And I'm not sure how to say it."

"It's okay, Elizabeth," she said with compassion, closing her laptop and pushing it out of reach. "I'm listening."

Elizabeth swallowed hard and closed her eyes and started to spill her locked heart.

"When I was twelve, during one of Dad's Fourth of July parties…" She stopped and shook her head. She had never said the words out loud.

"What happened, Elizabeth?"

Elizabeth still had her eyes sealed shut, but she could see the empathy in her words.

"When I was twelve, while the fireworks were going off," she stopped and opened her eyes. She wanted to see the eyes of her sister as she dove headfirst into this tragedy. She wanted to see her support because she was needing it more than ever.

"I was molested in Dad's office."

Veronica's mouth gaped open as her hand shot up to cover the shock on her face. She didn't say a word, but her face said it all.

"Dad walked in and caught us and told me to never say a word. I was scared and hurting, and all I wanted was for Dad to hug me, but he never did. He told me to get my clothes on and go out to the party while he talked to the man who hurt me."

"Oh, Elizabeth," Veronica moaned in pain as her eyes started to fill with tears.

"I'm sorry, V," Elizabeth started gushing as the tears started streaming down her face. "I'm sorry, I'm so sorry, V. I'm sorry that I haven't been a good sister to you. I'm sorry that you…" she started to say, but Veronica stopped her.

Veronica jumped out of her seat and knelt beside her sister, stroking her hair and embracing her so she could crash into a safe place. "It's not your fault," Veronica soothed. "I'm sorry I wasn't there for you. I should have been a better sister instead of always being jealous of you."

"But I was jealous of *you*," Elizabeth said looking into her sister's eyes. "I wanted to be just like you, but I couldn't. I wasn't strong enough."

"Oh, Elizabeth," Veronica cried. "If you only knew how many times I wanted to be like you. You were always so close to Mom, and I felt like I was the black sheep."

"And I always felt like I was the mutt who wasn't good enough since he dirtied me."

Veronica grabbed Elizabeth's face with both hands, cupping her cheeks like holding precious cargo. "You are more than enough."

"I never thought so," she cried. "I never thought I was good enough. You're the smart one. The lawyer. The prettier one. You were the one who graduated top of her class. Most likely to succeed. Look at your husband for God's sake!"

The two cried as the phone rang in the distance before the answering machine picked up.

"I just tried that hard because I thought I could earn his love," Veronica said. "But I've just learned this year that I will never be able to earn that."

"I'm sorry," Elizabeth cried as she wiped her eyes and her sister's.

"We are a sight," Veronica laughed as Elizabeth joined in.

"One thing I don't get," Veronica said, looking at her sister. "Who did it?"

"Charles," Elizabeth said, spitting out the name with disdain.

"Charles?"

Elizabeth nodded her head. "Charles Manfield."

"Dad's partner?" Veronica groaned in disgust.

"Well, he needs to thank me for becoming partner."

"Huh?"

"That's why Dad didn't press charges," Elizabeth said shaking her head. "He used me to become partner. He used me to further his career."

"He did *what*?" Veronica reacted with rage.

"Yeah, after Dad told me to go back outside to the party, I stood in the hall and waited. I didn't want to go back to the party. I was afraid. So I stood outside the door and heard him negotiate a promotion. Then when I turned eighteen, he made sure I couldn't press charges on my own by forcing me to sign a document, and Charles paid me ten million dollars to keep quiet."

"He silenced you?"

"What was I to do?" Elizabeth said. "Dad said that if I didn't sign the form, it would destroy his firm which would then destroy our family."

"He coerced you?" Veronica shook with rage. "He actually coerced his own flesh and blood to keep quiet to move up his corporate ladder."

"That's Dad," Elizabeth said, feeling like she was standing in the middle of rubble. But then Veronica looked at her and touched her hand and she knew. She knew no matter the destruction that was caused fifteen years earlier, she had someone who would be there beside her to help build it back up.

Brick by brick.

CHAPTER 113

I sat down at Miguel's and sipped my water while devouring chips, taking in the mariachi band music that played over the staticky speakers. I scrolled through Facebook, reading the latest thoughts from online friends I hadn't seen in six years.

"Are you waiting for someone else?" a woman asked as she walked up to my table. I nodded my head, texting Jeremiah about meeting him for a late afternoon tea or coffee.

"Yeah, a few more minutes," I said not looking up as the waitress stood at my table.

I realized I may have sounded rude and apologized. When I looked up, I saw a pair of eyes that I had seen a few times before.

"Fiona?" I asked, recalling various dreams from April involving this young woman who would have died from a shooter had Elizabeth and I not stopped it.

"I know you," she said, and I could see her trying to figure out how we were connected.

"I rescued you in the alley last April." Her eyes squinted as she looked at my face, trying to see the similarities from that darkened night. "Then my friend and I stopped the shooter from killing you," I added, unsure if she believed me.

"That was you?" she asked in shock as Wint walked up.

She turned around and recognized Wint immediately. Her face looked like her head was spinning from the memories of a frightening ordeal.

"Officer Cooper?"

"Wint, this is…" I started to say as Wint finished.

"I know Fiona," Wint said as he smiled. "How are you doing? Are you still going to therapy?"

She nodded her head with a pleasant smile. "I'm doing much better," she said as her smile started to glow. "Much better."

"So good to hear, Fiona," Wint said as she took his drink order and walked away.

"You know her?" Wint asked with a questioning gaze.

"Wint," I laughed. "Remember? Elizabeth and I stopped the shooter from killing her."

"That's right," Wint said, nodding his head. "I never understood why you two were walking that part of town so late at night."

"Now you know," I said taking a sip of water. "I told you it doesn't make sense."

Fiona came back with Wint's unsweet tea and took both of our orders.

"The first time I saw Fiona was an accident." I started retelling the story of stopping the rape in the alley, and how I knew it wasn't a coincidence because Elizabeth had dreamed about her too. I knew we had to help her, so we tracked her down to this restaurant and waited around until we could stop the shooting.

"That is unbelievable," Wint said, sitting on the edge of his seat. "So, how many dreams have you had?"

I looked at him and started to laugh. "How many dreams? I have at least one a night."

"You have these dreams every night?" he asked amazed.

"And Elizabeth usually has a different set of dreams."

"And you two do this every day?" He looked bewildered.

"Every day," I said with a smile.

"Doesn't it get tiresome?" he asked. "I mean, you're doing all this. You're just running around helping all these people. Do any of them pay you?"

I shook my head no. "Some have tried, but we just walk away."

"Solo!" he gasped. "How do you make a living?"

"I get by," I said tossing a chip in my mouth.

Wint took a drink of his tea and thought for a moment. "So, let me get this straight. You have these dreams and then you go out and stop them every day?"

"Well, we try to. Some dreams we can't stop because we can't figure them out. For example, the beatings this week."

"Is that why you've been visiting the guys in the hospital?" He gasped. "I thought you said you were doing a class project or something."

"I lied," I winced.

"So, you dreamed about the beatings?"

I nodded my head. "Yes. We dreamed it, but we couldn't stop it. Our dreams didn't show us where they were happening. We just knew the last guy was going to die in the subway station."

"So, what did you dream last night?" he asked like a child begging to be let in on a secret.

"That's why I asked you to come today," I said leaning down over the table. "He's going to attack again tonight."

"Get out!" Wint said, slamming his fist.

"But this time," I said grinning, "I know how to stop it."

"No way, Solo! No way!" Wint said. "Dakota and I have been tracking down a few suspects, but nothing has stuck yet."

"Meet me tonight and we can stop him. I'll send you a text where to meet me and when. Want Elizabeth to come?" I asked.

"Do you always do things together?"

"For the easier dreams we split up, but for a few we agree it is better if we do it together."

He nodded his head as he thought. "Yeah," he smiled. "Tell her to come. Tell her I'll be there too."

Fiona came back and delivered our orders. We exchanged some small talk since the restaurant was a little slow. I was delighted to see Fiona's gruff personality from a few months ago had faded into a friendly, young woman that seemed to have a bright future and a hopeful heart.

"One other thing," I said as Fiona walked away. "You got the wrong guy."

"Huh?" Wint asked, confused. "Wrong guy for what?"

"The guy you arrested for the murders in April," I started, "the drive-up killings."

"No, that guy did it. We had solid proof," Wint said. "He even confessed to raping the girls who were murdered."

"He might have raped them, but he didn't kill them," I said, taking a sip. "See, the dreams don't always give us enough information to stop them."

Wint ruffled his short hair as he replayed the case in his head. Even though he'd had many cases since then, some cases stood out. "What do you mean?" he asked, lowering his voice. "The killer is still out there? Fiona isn't actually safe?"

"Killers," I added. "It was four guys. Not one."

Wint's eyes went placid as the life drained out of them. "Well, what are we going to do?"

"I don't know. Elizabeth and I have tried to figure it out, but there's not enough information. We thought it was one guy doing the killing as well, but after you arrested the pawn, we each had a dream of the four guys destroying the car they used."

"Where?" he asked with determination. "Maybe we can figure it out."

"It was somewhere in New York," I said with a groan. "They dumped the car in the water. It's at the bottom of a river somewhere."

Wint looked at me aloof. He didn't look upset or sad or confused. He just looked like how I looked many days when I stared in the mirror at the end of the day and saw I hadn't accomplished what I'd wanted to. It was the look of failure.

"We have to fix this," he said. "Somehow we have to fix this."

CHAPTER 114

Ally McDermott started her daily anger therapy session with a few regulars walking in to take their seat. They were a few minutes early, and she knew the majority of the participants used this time as their lunch break and would be a few minutes late.

She usually didn't converse with her attendees, but the police visit had raised some concerns.

"Do anyone of you hang out with people in this group outside of these sessions?"

A few of them shook their heads, but the majority didn't respond. Just like during the normal session.

"Well, there have been three attacks this week involving people who have attended this group, and the police are investigating suspects. If anyone knows of anything, please reach out to the police," Ally suggested.

"Why?" Lex asked. "It's not like the police have ever done anything for me, except arrest me for bogus charges."

"The police are here to help," Ally refuted.

"They didn't help me when they believed my ex's story and not mine," Lex added. "They didn't even look into my story. She said I beat up her boyfriend. I don't even care about her boyfriend," he said raising his voice. "I didn't even know she was seeing anyone, and *I* ended it with *her.*"

Ally looked at her watch and noticed it was time to start. "Go on, Lex, tell us more."

"Well, my ex said I was stalking her, and I attacked her boyfriend outside a bar," he started, "but I wasn't following her. She was crazy, so I ended it."

"And how did that make you feel?" Ally asked, scribbling down some notes on this breakthrough.

"It felt good getting rid of her," he said with a grin. "Because if anyone is capable of attacking anyone, it's her. I bet she attacked her boyfriend and said it was me. I wouldn't put it past her."

A few other stragglers came into the room.

"I like a woman who takes control," Moe said.

"You would," Lincoln Pryce said in disgust. "Perv."

Moe Holmes looked over at Lincoln with angst, pursing his lips and making a mental note.

"This is stupid," Lincoln commented. "The cops don't care. You don't care. Most of the people in here don't care."

"I care," Ally lied.

"Sure, you do," Lincoln said cocking his head in disbelief. "How many repeat offenders have you had in your little anger management class, Dr. McDermott? What's your success rate?"

"I can't fix the issues if they don't want to be fixed," Ally answered. "I can only do what I can do. Just as you can only do what you can do."

"That's a cop-out way of saying you fail a lot."

"Cool it, Lincoln," Kristopher snapped. "Ally, I mean Dr. McDermott, is right. You have to want to change in order to change."

"Thank you, Kris," Ally said with a smile.

"Go on, drink the psychology Kool-Aid, Kris," Lincoln said, closing his eyes. "But you know this is just a bunch of bull. And anyone who thinks it's not is an idiot."

"Idiot?" Kris mocked. "The only idiot I see is you with your outburst."

CHAPTER 115

"I'm drained," Elizabeth said as she sat at Veronica's desk with the deli sandwich she'd paid to have delivered.

"Me too," Veronica sighed as she grabbed a few of her baked potato chips. "This week just needs to end."

"So, are you going to reimburse me for this work lunch?" Elizabeth grinned as she took a bite of her tuna sandwich.

"I'll add it to your paycheck," Veronica smiled.

"I thought I was doing this for free since I'm such a kind sister," Elizabeth said surprised.

"You are," Veronica kidded. "Thanks again for helping me. It's actually been nice having you here."

"Let's not go overboard," Elizabeth laughed. "I'm not looking for this becoming a full-time gig."

"What are you looking for?" Veronica asked. "I mean, I'm not saying you need a job, but don't you want something where you feel like you are making a difference?"

Elizabeth stole a few of Veronica's chips. "I feel like I make a difference most days."

"Besides volunteering at the school for a few hours here and there," Veronica said. "Don't you want something more out of life?"

Elizabeth looked back at her life over the last few months. Veronica couldn't see the change she had experienced or the effects of the chances she took, but she felt it. She saw the difference in her work with Solo.

"Actually," Elizabeth said, wondering if she was making the right choice. "I have a little secret," she said as Veronica's eyes widened. "I mean, a good one."

"Go on. Spill it," Veronica said as if they were young girls sharing a room, talking about life's dreams and goals in bed after the lights were out.

Elizabeth wasn't sure how she was going to react, but after yesterday's experience and this morning, she was feeling a little better about sharing her secret life.

"I'm actually writing a book," she said.

"You are?" Veronica said elated. "That's awesome, Elizabeth. That's really great."

"Really? You think so?" she said, relaxing her shoulders. "I thought you would think it was stupid."

"I would never think that of you," she said. "So, what kind of book is it?"

"Now, don't judge," Elizabeth said, getting in a defensive stance.

"Promise," Veronica said, rubbing her hands together to get the crumbs off her fingertips.

"It's a romance novel," Elizabeth sighed.

"Romance?" Veronica asked shocked. "Erotic, trashy, or Hallmark?"

"I said not to judge," Elizabeth winced. "You promised."

"I'm not judging," Veronica laughed. "I'm just asking which genre you are writing."

"Well, it's not erotic," Elizabeth said shaking her head. "My mind isn't graphic enough to write that."

"My sister, the writer," Veronica gushed. "When you start looking for an agent or publisher, let me read the contract. I'll watch out for you."

"That's another thing," Elizabeth said squirming in her seat. "I've already got one, and my book is going to be out later this year."

"Say what?" Veronica exploded. "Do you know how hard that is to do?"

She shrugged her shoulders. "Jeremiah got me a meeting with his publisher. They loved the idea. So, the book by Arose Seysmour Thornes will hopefully be out by winter."

"Arose Seysmour Thornes," Veronica said, nodding her head. "Interesting name. Playful and cute. But some people may not see it."

"That's fine," she said as she shrugged her shoulders. "But I'm taking a chance. Just like you."

"To sisters," Veronica said raising her can of Diet Coke. "May this be the year of our freedom."

"Here, here."

CHAPTER 116

I walked into our favorite coffee shop, ordered a green tea, and found Jeremiah reading a book as he waited in the quiet.

"What are you reading?" I asked, taking a seat as he slid the book away.

"Who's Arose Thornes?" I asked as the waitress brought me my tea.

"A friend's manuscript," he said as he put away the book in his messenger bag. "So, how are you doing?" he asked.

"Actually," I looked at him with a welcoming smile, "I am doing really well."

"Nothing on your mind today?" he prompted. "Nothing at all?"

Usually when we met it was a time to discuss philosophy or politics or anything else causing a division in the world. "I'm stress-free," I smiled. "I feel like a new man."

"You know," Jeremiah commented with a corrective tone, "a little stress is actually a good thing."

"Why do you do that to me?" I laughed. "Why?"

"I'm just trying to enlighten you," he grinned. "Most people assume stress is an evil ingredient in the world, but actually, if you ask most successful people, they will say they are energized by or welcome stress."

"Really?"

"I'm not saying to have enough stress to induce a heart attack, but stress releases a body chemical, dopamine, which causes motivation and reward behaviors. It's a normal thing. When stress happens, it causes people to react, to think, to dream, to project on how to eliminate the stress and better themselves. Once people stop trying to better themselves, they have lost the war. No one is perfect. No one. So, a little stress is a constant tool that is meant to sharpen us to a closer point of perfection."

"Fine," I grinned. "I'll find something to stress me out tonight."

"That's not what I meant," Jeremiah smiled. "But I see what you're doing."

"You're catching on, sir," I winked with encouragement. "So, do you have any new questions or thoughts? Are you researching any new book ideas?"

"Actually, I am still researching the class systems around the world. I'm still saddened by the caste system in India and the treatment of the Dalits, or untouchables as they are commonly known. No matter what caste someone is born into in India, they can never rise into another. No matter the education, wealth, even political position, if you are born as a dalit, you will die a dalit."

"I read that it is customary in some areas of India that after a dalit finishes their tea, they take their cup and smash it because it is considered unclean for anyone else to touch," I said shaking my head. "Yes, here we are in the United States, the land of freedom and opportunity. We may have an unwritten caste system, but people can rise out of it with determination."

"There is a growing trend in India to bring awareness to the discrimination, but it's going to take the next generation to break the cycle. Or even the next," Jeremiah said as he picked up his coffee. "But it is self-degrading to throw this piece of clay against the ground, acknowledging the fact that they are worthless in the sight of the world."

"I hope your book will open the eyes of its readers to rise up and make a change. A change that all men and women are created equal," I said as I sipped my tea. "If only."

CHAPTER 117

After my tea with Jeremiah, I decided to check on Elizabeth and Veronica. As I drove, I prayed that somehow they'd reconciled.

I walked into the office, but Elizabeth wasn't at her desk. My heart dropped as Veronica walked in.

"Oh, Solomon," she said, still reluctant to call me Solo.

"Where's Elizabeth?" I asked, not sure if I was embarking on shaky ground.

"She should be right back," she said. "She went out for a walk."

"So, you two are okay?" I asked, still unsure of the circumstances.

"Yeah," she said with confidence looking at me like I had a third eye. "Why wouldn't we be?"

"No reason," I answered. "So, have you received any other letters or emails from Jenny today?"

"I haven't," she said without a care. "Wint has surveillance at the jail, and they've been monitoring her activity. She's had no visitors the last couple of days and has only made one phone call. She called Milo, her old attorney, yesterday and she called a burner phone today. That call unnerves me a little, but we've installed a security system here and at home as a protocol."

"Better to be safe," I said as I rocked on my heels. Veronica and I had never had the best relationship. There was usually someone else around when we were together, so moments like this were incredibly awkward.

"I really like what you have done to this place," I said, looking around and noticing that nothing had really changed in the last few weeks.

"Thanks," she said politely. "It's getting there."

"Have you heard from your father on your counterclaim against your old work?"

"No, but these things take time," she said, grabbing the phone as it rang.

I was walking around the lobby area when a young gentleman with khaki shorts and a white polo walked in with a package. Veronica got off the phone and accepted the parcel. She examined the plain, brown box with the return address smeared and stopped the delivery man before he exited.

"Can you tell me who this is from?"

"I'm sorry," he said, shrugging his shoulders. "I don't have that type of record."

"Okay," she said with a concerned smile.

"Have you ordered anything lately?" I asked. She shook her head. "Do clients sometimes mail you boxes?" She shook her head once again.

"On rare occasions, but they usually tell me that they are sending me something," she answered as she set the box down on Elizabeth's desk. "Something just doesn't feel right."

"That guy wasn't wearing a uniform either," I said. "Did you notice that? Don't most postal carriers have a uniform of some type?"

"They do!"

"And sometimes they have you sign for packages they deliver." I ran out the door, almost knocking Elizabeth down as she grabbed the door handle.

"Did you see a guy in a white polo?" I asked as I looked around in all directions, not seeing a postal carrier vehicle on the street.

"No, why?" she asked, holding two iced coffees.

"Someone just dropped off a box, and it's unnerving us a little."

"Do you think it's Jenny?" Elizabeth asked as she entered the office. "We need to call Wint."

"Wint doesn't handle this type of problem," I said peering at the suspicious box.

"Neither do we," Elizabeth said as she called Wint. "Hey, um, Veronica just got a strange package. What should we do?" Her eyes widened. "Okay, we'll go outside."

"Outside?" I asked, reaching for the box as Elizabeth slapped my hand.

"You moron!" she snapped as she grabbed her iced coffee and commanded us to leave.

"I need to get my laptop," Veronica said.

"Do you need a hole in your head?" Elizabeth asked sharply, forcing us out the door. "Wint said to get outside now!"

We walked across the street and waited outside until a few cop cars arrived.

"It's inside on the desk!" Veronica shouted to them while Elizabeth worried more about her iced coffee, which seemed to be made with soymilk instead of fat-free.

"Really?" I asked in shock. "That's your concern."

"I paid $5 for this drink," she spewed. "How hard is it to make a drink the way I order it? How does yours taste?"

"I…uh…" Veronica stammered, more concerned with the bomb threat than her soymilk flub.

"Exactly," I agreed, looking down at Elizabeth. "This is more important."

"Fine," Elizabeth huffed as we watched a few police officers go inside. "Well, by time this is over, it will be the weekend," she said trying to make small talk. "Mind if I just head out now?"

"Really?" I once again asked in shock.

"I'm only kidding," she said with a wicked stare. "Just trying to ease her mind."

"Oh, you're doing an awesome job of that," I said, leaning against the building under the awning. "You're like a modern-day Mother Teresa."

"And you're like a modern-day Stooge."

"Why are you two always around one another?" Veronica started to laugh. "Sounds like you hate one another."

"Eh," Elizabeth shrugged. "There's levels of hate."

"Levels of hate?" I laughed. "That's a new one."

"Mrs. Cooper," one of the cops shouted from across the street as he motioned for us to walked over to him. "It's safe," he said.

"What was it?" Veronica asked.

"Looks like someone sent you a distasteful prank," the cop said as the other officers walked out of the office.

We waved at them and thanked them for their service as we walked back in to see the 'prank'. One of the cops followed us in and started asking us questions concerning the package.

Veronica lifted the lid and rolled her eyes.

"What?" I asked, straining my neck to see.

Veronica pulled out a can of exploding snakes the cops must have already opened, judging by the streamers and confetti on the ground.

"Jenny," Veronica said opening the card inside of the canister.

Boom. If I wanted you dead, you would be. But you're more fun to torture when you're alive.

"So, who is this Jenny, Mrs. Cooper?" the police officer asked. Veronica started telling him the short version as there wasn't enough time in the day to tell the full story.

After the police officer left, we picked up the office.

"Well, I guess you can rest a little more peacefully tonight, knowing she doesn't want you dead," Elizabeth said with a twisted smile.

"I guess that is one positive," Veronica said as she looked me in the eyes. "Unless she's lying."

I didn't want to scare her, but that was what I was thinking too.

Jenny couldn't be trusted until the day she died. Sadly, Veronica seemed like she was thinking the same thing.

CHAPTER 118

He watched as Lincoln parked his company truck, Clarity Plumbers, in front of his grungy apartment. He looked around the area from his vehicle, considering himself blessed for the home he lived in. But deep down, he was ecstatic with Lincoln's living arrangement. *He deserves to live like a rat*, he thought. *Especially with how to spoke to Ally today.*

He watched as Lincoln walked up the outside stairs to the second floor in his blue utility suit. He wished he had more information on Lincoln's timeline for the night. He didn't know anything about him, unlike some of his past victims. All he knew was he deserved to be punished for his outburst today.

He had never beaten anyone senseless in their own home, but based upon the lack of security he had staked out so far, he thought it would be possible. He didn't see any cameras, which gave him some assurance he would have a go at him that night. One thing he would have to do differently was beat him quickly so he couldn't yell. Nosy neighbors were always around. Apartment buildings were filled with them.

He grabbed the hamburger he'd bought on the way and savored the taste of the grilled meat. He could taste the heat of the flame, which he loved. He hated the taste of microwaved meat most fast-food establishments preferred for the speed; he didn't mind having to wait an extra ten minutes to get a sandwich that tasted good.

He had patience, unlike most people in the world. That was one thing the military had taught him. Not to jump too quickly, but to wait for the right time. If he jumped at the wrong moment, he could get hurt. Or die.

He despised the snowflake millennial generation that complained about menial topics as if their opinions were always right. He wished the government mandated young adults to have an automatic stint in the military like they did in Israel. That would fix a lot of the problems in the country.

But sadly, that would never happen. There would be too many people who would run to Canada and create a fake life up there to dodge the draft. Probably more in this generation than in any decade prior. Much more.

He took a swig of his Mountain Dew and swished the neon green drink around his mouth, tantalizing his taste buds with the sweetness. He had thought this night was going to be a dud, but he smiled as he took another bite of his hamburger and realized it was turning out to be pretty great.

The icing on the cake would be to see some blood from Lincoln dripping down his knuckles.

He might have killed Manuel the other night, but he wasn't going to let that scare him out of tonight's drill. He'd learned his lesson. At least, he hoped he did. Manuel was a small man, a muscular toothpick. He smiled as he watched Lincoln stand in his second story window with his shirt off.

He wasn't a shrimp like Manuel; Lincoln had some meat clinging to his bones. It looked like he used to lift weights but let the habit pass with age as most men did when they succumbed to the fact that a dad bod was in their future.

He pulled out a deep-fried onion ring from his paper bag and tasted the beer batter. He patted his stomach and grinned. He had good genetics that allowed him to eat like a pig every once in a while. Of course, he worked out often. He may actually work up a sweat tonight, unlike the tryst with Manuel.

He liked to sweat.

Real men liked to sweat.

CHAPTER 119

"So, when are we going to meet?" Wint asked as I sat on Elizabeth's couch talking on the phone.

"I'm at Elizabeth's now, so let's meet at my place around nine," I answered as she started another episode of *Orange is the New Black*. "Oh, no, that was only for yesterday," I said, turning my attention to Elizabeth.

"You know you want to," she grinned wickedly as she hit play anyway.

"Nine?" Wint moaned like a high school boy, hearing his parents say he had a curfew. "That's like two hours away."

"You're really getting into this?" I asked with a laugh.

"Oh, I am," Elizabeth answered, but I brushed her off, pointing to the phone. "Just tell him to come on over if he's whining."

"Elizabeth said you can come over here if you want to."

"No, that's okay," he said sounding disappointed. "I'd better stay here with Veronica for a little while."

"You're such a good husband," I grinned as Elizabeth looked at me with a gagging expression. "Stop that," I mouthed as I started to silently laugh.

She grabbed the phone from my hand. "Wint, come if you want to come or don't," she said point blank. "We don't really care. Just be at Solo's by nine. Got it?"

"I'll be there," he said with a downcast tone in his voice.

"You know, you don't have to," she snapped. "We got this. We've been doing this for a while now without you, and we can keep doing it on our own," she said with a grin, winking at me.

"No, no," Wint responded with a perkier tone. "I'll be there."

"Here you go," she said handing me back my phone.

"So, just show up whenever you want. You know where I keep my key," I said.

"Do you still have your key out for anyone to find?" Wint billowed like a nagging mom.

"You're the only one who has found it," I snickered.

"So you think," Elizabeth grinned facetiously. "So you think."

CHAPTER 120

Wint stayed by Veronica's side, trying his best to calm her fears. Even though she pretended to feel secure, he could see through her masquerade.

"I'm fine," she said in a solemn voice. "I'll be fine."

"Yes," Wint said coming up beside her as she did the dishes. "You will be perfectly safe. I promise. I won't let anyone hurt you."

"I know you won't," she said, turning her head to kiss her protective husband on the lips. "I love you."

"Love you too," he said starting to dry the clean plates and silverware.

"That may be the sexiest thing I've ever seen," she smiled, smacking his butt and leaning in for another kiss. "Who needs a crummy ol' dishwasher when I got you."

He looked at her with a playful grin. "I was going to surprise you, but I went out and bought a dishwasher a few days ago."

"Oh, thank God!" she said with an exaggerated laugh. "My hands aren't cut out for dishwater," she laughed at her shallow self. "They are already chapping," she said lifting her hands up to show the redness.

He laid his dishtowel down, took her hands into his, and lifted them to his lips, kissing and caressing them with tenderness and love. "They look beautiful to me."

She flung her arms around his neck, and they kissed like they were newlyweds as his phone started to vibrate.

"Go on, take it," she said.

"They'll leave a message," he said with a sexy grin as he started to nibble down her neck. "Nothing is going to stand in my way."

CHAPTER 121

Nurse Gina Tomlin held the phone up to her ear as she heard the voicemail recording to leave a message.

"Officer Cooper," she started as she looked down at the notes in her patient's file. "I had a note to give you a call whenever Tucker Stevenson gained consciousness. He is going to be here a few more days until all of his vitals have stabilized, but he should be able to answer some questions on the attack. His memory is slowly coming back, so we are hopeful by tomorrow his cognitive thinking will be much better than it is now. If you want come by tomorrow, that may be best to allow Mr. Stevenson to rest peacefully tonight.

"If you have any questions, you can give me a call in the ICU."

She hung up the phone and spun around in her chair as she heard a patient's alarm going off signaling their heart rate was crashing.

"Code blue!" she shouted into the intercom. "Code blue!"

All medical professionals on the floor ran into the room and started administering their lifesaving skills on Mrs. Kalenjin.

"Clear!" one of the doctors shouted, and everyone raised their hands from the patient as the defibrillator sent an electric current through the flat-lining woman.

"Come on! Come on!" another doctor yelled performing CPR to the beat of "Staying Alive" in her head.

Gina stood by, waiting to be told what to do as Mrs. Kalenjin was encircled by five pairs of hands.

She reminded herself there were only three more hours until the end of her shift.

CHAPTER 122

Elizabeth and I walked into my apartment at 8:44 and found Wint lying on my beat-up couch with a cheesy, satisfied grin.

"What's that look for?" I asked as Elizabeth rolled her eyes and plopped down on the couch beside Wint.

"I hid your key," he said, continuing to smile.

"You know the purpose of the key is so I know where it is in case I lose my other one," I said forcibly, heading to the bathroom to freshen up.

"Well, if you ever get locked out, give me a call and I will tell you where your key is," Wint yelled. "That's how good this spot is."

"I like your way of thinking," Elizabeth said, patting Wint on the knee. "We should team up against him more often."

"What did you say?" I asked, putting on a new shirt as I walked into the living room.

"Nothing," Elizabeth grinned as she gave Wint a conspiratorial look.

"Sure," I said disbelieving as I offered them something to drink and opened a bottle of water for myself. They declined as Wint started to ask a couple of questions.

I glanced down at my watch in the middle of his question. "Let's go on and walk down there and find our spots; we can work this out on the way."

"Is he always this pushy?" Wint laughed, getting up from the couch and pulling Elizabeth up with him.

"Always," she snarled. "It's like working with a Nazi."

"Anyways," I said as we headed out the door. We proceeded through the parking lot and walked a few blocks until we came to the park in my dreams.

"Is this where the magic is going to happen?" Wint asked in amazement.

I nodded my head. "He's going to come up and sit in the middle swing over there," I said pointing at the swing set on the other side of the park.

"You said the attacker is going to come at him from behind, so shouldn't we hide?" Wint stopped and looked around the park for a good hiding spot.

"Actually," I stopped him, "I think we should probably scatter in a triangle, so when the attacker tries to run off, we can surround him."

"It's not our first rodeo," Elizabeth chimed in. "When do you want to jump out? Right before he hits? Or do you want him to slug the guy so there is an actual witness who is awake and can testify?"

"Oh, I didn't tell you, Tucker woke up," Wint said. "I'm going to question him tomorrow."

"Then before," I said. "No use giving this guy a headache for no reason."

"And actually, if we stop the attack, there is still cause for me to arrest him tonight for attempting battery."

I smiled at his perspective and patted my friend on the shoulder. "I'm glad you're here with us tonight."

"You never say that to me," Elizabeth piped up with an attitude.

"No comment," I said with a mean smile.

She eyed me vengefully. "I'll give you something to comment about later."

"I bet you will," I said.

Wint looked at both us and started to laugh.

"What?" she asked as she looked and him and then me.

"You two," he said with a contagious laugh. "For months, I've been trying to figure out what type of relationship you two have, and never in my wildest dreams would I have come up with this."

"Well, to be honest, I would have never picked her to be my partner," I jumped in. "She asked to join."

"Asked?" she snapped. "Asked? Is that how you remember it, boy?"

I glanced down at my watch and suggested we get into our spots. We still had about thirty minutes before show time, but we weren't sure when the two men were going to be arriving.

Wint found a group of bushes he could hide behind near the swing set. I lay underneath the picnic tables in the shelter house, and Elizabeth stood behind a sturdy oak tree.

While I was under the gum-crusted table, I recalled childhood memories of me and Wint playing hide-and-go-seek in the summer months for hours on end. I turned my head and saw the bush he was hiding in and the tree Elizabeth was behind.

I started to smile at how precious life was to be living it with two of my favorite people on Earth.

CHAPTER 123

He watched Lincoln lock up his apartment and skip down his stairs with a pep in his step. He waited for him to get into his vehicle, but he didn't. Instead, he walked through the parking lot and headed down the sidewalk, walking under the darkened sky with streetlights leading him.

Lincoln stopped at a local convenience store and picked up something to drink as the man waited across the street behind a parked car on the curb, watching Lincoln's every move through the glass windows.

Lincoln started walking once again, pulling out his cell phone to make a call. The man stood up and started walking in the shadows of the trees that lined the street.

The stalker felt a rush of adrenaline he needed to release. He hoped the fight lasted a little longer than it had with Manuel. He shook his head in disappointment.

Why'd you have to die so quickly?

He watched as Lincoln ended his call and unscrewed the lid of his plastic bottle.

Diet Pepsi? Wimp. Maybe you're not going to put up a fight after all.

Lincoln stopped at a crosswalk and looked both ways. The light didn't tell him to proceed, but the road was empty, so he strolled across to an empty park with playground equipment. He entered through the gate and walked through the children's obstacles covered with invisible tetanus warning signs.

Lincoln took a seat on the swing and swayed with his back to the gate, lifting his feet and allowing the chains to follow the laws of physics with the pendulum of motion.

The man watched and surveyed his surroundings. There wasn't anyone around. He turned and noticed that most of the windows in the nearby apartments were black; only a few had a light on. He took a deep breath and looked both ways and crossed the street.

He lifted the handle of the gate, causing it to squeak. He stopped and looked up. Lincoln never moved.

He held his breath as he opened the metal gate, causing it to shrill in a high pitch. Once again, Lincoln never looked back.

He started to smile as he left the gate open and started to walk up to where Lincoln was sitting. He stepped over the plastic barrier keeping the woodchips of the swing set ground separated from the freshly mowed grass.

His foot landed on the wooden pieces announcing to Lincoln someone was behind him.

"You're early," Lincoln said as he turned his head. Shock went through him when he saw a grown man a few feet behind him.

"I didn't know there was a time," he smiled as he raised his fist.

"Freeze!"

CHAPTER 124

"Freeze!" Wint yelled, jumping out from the bushes and running toward the two men. "This is the police! Stop!" he commanded as he pulled out his gun, aiming it at the man behind Lincoln.

I rolled out from under the table and took off running toward the swing set as Elizabeth jumped out from behind her tree holding her pistol with both hands.

Lincoln stepped forward, away from the burly man, raising his hands in surrender. "Don't shoot!"

The attacker didn't have the same response.

"Freeze!" Wint shouted again as he took off running toward the open gate.

Shock was written all over his face when he saw me barreling at full force in his direction. His escape route was comprised, so he jutted to the right, but Elizabeth was running toward him with her gun ready to shoot.

"Stop!" Wint shouted as the three of us surrounded the panting man who looked like a trapped fox.

But he wasn't ready to lie down and die for our pack of bloodhounds.

He sprinted forward, seeing his only means of escape as climbing over the fence.

"Stop or I will shoot!" Wint shouted.

He didn't stop; he kept running toward the fence with full momentum; and for a large man, he was fast.

"Stop!" Wint yelled again.

"Well, shoot him!" Elizabeth hollered as she came running up.

The man made it to the fence and started climbing. I was still fifteen feet away, and he was making good progress when a gunshot went off.

The man froze on the fence.

He started to slide down, but I didn't see any blood as I got up close and grabbed his hands, pulling them behind his back and pressing his face into the fence.

"Are you shot?" I shouted. "Are you hurt?"

"No!" Elizabeth shouted as she ran up beside me.

"Elizabeth!" Wint shouted. "You could have killed him," he said as he started to Mirandize the attacker.

"I fired my gun into the ground," Elizabeth said, shrugging her shoulders. "Someone had to scare him."

Wint looked back and gave Elizabeth a look of both reprimand and gratitude.

"Call for police, Solo," Wint said as he cuffed the attacker.

"What, you're not a cop?" the man said in anger.

"No, I'm a cop. Officer Cooper," Wint said with a smile as he started to turn him around. "Nice to meet--" Wint stopped when he noticed he had met him before.

"Aren't you Dr. McDermott's husband? Gordon, isn't it?"

The muscular man huffed in agitation when he realized his days of wreaking havoc in freedom were over.

"Did she rat me out?" he asked in disgust. "It was her idea! If I'm going down, she's going down too!"

Wint looked at me and shook his head. "No," he said flabbergasted. "She didn't turn you in." He looked at me. "And tell the cops to pick up Dr. Ally McDermott for aiding and abetting." He looked at Gordon and

400

realized that was just a few of things they were going to be charged for that night.

I looked over and Lincoln still stood with his hands over his head, trembling with fear.

"He looks guilty over there," Elizabeth said. "Why do you think he's out here this time of night?"

"Probably up to no good," Wint said as we waited for the sirens to be heard in the distance.

SATURDAY

CHAPTER 125

"So, let me get this straight," I said as Elizabeth sat beside me on my couch talking to Wint on speaker phone. "The wife was really involved with all this?"

"It looks like it," Wint said. "I would have never believed it. I went to her house yesterday, and she didn't look like the type to have this level of anger, especially with people she was trying to help in her anger management classes."

"So what happened?" Elizabeth asked as she went to the kitchen to grab a bottle of water.

"Well, we haven't corroborated their stories, which are a little out of sync, but at first he was blaming her, and she was blaming him," Wint said from behind his steering wheel.

"Apparently, the husband has been battling PTSD for some time and has been taking out his anger on his wife. She's been covering for him by lying about accidents she was having, but she finally thought of a way to protect herself while letting her husband release his rage. She would give her husband the names of some of her least favorite clients. He would then go and follow them and attack them. He did admit to not meaning to kill Manuel; that was an accident."

"He was beating her?" Elizabeth asked in shook. "I wish I had shot him."

I looked over at Elizabeth and I knew she wouldn't have shot to kill. She would have shot to torture.

"So, he admitted to everything?" I asked, getting back on topic. "How often does that happen?"

"Well, when spouses are in different rooms, we have some liberties on creating a story to get the other one to talk," Wint said as he continued to drive. "After about fifteen minutes, he was telling us everything. He was blaming his PTSD, saying it wasn't his wife's fault, that he didn't mean to beat her, to not prosecute her, that it was all him."

"Well," Elizabeth said, "I guess I'm glad I didn't shoot him after all."

I looked over at her confused. "You know he did kill someone this week."

"But--" she started to say before I stopped her.

"No buts. He's a criminal."

"Well," Wint said with a tired yawn. "I just wanted to let you know how everything turned out. I'm about home, and I'm going to call it a night."

"Call it a night?" Elizabeth asked. "How can you sleep after something like that?'

"I'm a cop; it's what I do," he laughed.

"Actually…" Elizabeth started with an air of correction before I once again interrupted.

"You get some rest, man. See you tomorrow."

"Sure thing," Wint said. "'Night."

"Why did you stop me?" Elizabeth asked with some scorn. "He wouldn't have solved the case without us."

"He knows that," I said as I got up to get a snack. "We don't have to rub it in his face all the time.

"But it's so much fun."

I sat down on the couch, looked at the time, and realized I wasn't close to being tired.

"Want to watch your show?" I suggested timidly.

She gasped and smiled. "I thought you were liking it. I started to see you part your fingers a little more after the third episode."

"I was not…it's just that…" I started to say, but I couldn't come up with an excuse.

"Sure," she said, pursing his lips. "Your secret is safe with me, Jesus boy."

CHAPTER 126

"You got in late," Veronica said, resting her head on Wint's bicep as he caressed her arm.

"Yes, but the case is pretty much solved," he yawned with a sleepy smile.

"So, are you free today?" she asked with bright eyes fluttering with anticipation.

"I will be," he said, leaning over and kissing her. "I just have to run to the hospital to check on someone, and then I'll be all yours."

"All mine?" she smiled. "I like the sound of that." She kissed him once more before getting out of their bed.

He watched her walk away, tossing her head and humming. He had forgotten that sound. It wasn't beautiful to anyone else since she couldn't hit a note to save her neck, but he loved the sound of it. It was the sound of happiness.

He got out of bed and quickly threw on a pair of blue jeans and shirt before walking into their bathroom to brush his teeth as Veronica showered.

"I'll be back soon," he said after he gargled and spit his morning breath away. She stuck her head out and blew him a kiss.

He could get used to having such a loving wife.

He called Solo, but it went straight to voicemail.

"Hey man, give me a call when you get up. I'm heading to the hospital to question Tucker and then check on the other guy. Let me know if you need anything from me today."

He ended the call and felt like he was cheating on his other partner, Dakota. He quickly called her and caught her up with the details he could give without losing Solo's and Elizabeth's confidence.

She hadn't minded that he had a last-minute tip since she was out with Stew and probably couldn't have met him at the time anyway. He ended his call and felt better about himself. He didn't want to lie to anyone, but he was starting to see what Solo had been dealing with for the last nine months.

Some things were just easier to not tell.

That was going to be his motto from then on.

CHAPTER 127

Elizabeth drove away from Solo's apartment without feeling the walk of shame that so many other women were probably experiencing that morning. No, they fell asleep on the couch after a couple of episodes. She woke up hearing him snore and pictured him as an older, cute brother. But she would never tell him that.

She scribbled one of her dreams on a note pad and said she would call him later, but it wasn't urgent. The dream wasn't a matter of life or death, but to the person involved, it was monumental.

She proceeded down the road of great resistance. It was a journey she had never envisioned herself driving, but she knew she needed to clear the air. She needed to redeem herself. She needed to stand in front of the man who took away her childhood and tell him how she was feeling.

She gripped her steering wheel and practiced the lines she had been saying in her head for years when she would see his face in her nightmares.

"You can do this!" she said, cheering herself on as she drove through the prestigious subdivision where former presidents often lived after leaving their other mansion. It wasn't unusual to see the Secret Service jogging down the road beside an aging politician when they were visiting or doing their diplomatic duty.

She pulled in front of the house. A house that had caused fear and trembling in her soul for years. She looked into the rearview mirror and checked her lipstick and suddenly saw the image of herself as a twelve-year-old girl.

"I should have been stronger," she said to herself. "I should have protected you more."

She blinked her eyes and her preteen face vanished. She didn't see a pair of beady, petrified eyes that used to cry themselves to sleep. She saw the hopes of a warrior that sparkled and radiated bravery and redemption.

She opened the door and walked up the footpath. She took a deep breath and tossed her cell phone into her purse.

"You can do this," she repeated to herself as she rang the doorbell.

The door swung open and standing before her was the older version of the man she thought she could trust as a child. She looked into his eyes and saw the hollowness in them. Nothing had changed through the years. Just more wrinkles.

"Father, can I come in?"

CHAPTER 128

"It's early, Elizabeth," he said in his silk pajamas. "Your mother is still asleep," he said as his excuse. "Can this not wait?"

"No," Elizabeth said with force. "No, Father, it can't." She stepped into the home that still had the same iciness as when she grew up. The frigidness of never being good enough. The emptiness of never being able to reach his high standards. The solitude he manufactured by never allowing the women of the house to bond in their womanhood.

"What is it?" he asked as he stood in their foyer, closing the door behind her.

"We need to talk," she said flatly. "Well, I need to talk, and you need to listen."

"Elizabeth," he sighed, "I don't have time for this melodramatic nonsense."

"Melodramatic?" she huffed. "Was it melodramatic when Charles raped me in your office when I was twelve?"

"Why are you bringing this up, Elizabeth?" he asked in a condescending tone.

"Because it is time that you apologize for what you have done to me," she scolded.

"Me?" he scoffed with a haughty laugh. "Apologize? Why would I do that?" he asked looking blazingly into her eyes. "*I* didn't rape you."

"Not physically," she said, keeping her footing. "But emotionally you touched me places that no one should have ever touched me."

"You can't blame that on me," he said, raising his voice. "You were the one who walked into the room."

"Are you saying it's *my* fault?" she shrieked. "That a twelve-year-old girl deserved it?"

He looked at her and readjusted his shirt, making sure it was fully buttoned. "If you had just obeyed my rules and hadn't gone into my office, this would have never happened."

She laughed in his face. "Are you saying he wouldn't have stuck me in the linen closet if he had the chance?"

"We shall never know," he said with a menacing smile. "All we do know is you weren't supposed to go into my office, and you did."

Elizabeth couldn't believe her ears. She shook her head, wondering what she was expecting out of her cold-blooded father. No matter the hypotheticals she had played in her head, they had never sounded like this.

"Why didn't you do something?" she pleaded. "Why didn't you sue him? File charges? Instead, you just used it to catapult your career. Have you ever thought about what it feels like to see the man who raped you at your sister's wedding? Or having to hide in darkened rooms at birthday parties until I felt safe enough to come out? Or seeing your own father state your rapist was his best friend?" She stopped and looked into his eyes that were frozen. "Well, have you?"

"I was never raped," he said smugly. "So, no."

"But you were just as bad as him!" she shouted as she paced, catching the reflection in the mirror of a shattering woman. She looked into her eyes and knew she was done playing the victim.

She was done.

"Well, tell me, Dad, was ten million dollars worth my silence when you forced me to sign that clause?"

410

He huffed with a snicker. "I never asked for that for you," he said with a sinister grin. "He offered it to me to buy your silence."

"What?" she asked baffled. "You didn't ask for it?"

"Oh, Elizabeth," he said shaking his head. "Ten million dollars was nothing compared to what I was seeing in my future. If he wanted to give you that money so I could make more, so be it."

"So, you used me and forced me to sign it to keep me silent and to better your future?"

"You never object when you go out and buy a new car every other year."

"Just please," she said almost begging. "I just want to hear the words coming from your lips that you forced me to sign that form to keep me silent."

"Why does it matter to so you much?" he laughed. "It was over a decade ago. Just move on."

"Just say it!" she said, gritting her teeth until she tasted a drop of blood. "Just say it!"

"Fine!" he exploded. "I forced you to sign it! I forced you to keep silent because it was the best thing for our family!"

"Don't you dare say that!" she billowed. "Don't you dare say that my rape had a silver lining."

He thought for a second, rubbing his pointy chin and gave her a sideways glance. "Do you want to know the absolute truth, Elizabeth?"

"Might as well! What would be worse?" She laughed at the distaste in her words.

"I noticed how he was watching you," he smiled wickedly. "I had heard the rumors about him and didn't know if they were true. So, I

411

instigated a little. When I left the party outside, I knew you would come looking for me because you were always the nosy one. So, I waited. I heard you walk up the stairs. I heard Charles entice you into the room. I heard everything. Then, when I was ready, I came in to find him." He stopped and looked her in the eyes. "Was that really worth it?" he asked with a devilish grin. "To finally know the truth. Was it worth it?"

"You sick bastard!" she yelled. "You prostituted your own daughter for your own personal gain? How do you live with yourself?" she asked with nausea and disbelief mixing in her stomach.

"If you knew what I was capable of…" He stopped, leaned down, and whispered into her ear. "You haven't a clue, kiddo."

"And now you are suing Veronica too?" she exploded. "You couldn't just ruin my life, but you have to go after her now too!"

"It's nothing personal," he sighed. "It's just business, and she has taken some of my business away." He stopped and enunciated. "*My* business."

"Well, she said she never signed a non-compete clause, and you don't have any grounds."

He tsked and started to laugh. "Are you that naïve, Elizabeth?" he asked patronizingly. "I can't even believe you are my flesh and blood with your rose petal glasses."

"I wish I didn't have your DNA," she snapped.

"Ditto," he frowned. "It's totally wasted on you."

"You bastard!" she screamed again.

"Yeah, call me whatever you want, but at the end of the day, I will get what I want, no matter what."

"No matter what?" she asked, wincing at the words.

412

"Who will they believe?" he added snidely. "A respectable, life-long attorney who brushes shoulders with the upper class or a measly angry daughter?" He smiled at those words. "I bet the judge has a daughter who would throw him under the bus if she got the chance. So, I'm just watching out for myself." He leaned against the wall. "Survival of the fittest."

"So, you're really going to forge her signature on those documents?"

"It's already done," he grinned. "Signed, sealed, and delivered."

"How could you do this to her?" she asked with a renewed spirit.

He shrugged his shoulders. "When she left the firm, she became my enemy."

"But she's still your daughter."

He didn't respond to that line. He just looked at her with contempt.

"Anything else you want to know?" he asked as he placed his hands in his pockets. "If not, you can see yourself out," he said as he started walking to the double-sided staircase.

Elizabeth watched as her father walked each step without looking back. She wondered if knowing the truth was going to be worth it as she walked out the door. She promised herself she would never step foot in that dungeon again.

She pulled out her cell phone and stopped recording.

She had his confession for her.

And for Veronica.

CHAPTER 129

"I don't know," Tucker Stevenson stammered as Wint showed him a lineup of six pictures of men all similar to Gordon McDermott.

"Just think," Wint said. "We've already got him on other charges."

"You already got him?" he asked, looking up with his left eye swollen shut.

"We caught one of these guys last night about to attack another person," Wint said, keeping the details secret. "He admitted to attacking you," Wint said with honesty. "We just need you to point him out so we can close the investigation."

"If he has already admitted to it, you don't need me," Tucker said, resting on his pillow.

"This is more about you than it is about him," Wint said as he agreed. "You're right. We don't need you to identify your attacker, but there is something freeing about pointing out a person who assaulted you and knowing he can't ever hurt you again."

"I'm not afraid," Tucker scoffed as he shrugged his shoulders, changing his attitude from fearful to egotistical in the blink of an eye. "I just don't remember. He ran up behind me, and I never saw his face."

"Okay," Wint said grabbing the lineup and placing his card on the table. "But if you remember anything else, here's my card."

He walked out of the room as his cell phone rang from an unknown number.

"Officer Cooper," he answered, hitting the elevator button and waiting for the doors to slide open.

"This is Tami with Howard University Medical Hospital ICU. I have been notified to call you about Mr. Jed Poston."

"Yes, did he wake up?" Wint asked with a little optimism since Tucker hadn't panned out the way he wanted. Wint listened to Tami as she relayed her information. He shook his head as the doors slid open. "Thanks for letting me know," he said as he ended the call. He found a number in his phone and called as he walked into the empty elevator and pressed the button for the first floor.

"Cooper, what do you want? It's Saturday," Chief Johnson said disgruntled.

"I know. I'm sorry, Chief," Wint said undaunted. "I just wanted you to know that we need to up the charges for Gordon McDermott."

"Up the charges?" he said shocked. "What else do you got?"

"Another murder," Wint said as the elevators started to close. "Jed Poston died this morning."

CHAPTER 130

"Oh Elizabeth," I moaned into the phone at the horrific story she told. "I'm so sorry."

"I know," she said in a calm state.

"Elizabeth," I asked cautiously, "where are you?"

"I'm still sitting in my car in front of his house," she said stoically.

My thoughts started to spin, considering what I would do if I ever found myself in that situation when a loved one betrayed me. I couldn't grasp the emptiness she must be feeling. All I could feel was the rage boiling in my veins. With rage came bad decisions. With bad decisions came vengeful actions.

"Elizabeth, don't do anything brash," I said, grabbing my car keys and wallet. "Drive away now."

I could picture her reaching into her purse and pulling out her faithful friend. Even though I couldn't blame her, it still wouldn't be right.

"Elizabeth!" I shouted as I ran down the stairs. "Don't kill him."

"Kill him?" she said. "He's already dead," she said unfazed.

"Elizabeth, no!" I exclaimed, pulling out of the parking lot and driving like a crazy man. "Call the police and tell them! Elizabeth, it's not your fault!"

There was silence on the other end of the line as I heard her start the ignition.

"Elizabeth, don't leave!"

"Solo," she said annoyed, "I didn't kill him."

"Wait, what?" I said confused. "He's still alive?"

"Yes, he's still alive," she said, putting her car in drive and pulling away. "He's just dead to me."

I breathed out in relief. "You scared the…" I stopped.

"Go on, Solo," she laughed. "I know you want to say it. Say the big-boy word."

"Why do you try to corrupt me so much?" I asked with a smile, trying to let my heart rate jump off the cliff into a mellow, cool lagoon below.

"Eh," she said in disagreement. "I wouldn't say corrupt," she added as she thought. "Let's say I'm just testing you."

"How'd I do?"

"Oh, Solo," she groaned. "You always pass."

"With flying colors?" I laughed.

"Yes, Solo," she chuckled. "I'll bring you a ribbon so you can pin it on your chest for everyone to see."

"Geez," I smiled, feeling the love.

"I gotta go. Veronica is calling me," she said. "Bye."

"Wait, where are you going?" I quickly asked. "I'm driving, but I don't know where I'm driving to."

"Go home, Solo," she smiled as she ended the called.

CHAPTER 131

"Elizabeth," Veronica said through thick droplets of tears. "Why did you do that?" she asked after playing the recording that Elizabeth texted her.

"You needed it," Elizabeth answered, driving toward Veronica's home. "I'm heading your way."

"I didn't need it that badly," Veronica sighed.

"He wouldn't stop coming after you," she said. "He's that vile."

Veronica got up and grabbed a bag of Wint's Oreos in the cabinet to smother her emotions. "I could have handled it."

"V," she said calling her sister's bluff. "You are tough, but not when it comes to him."

Veronica stuffed a whole cookie in her mouth, enjoying the taste of Wint's guilty pleasure.

"I'm so sorry, Elizabeth," she cried, wiping her tears away. "I'm sorry."

"I know," Elizabeth said as her cheeks started to wet. "I know."

"If I knew you were going there, I would have been there by your side."

"I know you would have, but I had to do it by myself," Elizabeth answered. "He wouldn't have said all of this in front of you."

"He should never have said any of it!"

"At least we know more of the truth," Elizabeth said aloofly. "Our picture-perfect family is as messed up as anyone's."

"Worse," Veronica said giving her two cents. "We are way worse than any soap opera on TV."

"You know what they say," Elizabeth smiled. "Great art comes from great pain."

"You should get a Pulitzer then," Veronica said with a depressed croak in her voice. "I'm so sorry, Elizabeth."

"It's in the past," she said. "I'm done living with it."

"I don't know how you will ever get past what he said."

"Just play the recording during your disposition so it is documented for all eternity in court records," Elizabeth grinned. "You could have the firm if you wanted it."

"I don't want it," Veronica sighed as she watched Wint come in through the front door. "I got what I want. You."

"Are you talking to me or Wint?" Elizabeth laughed.

"Both," Veronica said as she wiped away her remaining tears. "See you soon."

Elizabeth came to a stop light and looked up her financial advisor's number.

"Mr. Archer, how are you doing this fine Saturday morning?"

"I am doing well, Elizabeth. How are you?" he asked. He hadn't recognized her voice, but he had every one of his client's numbers saved in his contact list on his phone.

"I am feeling extremely generous today. I want to transfer some money out of my account," she said, looking down at her passenger seat with two bank routing and account numbers.

"Okay, give me your information. I can't do it until Monday," he said, "but I'll give it to my assistant who will take care of it first thing."

"Perfect."

She gave the two different account numbers and the dollar amounts to transfer.

"That is a lot of money. Are you sure?" he asked. "Once we transfer it out, it's always uncomfortable to ask for it back," he snickered.

"Yes, one million dollars to each," she smiled. "They deserve it."

"Okay," he said and repeated the routing and account numbers back to her.

"Yes, that is correct," she smiled, feeling the joy of giving.

"So, once again, just to confirm, we will be depositing one million dollars to Veronica Cooper and one million dollars to Solomon Davis?"

"That is correct," she smiled as she ended her call.

The money was for her silence.

Who better to share it with than the one who helped her open up and the one she opened up to?

CHAPTER 132

Mikhail parked outside of the Washington D.C. jail that housed Jenika. He texted his father, making sure he was on his way to his location.

I'm almost there, his dad responded as Mikhail smiled thinking of the fruition of their plans.

Mikhail texted two other partners in this elaborate scheme.

Ready? he sent to both of them.

One quickly responded, *Affirmative.*

He knew the other one was probably driving toward the jail.

Everything was going as planned.

Mikhail looked down at his clock radio, and it showed they still had fifteen minutes until Milo was supposed to be arriving at the jail to meet with Jenika.

He smiled as he looked down at the text he'd sent his father the day before. To some it would look like just numbers: a bank account, a password, a code. But he knew what 06071400 meant.

He looked down at this phone as his clock signaled the time, 06071347. He only had thirteen minutes until Milo was supposed to be meeting with Jenika. Sixth of July at fourteen hundred hours, or as Americans would say, July sixth at 2 p.m.

Then, depending on how long the meeting lasted, that was how long he had left to breathe.

He still couldn't believe when Jenika called yesterday with the time. Especially one that was so close. Mikhail had wondered when Jenika was going to lure Milo into their spider web, and his heart skipped a beat when he realized the time had finally come.

He was ready to watch Milo's smug expression get pierced with a bullet. He just wished he could be the one to administer the deadly kill shot. Unfortunately, he didn't have the skill level of some of the others who'd had sniper training longer than he had been alive.

He looked down at this phone as it started to chime.

"Hello?"

"You got it?" Jenny asked into the phone as she made her one allotted daily phone call.

"Jennifer Ascot!" a police officer shouted behind her. "You have a visitor."

"You only have one chance, so you'd better make it work!" she hissed as she slammed the phone down on the receiver.

"I have a visitor?" she turned around in surprise. "I wonder who it could be," she said with a quizzical look. "I guess I'll go find out," she winked to the guard at the phone.

She walked down the hallway, her hands shackled together with a long chain connecting to her shackled legs. The chains rattled and clanked a beautiful melody to her ears. She loved the sound of the scraping metal against the hard, cold concrete.

"Look where you're going," the guard said as she walked with her eyes closed.

"I know where I'm going," she smiled wickedly. "Six more steps and then we will turn right," she said without opening her eyes.

The guard looked at her with interest.

They came to the turn and she blindly twisted her body in the correct direction. "Told ya," she said unfazed as she took two steps forward without hitting a wall. "I have this place memorized," she smiled as she turned her face toward the guard without opening her eyes. "So, you'd better watch your step."

The guard huffed. He was used to dealing with criminals who got their cheap thrills from bluffing and terrorizing the employees of the jail, so he wasn't going to cower to her comments. She was locked up like a mutt on a leash.

He smiled at the thought of leaving the jail in a few hours when his shift was over. He smiled more knowing she would be stuck in her cell until her sentencing since everyone knew she was guilty.

She should have been sentenced with all the killings last October, but somehow, she got off.

But not this time.

This time everyone on the police force was willing to do whatever it took to make sure she wouldn't see the light of day for a very long time.

He opened the door and escorted her to her chair, leaving the chains on her hands and feet.

"Thanks, dear," Jenny said with a playful grin. "See you shortly, hot shot."

He walked away, feeling disgusted. But it wasn't her words that irked him, it was the visitor on the other side of the glass. He wished he had the guts to shoot him between the eyes, but he would lose his full retirement benefits, and he only had six more years.

Maybe later.

"Well, hello, Milo," Jenny said picking up the phone with a charming smile. "Good to see you again."

CHAPTER 134

"Do you ever get a weird feeling that you can't wrap your head around?" I said, calling Elizabeth. I had already settled my minor dreams that morning and I had the rest of the day to celebrate, so I decided to pay my respects at the Congressional Cemetery. I went to Arlington multiple times a year, but I hardly ever thought of going to this one. After I was done, I decided to wander down a few streets.

"Occasionally," she said walking around southeast D.C., window shopping with Wint and Veronica through some quaint new stores off Massachusetts Avenue. "But I wouldn't let it worry you," she said looking into an antique store as something caught her eye.

"Yeah," I said a little unsure. "You're probably right."

"Probably?" she laughed. "Don't you know by now that I'm *always* right."

"Don't you know by now you always *think* you're right?" I countered as I strolled down the sidewalk with an ice cream cone in my hand.

"I think, therefore I am," she said walking into the antique store as Wint and Veronica slowly followed her in.

"You're full of it," I said as I ended the call. I didn't want to think of anything other than the melting chocolate-vanilla soft serve swirl dripping down my knuckles.

I smiled at any passerby that looked me in the eye. Only a few acknowledged me, but those few looks helped forget about the nagging thought that something wasn't right.

I stepped into a bookshop and browsed the new releases, all of which seemed fascinating, even though I knew I would never get past four chapters. It didn't matter how good the book was. I had been reading Jeremiah's book for six months and still hadn't finished it, so I knew I didn't need to buy anything until I could cross his works off my list.

I nodded to the cashier who sat behind the counter, playing on her cell phone. It seemed comical to me for her to be playing Candy Crush, when there were thousands of books she could be reading for free, but I understood the charm of diving into an addicting game.

They were always more fun than reading pages with only black text printed on them.

I stepped out and bumped into my adoptive family.

"Are you stalking us?" Wint smiled as he held two bags, one in each hand.

"Looks like he's stalking the ice cream man," Elizabeth said, wiping off my chin with her thumb and pointing out a dirty spot on my white t-shirt. "Looks like you'll need to buy another one. Next time, don't shop on the clearance rack," she winked. "You deserve something nice. Splurge a little."

"That's what she is telling me too," Veronica laughed. "And I'm following her orders." Wint lifted the bags as if they were dumbbells.

"What are you all doing?" I asked, wiping my face like an eight-year-old.

"Looking for some office décor," Veronica said. "Elizabeth said I needed to spruce up my place."

"Of course, she did," I grinned. "She's good at spending other people's money," I winked.

"Always," she said with a twisted smile.

"Finding some good deals?" I asked as Elizabeth started to smirk.

Bang!

Bang!

Bang!

CHAPTER 135

Three rapid shots fired. Wint and I enclosed the girls, using our bodies for their protection.

"Go inside!" Wint shouted, handing Veronica the bags as he started looking up and down the street.

I stood outside with him as the ladies scurried into the bookstore, trying to see where the shots were fired.

Bang!

Bang!

Bang!

Bang!

He looked at me doubtfully. "Did you know about this?"

"No!" I said with shock in my eyes. "I was just enjoying a Saturday afternoon."

Bang!

Bang!

"There!" he shouted pointing to a crowd of people running toward us. We took off running in their direction as Wint pulled off his badge attached to his blue jeans belt loop.

We continued to run as the stampede of people started to pass us. "What happened?" Wint shouted.

One of the fleeing women screamed and pointed behind her. "The jail!"

We sprinted a few more blocks. A black sedan squealed its tires, running through the red light, turning instantly while revving its engine.

"Did you catch the license plate?" Wint asked me. I shook my head no.

Three patrol cars flew by the street as we ran upon the scene of the crime.

We saw shards of glass sprinkled on the ground beside an old red four-door Acura. "What happened?" Wint shouted to one of the cops running out of the jailhouse.

Wint approached the vehicle and saw a young man with two bullet holes in the side of his skull. He looked closer and thought he looked familiar.

"Is he dead?" I asked as Wint nodded his head while uniformed police officers took over.

"I heard about ten shots," Wint said to the officers.

"Nine," I corrected. "There were nine."

"So, where did the other shots go?" Wint asked. "There were only two shots there."

"Hey, there's another dead body over here," one of the officers shouted at the corner, "in a black Lexus."

"I found another one," another officer said through his radio, "in a black Escalade."

"So, three dead bodies?" I asked.

"Someone just called in that a black sedan just dropped off a dead body off South Carolina Avenue," a dispatch operator announced through the radio.

"Four?" I asked. Suddenly, my gut feeling seemed true.

Something bad did happen.

CHAPTER 136

Jenny lay on her bed and waited for the glorious sound. She hoped the fortified walls weren't that thick. She didn't think they were because on quiet nights she could faintly hear the screaming matches of residents of the nearby apartments.

Suddenly, the silence was broken by nine shots.

She smiled, thinking of the looks on the faces of the men she wanted dead. Her memory trekked back just twenty-five minutes when she'd made her last telephone call.

"Pyotr," she'd said with influence as she continued in Russian. "This is Jennifer Ascot, or Jenika Lechkov. You have to listen to me, but don't say anything."

"Mmhmm," he'd said.

"This is a setup. They want Milo silenced. Are you in the car with Milo?"

"Mmhmm."

"Is Pavel driving?"

"Mmhmm."

"Pavel is in on it," she'd said. "You better take care of him before he takes care of you. When Milo comes in, you better do what you need to do."

"Mmhmm."

"You may not trust me, but Mikhail Lebedinsky and his dad are wanting to silence Milo so they can take control. You have to stop them. Do you know Mikhail?"

"Mmhmm."

"Good," she said looking over her shoulder. "I don't know who the fourth person is, but there should be a fourth."

"Mmhmm."

"You got it?"

"Mmhmm."

"You only have one chance, so you better make it work!"

Jenny closed her eyes and wondered if her plan worked. She needed to get rid of her competition.

If she wanted Milo's spot when she got out of jail, she needed to make sure they knew where her loyalty laid. People didn't easily forget things like this.

Her smiled broadened as she drifted off into a sweet dream.

Rest in Peace, Mikhail. You were never going to be my brother's replacement, no matter how hard you tried. Or Milo's.

I see a queen in their future.

CHAPTER 137

"Thank you for protecting me, Pyotr," Milo said from the backseat of the black Lincoln Continental.

"It is my duty, sir," Pyotr said as he drove away from the scene of the backstabbing bloodbath.

"How did you know?" Milo asked, wiping his hands of Pavel's blood from when he pushed out the dead man on a side street when Pyotr stopped the car.

"Jenika called and said it was a setup," he said as he proceeded to their next stop.

"How did she know?" Milo asked.

"I don't know, but she told me there would be four men to ambush us. When you went in for the visit, Pavel seemed strange. So I slit his throat," he said casually, as if telling his wife the events of any normal day. "Then I called Artem and Ivan to come and help. They were here in ten minutes. When I saw you coming out of the jail, I commanded them to kill their marks. Artem killed Alexandr, and Ivan killed Anton."

"I can't believe Anton and his son would be out to get us like that!" Milo said in disgust. "But I appreciate you allowing me to kill Mikhail. He's been a troubled youth for a while now. It was time to stop him."

Pyotr's first stop was Mikhail's apartment. Milo walked into his bachelor pad and found multiple laptops scattered on his unkempt table.

"What's this?" Milo asked, looking at the desktop screen with various files labeled 'Veronica'. He clicked on one of the files and opened a video. He smiled as he watched his old legal counsel partner on the screen. "Pyotr, do you know what this is?"

Pyotr walked over to the laptop after he ransacked the living room. "It looks like he had been surveilling Luther Hyde's daughter," he said. "I'm not the best with computers, but it looks like he hacked into her computer and…" He stopped and took over control of the laptop, clicking on a button on the taskbar. It opened a new video that appeared to be in real time.

"Well, isn't he a smart one," Milo said with a twisted smile. "Sad that we killed him a few minutes ago. We might have actually been able to use him."

"Nah," Pyotr gruffed. "We can get any peon to do that."

Milo grabbed the laptop and instructed Pyotr to grab the other ones. "We may be able use this to our advantage in the future," Milo smiled wickedly.

They got back into their car as Pyotr called Artem. "Did you and Ivan take care of the others?" he asked. "Okay, we will go there now." He ended the call and turned to Milo. "All of Anton's kids are dead. They thought you would like to do the honors of his wife."

"That will do," Milo said, leaning back in his seat as he continued to look at the videos of Veronica. "Very interesting indeed."

It was a short ride to Anton's house, and soon Pyotr parked the car in front of the three-story picture-perfect home.

"We are here, sir," he said.

Milo laid his new favorite toy in the seat beside him and picked up his gun. "It's only fitting to kill her with the same gun I just used to kill her son, don't you think?"

"Da," Pyotr said.

Pyotr waited in the car a few minutes until Milo came walking out of the house looking dignified.

"It's all done, sir?" When Milo nodded, Pyotr drove away down the quiet suburb. "Anywhere else you need to go before I take you home?"

"No," Milo said leaning his head onto the headrest. "That will do." The ride was peaceful. Pyotr turned Tchaikovsky on Pandora as they both breathed the sweet relief of another day almost over.

"Oh, Pyotr, after you drop me off, make sure to dispose of the vehicle. I would hate for them to track us down."

"I'm already on it, sir," he said as had already contacted his brother's chop shop while Milo was finishing Mrs. Lebedinsky. "No one will be the wiser."

Milo closed his eyes and imagined himself playing the violin with Tchaikovsky. He started to grin when his thoughts turned to the girl.

"Jenika," he said with a laugh.

"What about her?" Pyotr asked.

"Do you think I should defend her again, Pyotr? I respect your opinion."

"Without her we would both be dead," Pyotr said bluntly. "So, I don't see why not."

"Yes, but she has a way of playing people. I wonder if she was the mastermind behind this setup," Milo said with a gleefulness in his voice as he once again picked up his imaginary violin.

"There is no telling, sir," he said continuing to drive through the back streets of Washington D.C. "Her father was one I never knew whether I could trust."

"Are any of us really trustworthy?" Milo asked with a wicked smile as he lifted his head, laid down his invisible violin, and started to clean his gun.

"I guess time will tell, sir," Pyotr said unfazed. "Only time will tell."

Milo polished his gun, thinking of Jenika with each swipe.

She may have played them that day, but she'd better not play them anymore.

SUNDAY

CHAPTER 138

"So, have you come up with a new plan?" a man's voice asked in the darkness.

"I think I'm getting close to something," a different man answered.

"Well, can you give us some details?" a man with a British accent asked.

"Not yet," he said. "I don't want to jinx it, and I'm still trying to work out some of the scenarios."

"You know, Grant, we can help you," a different man added.

"I know. I know you can," Grant answered. "I'll definitely let you know soon. I just don't want to get your hopes up."

"So, are you going to let me finish Fiona once and for all?" the first man asked.

"Collin, you need to move on," the man with the British accent said. "You had your chance, but it won't look right since Simon's in jail."

"I promise," Collin said. "I'll finish her next time."

"No," Grant answered. "Stewart's right. Fiona's in the past. We can't pin these murders on Simon anymore."

"I guess you're right," Collin groaned. "And wipe that smug smile off your face, Jordan."

"What smile?" Jordan laughed as the group burst into laughter.

"Plan B is starting to come together, boys," Grant said in a deep, sinister bravado. "Are you still in?"

"Definitely," Stewart chimed in first.

"Oh, yeah," Collin joined next.

"Of course," Jordan said with conviction.

"Okay. Because if you want out," Grant started, "you better tell us now."

There was silence.

"Good," Grant said. "That is very good."

I woke up with déjà vu of a similar conversation last April. It was the same names, same voices, same situation.

I grabbed my phone and started to text Elizabeth when I realized I needed to add another name. I typed Wint to create a new group text for the three of us.

Just wanted to let you know, I started to type. *I just had a dream with the drive-by killers from April. They are at it again. I don't know when it will happen, who they will kill, or how they are going to do it. All I know is they are planning it now. Grant, Jordan, Collin, and Stewart are back. We have to get them this time.*

I hit send and laid my phone down on the nightstand.

3:43 a.m. shone brightly on my alarm clock until the red numbers faded for another few hours of sleep.

www.ingramcontent.com/pod-product-compliance
Lightning Source LLC
Chambersburg PA
CBHW070614260626
47161CB00007B/2430